PRINCE OF CLAY

PRINCE OF CLAY

THE DRIFTING LANDS
BOOK THREE

JOSEPH BRASSEY

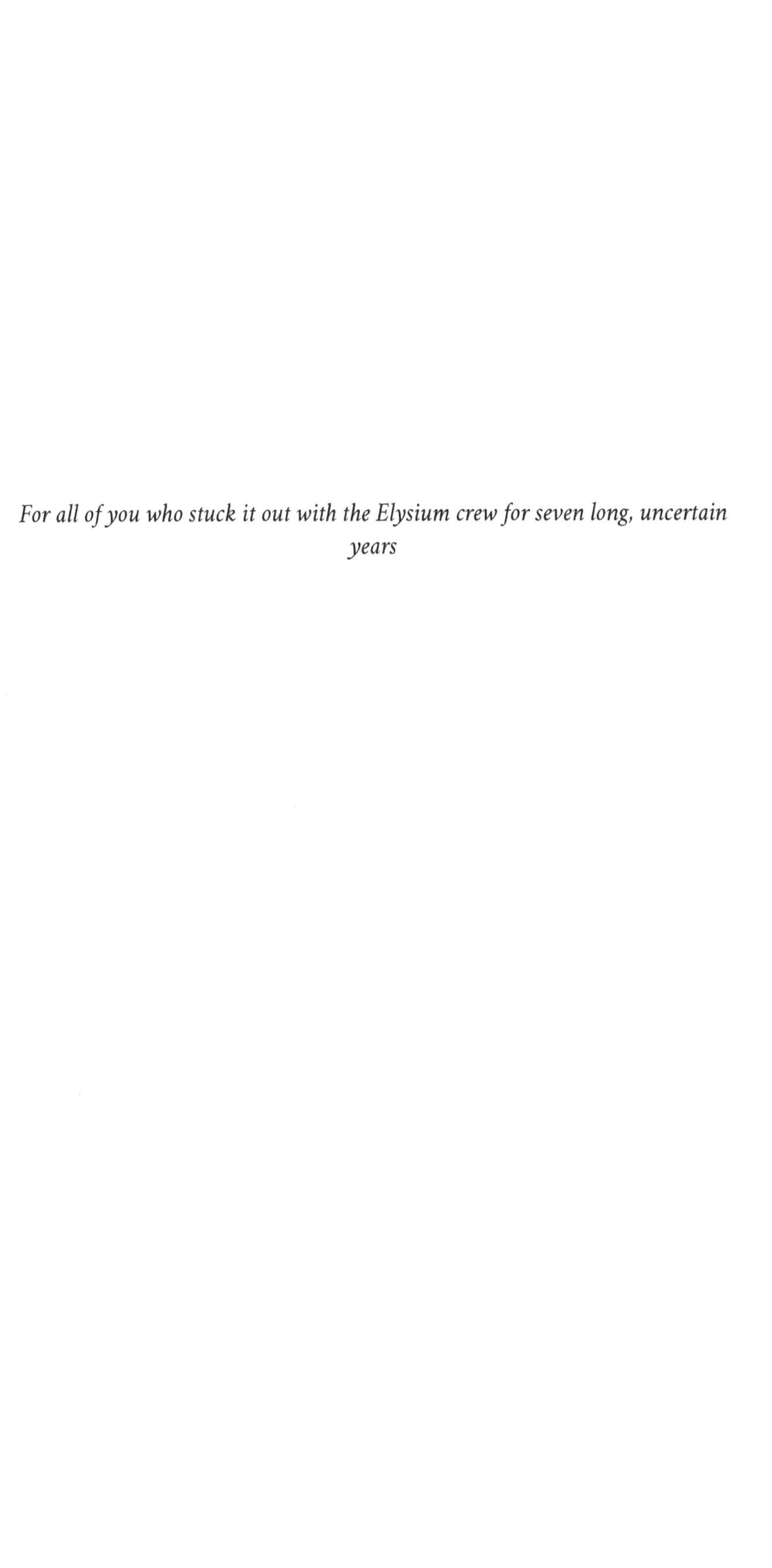

For all of you who stuck it out with the Elysium crew for seven long, uncertain years

Every saint has a past and every sinner has a future.
~Oscar Wilde

PROLOGUE

'NEATH GNARLED AND TWISTED BRANCHES

He took an experimental breath of the strange, cold air. A first blink. A second. A third to bring the world into focus, and his mind caught up with his perceptions. There was a river. There was ground beneath his feet, and a surge of elation pierced the rage and despair that had dwelled within the grey sage named Silas for the first time in months. The ritual had worked.

Straightening, accustoming himself to the realities of the mystic projection, the old sage gave a few more experimental breaths, closed his eyes, then opened them again. Before him the black river cut through the mirror earth with a slow and steady rustle. That was good, it was the only thing about this place that seemed normal at all. The mirror plane was ringed by a distant circle of jagged, black peaks. Above his head, a heaven filled with strange stars spread across his vision, dotted with constellations the learned man did not recognize. The air was stale and sickly sweet, redolent of funerary oils and flowers mingled after a thousand years.

But what pulled his attention was the vast, obsidian facade of the catacomb which dominated the valley's center. At the mouth of the river it crouched, black and fungal, its edifice a facsimile of some long-fallen, rotted tree-stump whose exposed roots cut across the mirror surface for what must have been miles in every direction. Something had broken it long ago and its apex was all jagged charcoal lines against the surrounding mountains. Even from this far away it filled the space with a sense of incomprehensible sadness and quiet, despairing enmity. Silas froze in place at the wave of crippling sorrow that washed over him the moment he took his first step.

The sage staggered. Nearly fell to his knees. He breathed in the cold, alien air and clenched his fists as the magic that kept him here wavered. He had come too far and sacrificed too much to stand on this distant, profane ground. Silas steeled himself and strode across the landscape towards the mouth of the water. It was time to enter the Barrow of the Twelfth Night.

It was hard to breathe at the base of the labyrinthine tangle of black roots. A wall of darkness rose before him to choke out the air. The sage paused to slow his pounding heart. Somewhere nearby, the dark waters churned from the base of the tomb, their echo similar to the river near the Port Providence homestead of his childhood. The memory was like a knife-wound: a prick and a small impact was all he felt at first, then reality pulled it away, and the pain dropped him gasping to his knees. Further. He had to go *further.* The spell had drained him, and he had already paid so much in costs to his soul that the order of sages would throw him from their temples, when they learned what he had done.

Silas raised his eyes, pushed himself to his feet, and flexed his fingers. *When I am done,* he thought, *there will be no sages. No nations. No Prophecies to break or legends to tell.* Then the old man let go of his last ounce of shame and pressed his hands to the cold mass of darkness before him. The sensation was jarring—frigid stone and hardened sap. And beneath, a stirring of something cold and empty.

"The legends were wrong," Silas whispered, his words bitter in the half-light. "You Whose Name Itself Has Perished, if Pride and Vengeance yet stir within you, I offer up this prayer: not all have forgotten, not all roads have closed. Heed me, and I shall be your stavrophore. I ask only for the power to right what has been made wrong."

Nothing. The waters droned on and the alien stars wheeled overhead.

Silas' breath, halting and ragged, echoed in his ears. Fear. How much had he paid to be here? His hands shook. What had he given up, for nothing?

"No," he breathed. "Please, I beg you, wait—"

The wall of darkness before him erupted outwards. Shadows spewed from the tomb-wall in a mass of black blood from a thousand wounds. It seized Silas and pulled him screaming into a gaping, frigid maw. Countless images flashed through his mind. Vistas. Grandeur beyond knowing. An ocean of behemoths moved through a cyclopean eye, greater than the vastest of continents. A flock of amaranthine birds fled a darkness that ate the stars. White knights, pale swords, knives in the dark. A broken tree burned. Swords cut the bark, ripped the soul, set the branches ablaze. The cut was a wound. The wound was an abyss. A chasm without end. It wasn't a voice that rose from the depths, but the one-time sage felt the agony of understanding burn through him as he hovered at the edge.

Bargain struck.

Silas fell.

The old man gasped awake with a ragged scream. The strange perfumes of the distant valley of the barrow fled, replaced with the familiar stink of his sweat and blood-sodden cabin aboard Coulton's flagship. The ache came next, starting in the crown of his head and rippling down his body in the wake of the incredible strain. He rolled onto his side, groaning in the dark. The ritual circle, so carefully plotted, was a charred ruin burnt into the wood of the deck, the candles scattered, the powders turned to ash. The only sound was the rain pelting against the windows and the intermittent roll of distant thunder. And his breathing. Focus. How much of it had he kept? How much was retained? Silas was not a natural at the arts of sorcery, and the ritual had drawn out every ounce of cunning and meager magic he himself possessed. His memories of the encounter were already distant, dream-like.

Focus. If the bargain had worked, he would know what to do. There was a slight itch in his chest. He ignored it. The act of trying to focus his thoughts made him dizzy, and he fought the urge to void his stomach all over the floor. Then, painful understanding.

Will it, stavrophore.

The first creed of the sages: nothing was true until tested. His breath quickened. The man who had never been a true sorcerer reached out with his hand and willed the magic to form. The room spun. A surge of power unlike anything he'd ever felt roared forth from the old man. Every candle in the wretched cabin sprang to light at once. The itch in his chest intensified. Silas absently scratched it as he rose, turning in a circle, surrounded by a hundred gleaming lamps. His laughter, harsh and delighted, was so loud it brought a deckhand banging at his door, and when it opened it, he must have looked a fright, for the boy took an involuntary step back in fear.

"…Your wisdom," the young soldier said. "Are you alright? I heard… noises, and…my lord, are you ill? Your chest…"

Silas glanced down. The spot that itched was black, as if a reflective chunk of obsidian had embedded itself in the flesh. There was no pain. It didn't matter. Images were already flashing through his mind, secrets beyond count, flowing as powerfully as any river, direct from the heart of the Barrow. It had worked.

"…My Lord?" the boy asked again.

"I am well," Silas said, smiling as he hadn't since the days before his kingdom fell. "But I need you to send for the royal guards. Tell them to rouse King Coulton immediately, for my research has finally born fruit. If he wishes to know of what I speak, tell him that I am going to save us all."

QUEEN IN ABSENTIA

I'm not going to argue with you anymore, grandmother." Coulton said. He stood at the far end of the royal suite, half bathed in the sunlight that poured through the leeward window of Alahna's cabin, and half cloaked in shadow. Her grandson had grown in the year since their homeland was destroyed, she reflected, and that hardship had been baked into him, a cynicism calcified in his heart that wasn't there before.

Even through the haze of pain the Queen Mother felt lying in her bed, that somehow cut deeper still. He was a gaunter, angrier version of his dead older brother, now, with a gentle heart made guarded and fearful by everything their people had suffered. And now the exiled king of Port Providence was about to doom himself on the words of an advisor Alahna no longer trusted as far as her tired arms could throw.

"You're listening to Silas," she said. Her own voice was ragged in her ears. Hoarse. The damned wasting sickness had taken much from her, this past year, and now it was attacking her throat. "And what little good remained in him is as dead as your father." Her fingers clenched.

Her handmaid attempted to urge her back to her pillows. "Queen Mother," she pleaded. "Please, you're not well."

Alahna swatted the younger woman's arms away. "Dammit Anna, I'm sick, not invalid. Save your clucking for the servant boys. I'm not done with my grandson." She fought with a painful cough then stared Coulton in the face. "Silas does not have our best interests at heart. Do you understand?"

Coulton turned. The newly minted King had his father's obstinance and his mother's compassion, but here and now, after the loss of his kingdom and under the pressure of his advisors, the former had convinced him that the latter was his greatest weakness. "I understand," Coulton said at length, "that we are a people without a homeland. Listless, adrift on the winds. In such times as this, the grace of kings past is not something we can afford."

"Coulton—"

"No, Grandmother." The King cut her off. "Silas has spoken, and my generals agree with him. There are other plans, yes, but none that grant us revenge for our slain people, restoration of our ruined homeland, and the ability to look at our own reflection again without shame." Alahna could see the fight in his eyes. The fear, as the boy's heart told him something at odds with what his every advisor urged: anger as balm for pain, action as balm for fear, war as balm for national pride shattered past repair.

He was close now. The Queen Mother reached out with a hand that felt so much weaker than she needed it to be, and took her grandson by his trembling, sweat-damp fingers. "My poor boy," she murmured. "Did you learn nothing from your father, from your brother, from me?" A cough lanced through her and she tasted blood in her mouth. "Our people are so much more than what victory they win through blood. Coulton, we were singers before we were warriors. Poets before we were killers. The Eternal Order destroyed our home, not our soul. That is something only we can kill. You have it in you to be the King that reminded us who we are. Don't be the one that drowned us instead."

Coulton met her gaze. His eyes were wide, wet, and afraid. Of failure. Of shame. His lower lip quivered, and in the moment, he was at once the little boy chasing his older, stronger brother through the castle halls. The boy who loved music and dance and had run to his grandmother's bed in the night at the first sound of thunder rolling in from the eternal sky.

"Please," Alahna pleaded. Her voice was a whisper. Coulton closed his eyes, and tears ran down his face. He took a shuddering, fortifying breath, then squeezed his grandmother's old, failing hand. Then he kissed her forehead.

"Thank you," he whispered. "For reminding me what I am fighting for."
No.

Coulton straightened. Released her hand. The King's eyes opened, and he stood, donning the cloak of an ill-fitting manhood as he turned away.

"Coulton, please," Alahna's voice caught. Not strong enough. Weak. Failing.

"It's a new age, grandmother," he said. "Don't be afraid." He walked towards the door. An armored guard opened it, his hand on a shock-spear. Framed by the light pouring in from outside, the King covered his doubt and fear with a mask-like smile of bravery. "When this is over, you will see. Silas is right. I'm going to save us all."

Coulton stepped through the door, and Alahna heard it slam shut like the crashing of a portcullis. She fell back onto her pillows. Her fingers gripped the sheets as she fought back tears of frustration and grief. "Dammit," she breathed through a cough. "Dammit all to hell."

"Queen Mother," Anna pleaded. "You need rest."

Alahna took a few more shaking breaths until she was sure that no more coughs were imminent. Then she opened her eyes and seized her handmaid by the wrist. "To hell with rest," she said. "Help me to my writing desk. Now."

Crossing the room was so much harder than she ever remembered it being. The pain was a series of stabs through her wasted legs, needles jamming their points through the soft parts of her tired joints. Every breath was an effort, and every effort left her dizzy as she leaned on the younger woman's shoulder.

"The King would not approve," Anna murmured.

"The King is a fool," Alahna answered. "In thrall to a madman whose lost his grip on reality. My chair. Pull out my chair."

She sagged into it as soon as Anna pulled it out. The cushion was barely enough to ease the pain of bending her body to sit. Breathing was still difficult. Youth was wasted on the young. "Ink," the Queen Mother breathed. "Parchment."

Her fingers ached. It had been months since she'd held a pen. Would she be able to? She clenched her fist, and stars of white pain blasted across her vision. *It doesn't matter,* she thought. *If it will save the boy, I can endure anything.*

Anna laid a sheaf of parchment in front of her as well as a fresh pen and ink-well. Alahna's fingers closed around it, dipped it into the ink, and —with pain coursing through her hand—started writing.

As far as treason went, the letter was short. Terse. Her aching hand allowed for nothing florid, and by the time she signed her name, beads of sweat stood out on her brow from the knives pushing their way up through her fingertips.

She laid down the pen and closed her eyes. "Anna, I need you to find Helena. She must take this to its destination, and she must go alone. Anyone else and my grandson's agents will follow, and stop them."

"It's been years since she went on a mission, Queen Mother," Anna said, hesitating. "She's been retired since his grace was in his swaddling clothes. Has washed her hands of killing."

"She will come forth for this," Alahna breathed. "She was my champion for twenty years. For my sake, she will come."

Alahna's chair rolled down the hallway of the skyship's lower levels, passing portholes that looked out over the open heavens. It had taken nearly a week to set this meeting up, and now the Queen Mother and her handmaid made their way towards a small bay, relatively unused since the ship was last in port, to make complete their treason against their fallen kingdom's new monarch.

The walls weren't well insulated, down here and the wind whipped fiercely at the wood panels, making the beams about them groan in complaint. Up over their heads, a flock of gull-rats nesting in the rafters let out a chorus of quorking noises. A squall was approaching, and the dark thunderheads were visible in the distance, bisecting the visible sky between sunset and a night black as ink. When the door to the bay creaked open, Alahna braced herself for the wind that howled past. The interior of the space was a mess, a battered, rubble-strewn loading dock long ago stripped of anything that could be of use for Coulton's war. And at the far end, a two-man gunboat sat, the heat from its single glowing exhaust port making the cold air shimmer.

As they approached, Alahna's breath quickened, until the cockpit hatch opened, and a tall, lithe figure in silver mail and a grey cloak sprang free. The hood tumbled back as she approached, and white hair fell about an aging, noble face set with sharp hazel eyes, but the Queen Mother didn't need any of that to recognize the woman before her. She'd have known Dame Helena Greyspear in any crowd by the way she moved: straightforward, confident, catlike. Her seventy-two years had done little to dull that step, and the look she fixed Alahna with was familiar and fond.

"It was not my desire that we meet again like this," the Queen Mother said. "I am—"

"Save the apologies, my queen," Helena answered. "Had the summons been frivolous, I'd not have come. Tell me what you need."

"I need a message delivered," Alahna said, and, reaching into the folds of her robe, produced the envelope, sealed with her royal device. "And quickly, to ones who will not be easy to find."

Helena reached out and took the envelope with a hand wrapped in a leather glove. She turned it over in her hands before meeting Alahna's eyes once more. "Dare I ask what it concerns?"

"The less you know the better," the Queen Mother replied. "But briefly, my grandson is under the thrall of Silas, and has lost his way. The people I am sending you to find may be the only ones who can save him—and all of us by extension—from himself. Find the skyship *Elysium*, and deliver this letter to Harkon Bright, Aimee de Laurent—" she paused, the last name was hard to say "—or Elias Leblanc."

The warrior's eyes narrowed. "Silas…the grey sage who advised your family?"

Alahna reached out and grasped her one-time champion's hand. Her voice was hurried. "The same, but a sage no longer. He has… done things to himself. Experimented with some devilry that's turned the madness of his grief into something as dark and terrible as the Eternal Order. Do not listen to him. Do not trust him. Do not accept aid from any who owe him allegiance."

"Really, Majesty." The new voice cut across their conversation, freezing Alahna's heart. Silas stood in the doorway through which they'd come, barring off their exit. "You overstate my influence."

The past year had twisted him from a kindly teacher to a ragged madman to the figure that now approached: gaunt and hard, his gray hair pulled away from his face and his hungry frame wrapped in warm sable robes. The greatest change of all, though, was his eyes. They were dark, now. The irises the color of jet, and at times, darker still, as if smoke moved behind the whites.

"Dame Helena," he said respectfully and bowed. It's been a long time.

Now please, hand over that letter. The Queen Mother is not well, and I do not believe she should be sending official communiques."

Alahna didn't look at her champion and old friend. She merely met the old sage's eyes, breathed in a painful breath, and shouted, "Helena, run!"

Silas's face twisted into a frown. "Fine."

The spell hit Alahna so hard the wind was knocked from her. Bands of unseen force clamped around her limbs, spiraled around the base of her chair, and lifted her slowly into the air even as her throat began to close. She gasped, clawed for breath. Silas had neither moved, nor made a gesture.

"I didn't want to do this," the sage said. The smoke filled his eyes now, rendering them ink-black. Veins of night stained the skin around his brows. "But you people just will not leave be. Dame Helena, the letter, if you please. Give it to me, or I'll be forced to damage the Queen Mother."

"Harm her," Helena snapped back, "and I'll carve your heart out and burn it."

Alahna couldn't breathe. Anna was screaming. The world was tilted as her vision went strange colors around the edges. "Go ahead," Alahna choked. "Kill me. My ghost will love watching my grandson keel-dragging you through a hailstorm."

"Shut up," Silas said, his eyes snapping up to look at her. "Just shut the fuck up, you arrogant, insipid bi—"

Helena exploded into movement. Alahna saw the warrior's hand flick, and a flash of silver between them before Silas screamed in pain as a large throwing knife embedded itself in his shoulder. The spell ceased and Alahna's chair smashed to the deck and toppled sideways, spilling her onto the floor of the deck. Pain blasted across her vision. "Helena!" She screamed with all her effort. "Leave me and go!"

Two men surged past Silas—soldiers wearing Coulton's livery. They closed on Helena, arming swords and steel-rimmed shields in their hands. Helena's arm swept behind her, produced a silver handle from the folds of her cloak, and with a flick of her wrist, the two halves of a six-foot stave capped with a glimmering silver blade flashed into existence, crackling with magic. She sheared the first one's shield in half, slammed the butt of her glaive into the head of the second, and sent both men sprawling.

"My queen," she grunted. "I cannot—"

Silas surged upwards, and abruptly a crackling gunshot struck the deck between champion and fallen sage. Helena's co-pilot had emerged from the hatch of their gunboat, and was reloading a long, black-barreled rifle. Alahna rolled onto her back as the sage summoned a powerful shield spell between himself and the knight.

"Go!" Alahna said. "That is a royal command!"

Helena ran. A second gunshot made Silas's shield spell ripple. Then another. And another. Silas lurched forward and the shield moved with him, one of his hands clutching at the bloody knife protruding from his shoulder. Helena had reached the gunboat now. The hatches slammed closed and the bay was filled with the roaring noise of the drive firing as the brown vessel lifted off the deck and surged into the open sky.

"No," Silas shouted. "No no no no no!" He stagger-dashed towards the bay door, a dark shadow in Alahna's vision, neither accustomed to exertion nor the tremendous power suddenly at his fingertips. He skidded to the edge as the Queen Mother rolled onto her side. Then he let out a roar, a sound unlike any Alahna had ever heard the old man make, terrible, deep, and rending. The birds overhead, startled by the sound, took rustling flight. A coruscating mass of darkness flared out from his frame, and with a primal scream, he sent a massive crackling bolt of night into the sky. Alahna felt her ears pop and her skin freeze as the effect of whatever horrid magic he'd just used washed over them. The blast missed Helena's ship and the sage fell to his knees on the deck.

She felt Anna's hands on her shoulder, trying to help her up. The first of the birds dropped from above, its corpse landing a few feet from where Alahna lay. The Queen Mother's breath came in ragged gasps. The light was fading. Every part of her hurt so badly that it was a wonder she was still conscious. Through the haze of her bleary vision, Silas approached, his sable robes stained with blood and his face a mask of quiet fury as dead, white-feathered birds rained down around him.

"Stay away from her!" Anna shouted. Silas waved a hand and the girl was thrown through the air to the deck. He made another motion and Alahna's chair was righted, and the Queen Mother seated within it. Pain. Everywhere.

"You were right," the old sage said in a shaking voice. "I can't kill you. I need your grandson too much, and he might stray from the path we've set for him if granny dearest were to suddenly perish."

He crouched before her, now, and stared into her face with his eyes made of night, and when her family's old advisor spoke, Alahna could now hear a second voice, a rasping whisper, underlaying the sage's own. "But it doesn't matter. That letter will never find who you've sent it to, and none whom it might reach has the slightest chance of stopping what is coming. Do you understand?"

Alahna drew in a deep breath, gritted her teeth through the pain, and spat blood into the old man's face. Silas's hand shot out and seized her by the chin. "I will avenge Port Providence, my queen. On the whole world, if needs be. On every single stretch of wretched land. I will have it for what was done to us. I will use your grandson to do it."

He leaned in, and the Queen Mother smelled rotting bark on his breath. "And you will watch."

This is **Aimee de Laurent.** Only child of a financier and a water baron's daughter, her life was laid out for her by the rules of high society before she was born. And every instance, every moment she has breathed, she has defied everything and everyone that has sought to define her. A rebel in charm-school, first to argue protocol, last to be suppressed, where she encounters a rule she cannot break, she bends it to her will. Weaponizes it. Turns what would suffocate her into armor.

This is Aimee de Laurent.

Of average height, she has a presence that outsizes her stature. Claims the room. Wrests attention with blue eyes that inquire, pierce, and accept no lie. Voracious in her hunger to learn. Aimee de Laurent is a woman who has thrown salt in the face of aristocratic and academic men who sought to silence her voice. Who has broken tradition and suppression over her knee.

This is Aimee de Laurent.

Skysplitter. Student of the Mage who Meddles. Apprentice coming into her own. She has killed demons with portals, defied captains, politicians, and tyrants. Her blonde hair as often braided as it is worn loose. As at home weaving wondrous and powerful spells as she is wearing a ballgown and heels. Her ambition is as limitless as her courage, and proven now, over and over. She lives to seek. Learn. Explore. Fight. Strive. And as the skyship *Elysium* docks at the port of Whitefeather, she dons armwraps and fatigues to do as every learner poised towards greatness does:

Aimee de Laurent steps into the role of student, and she trains.

2

LAST CALL FOR UNDERDOGS

Aimee dropped back into a crouch, then straightened, taking a moment to wipe sweat from her forehead as she circled her opponent. Elias prowled across the makeshift ring from her. Half in shadow, the tall, angular man cut a jagged profile that moved fluidly as he approached, the look on his face intent and burning. "Good," he said as he shifted to a sidestep, circling around to Aimee's left flank. "But watch your lines."

Her fingers flexed as she shifted into a balanced stance, raised her hands, and grinned. She shifted her weight, pivoting to keep him in her sights. Her training fatigues were loose, permitting her a comfortable ease of movement, and she'd discarded shoes, preferring the feel of her bare feet on the floor. Her gold hair was pulled up behind her head in a messy bun. His green eyes flicked to her center of mass as he took another step, and she caught a ghost of a half-smile at the corner of his mouth.

"Watch your own, Elias Leblanc," she said, and exploded forward. He turned aside the first punch, and the second. She threw a third, shifting her stance as she advanced to change the angle and he caught her arm, pulling her in. She bent her elbow and dropped her weight as Bjorn had showed her, denying him leverage. She heard him grunt in surprise. The motion slammed her closer, and Aimee tucked her chin and jammed the top of her head into Elias's neck, pushing him back. This time he stumbled, made a sound of surprise. Aimee grinned, snaked her hand between their bodies and shot her left leg between his to find the back of a knee.

Instead, she felt two vice-like arms close around her middle. Shit. They teetered back and forth, struggling for advantage. Elias was significantly stronger, but having to cope with that edge had forced Aimee to learn quickly.

She shifted her foot, felt him sense her moving and reflexively shift his weight to throw her. Aimee dropped every ounce of her weight into the floor and tried to heave him over her shoulders.

Halfway down, his grip tightened. They both lost their balance at once. She had time to hear her sparring partner squawk and to let out an ungraceful squeak herself before they slammed to the deck in a pile of flailing limbs.

He lay on his back. Aimee pushed herself up on her elbows, then scooted quickly to plant her weight on his shoulders and look down at his face. "I win."

His green eyes blinked twice as he blearily shook his head before making a small, pained sound. "And I think I have a concussion," he replied before holding up both hands in a sarcastic, celebratory gesture. "Yaaay."

A small, guilty giggle escaped her and she folded her arms on his chest before asking "Are you okay?"

He rubbed his face with both hands. "Oh yeah, I've been hit harder. That was really good, just promise me that if someone my size ever grabs you like that you'll just set him on fire or shank him, okay? Falling down like that is…not ideal."

Aimee made a fist of her right hand and mimed driving a knife into his neck. "Shank. Shank." She deadpanned. "You're dead now."

His pained laughter shook his frame beneath her. Instead of rising, she caught one of his hands in hers. "Are you okay, though?" she asked more earnestly. "The truth, now."

Elias lifted his head and pushed himself up until he rested on his elbows. Aimee shifted back to a sitting position on her heels, but they were still very close. "Oh yeah," he said after a moment, still blinking. Then his eyes settled on hers. In the year since he joined their crew he'd gone from gaunt and hollow to recovering much of his former strength. The ghost of a beard edged his sharp jawline these days, and his unruly dark hair wasn't completely contained by the knot he used to pull it back when they trained. One thing hadn't changed: the dark circles around his eyes. Elias Leblanc always looked tired. "Really, I'm fine," he said. "You?"

Aimee cleared her throat, leaning on one arm and cocking her head to regard him with a sideways smirk. "Never better," she said. *Now,* some part of her brain begged her. *Just do it now.*

She was about to lean in when the door to the cargo hold slammed open, and Bjorn's big frame filled the entryway. "Hello? You two kids in here?"

The two of them scrambled to their feet. Moment broken. Aimee frowned and fought back the urge to summon up a wind to throw the big man back through the doorway. *Dammit.*

"Over here," Elias said, leaning against a wood crate. Aimee flashed him a small glare over her shoulder. The look he answered it with could've been amusement or confusion. It was hard to tell.

"Oh, there you are," Bjorn said, his expression even and congenial. As if—Aimee thought—he hadn't just interrupted something important. "It's time to go portside," the big man finished. "We've got several hours to kill before chow's ready."

Clutch emerged from behind the big-framed cook and ship's gunner. Her dark face wore a cat-like grin beneath her shock of blue hair. "Assuming the two of you aren't otherwise occupied."

"Just sparring," Elias answered, and Aimee saw the hint of a laugh play at the corner of his mouth. "Anyone else is welcome to try." He paused, fetching his shirt from atop the crate where he'd laid it. "But she'll probably beat you."

"My Gods," Clutch said behind them as they walked up the stairs to the central corridor, "I think he's growing a sense of humor!"

The port in question was called Whitefeather, a city crouched upon an outcropping at the far end of a peninsula in the northern reaches of the Kiscadian Republic. Aimee's new leather boots thumped down the gangway as she walked, pulling her worn blue coat about her shoulders with hands threaded through fingerless gloves. The familiar weight of her portalmage's apprentice badge rested against the top of her neckline, and at the bottom of the ramp she took in the sprawl of ramshackle buildings spreading out in every direction. It was just before dawn, and everything was lit by the thousand wires holding paper lanterns that rustled in a cold wind.

Behind her, the slender knife of the skyship *Elysium* floated, secured to the skydocks by its mooring lines. A few feet from where she stood, the dock's edge dropped away into the open sky. It was cloudy this morning, and the ship's running lights illuminated the open air before it only a short distance.

"Lost in thought?" Elias asked as he came down the gangway towards her. He'd donned the black and green coat lined with fur that he'd gotten before they left the behemoth called *Iseult* ten months ago. His left hand rested on the pommel of Oath of Aurum, the enchanted longsword he carried with him everywhere he went. They stood together at the base of the ramp for a few seconds before she realized she was staring at his face and remembered she was supposed to answer. Her cheeks burned. *Not exactly.*

"It's been a year," she said. "Since I joined the crew, I mean. I was just thinking about how different of a sight that cargo bay is now. And…how much it's really not."

His eyebrows raised. "Then for me it's been about the same," he mused. "Minus…a week?"

"You're splitting hairs," Clutch said, coming down the gangway behind them. "You basically came on around the same time, albeit under wildly different circumstances."

Just behind her came the twins. Vant and Vlana were shorter than the dark-skinned pilot, and both had brought satchels slung over their shoulders. "Before you ask," Vant said, "we're not getting out of haggling with the spice merchants. Bjorn has been insisting on refilling the cabinet with hotter peppers ever since someone—" he glanced at his sister "—implied his cooking was bland."

The engineer's expression was half a grin and half a grimace. "So, intrepid friends: who's going with me? Everyone can't say no."

"I'm going to look for some other stuff," Vlana laughed. "Spices are your problem."

"We are," Aimee said, looping her arm through Elias's elbow. The engineer would likely haggle with the merchants for hours when they got there. Elias arched an eyebrow at her and she grinned back up at him. "I've never seen the spice agora. Come on, we can bring something back for Bjorn, and we've got the thyme to kill."

Elias caught the pun, and stared at her for a few seconds before cracking a smirk. "Seriously?"

Aimee swallowed, blushed, and stared straight ahead. *Why in the abyss did I say that.* "Just walk," she muttered.

Since Aimee de Laurent had joined the Elysium's crew as the apprentice of its owner and portalmage Harkon Bright, she'd been through hell and back. After the war in Port Providence and the month of intrigue and peril aboard the *Iseult*, the near-death experience of braving the Maelstrom and the skykraken called *Grandfather*, the past ten months had been almost peaceful. Surveys. Exploratory journeys through the unclaimed. She'd seen grey towers circling the high manses of the kingdom of Albatross and witnessed wild portal-storms at a distance near the edge of the Argathian Gauntlet, where two continents were locked in a cycle of mutual obliteration. She'd honed her magic, stepped up her fitness, and started training close combat under Bjorn and Elias's supervision.

And now, as she walked down the long, winding path of yet another port in the lantern-glow of the pre-dawn dark, moving past stalls and vendors and smoking coals, her mind was really only cooking over one thing: how was she going to get Elias Leblanc alone?

Just ahead of them, Vant's over-large satchel made repeated thumping noises against his back as he walked. Elias shot her a sideways glance before he asked "… just how many spices are you planning on getting?"

The grunt with which Vant responded bespoke boundless determination. "Enough."

Elias laughed—genuinely. It was a rare sound, but so at odds with the man he'd been a year ago, before their mutual contact with the enigmatic Axiom Diamond had freed him from the Eternal Order's mental control.

Aimee couldn't quite keep the affection from her face as she looked up at him. "Clutch was right," she said, gently nudging his rib with the elbow tucked inside his arm. "You are growing a sense of humor."

He looked momentarily self-conscious, and his free hand reached up to scratch the back of his head. "Think so?" he answered. "Is it terminal?"

Aimee laughed, the sound a little more nervous to her ears than she preferred. She gave his arm a squeeze. "Positively fatal."

Moments later they reached the agora, nestled between a high vaulted roof upheld by chipped and battered pillars. The lights of a thousand-plus lamps and lanterns glimmered alongside the shimmering haze of smoke and heat and small mystic furnaces keeping booths warmed against the cold. People without number moved past, a churning mass of patrons visiting the swath of vendors.

"Oh, damn it all to hell," Vant sighed. "Alright, come on."

They found a tall, walled shop that smelled intensely of spiced tea when they stepped through the door. Rows of shelves filled with large glass jars were labeled in dozens of languages. "Meet by the door," Vant said. "I gotta go haggle with the owner. See if you can find gnarl-root and sunflame powder in the meantime, yeah?"

There was her chance. "Understood," she said, and took Elias by the hand, pulling him further into the mass of shelves and the back aisles.

"I'm pretty sure," she heard him say, "that this isn't where the gnarl-root or sunflame is."

At the end of a row she turned around, pulling him with her. He stopped a little awkwardly, and the action brought him into her personal space. She didn't step back. Elias looked at her now. He'd gone very still, his hand still holding hers. A small smile quirked at the corner of his mouth. Acknowledgement. "Ah," he said, quietly.

"Is this okay?" She asked, frankly, lacing her fingers together with his. "This?" Her heart hammered in her ears. Reckless. Stupid. She didn't care —only needed to know that it was alright. That she wasn't crossing his line. His eyes closed for just a moment, and he breathed out.

Then he looked at her, and for just a second, she felt like his eyes were going to burn her alive. "That depends," he murmured. "On what you do— or don't do—next."

She was done waiting. "Good," she breathed. "Because I don't want to talk."

Her free hand reached up to bury in his hair, she pushed herself up on her toes, and pulled his mouth to hers. She felt his lips—soft. Felt him suck in a breath—then respond, as if he breathed her in. His fingers tightened in hers, and his other hand reached up to brush the side of her face with a callused palm. It was brief, tentative, inquiring, and when it ended, she pulled back slightly to watch his eyes. *Please,* she thought. *Tell me that was the right choice.*

He watched her quietly for a moment. Intensity. Surprise. She caught a flicker of something in his expression. The start of a smile—was it?

"That," he breathed, "was—"

Then someone screamed, "grenade!" and an entire rack of shelves two aisles over exploded.

They crashed through the stacks. Glass jugs burst open, spilling a cloud of mixed spices into the air. Aimee summoned a shield spell with a gesture and a hasty word, and it caught the second wave of debris that washed over the two of them. She pushed herself up on her knees, reached for Elias. "Are you alright?"

Beside her, the tall warrior rolled into a crouch. The shoulders of his coat were dusted with red powder and there was a cut on his forehead. "Everything's fine from the neck down. Where's Vant?"

"Shit," Aimee swore. The room was eerily quiet in the wake of the blast, the first groans that signaled the injured coming to their senses filling the air. "Vant!" she shouted, letting the mystic barrier dissipate. Elias moved past her, drawing Oath of Aurum from its sheath in a smooth arc. The broad, diamond cross-sectioned blade of the enchanted sword painted half his frame in soft light.

"Is anyone hurt?" His voice echoed through the room.

"This man over here," came a voice from off to the right. As both of them turned, Aimee's heart froze. Vant lay next to the ruins of the merchant's counter, blood seeping from a wound in his head. She vaulted over the debris, scrambling as Elias followed. Standing over the engineer was a gray-haired woman in a long coat. She shifted to let Aimee pass and she glimpsed the shimmer of steel rings beneath it.

"He lives," she said, as Aimee crouched. Vant's eyes were closed, but his breathing was steady and even. "But he'll need a healer."

"What happened?" Elias asked, as Aimee ran her hands over the sides of the engineer's face. "Did you see who did it?"

"I didn't," the woman said. She watched the door hawkishly. "And I'd rather not to stay to find out. Can you move him?"

"Give me a moment," Aimee murmured. Breathe. She could do this. She felt for the damage. Then she summoned up the stopgap spell with a swift series of gestures and pressed her hands to the sides of his head, speaking the words. The engineer breathed easier. "We can move him now," she said, rising, "but we need to go quickly."

"Yes," the woman said, before looking at Elias. "Can you carry him?"

A suspicious look flashed briefly across the green-eyed man's face. "There are other people hurt here. We can't abandon them."

Aimee looked around. Amidst the mass of collapsed wood and broken glass, the wounded were crying, now. A chorus of pained voices wailed around her. In the distance there was the pounding of feet and the raised shouts of the agora watchmen running towards the blast zone. Watchmen meant questions. Questions meant not getting Vant back to the ship in time.

"The guards are coming," Aimee answered. "And if we don't get him back to the infirmary now he's going to get worse." *I wasn't paying attention*, she thought. *Vlana. Gods.*

"Commendable as your virtue is," the woman said to Elias, "the sorceress is right. We need to leave. Now."

"Who are you?" Elias demanded. His hand was still on Oath of Aurum. The blade glowed brighter. "The truth."

The woman sighed, and closed her eyes. "Fine," she said. "The full truth: my name is Dame Helena Greyspear. I was the champion of Alahna of Port Providence for twenty years until I laid down my glaive." She turned and fully regarded them. "That," she gestured at the glimmering blade, "is Oath of Aurum, last held by my queen's late grandson, crown prince Collum, which means you are Elias Leblanc." She turned to look at Aimee, her hazel eyes cool and direct. "And you are Aimee de Laurent. Now I am more than capable of handling the men coming to kill me, but nothing is a guarantee, and I have sworn to see my queen's message delivered to you and your teacher. Now for the love of all the gods, children, you owe my people this much. Let's get out of here before things get worse."

Elias looked as though he'd just eaten a punch to the face. Pale. Eyes wide. Then he moved to Vant's other side. "I've got him," he said, and sheathed his sword before lifting the engineer like an oversized baby. "Fair warning," he grunted. "I can't fight very well like this."

Dame Helena smirked. "Don't worry, dear boy. You won't need to."

"Well, that was the easiest introduction I've ever had," Aimee said, grabbing up Vant's satchel. What she'd seen was impressive, but she hadn't survived the past year by trusting without reservation. She headed for the door, jumping over debris where it was needed. "Keep up Ma'am," she said. "And if you betray us, I'll set your face on fire."

They moved through the door and through the chaos of the crowd outside. Now free of the building's interior, Aimee could tell that something else was wrong. People weren't just running towards the spice-shop, they were running everywhere. She felt the chill wind and smelled the scent of burning wood and sulphur. The pre-dawn sky was marred by shimmering pillars of smoke that rose from several different places across the city.

"What in the abyss…" she started.

The pause saved her life. A blast of light sparked against the street right where her body would have been had she taken another step. The defensive spell came reflexively, mingled with the voiding backstep she'd learned from Bjorn and Elias months ago. A whirling wall of diluted force spun from her hands as she angled it between herself and her companions in time to catch the second blast. The shooter was a man of middling height dressed like any other of a thousand agora patrons, save for the light dancing around his outstretched fingers. Hedge-mage. "They're flushed!" the man screamed. "Now!"

Elias twisted behind her, shifting Vant just over his shoulder like a sack of potatoes. Four men charged them, two from the right and two from left. Elias pulled his sword with his right hand, keeping Vant over his shoulder with his left. The glowing blade was half out of its sheath when it caught the first assassin's axe with a ring. The second darted in on his flank and Aimee snapped her left hand to summon a spell of wind, but she didn't need to. Dame Helena was suddenly between them. A metal rod flashed in her hand, and the length of a six-foot glaive with a sharp blade at one end sliced out as if summoned with sorcery. The blade punched through the throat of Elias's second attacker and the butt struck one of the Dame's attackers full in the face. She spun. One man fell with a slashed neck, the second clutching a ruptured eyeball. A third spell tore outward from the mage, just beyond the reach of Aimee's shield. It barely missed the older woman's shoulder.

"Miss Laurent!" Helena shouted. "Be a dear and deal with the damn sorcerer, would you?"

Aimee dropped the shield spell, snapping over her shoulder "I'm not your damn granddaughter!"

She surged forward. Her enemy backpedaled, weaving awkward gestures she recognized even as they sparked the light of flame-spells into existence. Aimee's hands dashed through the counters, split the first attack down the centerline, dodged the second, and closed on her assailant with a fist sheathed in crackling lightning. He screamed.

Aimee spun back as the hedge-mage dropped smoking to the street. The remaining assassins were down, and Elias was sheathing his enchanted steel. It looked as though he hadn't drawn blood.

"I wasn't joking," Helena said, retracting her glaive once she'd wiped the blood from the steel. "Now the ship. Please. There will be others following."

Aimee didn't wait. She started back towards the ship at a jog, hoping that the others were all right. "Then keep up, granny. I'm not slowing down."

23

3

BREAK THE SPINE

What in the name of the fucking abyss is going on out there?"

Bjorn waited for them at the top of the ramp by the time they made it back to the ship. "I told you to find spices," the old warrior said. "Not set the city on fire."

Still carrying Vant over his shoulder, Elias let out a grunt. "You weren't specific enough."

"I need the infirmary ready," Aimee said, storming up the ramp. Dame Helena came behind them both, taking the measure of the ship with a glance. "The stories do not overstate," she mused out loud. "She's beautiful."

Elias was halfway up the ramp when Bjorn—noticing Vant— stepped between the young warrior and the older woman trying to follow him. "What in the abyss happened to Vant, and who in the abyss are you?"

Helena stopped just short of the old man, sizing him up, then she arched at eyebrow at Bjorn. "He was caught in the blast radius of a small detonation. He should live, if your sorceress friend can get him healed in time."

"That's not a full answer," Bjorn said, checking her shoulder with his palm.

She glanced down at his hand. "Touch me again and lose it."

"Bjorn!" Aimee shouted from the cargo bay. "Not now!"

24

Elias turned away from the pair. "Nobody dies," he said over his shoulder. "And nobody loses body-parts. Clear?"

They got Vant to the infirmary, laid him out on a cot, and Aimee set to work while Elias stood back in awkward, concerned silence. There hadn't been time to process what had happened, only the sudden awareness of her physical presence as she'd stepped closer and asked permission—something that, itself, meant the world to him, even if he lacked the proper words for it.

After a few moments she sagged back, folding her arms and breathing out. "He'll be alright. He'll have one hell of a headache when he wakes up… but he'll be alright."

She looked at him, then, and for a moment they stood in awkward silence opposite each other. Elias had never seen Aimee's eyes so wide, or so nervous. His own nerves were raw, and he didn't know if it was from the near-death experience, or the fresh memory of her fingers at the back of his neck. "Listen," he started to say. "About… about what happened back at the agora, before—"

"I'm sorry," Aimee said. Reflexive. Compulsive.

Elias frowned. "What?"

"I didn't mean." She started stumbling over her words. It was the strangest thing he had ever seen. "That was… I don't want you to feel like I wasn't…" she dropped her arms helplessly to her sides and she looked at him with her heart in her eyes. "Dammit."

Elias just stared, having gone from nervous to confused, to more confused. He let out a breath, then shook his head. It didn't matter how well trained he'd been in social interaction, or for how many years. The lessons on how to read another person which he'd received for over a decade were rendered useless when they were intimately tied first and foremost with understanding how to manipulate, hurt, or kill.

You didn't hurt me, he wanted to say. *I want this.* But his tongue kept tripping over his intentions.

It was needing to speak plainly while still re-learning how to talk at all.

"Aimee," he started, taking a step forward.

"Vant!" Vlana burst through the doorway. Elias flattened himself against the wall and barely avoided being trampled. The navigator staggered to the edge of her brother's bed. Half her face was coated in rock-dust, and there was blood on her left hand, but she looked better off than her brother. "What happened?" She demanded of Aimee. "Is he alright?"

Just outside the door, Clutch could be heard running to the bridge, a stream of curses echoing behind her.

"He's going to be fine," Aimee had already turned her attention to the engineer and his sister again. Elias thought he caught her wiping the corner of her eye very briefly. "We were hit with a small explosive charge but it didn't catch him directly. I've mended most of the damage, but what he needs most right now is rest, okay?"

Vlana breathed easier, nodding, closed her eyes, and knelt beside her brother's bed. Aimee shot Elias a look. Apologetic. Searching. He managed a small smile, then stepped out of the room. *Later. We can talk about it later.*

For now, there were urgent questions that needed answering. By the time Elias made it back to the cargo bay Harkon had emerged from his cabin, and now stood beside Bjorn as Helena spoke with both at the top of the ramp.

"Elias," Harkon said, turning towards him. The look on his face was worried—and grew more so when he caught the look on the green-eyed man's face. A letter was in the old sorcerer's hand, the red wax seal upon it broken. "Before you ask—"

"You mentioned the Queen Mother," Elias said, his eyes locked only on the warrior woman that had just upended his thoughts so thoroughly that even Aimee's kiss couldn't stay in the forefront of his mind. "You mentioned Alahna," he finished, coming to a stop just short of the edge of her personal space. The last time he had seen King Coulton's grandmother had been in the depths of the Iron Hulk, when he freed her from a captivity he had only days before enforced upon her, when he'd been the black knight known as Lord Azrael.

She had been the first to see something else in him, and the first person—other than Aimee—to believe him when he had thrown everything away.

"Dame Helena," Bjorn started. "This—this is a lot, at once."

"My queen remembers you," Helena said, talking over the warrior. "And now that I've read her letter as well, I believe that no matter what these two say, you must hear it now: her grandson has fallen under the thrall of Silas, the one-time grey sage. He has made blood pact with something ancient and evil, in return for terrible power the likes of which I have never seen in all my years."

Out of the corner of his eyes, Elias saw Bjorn close his eyes and bow his head.

"Her Majesty has sent me to beg you remember that whatever else he is, Coulton is still a child. The last scion of his line, and the hope of his kingdom. But more than that, he is her grandson, and all that remains to her." Helena's eyes burned into his. "My queen would have you find him, before the madness of this vendetta consumes him." She paused. "She would have you save the boy from himself."

Silence fell across the bay. Elias felt three pairs of eyes upon him. Behind him, he heard Aimee's footfalls at the door to the cargo bay. After a moment that seemed eternal, he heard Bjorn start to speak again. "Lad," the old warrior murmured. "You should take a moment to breathe. You don't have to—"

"There's nothing to think about," Elias said. "I'll do it."

"What in the abyss did you just agree to?" Aimee's voice echoed behind him.

Elias paused, the deeper implications sinking in. "I… have no idea." He turned back to Helena. "I don't know what it could possibly entail, or why he might listen to me of all people…but I will try."

At the edge of his vision, Elias could see Harkon watching him with a level gaze, and Bjorn closed his eyes, bowing his head for a moment, as if crushed momentarily by an inexpressible grief.

There was a beat. A pause, as the room absorbed what he'd said, then Elias heard Aimee speak again behind him. "Then I'm going with you. All of us are."

He didn't know what he'd expected to hear in response, but it hadn't been that. For the few seconds that followed, he couldn't speak around the lump in his throat.

"So the next question," Aimee said, looking at Helena, "is where in the abyss are we going, anyway?"

Helena paused. "We have to find him, first."

And that was when a loud crash of rending metal sounded outside, and the *Elysium* shuddered at the nearby impact. A groaning noise followed, rending, metal crying out as its structural integrity buckled. Elias dashed to the stern ramp that led down to the skydocks from the cargo hold. Outside, a chunk of the docks two berths down from the *Elysium* was a smoldering, twisted ruin of mangled wood and melted steel. Two more blasts sounded further down, and Elias saw detonating flashes of ether-canon blasts slamming into the thicket of docked skyships. Burning wreckage sloughed off into the abyss, and a chorus of cries and shouts now rose in the wake of the first impacts.

Elias raised his eyes to heaven. The pre-dawn sky over Whitefeather burned. He heard the others emerging behind him, a dozen exclamations, theories, and curses rising in his ears. Elias shut them out, searching the heavens for two things: the familiar sight of fast-moving black gunships, and the tail-smoke from the swift craft he knew too well.

"Who the fuck has the balls to raid Whitefeather?" He heard Bjorn yell.

A loud roar sounded from beyond the docks, and as Elias looked up, a black, knife-like frigate roared overhead, faster than any ship its size had a right to be. The red flare from its exhaust vents and the swift turn of its graceful arc chilled the green-eyed young man to his core. It had been over a year since he'd seen that make, but it was as intimately familiar as the sight of his own hand.

"The Eternal Order," Elias answered. The bottom dropped out of his stomach. "They're here."

"We need to go," Helena said. "Now."

"Agreed," Elias heard Harkon say. High overhead, a larger warship, a sleek, immense dreadnought sliced through the clouds, its running lights glimmering in the darkness as it came to a stop over the center of the city. Not an Iron Hulk, but a monster nonetheless. The graceful arc of its cloud-cracker was like the spine of some murderous vulture, its maw shimmering with the heat of chained fire.

Then multiple beams of light lanced across the heavens, forming the image of a pale face with red-rimmed eyes, the mark of nine black stars stamped upon his head. Elias's mouth went dry, as the projected voice echoed across the savaged, confused districts of Whitefeather.

"People and government of Whitefeather. I speak on behalf of the Eternal Order. Your esteemed city harbors a man named Elias Leblanc. He has taken sanctuary aboard the skyship *Elysium*. Know that he, and the friends, family, and loved ones of any who harbors him are marked for death."

The image shimmered, and Elias stared, wide-eyed, into the image of his own face, projected across the sky. "Whomsoever delivers him to us, or any information that leads to his capture, shall know riches beyond the dreams of emperors."

A strong hand grasped his shoulder, and spun around, Elias found himself staring into Bjorn's face. "Don't even think of turning yourself in, boy," the old warrior growled. "They'll just kill everyone anyway."

Elias's throat was dry, his heart hammered at panic pace in his chest. "I can't—" he stuttered "—I can't just let them do this."

"We're not 'letting' them do anything," Harkon said. The old sorcerer stared at the sky, a fury in his eyes such as the black knight had never seen. "This is not New Corinth, and we are not helpless as we were then. Get inside. We're taking off."

Elias swayed on his feet as he followed. "We can't just leave these people at their mercy!"

The old sorcerer glanced back over his shoulder as they all followed him into the ship. "We're not slinking away, Elias. We're going to fly up there and bloody the beast in the nose. Then we'll flash them our exhaust vents and have them make chase. Helena—" he addressed the old warrior woman "—Get me coordinates for the nearest thing to Coulton's last known location. Aimee, be ready to portal us out of here as soon as I give the Order."

"Hark," Bjorn swore. "You may have noticed this, but we're temporarily down an engineer."

"No," came a voice from the door to the corridor that spanned Elysium. "You're not. At least... not exactly."

Vant leaned heavily on his sister's shoulder, his eyes half-focused. The engineer's face lacked color, and he looked as if every last ounce of whatever he had had been used to drag himself from the bed against Vlana's protestations. "I just...just need someone to be my hands," he said. "Someone to do what I tell them."

"You shouldn't be doing anything," Vlana pleaded.

"Prolly not," the engineer groaned, rubbing the side of his head in obvious pain. "But if I don't, we're all gonna die. So that's not exactly a choice, is it?"

"I'll go," Elias said, wrenching himself free from Bjorn. Ascending the steps, he shifted in under Vant's other arm. Vlana stared uncertain daggers at him. "They need you on the bridge," Elias said. "I only know the very basics about metadrives, but I'm quick, and I can follow orders."

"Hear that?" Vant half-chuckled. "He's gonna follow my orders. See Sis? He'sss like a brother already. Now stop treating me like a newborn squitten and go do your job."

~

The heart of Elysium was its metadrive chamber, and when he saw it for the first time, Elias had to tilt his head to ensure that what he perceived wasn't wrong. There was no floor to speak of—instead, on the other side of the door the space was a large, multifaceted sphere set with a lattice of brass bars. And from one end of the room to the other, a single metallic column bisecting the space with a large orb of black-veined white stone, etched with numbers in repeating lines.

No, Elias realized after a half-second of staring. The lines of text were shifting back and forth in rows above and below one another. With each ripple of intense magic that emanated from the heart of the ship, numbers changed, runes twitched left or right, and the whole orb rotated.

"Yeah," Vant murmured, leaning on his arm. "I know, it's a bit different. The *Hulk's* drive was a giant, glowing orb of contained mystic fire, and *Iseult's* cores were glass tubes filled with purple light, but *Elysium's* heart is unlike anything else in the Drifting Lands. One of a kind. And she's a helluva thing to use: one part abacus, one part puzzle-vault, channeling a soul of limitless potential. The ship spins so much that it doesn't make sense to stand on the floor, so you get around by holding the bars. Half this job is doing high level arcanology while hanging upside down by your knees."

The engineer coughed. "It's the only part of this ship built around the fact that sometimes we have to be upside down or sideways. I hope you can keep your constitution together and follow orders while doing a handstand. And if you can't, well…puke bucket's over there. Okay, put me down there."

Elias helped the engineer to a set of handholds that gave him a perfect view of the whole of the metadrive. "You're going to have to allow for a second delay on everything," Elias said. "I know my basics, but this is… something altogether different."

"Also not designed to power continent-killing super weapons," Vant grunted.

"That too," Elias answered.

There was a crackling noise, and Elias heard Clutch's voice come echoing down through the communication tubes. "You two situated down there? We've got frigates coming around for another pass and could really use the boost."

Vant groaned as he tightened his grip. "You're gonna hear Clutch scream 'hard burn,' soon. Then she's gonna start yelling for it every twenty seconds. Suppress the urge to kill her, but cuss at her all you want."

Elias shifted towards the sphere. "Okay, how do I do this?"

There was a shift beneath his feet as the Elysium swung loose from her moorings and tilted into the open sky. Outside, the rhythmic thump of ether canons filled the air.

"When she calls for a hard burn, put your hands on the first row and shift it two notches to the left. Less and the drive will underpower the burst. More, and we might fly right through one of their cruisers like a spear. Not good."

"Two notches," Elias nodded, flexing his fingers and making sure his weight was settled and evenly balanced between his heels. "Spear not good. Right."

"Don't sweat this," Vant said, trying to sound helpful. "If we die it will happen very quickly and both of us will be incinerated first."

"Oh," Elias said. "Um. Good?"

He had just gotten his balance when he felt a ripple of potent magic surge outside the Elysium's hull. A communication spell—amplified by degrees that made the black knight dizzy to contemplate.

A half second later, a voice filled the air—forceful, unrelenting, blunt, and all-too familiar. "People of Whitefeather, I am Lord Ogier of the Eternal Order. Your city has given sanctuary to the crew of the skyship *Elysium*. Turn them over to me, or I will kill every living soul in this city and melt what remains into slag."

Elias's breath quickened. His hands went cold and clammy against the warm sphere and he tried to keep his focus on the here and now, even as he grappled with twin feelings of fear and relief. Not Roland. Ogier.

"You alright?" Vant said behind him. Then, after a pause, "is…is that your teacher?

"No," Elias answered as Elysium turned in a slow arc. "He was Malfenshir's."

Silence. Muffled explosions sounded outside. Then Clutch's voice came down the tubes.

"Boys," she said. "Hard burn."

Elias pressed his fingers to the row and turned. Two notches. It was as if two separate flood doors had been opened. The light in the room brightened to blinding for a half-second, then the whole metadrive chamber rotated, and mystic force surged down the column with such force that Elias nearly dropped to his knees.

"Oh yeah," Vant laughed behind him. "Here we go."

Elysium exploded forward. Elias held on for dear life as the metadrive chamber shifted and rotated. Behind him the engineer cackled as the slender skyship turned sideways, dove straight down, then surged into a nearly vertical climb.

"In just a second," Clutch called down, "we're going to level off and come right down on that capitol ship they came here in."

"We're suiciding into a dreadnought's spine?" Vant yelled back. "Is that what you're saying?"

"Please," Clutch's voice came back. "The second we go level I need you to open up all vents and flood the guns. We're gonna strafe the bastards, then we're bolting as fast as we can."

"And you want me to do this secondhand?" Vant snapped back. "With fingers that aren't mine?"

"Look," the answer came back. "You're the one that said we could do this, so put up or shut up, hull-rat."

Glancing over his shoulder, Elias saw red flash across Vant's eyes, and the engineer suddenly found a surge of energy, grabbed the communication tube and screamed into it. The stream of invective that followed was the most inventive thing he'd ever heard.

"Okay," the engineer then said as the room tilted and Elias started to feel sick, "You're gonna have to get right up against the sphere. You flood the vents by shifting the row two notches back, the one underneath three notches to the right, then pulling the lever on the left side of the column, all in rapid sequence. Understand?"

"Wait," Elias said, lurching back. "Give me that tube."

He lurched over and snatched the aperture from the engineer's hand, speaking quickly and hoping the people on the bridge would understand him. "It's Elias—listen. If that dreadnought is Ogier's flagship, its name is the *Atrocity*, and it's armed with a spinal cloud-cracker that can turn Whitefeather to molten rock. Ogier will do it. The second he thinks we're running, he'll fire. You have to disable the gun, or thousands of people are about to die."

The sound of hasty talking echoed from the far end, then Clutch's answer came back. "Be ready to flood those vents, pretty-boy. And we'll light these bastards up."

Behind him, Vant laughed. Elias answered quickly. "Three silver rings. They're small. They mark segments along the dreadnought's spine. They're accelerators and amplifiers, and the beam has to pass through each to hit full strength. Hit each of them as hard as you can, and it'll take the gun out for hours. Possibly days, if the damage is deep enough."

"Elias," the terse answer came. "Thank you. Now get to the vents."

The ship surged level. Vant yelled "Quick! Do it quick!"

Elias leaped across the space. The ship started to tilt forward. He misjudged the distance and slammed into the sphere, pain exploding across his face.

"Oh God," Vant groaned behind him. "You choose now to fall on your face?"

"Shut up!" Elias pushed himself up, struggling through a haze of dizziness to perform the task given him. Two notches back. One notch right. The ship was in free-fall forward, he heard Clutch screaming over the tubes "Now means now, not after we die!"

Elias thrust his hand down and snapped the lever down so hard he lost his balance and tumbled to the edge of the chamber. The Sphere surged with light, as every single etching upon its manifold rows glowed from within. There was a rush, as the column shifted with a roar as the full power of the ship's metadrive was unleashed through the system, simultaneously surging to weapons and engines.

Elias grabbed two handholds, though he needn't have. The force of their descent pinned him to the wall of the chamber. Down. They were flying straight down. The arcane power all around him made him nauseous. The dull thump of ether-canon fire from outside filled the air, and in his mind's eye he could almost see the black specter of the *Atrocity* beneath as the *Elysium* surged downward.

Then with a jerk that made him sick, they leveled out. Elias's tenses tingled and he gripped the bars to keep from being violently flung around as the ship's own guns sprang to life, and the ripping crack of shredding bursts of arcane fire filled his ears. Three, four, five times, then a rending explosion. A half-breath. The ship veered, likely around a control tower on the vastly larger vessel. Elias held on for dear life as the guns roared to life a second time from both front and rear. A second explosion. They were almost there.

"Get ready to amplify and flood all power to engines!" Clutch yelled.

Elias pried himself from the handholds, forcing himself back towards the sphere. "Pull the lever back up, then straight out!" Vant shouted as a third salvo of gunfire followed so fast on the tail end of a second explosion that the two sounds were nearly one. They'd hit the second ring along the *Atrocity's* cloud-cracker. Elias pictured the black plates of the killing warship's spine perhaps less than half a ship's length beneath them. Almost to the third.

He was almost at the base of the sphere. Every movement of his hand was like dragging through water. His head was too addled to summon the requisite spells, and the amount of magic surrounding him was making him violently ill. The lever was there. Reach. Reach!

He heard the third ring explode with a rending crash, and a much deeper blast echoed far-too-close beneath. Screaming, Elias pushed the lever back up, then pulled it out. He felt the flow of power reverse direction as if the bottom had dropped out of his stomach. *Elysium* shot forward with the sound of a detonation astern. There was a rush of magic upwards as one of the mages summoned their portal into the sky, then the familiar surge of speed and disorientation as the vessel shot through it.

"Back in!" Vant said. Elias obeyed. Returned the lever to its original position. The lights on the drive dimmed, and the overwhelming rush of magic began to ebb away as it was contained within the heart of the *Elysium's* core.

Elias lurched sideways. He grabbed the puke bucket in both hands and let go of everything he had with a loud, violent croak.

Dimly, through the coughs, the green-eyed warrior was aware of Vant's hand coming to rest on his shoulders.

"It's alright," he heard the engineer say. "Not everyone can do my job."

4

THE TIRELESS

I told you, majesty," Silas said. "That I would find the means to save us all."

The interior of the hold was dimly lit by lamp-strands high overhead. The belly of the royal flagship of Port Providence was a cavernous space, but the central bay of the hauling barge put it to shame. The space in which they now stood could have housed multiple legions at attention plus whatever support equipment they'd brought with them.

Which was fitting, Silas mused, since the secret he had brought before his liege took up the same amount of space, but was worth so much more than any mere army of men. They stood now before a mass covered in the shroud of a canvas tarp tied down with thick hemp ropes. One of many. The King stood just a short distance back, his long coat ill-fitted to his narrow shoulders. Seventeen had not seen Coulton grow into his full stature as yet, but Silas had every faith that the boy would do admirably, so long as he listened.

So long as he obeyed.

Coulton slowly stepped forward. His guards stood just back, nervous, uncertain as to whether they could stop him. They regarded Silas with measured suspicion. Silas smiled.

"They're larger than I expected," the King said. He held up a hand to touch the tarp, but hesitated before looking at the old man with the face that bespoke the trust of a student in his faithful teacher. Looming over him, the vaguely man-like shape of the figure projected an ominous, patient quiet.

"Can I touch them?" Coulton asked with jarring innocence. "Is it safe?"

"They were dormant when we found them," Silas said, "and the power I have been granted allowed us to transport them in that selfsame state, so yes, your grace. You may. When the time comes to wake them, that touch will be absolutely crucial. These are to be your mightiest servants and loyal champions, my King. Best you become acquainted."

The ritual had very specific requirements, the knowledge within Silas reminded him—that small voice present since his communion with the Twelfth Night that never left, and sometimes added its voice to his own. It had to be Coulton. It had to be the blood of a king. And as Silas watched, the canvas rustled at his majesty's touch. Coulton's eyes closed, then opened. He smiled. "Silas," he said. "I can *feel* them. I thought you said these were just…what was the word—automatons?"

"Yes, Majesty," Silas answered. "This is good, it means your bloodline is sufficiently strong, your claim to royalty potent enough to exert the requisite will upon them. If you are ready, I can perform the ritual that shall give you direct command over not just one, but all of them. A legion of adamant acting upon your very thoughts. It will tax you, my boy. There is always a cost, but the gains cannot be overstated."

Coulton stared up at the masked face beneath the fluttering canvas. Silas held his breath. Willing. It had to be willing. Everything now rested upon the boy's choice.

Silas watched the fear, the hesitation, the would-be gentleness rise up in the boy's face…then he watched as Coulton's fist tightened, driving it down. Crushing it beneath his youthful will. "Do it."

"Seal the doors," Silas said to the guards. "Everyone outside but the King and myself."

Nervous looks were exchanged between the courtiers and the remaining generals. One started to object. "Highness," he said, "you have fighting men remaining, ships, a fleet, however small. These…steel servitors are not flesh and blood."

Silas turned, smirking, and looked at the battered old fighting man. He didn't even remember the older noble's name. "All the better, don't you think? These ancient titans of Varengard, this legion of Tireless from the golden plains saves countless lives for every one used. They do not tire. They do not slow. And when one falls, we have lost none of our precious sons or daughters."

The general cleared his throat and started to speak again. "A warrior is more than strength and power," he said. "More than the will to conquer and the skill to kill. Our people have never believed in doing things the easy, convenient way. Majesty, please, your late father and brother knew that victory must never be attained at the cost of our people's souls. It is why they fought when they could have yielded easily to Lord Azrael's demands—"

"Do not speak to me of Lord Azrael," Coulton's reply was a sharp, pained retort, as if the name had stung him. Silas could hear the boy's heart breaking as he spoke. "You're right, general. My brother believed in an antiquated, straightforward honor, and in doing things the hard way... and it landed him dead, and his enchanted sword in the hands of the man who killed him. I cannot be my brother, or our people will never know victory, or satisfaction, or safety, again."

As Silas watched, the boy took a breath. "Guards, escort my court from the room. Silas has a ritual to perform."

~

They walked alone through a room filled with silent titans. Silas breathed in the cold air, tinged with the faint hint of dirt and a low buzz of magic energy the one-time-sage had never been good at detecting before his bargain. *Stavrophore,* he reminded himself. *First priest of the Twelfth Night to walk the Drifting Lands in over a millennia.*

"I commend your strength of will, majesty," Silas said as they walked past countless silent ghosts in canvas shrouds. "There was a time, not so distant in memory, when such power of mind in its King was all a nation needed to prosper."

Beside him, the young King took a fortifying breath. His fear was apparent to Silas—his doubt in his decision to dismiss his generals, and in whether or not he was strong enough to meet the challenges ahead.

Turn him from the former, the voice whispered in Silas's mind. *Set fire to the latter.*

"I am trying," Coulton said, earnest and pained.

"Majesty," Silas said. "Do not doubt yourself. You are making your ancestors brim with pride."

The King paused and looked at Silas's face. "Then why," he said, quietly, "do I dream of my late brother's face, staring at me with sorrow and grief?"

Silas placed a hand on the King's shoulder. *Why indeed?*

"My King," the Stavrophore said, "your brother is as yet unavenged, and his enchanted sword is wrongfully resting in our enemy's hands while his people wander in exile, their future uncertain. Why wouldn't he grieve? But fear not. Together, we will make it right."

He had prepared the ritual circle meticulously, a near twin of the one that had taken his consciousness to the barrow of the Twelfth Night. But bigger, grander, and from its edge, thousands of individual lines linked it to smaller marks beneath the feet of the forest of shrouded figures that surrounded them, now. Months of work—each one of these creations dug painstakingly from the earth—now culminated in a single set of magical activations contingent upon one young man's compliance. Coulton stopped at its edge, staring at the platinum dust and the scratched singles incised into the floor.

"It's…frightening," the young King said. "Unsettling to behold, but also beautiful, in a strange way."

"Your majesty has the right of it," Silas answered. "This is old magic. These Tireless were once but a footnote in the armies of long-lost Varengard. But against today's military might, it would put even the Eternal Order's mighty knights to the test."

"How many," Coulton breathed, "do we have?"

Silas smiled. "Five thousand, majesty. And once I have performed the ritual, they will all operate at your every command. Now please, my King, step into the circle."

Coulton's careful, obedient footsteps were like hammer-blows of destiny, and Silas felt his heart rate increase. *Yes,* said the voice. *They will pay.*

The King stood in the center of the circle, now. His feet found the right place to stand, as if he was destined to occupy that space. Silas paused, briefly disoriented. In that instance, Coulton suddenly looked neither like a king nor even like a brash young man of determination and will. What stood before Silas was the young boy he had tutored and taught in the sunset kingdom of Port Providence. The boy that had preferred literature and painting to war, even as he furiously chased after the ankles of his older, more famous brother.

And as he looked, the boy's composure cracked, for just a moment. "…will it hurt?"

Deep within him, some vestige of defiance rose. A beseeching whisper, pleading with him even as the pathway to his vengeance stood before him. *Please,* it begged. *Don't do this.* Silas took a shuddering breath. Then the visage of Lord Azrael stared back at him, a year ago, from the floor of the Axiom cavern, bound yet still toying with him. *You're not accustomed to the idea of killing, are you?*

Silas swallowed. Fortified. In his heart, he grasped hold of that last quiet voice of resistance and drowned it.

"I believe that it will," Silas answered. "But it is all for good, majesty. By taking on this burden, you will set great things in motion." He pressed his hands to the edge of the carefully drawn circle, felt the power stir within him, the ambient strength of his patron calling to him across incalculable distances. The itch in his chest intensified to an ache. As if it would leap forth from his body, if it could.

There were no words necessary. Silas pressed his hands to the circle and willed its magic to activate. Darkness threaded forth from his fingers, filling the lines of the circle like water chasing the length of a channel. Coulton's face flashed with fear, and Silas watched.

The lines coalesced. A cold wind blew through the vast bay, stirring the shrouds of five thousand adamant ghosts. All Silas could hear for an agonizing second was Coulton's terrified breathing, then a black limb thrust from the circle before the King's frame, the substance of which was not quite shadow, not quite flesh. The scent of funerary oil and candle-smoke smothered the senses, and Coulton had a half-breath to scream before the limb lashed him across the face. Drops of royal blood splashed upon the floor, and the lines of the circle turned red. Rushed outward. Raced across the floor in every direction, striking five thousand circles beneath the frames of hulking, shrouded shadows. As swiftly as it had appeared, the limb melted to nothing, and Silas turned as his king fell to one knee.

There was a great groan, the sound of metal bodies without number shifting their stance, and beneath the cowls of countless shrouds the crimson glow of eyes ignited. Silas felt his breath catch in his throat as he turned on his heels, arms spread wide. "Behold, my King," he breathed in the red-tinged darkness of the bay. "The pride of lost Varengard. Behold your legion of Tireless."

Coulton swayed on his feet, still clutching at the cut on his face, then staggered backwards. There was a loud clamor as one of the twelve-foot golem-soldiers shifted, discarding its shroud. One of its four adamant limbs caught the King as he fell, preventing his head from striking the bay floor. Silas had never seen anything move so fast.

But it was neither the sound of his king's voice, nor the presence of the newly awakened ancient war-machines that pulled Silas's focus to a pinprick. It was the sound of clapping. Across the floor, coming from the direction of the door the stavrophore had believed to be closed, a figure approached. He was tall, with the strong frame of a fighting man. And though he was older by two decades than the last person Silas had seen wearing that armor, it slowed him not at all. A longsword was strapped to his left hip, and there were white streaks in his black hair. Yet it was the face that pulled Silas's attention. Utterly unconcerned. Pale. Set with eyes like cold, distant stars. He smiled, and it was somehow both placid and crooked at once. The darkness within Silas stirred in recognition.

"Impressive sorcery," the stranger said. His voice was deep. At ease with his surroundings. "Do watch over the boy, though, in the days to come. Rituals such as this take such a toll on their subjects."

He should have obliterated the interloper with a gesture, yet something within Silas made him stop and speak before his hand spat the sort of darkness that had nearly destroyed Helena's ship, weeks ago. Instead, he turned to face the intruder. "How did you get past his majesty's guards?" .

"Come now Silas," the man said, still smiling. "Surely your bargain has not made you ignorant of reality. There isn't a single fighting man or sorcerer on this ship able to prevent me from going anywhere that I wish."

"You," Silas hissed, and his hand raised. "I should burn you to paste for daring to enter my presence."

The man waited, smiling, for a blow that never came. And after a moment of standing, staring at this figure who refused to fear either force or strength. Then, at last, Silas lowered his hand. "Why are you here?"

"That's better," the man said. "Proper introductions first. I believe in formalities. I am Lord Roland of the Eternal Order. I have come to offer you a bargain."

5

THE DE LAURENT MANEUVER

The bridge shuddered as another ether canon blast painted the sky ahead of Elysium the color of blue fire. Aimee gripped the rail to keep her balance, and at the wheel Clutch snarled "This makes seven jumps! How the fuck do they keep finding us?"

"Hark, I thought you said the *Elysium* could outrun Order skyships!" Vlana barked from the navigation console.

"The *Atrocity* is newer," Bjorn grunted, running towards the door to the spine corridor of the ship. "At least that's what Elias said. Only a few years fresh from the House of Nails shipyards."

"Yes, well," Harkon growled from atop the portal deck. "I suppose after seventeen years they're finally starting to catch up."

"Oh, you wanna bet?" Clutch said through clenched teeth before she shouted into the tube "Boys!"

"Clutch, I know Elias and I look very similar," Vant's deadpan sarcasm came back, "but please remember that we have names."

Aimee surged backwards towards the door of the bridge. "Helena!" She yelled back through the corridor. "How's it coming with those maps?"

"We're still two more jumps away," Helena snapped back from the galley. Aimee followed her voice, jogging down the hallway as the muffled sounds of ether-canon blasts thudded outside the hull. As it turned out, Helena Greyspear did not know the precise location of Coulton's people

—only rumors, and a name she'd been hunting the skycharts for: *Lia's Rest.*

"But do you know this time?" Aimee fired back. A spark of hope lit in her chest. A destination, finally.

"I'm as near to certain as I can be," the warrior woman replied. She dashed up the corridor and pressed a piece of paper into Aimee's hands. Coordinates. "Please," Helena said. "Get us away from that damned vulture of a warship, will you?"

Aimee staggered back onto the bridge just as Elysium blasted her engines again. They'd been at this for what felt like days. Every time they made a portal jump, the *Atrocity* would appear within a few hours on the other side of the portal, somehow tracking them from place to place, hunting them without surcease. "I've got the numbers," she said, rushing back onto the bridge. "The problem is, we can't tell how they're tracking us. Without knowing that, we might as well lead them right to Coulton's people."

"Something about our metadrive, maybe?" Vlana suggested, crouched over the navigation console. "The *Atrocity's* from the same shipyard, yeah?"

"Possible," Harkon murmured. "Yet we can't kill the engines to lose them."

Aimee chewed on her lip and wracked her brain for options.

"If you don't mind," Bjorn's voice came over the tubes, "they're gaining on us."

"I liked this gig a whole lot better when we were still the fastest ship in the Unclaimed." Vlana grumbled.

"Vlana," Clutch jabbed a finger in the navigator and quartermaster's direction, "I don't care if we're dropping out of the sky on fire. Never insult my girl like that again. Understand?"

Something clicked in Aimee's head. A historical footnote from her classes at the academy, well over two years ago. Of course. She'd been stuck looking for solutions other people had already come up with to problems that weren't this one.

The answer—crazy, dangerous—lay in one of the most spectacular failures of portalmagic in recorded history.

"Harkon," Aimee said, grabbing her teacher by the shoulder. "We need to outdo the *Rosswen.*"

Harkon Bright turned to look at her, an expression halfway between shock and contemplation on his face.

"Rosswen," Vlana gulped. "Like...the lights?"

"I think I can make it work," Aimee answered.

"Rosswen," Vlana continued, "as in the trapped-in-time-disintegration called the Rosswen Lights?"

"Yes," Aimee said over her shoulder. "Except, we don't disintegrate. Understand?"

"How exactly?" The navigator shot back.

"Simple," Aimee said. "We don't make the same mistake."

"Any idea what that was?" Clutch spoke this time. Her voice was focused—incredulous.

"Nobody knows," Vlana said. "The only ones who do are dead."

"I have a theory," Aimee answered.

"Would someone mind clarifying what on earth you're all talking about?" Helena interjected.

"The Rosswen Lights," Harkon explained, "You've heard of them?"

"Of course," Helena answered. "The three odd peaks in the Sparrow-teeth mountains?"

"They're named for a portal accident," Harkon said. "The crew of the *Rosswen* attempted a specific sort of jump, where a portal is opened, and a second is immediately opened on the other side, cast through the first. They failed."

"They're called the Rosswen Lights," Vlana said, voice shaken, "because the sky above them glows with the reappearance of a lovely four-dimensional debris field that intersects the highest peaks of those three mountains every ten days, thirteen hours, two minutes, and twelve seconds. People keep finding debris from the crash that vanishes and reappears where they found it, each time it cycles in."

Her eyes were haunted. "The bodies don't even rot. Stuck in time."

"We jump to a random location," Aimee continued, "we feint—and shoot the second portal through the first to the actual coordinates Helena's provided. However they're tracking us, I doubt they can follow us through that."

Harkon nodded. "Until we know how to track them, we don't dare stop."

"Then don't," Aimee said. "Just long enough to drop a few of us on the ground. Elias, Helena, me. We'll make contact while you keep the *Atrocity* off for a few days then swing back when we've learned what we need."

Silence hung on the bridge for an agonizing moment. The thud of ether canon fire echoed outside the hull, and Elysium shuddered and leaned as Clutch pulled the vessel into a long turn.

Then Harkon nodded. "Make the calculations."

~

Aimee's feet shook on the portal deck. The loud explosions sounded. She didn't even know where they were, only that they'd lost track of after numerous jumps and terrified scrambling. The first location was less important than the second, so she'd picked a spot somewhere just outside the Violet Imperium's borders. Sending the *Atrocity* somewhere likely to force them to take fire from irritable Imperial dreadnoughts seemed like a fine middle finger to leave their pursuer with. Glimmermere, she thought, as lenses lowered and she stepped onto the dais. The feel of the enchanted stone beneath her boots was a tease to the senses, and her palms sweated with the insane, stupid danger.

Her theory had to do with a simple matter of timing. Basic, inane timing. The crew of the *Rosswen* had been so set upon their goal that they lost sight of the mundane. One number exchanged for another in the mind of a portalmage, and brilliance had become horror repeated age over age, instead. If they could space it out right. If she didn't slip, or collapse into a fit of nerves. If if if.

The magic of the metadrive surged beneath her feet, smooth and potent. A rich resource promising a thousand possibilities. Aimee forced her mind to focus only on the one that mattered. Glimmermere. She summoned the blue flame with hands upraised, and shouted the words, sending a bolt of magnified light into the infinite sky. The blast of the newborn portal followed the flare of light and the glittering, kaleidoscopic eye that split the heavens, and Elysium surged forward again. Aimee silently counted down from seven. It had been seven.

It had to be.

Then she dropped back, and rolled out of the way, her fingers holding the spell in place. "Now!"

Harkon Bright leaped onto the dais and whipped his hands through the precise gestures of portal-casting, so fast that Aimee's eyes could barely follow. She was good at her chosen profession, swifter on the dais than any of her classmates, and since her first trial by fire in Port Providence a year ago, Aimee had cast portals in storms, in calm skies, in the midst of gales and during firefights. She was coming into her own.

Watching Harkon Bright at that same craft reminded her just how much she still had to learn. This second portal was by far the more difficult, having to be cast through the first. The slightest dimension off, and there would be a second haunting ground of eternally disintegrating wreckage named for whatever the people who eventually found them chose to call it. Idly, Aimee wondered if it would be insulting.

Then the metadrive gunned beneath them as Harkon held the spell suspended. They roared towards the first portal. Aimee counted down, keeping her spell going, this time out-loud.

"Seven."

A blast of ether-canon fire painted the sky before them green and red.

"Six."

Clutch gripped the wheel below as the engines roared their fury at the billowing clouds.

"Five."

Vlana shouted something below, or perhaps she prayed. Aimee's ears rang with the rush of her breath and her own pounding heart.

"Four."

Vant's voice echoed upwards, something halfway between a shout of fear and a cry of exhilaration.

"Three."

Her hands ached from holding the portal open as fire sparked between Harkon's controlled, frozen hands. The cyclopean eye filled their vision.

"Two."

Out of the corner of her eyes, she saw Elias burst onto the bridge, saying something. Their eyes met.

"One."

Silence. Eternity. A single breath. Then Harkon released the spell. Simultaneously they passed through the portal. Aimee set her teeth, her fingers feeling like twigs straining to contain hurricane winds. The glimmering tunnel whirled around them in its wheel of impossible color, and Harkon's beam of perfect light blasted through its center as the *Elysium* shot forward on the strength of its first engine burn. They tore through the other side, amidst a thundering gale that buffeted the ship with wailing winds. Lightning forked as the second portal burst into existence and the engines burned again. Aimee slammed her first portal shut with a clap of her hands as Clutch screamed against the wheel and the skyship hurtled through the second portal—silver lightning shot from the bow of the gods.

The darkness of the stormy sky was suddenly light. Harkon closed the second portal behind them. A thunderclap sounded, and the ship drifted free in a sunset sky, coasting off its last burn through an arch of gold-edged clouds. Aimee fell back against the rail of the portal-deck as her teacher stepped down, and they shared a grin before he helped her up.

They weren't dead. They weren't trapped or scattered across several different iterations of time and space.

"Congratulations," Vlana said with genuine relief, "you just outdid *Rosswen*."

"Rosswen nothing," Clutch laughed, leaning on the wheel and grinning up at the portal deck. "It doesn't matter who first theorized or fucked it up. They're gonna call that the de Laurent Maneuver long after we're all gone."

"It was a team effort," Aimee said, flexing her aching fingers. She was going to need to be careful, or she'd overclock herself again.

As she descended to the main floor of the bridge, Elias smiled, warm, genuine, and everything she needed in that moment. "Nice job," he said.

She was about to answer—or maybe throw her arms around his shoulders and collapse—when Helena stepped between them and towards the main viewport of the bridge, a map in her hand. "There it is."

Everyone's attention swung back to the infinite, sun-tinged sky, following the old warrior-woman's outstretched finger to the stretch of land that emerged from behind a distant cloud-bank. Dusty, brown, and suspended in the heavens. "That's it," she said.

"Lia's Rest," Aimee breathed.

"No," Helena explained. "I've looked over the maps again. Lia's Rest is the settlement, the old ruins where Coulton stowed the majority of Port Providence's people who traveled with him for the time being, but the landmass has another name, much older and perhaps more significant."

Helena glanced over her shoulder at Aimee and Elias, and her eyes darted briefly to the sword on his hip. "As it turns out, this isle's original name is the Plains of Aurum."

The ramp thudded down. A wave of ochre dust billowed into the cold air. Aimee's boots crunched on gravel and sand, and she pulled the collar of her coat up, tightening the scarf about her neck. Helena's long coat fluttered in the wind, and behind them, Elias was dressed in yet a third duster, Oath of Aurum belted at his waist.

"Are you sure you want to wear that sword openly?" Bjorn said from further up the ramp. The old warrior's face was worried.

"If they're going to recognize me, they're going to recognize me," Elias answered. "I'm not here to hide from them. You don't make amends by lying."

Aimee shot him a sideways glance. "You don't owe amends for things you did while mind-controlled," she said with iron in her voice.

"Try telling them that," Helena answered quietly. "I imagine it won't go over well."

Harkon descended the ramp next, looking like a man on a mission. He walked up to Aimee, held out a gloved hand, and pressed something in a leather purse into her hands. She didn't need to ask. She immediately felt the familiar warmth of the Axiom diamond. "You're going to need it," her teacher said.

He then turned and looked at the three of them. "When you've either found Coulton or discerned his location, send a communication spell. We're going to take to the air again for the time being. The Eternal Order is chasing the *Elysium*, so far as we can tell, and will have no reason to come here so long as we're absent."

A few moments later, they stepped back, a wall of dust blown up as the *Elysium* lifted off and into the sky, its twin exhaust ports flaring with blue light before it surged upwards and away, then dove sideways and dropped beneath the lip of the land's edge.

Aimee stood amidst the settling dust, then exchanged a glance with her two companions. "Alright, Vlana said the settlement she detected was about two miles from here," Aimee said after a moment, then shouldered her bag. "Best we start walking."

The landscape was barren. That was the first thing that jumped out at Aimee as they strode across the dusty, rocky path that wound between the jutting thrusts of orange-colored stone. Every so often she noted old carvings, wind-blasted and time-faded, scarred across old rocks or half-buried by sand. Aimee paused to examine one of them, poring through her memory of arcane symbolism. There was only the faintest familiarity that leaped out at her. As far as the eye could see, the same stretch of endless, desiccated landscape stretched out—save for a single spire of orange rock that stood out in the distance.

"They'll be clustered at the base of that," Helena said. "Prince Collum came here once, long ago, some time after he found the Oath. He had a fascination with it, and the old myths and legends that cluster around these dusty rocks."

Aimee looked sideways at their guide, then at Elias, who had paled visibly at the mention of Coulton's dead older brother. Dead, as it happened, by the hand of Azrael, the dark knight that Elias had been before the Axiom Diamond burned away the mental conditioning with which the Eternal Order had enslaved him for sixteen years. Elias kept walking, one hand gripping the sword's hilt as if it could grant him the strength to keep walking.

"You knew him well?" He asked Helena at length. "Collum, I mean."

Helena looked over her shoulder at the one-time black knight. Then she simply said, "I trained him."

Elias looked as though he'd nearly choked on what he was about to say next. Then, after a moment, he looked at the old knight and said, "I'm sorry."

Aimee held her breath for a moment, watched Helena's face carefully even as she fought down the urge to correct the noble, foolish young man beside her.

Helena just stared at him for a moment, then said, "We need to keep moving if we want to be there before nightfall. It's not pleasant here after dark."

"How are we going to approach them?" Aimee asked after they'd walked for hours. The lights at the edge of what looked like a settlement of hastily constructed homes and very old buildings could be seen drawing near. "I imagine just walking up and asking where Coulton is won't be received well."

Helena turned her head, her severe features cast half in shadow as the sun set behind them. "Oh, I wouldn't worry overmuch about that," she said. "They're about to find us."

"No one move." The command cut off Aimee's response, accompanied by the sounds of thrumming shock-spears being primed, and the hammer-click of slug-throwers being cocked. Aimee let out an irritated sigh, her fingers freeing themselves for swift spellwork. "This," she growled, "is not how I wanted this to go."

"Aimee," Elias murmured beside her. "Don't."

Aimee turned on her heel. They came from the surrounding rocks, stepped from the shadows. None of the faces were familiar, but Aimee knew the kilts and tartans, the ornamented make of the shock-spears and the occasional noble crests stamped on the hilts of swords all too well. Defenders of Port Providence…though these were rather more ragged than the last she'd seen. They were either older or younger than the average soldier, and their faces were dust-painted, worn and weathered by grief and war and terror.

"Coulton took nearly every person of standard fighting age with him, I see," Helena said. "Who commands here? And put down your damned weapons." She threw back her hood. "I am Helena Grayspear. You know me."

"I command," came the same voice that had spoken, and Aimee watched as a young woman emerged from the cluster, no older than sixteen, with red hair and brown eyes, a long rifle with a wicked bayonet at its end leveled at them. No, not at them. At Elias's head. "And you are known to us, Lady Grayspear. But you also came here in the company of the thief who stole our greatest national treasure, and the monster that killed Prince Collum and destroyed our home."

"Put the damn gun down, child," Helena's irritated voice rose in volume.

"The sorceress agrees to be cuffed, or no deal," the girl said. "And Lord Azrael gets on the ground. Now."

"Not happening," Aimee snapped.

The sound of shuffling feet echoed around them as weapons were readied.

"Your choice," the girl answered. Aimee's eyes darted to Elias. He could dodge the bullet or get his sword out in time to parry it. He was fast enough. She'd seen him do it before—

Elias reached for his sword.

"Not another move!" the girl screamed.

Elias had moved too quickly. Oath of Aurum sang free from its sheath, glimmering like pure starlight tinged with sunset. It was in his hand.

Then he opened his fingers, and the blade clattered to the ground.

The girl's shoulders rose and fell, sweat marking her brow. "… Are you deaf?" she snapped in bafflement. "Do you want to die?"

Elias met her eyes, and the expression on his face broke Aimee's heart. "Sometimes."

Helena stepped forward, now. "I come here on command of Queen Mother Alahna. Do you understand?" Her voice, angry before, was calmer now. "The boy's thrown down his sword. Lower your damn guns so we can talk."

Tense silence hung on the air. All around Aimee armed people—too old or too young— waited with tense, air-thickening fear. Aimee stretched her hands out and opened her palms. "I don't want to hurt anyone either."

"I would die," Elias said, almost too low to hear, "before I let myself wound even one more of your people."

The girl looked from one to the next of them, then took the sort of deep, fortifying breath that told Aimee she was agreeing to something counter to her every instinct. A small pang of sympathy reverberated through the young sorceress.

"Weapons down," she said, before looking at Elias as if she was trying to dissect his face. "You," she said, "are living entirely on my respect for Grayspear. Don't forget that."

Elias gave a slow nod. "I don't deserve it," he said. "But thank you."

"Don't thank me," the girl said, "Because you're right. You don't. My name is Lady Grace of House Hamlin in Land's Edge. Captain Gara was my sister."

6

THE CANYON AND THE QUESTION

G race knelt, her eyes still on Elias, and reached for Oath of Aurum's hilt. Elias kept his hands in the air, non-threatening. Aimee stared at him out of the corner of his eye as if awaiting whatever plan he had in throwing his sword on the ground. Elias gulped. There was no plan. He knew there should have been, but there wasn't.

In the burning moment, there was only the desperate need to show these people that he refused to hurt them anymore. No matter the cost.

"That sword doesn't belong to you," Helena interrupted, and Grace looked up at the exponentially older woman, a flicker of uncertainty on her face.

"It's King Coulton's property," Grace recovered after a moment. "His inheritance. If this...person—" she looked at Elias "—wants to make amends, he can start by returning our late prince's sword."

The light of Oath of Aurum still glowed. Normally the blade only shimmered in Elias's hands. That wasn't right. And more than that, he felt a tingling sensation. An ache in his sword hand, a pain in his head that seemed, somehow, to emanate from the steel. Grace reached down again. "Lady Hamlin," Elias started. "I don't think you should—"

Grace's hand closed around Oath of Aurum's handle, and there was a flash of light. The sixteen-year-old leader staggered back with a sharp cry of pain, and the guns were once again on them.

"Milady!" One of the other Port Providence men shouted. "What happened?"

"It...burned me," Grace said in shock, almost to herself.

Elias's head hurt. He swayed on his feet but forced himself not to stumble. Two of the warriors had their guns trained on the blade now.

"Oh, of all the fucking absurdities," Helena groaned. "Put the damn guns down. What are you going to do, shoot a sword?"

"That's not possible," Grace breathed. "Collum was the one the prophecy referred to."

"I don't give a damn." Helena said.

Grace flinched. "The prophecy—"

"It wasn't about him," Helena answered. "Collum should've known better, and so should you."

Grace stood, still holding her smarting hand. "Have a care, Dame Helena, how you speak of Prince—"

"I trained him!" Helena thundered, and every soul in the small clearing fell silent as if chastised by a roaring wind. Grace blanched as if the elder woman had physically slapped her, then the Grayspear's shoulders dropped and she sighed. "Do you truly imagine, Lady Hamlin, that I did not know my own student? I knew him when he was an eager-eyed boy, an earnest teenager, a forthright man, and a bold adventurer. Collum was energetic, he was generous, he was high-minded, and he was far more interested in chasing relics and prophecies than he was in learning how to rule. Honor him. Remember him. But you dishonor his memory when you make him perfect in your recollection. He listened to a prophecy that wasn't about him when he should've thought of his people. He fought when he should've run, believing the words of some prophet made him invincible. He would have been a shit king. And that sword? Had nothing to do with him, or with our homeland."

"Though I think," Aimee said quietly, "that it has something to do with this place. The name can't be a coincidence."

Grace stood, keeping well back from the blade. Oath of Aurum's glow faded slightly. Then the young noblewoman looked between the three of them and said, "Why are you here?"

Elias finally found his voice. "To save your king from Silas—and from himself."

A tense silence followed. Elias heard shuffling, felt the tension rise as the words rolled over the people around him. Some raised words of harsh objection, others stood in the halting, arrested silence of those who have heard the fears they forbid themselves to express spoken aloud. Elias stood his ground, doing his best to manage his pounding, fearful heart, and kept his eyes on Grace.

"Silas," she said with the voice of one trying to hold on to a beautiful lie, "just wants to protect us."

"He's lost his grip on reality," Aimee said, just as plain and clear. "And the Queen Mother knows it."

"Lady Hamlin," Helena said with quiet intensity. "I watched him wield magic that turned his eyes black as coal. He tried to kill Alahna, tried to kill me…and when we fled, he sent a killing bolt of darkness into the sky that nearly sent my skyship plummeting to the abyss. His assassins chased me all the way to Whitefeather. He's spun a beautiful lie, and even the King believes it, but he's made bargains with things no person should trifle with. What is our survival as a people worth, if it costs us our souls?"

Grace looked back and forth between the three of them. Someone to the side of her begged her to put a bullet through Elias's skull. Another chided the other to be silent. All the while, Grace struggled, searching their faces each, and finally settling on Elias. He felt an unspoken question and gave the only answer—agonizing as it was—that he could.

"He's broken," Elias said as he looked her in the eyes. "Beyond repair. I know, because I'm the one that did it. And it seems that mere minutes before the Axiom Diamond revealed the truth to me, the darkness I abetted found a way to reproduce itself."

Grace closed her eyes. Elias couldn't help but notice how much she looked like the sister he'd killed. The memory of the act was like a knife across his thoughts, and he suppressed the urge to flinch with physical guilt. The arguing of her people seemed to grow louder.

"That's enough," Grace said, at length, with enough command to quiet the objections. Then she looked at the three of them. "This isn't the right place to talk. If you were going to do us harm, you'd have tried already… so you may as well come to the settlement proper. There's no sense in talking here."

As her people moved to follow her orders, Aimee and Helena looked at Elias, the expression on the face of the former pained, the latter tired.

Then Grace spoke again. "And pick up your sword. Whatever your name is now, it apparently isn't Azrael."

"You need to stop apologizing," Aimee said as she fell into step beside him. They'd been walking for nearly an hour. Elias glanced at her. The sorceress wore a look of mingled concern and irritation. They walked amidst the cluster of Port Providence refugees and defenders towards the lamps of the settlement up ahead. Back at his hip, Oath of Aurum was a comfortable presence once again.

"Would defiance have helped us here?" He finally asked, uncertain how to put her at ease.

"That's not the point," Aimee said. He could feel her blue eyes burning upwards at him. "You were as much a victim as they are. You're not responsible for the crimes you committed while you were brainwashed."

Elias looked ahead. The vast upthrust of rock that dominated the landscape was growing closer—or at least near enough for him to have a sense of how incredibly vast it was. The settlement that had seemed at first to cluster at its feet was closer to a mile from its base, and clouds clung to its upper reaches, small against its breadth.

"I remember doing it all," Elias answered, finally. "Every act. Every crime. All of it. Maybe I was a slave, but I still carry the memories. Is there truly much of a difference?"

Aimee took a deep, irritation-suppressing breath and stepped closer to him. He felt her fingers slide between his, and this time when she looked up at him, it was impossible to avert his gaze.

"There is to me," she said. "And it's not just affection, Elias. I'm a sorceress. A portalmage. Deduction of truth, of process, is important to me. Because there is an objective truth, and it matters."

Elias squeezed her hand. He didn't know what to say to the intense young sorceress beside him. There didn't seem to be sufficient words in his repertoire to explain that it seemed she could both be correct, and that being blunt in the moment could also be a terrible idea. So instead, he looked sideways at her—hoping he appeared more certain than he felt—and said, quietly, "Thank you, for standing up for me—even to me. I don't deserve it, but I'm grateful."

She looked up at him again, meeting his eyes, and there was this look on her face—a singular mingling of indignation, exasperation, and something else. Burning. Deep. Fierce.

"I love who I love," she said with sudden intensity. "Deserving doesn't enter into it."

Silence. Elias's mouth hung briefly open as the words hit him in the chest, and Aimee's free hand clapped abruptly over her mouth as her pale face turned bright red.

"We're here," Grace said, and looking forward again, Elias nearly walked into the Port Providence armsman just in front of him. The buildings of the settlement closed about them, casting long shadows in the evening light. Calling it a settlement was both charitable, Elias reflected, and a tremendous understatement. The walled space was dotted with hovels and a handful of larger buildings repurposed from old ruins that jutted from the earth. Elias glimpsed columns that had once been magnificent, and stone walls worn smooth by wind and time. Not much grew here, it seemed, though despite their roughened, battered state, the people didn't seem starved.

"Hurry," Grace said, as she led them down a long thoroughfare lined with curious faces and the bustling activity of a refugee camp. Elias felt his nerves tensing ever more the further they walked. There were far more people here than he'd originally thought. Most of them, like the defenders that had intercepted the trio, were too old or too young. But he saw families, as well. Wounded. A group of kids sitting on the back of a wagon while the ruins of a tattered shirt were used to wrap their feet in place of lost shoes. The smell of shit and piss mingled discordantly with the sooty smell of guttering cook-fires. If it weren't for the fact that Elias had seen and smelled worse in his time, he might have retched.

At length they came to a large facade hewn directly into the face of a rising hillock of brown, wind-blasted stone. This far into the settlement, the large upthrust of the immense spire that dominated the landscape obscured half the sky. Two kilted men armed with battered swords flanked a doorway at the stop of a series of carven steps, and beneath, a cluster of people spread out in makeshift tents, wagons, and a small number of livestock.

"How many people are here?" Aimee asked. The tone of mixed curiosity and horror in her voice told Elias that many of the same questions in his mind were also in hers.

"Ten thousand," Grace said over her shoulder.

"How in the heavens are you provisioning them?" Helena asked.

At the base of the steps before the stone doors, the young woman looked over her shoulder. "That's complicated, and not everyone here understands. I'll tell you inside. Just know that it's as strange to us as it is to you."

The guards stood aside for her, and the group passed through the doorway into a dim, vast chamber lit faintly by tallow torches that made the whole dusty space stink of animal fat. Grace threw down her cloak and turned to face the trio after ordering the rest of the patrol back out again. "I need explanations," she said. "And I need them quickly. Sneaking you all in wasn't very well an option with how this place is laid out, and there's no telling what might happen if someone out there recognized you lot. The first thing you need to know is that these people are starved of hope, their pride obliterated, and they will latch on to damn near anything that offers them a taste of either. Silas has given them that, even if they're afraid of him."

"What's he given them?" It was Helena who pressed, now. Her expression intent and tired of argument. "Come on, Lady Hamlin. You've been dancing around it since we met you. Why would Coulton take so many of his people here? Why this desolate wasteland?"

Grace looked back and forth between the three of them, then said quietly, "It's where he found the metal soldiers."

Elias's eyes widened. Memories flashed to the forefront of his mind. Roland, ever the savant of ancient myths and old, forbidden secrets, had known of this. He took a small step forward. "The Tireless," he said. "Did he call them the Tireless?"

All eyes were suddenly on him, again. The sensation—once a fact of leadership and life—was intensely uncomfortable.

"I...I think Silas may have," Grace said. "Once or twice. Why?"

Elias closed his eyes and spat a stream of emphatic curses into the dry air. "How many?" He asked, looking the young leader in the eyes. "How many does he have?"

Grace swallowed. "A legion, I believe. That's what I heard the quartermaster saying."

"I don't understand," Helena said. "It's not a name I'm familiar with."

"They're an old fable," Aimee said. "Or that's what I remember. A bedtime song about an old king named Nemahs who defied the gods, so they sent the Tireless to raze his palace to the ground. It's a very old story, the sort parents use to get their kids to behave."

"They're not stories," Elias answered. "At least, the Tireless aren't. They're long-lost super-weapons from ancient Varengard. Automaton soldiers, twice a man's height, faster, strong enough to crush stone in their palms."

Silence settled. Aimee's eyes were wide, and Helena's eyebrows had climbed up her forehead.

"Well," Grace said after a long, unsettled moment. "They were tall."

"Where did you learn about this?" Aimee asked.

"Some from my former master," Elias answered. "Lord Roland was obsessed with anything mythical and ancient, with hidden secrets and old treasures. The rest..." here he paused. He'd hardly spoken of this since the group had left *Iseult* a year ago. "From the books that Belit gave me."

"They're gone, now," Grace said with a sigh. "Silas took them all, loaded them into the bellies of the fleet."

The winds without blew through the cracks in the stone structure. Then Aimee broke the silence. "If I could see where they came from," she said, "I could tell you a lot more."

Grace went quiet, looked inquiringly at Helena.

"I wouldn't have brought them," the old knight answered, "if I didn't think they could be trusted."

"There's...there's a ravine," Grace said at last. "Out on the plains. A rent in the earth, where they found them beneath rubble. They...dug a pit."

"Please," Elias said. A knot churned in the pit of his stomach. "Take us there."

An hour later, the dirt crunched under Elias's boots as they walked out over the strange, dry plains outside the settlement. The sun was near to setting, and the wind that blew across the flats was cold, cutting through the heavy canvas cloaks Grace had loaned them to make the trio less conspicuous. The hills about the spire fell away, and an endless, unsettling expanse of flat settled, a silence laying down upon them broken only by footfalls and a ceaseless, low drone of breeze.

Up ahead, a black line split the earth. The closer they drew to it, the dizzier Elias felt. Something about this place pulled him in a hundred different directions, smothered him with the intense feeling of being watched and pricked with a low-level charge at all times.

It was as if his blood sizzled at the touch of the ground beneath his boots. Sweat formed on his forehead, and he took a long, stabilizing breath as they walked.

"Are you okay?" Aimee asked beside him. It wasn't until he looked at her that Elias realized he must've looked horrible.

"I did this," he said quietly. "These people. I made them homeless." Before she could argue, he looked around, from the tortured plains of these strange lands to the settlement behind them, then back at Aimee. "What did you say this place was called?"

"Lia's Rest," Helena answered from just ahead.

"But you also said that Collum came here," Elias pressed. "And someone said before that this place was once called the Plains of Aurum."

She picked up on the connection point he was getting at. "Collum noted that as well. It's why he came here. He believed that something in the name made this place the key to unraveling that old prophecy about awakening the blade. Clearly he was wrong."

Grace flinched slightly. "You should know," she said, "that Coulton insists he wasn't. Silas has spread the word that whatever you've done is a form of seditious magic, and that whatever the sword is doing is a lie."

Elias glanced down at his boots. In that moment, the memory of the dark cave, when the man named Azrael had pressed the old sage named Silas until his spirit broke, was like a knife through his mind.

"Silas," Aimee spat the name like a curse. "When I knew him he was a shriveled old man frightened of his shadow and broken with grief. Since Helena found us, I've had only half-tales and hints. How did that become something that could terrify a warrior people and nearly bring down a ship on his own?"

Grace looked over her shoulder at the two of them, and this time Elias saw the fear in her eyes. Deep. All-consuming. "...I don't know," she said finally. "Except that it reminds me of my grandmother's stories of some old practice of fixing a broken piece of pottery with veins of gold to make something new and beautiful. But this isn't like that at all. That shriveled man let the Night into him. It filled in all the broken cracks and took away his fear. And everything good in him, too."

Elias considered that, wracking the corners of his frayed memory for any hint of what thing might have been bargained with to render Silas so seemingly powerful. "Had he skill with sorcery before?"

"No," Helena said. "None beyond the dabbling of the mildly talented."

"And I sensed nothing, saw nothing, when we were side by side with him," Aimee added with a shake of her head. "I know he kept secrets." The way she said that last bit was full of bitter anger. "And he's a gray sage, though I don't know why that matters. They're an order of advisors and historians, aren't they? Observers and all that."

"It's...more complicated than that," Elias explained. His head was starting to hurt as he thought back over his years of training, of Roland's instruction and the classical education burned into him. "The sages go a long, long way back. They're nearly as old as the Eternal Order, and there are some secrets about—" he had nearly said 'our history,' and the thought chilled him, "—about their history that only the Eternal Order and the sages know."

They stopped walking. All eyes were now on him. Elias shook his head. "I don't know those," he said. "And I can't parse the lies from the truth. I know that once the Eternal Order believed that the Axiom belonged to them, and that they say the sages stole it and hid it away. I know that the reason Roland wanted it was to find long-lost enemies he believed were a danger to his plans."

Elias had never truly understood who those foes were—his one-time master had not deigned to share such secrets with his foremost apprentice, but after their time on the Behemoth called *Iseult* a year ago, and after his brief studies of the book Belit had given to him, he was starting to guess who it might be.

"But I have no idea what he might have bargained with. None of the stories I remember mention anything that powerful."

Grace shook her head and they started walking again. Eventually they reached the lip of the ravine, and Elias saw a vast stretch of torn earth before them. No water had cut this over thousands of years, however. It was not made by the slow weathering of time. The edges were jagged and warped all the way down, wrenched apart and scorched a long, long time ago.

"This isn't natural," Aimee said, crouching. Her eyes searched the vast rent in the isle beneath them. "Some magic did this," she said. Her eyes were wide. "Powerful sorcery, well beyond any mage I know of."

"There are stairs down," Grace said, and she led them to a place where the lip of the canyon gave way to recently made steps in the rock that let the group begin the slow descent. At the edge, Elias paused. Something about this place disquieted him, even as it pulled at him to continue. The walls of the ravine were dark, and Elias felt as if they watched him with weighted patience.

If I go further, a part of him whispered, *the luxury of not knowing will end.*

Not knowing what? He couldn't say, but at once, the possible answers terrified him.

Up ahead, several feet further down the steps, Aimee seemed to suddenly sense his hesitation, and she turned. Her blue eyes met his, and though she said nothing, there was compassion, there. Questioning.

She held out her hand to him. An offer. Reassurance. Fortification. A reminder that neither of them were alone. A hint of fear was in her face, as well.

Elias let out the breath he'd held, took a step forward, and took her hand, lacing her smaller fingers in his own. The small smile she gave him was enough.

The truth will set you free.

Hand in hand, they followed Grace and Helena into the shadow of the canyon.

This is Clutch. Pilot without peer. Born from strife. Forged from the moment of her adornment with the glyph of Guild-Sanctioned Pilot by the need to survive against a world that doesn't want her to exist. Clutch is nothing if not cunning. Wit and nerve have carried her through a forest of jagged stones, across storms and between the lancing bursts of skyship gunfire across countless aerial battlefields. But nerve has its limits, and the endless sky is full of challenges that no amount of guts will overcome.

Not on their own.

And this is why Clutch loves. She has tasted desperation and hunger and pain and betrayal. Clutch has known what it is to sleep under bridges and hastily scarf dumpster food in a cargo-hold between shifts.

And it has never shadowed her soul.

She learned long ago that in an unforgiving world, it is those that hang together who survive, that the vessel moving at her touch and the crew around her are more precious than the breath in her lungs and the very feet with which she has gripped the deck in a hundred gunfights. Devotion and dedication have carried her through nightmares and into sunrises across a thousand horizons. Her strong, dark face framed by blue hair has watched clear skies and hurricanes with a flashing smile that she wears by choice, day after day. Whether caustic or bold, warm or frigid, steely or soft, her dark hands have guided her home, her ship, her beloved, and the crew she adores through storms and shadows and past dawn after dawn, not because of stone hearted stubbornness, though she is surely stubborn. It is the opposite of a dead heart that still carries her through, even as she must do it all again.

Because Clutch, pilot without peer, loves.

And that is how she wins.

7

SECOND TIME'S THE CHARM

Clutch sat in the darkness of the bridge, watching the silhouette of the wheel against the twilight clouds outside. The lights were doused, the consoles dark. Against the frame of the *Elysium's* hull, the wind was a slow, ominous creak.

Just enough power flowed from the metadrive to keep the ship aloft and stable in the debris field where they'd chosen to lie in wait—a place where ambient magic kept wreckage from falling into the endless abyss, holding it suspended forever in the air. The girl still lived—silver and thrumming—and that kept Clutch's nerves from raking themselves raw in the darkness. Still she stared, hunting the sky with her eyes and waiting for their enemy to appear.

"C'mon," her whisper pierced the quiet. "Don't tell me the ship named the *Atrocity* has lost its nerve." Each whispered word was a dare to keep the roaring, barely-caged fear at bay. "Come out to play."

The others had retreated from the bridge—to rest, to eat, to recover what strength they could before their enemy appeared again. Harkon had jumped so many times since they left Aimee and Elias at Lia's rest that he needed to lie down. Bjorn was seeing to their weapons in case they were boarded.

None of this appealed to Clutch. Waiting was a bitch, but instincts gained in her first years as a pilot now compelled her to lie in wait. Some bastard was hunting her, and she'd be damned if she or her family were caught unawares.

"I can wait," she addressed the dark and quiet. "I'm way more patient than you, and a helluva lot meaner."

"I believe you," Harkon said. Clutch didn't look away from the sky, only heard the old sorcerer taking a seat to her left. He sounded a little more awake, now, but the hint of an old exhaustion still hovered at the edge of his voice. The man was older—by far—than he appeared. Clutch was one of the few who had guessed near to how much, and she tried not to think about it.

"You nap quick," she answered.

"Acquired habit," her employer answered. "It's the waking that's harder, these days. I'd rather be alert when they come upon us."

"Vlana thinks they might give up," Clutch murmured.

"Someone must retain their optimism," Harkon replied. "It keeps us all alive."

"I'd rather they hurry up and get it over with," the pilot sighed after a short span. "I've lurked under the bellies of kingdoms, waiting for contraband to be fed into my cargo holds upside down." She chewed her lip. "This is worse."

"They're worse," Harkon said. "And for this long we've been able to outrun them. But it seems that after seventeen years, the yards of New Corinth at last yielded up some of their secrets. They're catching up."

Now he looked at her, and Clutch couldn't avoid his eyes without disrespect. "I do regret, at times," he said, "that joining my crew has meant all of you being in the middle of this."

Clutch took that in, then shook her head, and ran her hand over the lines of the hull beneath her. "You took in a failed pirate and introduced me to the love of my life, Hark. Don't you ever apologize for that."

She looked back out into the sky and blew out a sigh. "You think they can do it? Those damn kids we left on that empty rock?"

"I do," Harkon said. "They'll find out where Coulton is, and what he and his advisor are planning…but before we can worry about that—"

"—we've gotta survive," Clutch finished. "I just wish the bastards would catch up already. The waiting is killing me."

"You're still too eager for a fight," Harkon said.

Clutch just looked at the dark-skinned man beside her, grinning. "I learned from the best."

Her eyes were suddenly drawn upwards as a flash of light flickered somewhere in the sky. The telltale sign of a portal opening and closing. A crack, like distant lightning, followed a few seconds later as the sound rolled across the heavens.

"They're here," Harkon said.

Clutch reached for the tube, but the old sorcerer stayed her with a hand on her shoulder. "Not yet. I want to see her properly first."

The pilot's knuckles whitened on the wheel. She hated when he did this. Trust—and only trust—kept Clutch from wrenching that tube up and telling Vant to burn for a rabbiting, but Harkon Bright knew what he was talking about. So they stood and watched as the dreadnought called *Atrocity* slid into view.

It looked like a vulture. Twin wings fanned out, sloping gently forward from a central frame, vast, and knifing to a jagged, hooked point. The length of its spine was a long, jutting line that terminated just above the faint glow of its exhaust vents and above the distant, faint light-line of what must have been its bridge.

It was red and black. Blotched in paint made to look like its namesake. A flying war-crime in waiting. Aggressive and genocidal in its hunger. It was almost comical, how far Lord Ogier had gone to transform his flagship into a monument to cruelty. And yet, looking upon it, Clutch audibly gulped. There was no lie in any inch of the macabre detail etched into the stalking hunter moving inexorably towards them.

"Tell me something Hark," she breathed in the silent darkness. "The things they say about Lord Ogier. Are they true?"

Harkon Bright's eyes were fixed on the approaching ship. Clutch had never seen him afraid, and it would be wrong to say that he was now. Nonetheless, what he said as his eyes fixed on the dreadnought chilled her.

"Every one."

And then every warning sensor on the bridge went off at once, triggered as the distant vessel's scanning alighted upon them. Vant's voice shouted up through the tubes in a combination of panic and anger. "A bit of warning would've been nice!"

Clutch dashed across the bridge and shouted back, "They just got here. Now quit complaining and get everything up and running!"

Vlana exploded onto the bridge. "Fuck, fuck fuck fuck fuck!"

"Calm," Harkon said. The sorcerer was already moving to the portal deck.

"Hark no," Clutch said. "Not again."

Looking at the maps and charts with new eyes, she'd remembered something. The heart of an old boast that suddenly seemed like the most insane potential win she could summon up from the depths of a hopeless situation.

They couldn't run forever.

And she knew where they were.

The sorcerer had stopped, and Vlana looked supremely nervous. From the doorway, she saw Bjorn's face blanch. She was the only one on the crew who could pull this, she knew, which was why she did it only rarely.

"We're near the Gauntlet," Clutch said. "Let me do this. I can lure them in. Trap them."

Harkon watched her as klaxons blared in their ears. Then he nodded and said, "Do it."

They shot out from under the debris field. A burn so hard it shifted the deck beneath Clutch's feet. She gritted her teeth, practically felt the *Atrocity's* guns coming to bear. "Three," she breathed. "Two."

A high-pitched whine teased her senses.

"One."

The beam lanced through the sky, ripping up debris, and missing the *Elysium* by bare inches. She pushed the wheel forward. Rolled sideways. The crew gripped the rails and *Elysium* danced like a ballerina on point.

"Weak, weak!" Clutch snarled between her teeth. "You're a flying blood bruise with a barely competent pilot and a gunner scrambling to hit my contrails!" A second beam fired. She anticipated. Rolled. A suspended piece of shattered bulkhead hanging in the sky came apart in a crack of light and ripping sound. Vant burned and Clutch shot the vessel forward.

"Alright Mr. Lord Ogier of the Eternal Order with your fancy, fast-as-shit tricked out capital ship." Her fingers flexed on the wheel. "Show me what you got."

The *Atrocity* gave chase. Bursts of light cut across their weaving path, shredding up debris. Vlana found her station, and soon she was barking out sensor readings as Bjorn dashed back to man the rear guns. Seamless. The dull thud of their aft barrels lobbing off shots at the pursuing dreadnought soon filled her ears.

"They're not falling behind!" Vlana shouted.

"I'm headed aftward to give us some shielding," Harkon said. Looking Clutch in the eyes, he nodded. "She's yours."

The pilot's fingers clenched around the wheel, and she gave a small nod before turning her eyes back to the sky. They arced around a vast slab of broken hull. Clutch could feel the tug of the winds now, just the faintest tease of what they'd be in a few moments if she kept her present course.

And then Vlana realized what she was doing.

"Clutch," the navigator breathed. "Where did you say this place is again?"

Clutch turned them slowly, into the pull of the wind. Her voice was low. Bits of debris now moved past them, whirling through the air towards a pair of vast, slowly-rotating shapes a distance away that was all too close for any sane person's comfort.

"The Tyrith Wastes," she breathed.

Out of the corner of the pilot's eye, Vlana turned pale. "The graveyard of ships," she said. "You...you've been here before, right?"

Clutch gulped. "Just once."

Ahead of them, two vast aisles, each of them bigger than Port Providence, sat locked together by some invisible force in the space between them. End over end, they slowly rotated, and in the space between them a vortex of wind, debris, and dark clouds swirled about a dark pinprick of pure shadow dappled with flashes of intermittent light.

"And that's..." Vlana trailed off.

"The Argathian Gauntlet," Clutch breathed. "Yeah."

"You've flown it before, right?"

"I was drunk," Clutch said. "I barely remember it. But yes. And now I'm going to do it again."

"That—" Vlana stuttered "—t-that's fine. I'm sure plenty of pilots have pulled repeats, yeah?"

"I'm hoping to be the first not to die in the second attempt," Clutch breathed. Her fingers were cold on the wheel. "Come on girl," she whispered. "We can do this. We can do this."

Another beam. Closer this time. "Alright," she said into the tubes. "Vant, I need you to listen to me very, *very* carefully. I'm going to need micro-burns every ten seconds in about thirty. The winds are about to get bad, and our adjustments are going to have to be minute and constant or this ship is going to be shredded into a million pieces by debris. Understand?"

"You know how to sweet-talk a guy," came the reply. "Beginning micro-burns in thirty."

Clutch's fingers flexed on the wheel. The spiraling void drew closer. "Okay," the pilot said. "Vlana, give me readings."

"The *Atrocity* is right on our tail," the navigator's fingers flew over her control station. "Clutch, I've never seen windspeeds like this. And whatever magic is keeping those isles locked together is pulling everything that crosses a barrier point about one minute ahead of us through that vortex. We're not going to be able to burn our way out of this."

Clutch smiled as the first microburn hit. She dipped them down, fluttered around a slab of rapidly rotating stone and shot past the other side. "Dodge that, dipshit."

"I know," she continued as the winds pulled them faster. "I'm counting on precisely that."

"That's not a comfort, C," Vlana's voice cracked.

"Just focus on giving me those readings," Clutch said. "Space them, keep it quick and brief. When I say to shut up, just hold the fuck on because at that point it won't matter."

"Was it like this last time?" Vlana breathed. Through the viewport, the vortex loomed large, a spiral like an aerial maelstrom filled with crashes of lightning and periodically vomiting a stream of debris that ripped stone and ship-wreckage apart before swirling once more into the void.

"Last time I was in a stock freighter," Clutch murmured. "*Elysium* is faster. More responsive by a lot."

"Well…that's good."

"Not necessarily."

"What?"

"Well," a gulp followed and the pilot wiped her brow. "Its responses were slower, so when I remember this damn run, all my reflexes are keyed to a slight delay that could fuck me if I move too early. It's not a big deal. Don't worry about it."

Out of the corner of Clutch's eye, Vlana turned green. "That is not the sort of statement you follow with 'don't worry about it!'"

"Sure it is," Clutch laughed. "Otherwise you'd worry."

"What is wrong with you?"

"You want the list? Cuz I can't do that right now. Let's just go with blah-blah-blah-numbers."

Vlana grabbed the control station next to her for support. "I. Am going. To kill you."

"Good," Clutch said. "Determined to live—that's the spirit!"

Vlana's only answer was an unhinged scream as they veered around another whirling chunk of debris.

The field opened up, and Clutch caught a glimpse of the vortex.

~

Clutch veered the ship sideways. The bridge tilted violently and Vlana clung to her station. The winds pulled at them, now. Dragged across the hull and the bucking of the storm made the wings creak and the hull groan.

Up ahead, the heart of the storm loomed. Concentric clouds lit with inner flashes of lightning twice the size of a dreadnought swirled between broken isles, siphoning debris into streams that raced down the darkness at the nadir of the nightmare.

"Hello, beast," Clutch said under her breath as the winds caught them. Pulled them in. "Can't say I've missed you."

"*Atrocity's* bearing down on us still," Vlana managed, holding on to her station. "She's accelerating!"

"Should be within range in half a minute!" Bjorn's voice came over the tubes.

"Vant, hold the burn!" Clutch shouted into the rubes. "We're letting the winds take us in!"

"Are you fucking out of your mind?"

"Do you even have to ask?"

"I'm doing this because I trust you."

"Good. We're going to get through this." Her fingers tightened on the wheel as the ship started to pull towards the aerial maelstrom. "I promise."

Closer now. The hull creaked and the roar of the winds filled their ears even through the viewport of the bridge. Clutch's hand deftly adjusted the wheel by millimeters. Shredded remnants of obliterated skyships hurtled past.

The abyss yawned before them, side-on, and she held them in place, straining at the pull. Holding on for the right moment. The breath before the plunge. She'd done this before. She knew the method and the madness.

"Clutch," Vlana's voice shook with fear. "Please."

On the opposite side of the viewport the *Atrocity* loomed, growing ever closer. *Come on,* Clutch held the wheel. *Closer, you bastards.*

The vulture-like vessel filled their vision. Winds pulled them from every direction. "When I say burn," she breathed into the tubes, "give me everything you've got."

Her fingers twitched on the wheel. Ten seconds. Nine.

"Clutch!" Vlana shouted. "We're sitting sparrowducks!"

Eight seconds. Seven.

"Clutch!" Vant shouted. "We can't fight these winds!"

Six.

Five.

Four.

Three.

Two.

"That's the secret of the Argathian Gauntlet," she said. "You don't fight the winds. You ride them."

One.

"Vant. Hard burn."

Elysium's metadrive roared. Clutch spun the wheel, and they toppled into the vortex. The wind blasted them left. Clutch spun left and up. They surged, speed increased. Into the wind. Into it. She turned. Turned. There. There!

The gust caught them from behind, and the *Elysium* shot forward and into the wall of the whirling vortex. The buoying gale-force surged behind them, and Clutch came alive. This was freedom and thrill. This was the blaze of flight. The *Elysium* spun under her control. Danced as the fired engines blazed their fury into the twisting storm. They roared downward, spiraled into the abyss.

"Kill it!" she shouted. They had enough of a boost now. It was sail, sail and twist and pray. She held the wheel and steered. The engine died as the burn stopped. There was only the roar of the wind and the twitch of the controls. They neared the vortex. Clutch spun them out of the path of a whirling chunk of debris, staring into the darkness that pulsed with flashes of lightning. The *Atrocity* loosed a gun barrage at them and the winds ripped the bursts apart, sending shots harmlessly piercing through debris-filled clouds.

And at the nadir of the gauntlet, the gusts whipped them. A flag in a gale. Clutch sensed the pull and followed it. "This is about to make everyone sick!" she shouted, and pulled the ship into a corkscrew as they lanced into the shadows. The *Elysium* started spinning. Chasing the whirling vortex until all Clutch could see through the viewport was the eye of the maelstrom, a pinprick of darkness illuminated by the ship's running lights as they shot faster and faster, end over end. Through. She gripped the wheel, now. Letting the wind pull. Making minute adjustments as the winds twisted them. Pushing the vessel to her limits.

"Clutch!" Vlana shouted. "For the love of all the gods!"

"We're almost through!" Clutch shouted back.

There. At the far end. A pinprick of light. "Vant! Now!"

The engines roared and the vessel came straight, and Clutch shouted in pure, unabashed triumph as *Elysium* shot out of the far end of the vortex and blazed across the skies, diving deep towards the abyss.

Pull up. Pull up! She pulled the wheel back. Brought them in a burning arc that left blue-lit flame-streaks across the sunset heavens. "Hark!" she shouted. "You ready?"

And atop the portal deck, Harkon Bright's hands flashed through the series of gestures before the portal-generating beam lanced across the heavens. The *Elysium* surged out of the deepening dark, rising into the middle sky as the eye of light ripped open, and in the blink of a blaze they passed through.

They slowed as the burn died down, and Clutch sagged against the wheel. They needed time to cool off. The drive would be heated, now, and she had no doubt that the exhaust ports of the ship were glowing red. The hull shuddered, and looking forward through the viewport, Clutch saw the edge of land, glimmering bright under the sunset. A beautiful stretch of continent reaching off in both directions and sailing into the distance. And at its edge, a city spreading out, the gateway to its main port set with vast banners of bright purple.

They had come to Caritas. The gateway to the Violet Imperium.

"Good choice, boss," Clutch breathed. "The Eternal Order will be reluctant to come here, and they certainly won't dare threaten a military port. Not yet, anyway."

"Gods," Vant's voice came through the tubes, and Clutch's blood went cold at the next words out of the engineer's mouth. "I hope not. That last jump and burn overclocked the drive. We've got enough to limp into dock, but I hope to high heaven that Aimee and Elias are safe." The gulp that followed was audible. "Because we're not going anywhere for a bit."

Clutch stared at the communication tube in her hand. Opened her mouth.

Vlana said it first. The navigator blinked several times, met Clutch's eyes and simply said, "Fuck."

8

LIA'S REST

imee felt like a gnat upon the face of a vast cathedral rose-window, attempting to consider its design. The base of the canyon spread out before her—huge and overwhelming. Yet it wasn't its size that left her arrested and unsettled, but the weight of pressing despair that suffused the very stones about them. When they reached the bottom, she'd stumbled for a moment, letting go of Elias's hand so she could catch herself on a nearby rock. A powerful sense of emotion surrounded them, thick as a choking fog, and each of them had to catch themselves before they learned to breathe again beneath its weight.

Grief. Overwhelming grief. Aimee's fingers curled against the ancient stone and she breathed out the imposition of feelings that weren't her own. She'd read about this, back in the academy—how places stained by that unique mingling of magic and tragedy bore the scar ever-after. There was even such a place not far from her home-city of Havensreach. A desolate stretch of ruined, blasted earth that local legend called the Cairnlands.

"Yeah," she heard Grace say behind her. "This is why we haven't come down here much. It feels like a thousand ghosts stalk your every step."

"It's not ghosts," Aimee said, recovering her breath and straightening despite the oppressive cloud around her. "It's a lingering magic stain on the land. The echo of past crimes committed. But that's all it is—an echo. And damned if I'm going to let a grief that's not my own stop me."

She stormed forward. Footfalls crunched over loose stone on hard earth. Downward the pace of the land evened out into the deeper canyon through which an uneven dry riverbed cut. Apparently at one point in the past this aisle had gotten a higher dose of rain, but based on the accumulation of dust and sediment hardened to stone, it had been a long time since any sort of water had flowed freely here.

Elias sagged briefly against the wall of the canyon behind her, and she saw him gripping the hilt of Oath of Aurum as he sometimes did in moments of flagging strength. "I'll be fine," he said, holding up a hand to forestall worry. "I think...it's something about the way my magic works. It's very loud here."

Aimee reflexively lowered the hand that had risen. Stuffed it in a pocket of her coat. Awkward. "We'll—" she fumbled, "—be through it in just a second."

She turned back around. Fuck. The kiss back in Whitefeather had only put her on more of an emotional hair-trigger in a relationship that was even more ambiguous than before.

At least there was plenty to focus on. To make herself focus on.

Come on. Aimee. Focus.

Up ahead, she heard a moaning creak on the wind. The ground trembled slightly.

Forward.

To her left and right, she could see signs of recent excavation. Older and newer—one in the past four years, the other...less than a week since the carving was done. The second thing she noticed was the perfectly flat planes of some of the hews into the stone and the dirt. A sizable amount of the newer work had been done with magic. Hastily. They made their way into the canyon, across the floor. Up ahead, the ground abruptly dropped away, and Aimee sucked in a breath.

An entire segment of the valley floor had been carved away into an immense jagged open pit-mine that dropped down in a funnel shape of carved steppes riddled across with hive-like hexagonal apertures at evenly spaced intervals. A howling sound—deep and mournful—echoed in her ears, and crouching at the lip of the huge hole let her squint enough to see why.

Far, far below, at the very base of the pit, the diggers had pierced through the bedrock of the aisle. The cracking groan she'd heard before echoed in her ears as another chunk of ground at the bottom of the mine shuddered, cracked, and fell away. The hole into empty sky and fathomless abyss grew several feet wider.

"...Gods," Aimee breathed. "They've destabilized this entire island's integrity."

"That hole," Grace breathed. "That...that wasn't there when we were last here."

"This hole is going to expand," Aimee said, turning to look at the sixteen-year-old. "It might be weeks, it might be a year or more, but it's going to split this isle in half."

"And when an isle breaks," Helena added, "it's anyone's guess whether it will split into two parts or shatter into fifty."

Elias walked up to stand beside her. She was at once acutely aware of their proximity. His green eyes fixed on the vision before them. "That is a lot of Tireless."

Then he looked up, his eyes fixing on something straight ahead. Across the lip of the huge hole in the earth. Aimee squinted, then wove a spell of sensing and revelation. "Show me," her words echoed with power, and the ripple through the air stirred dust in its wake.

It ghosted against a field of illusion wrapped like tight mesh around something that looked like a simple flat face of canyon wall.

The illusion trembled, but it didn't break. Aimee's eyebrows raised. "Come on," she said. "We need to get over there."

The walk was treacherous. The mine's lip ran right up against the wall of the ravine, leaving only a narrow pathway to walk. The wind howled up from below, and Aimee fought the urge to peer over the edge. Staring into the abyss was something she'd done enough—had nearly tasted falling from the prow of the Behemoth *Iseult* one year ago. She still had nightmares about those moments when she'd believed she was lost to the endless depths from which only horror stories returned.

"Can you tell me what you sense?" She glanced briefly back at the green-eyed man making his way along the path behind her.

"Something big," Elias breathed. The man looked nauseous, following in her wake. A hand in fingerless gloves pressed against the stone to steady himself. "Old, too. It has that feeling of something...buried out of sight. Undisturbed. For a long, long time."

Then he looked back at Helena. "You said Collum came here?"

Helena's eyes looked distant as she picked her way along the narrow stone path. "To learn what he could about awakening the blade. Yes."

"Obviously he didn't find much," Grace pulled herself along, using the butt of her rifle to balance herself. An exhausted look painted her face. "There…aren't words for how much my people feel robbed of what was supposed to be a golden age."

"I've never believed in those," Aimee put one deliberate foot in front of the other. "One person's halcyon is another's hell."

"Easy to say," Grace's boots crunched over stone. "For the upper class Havensreach woman."

Aimee almost stumbled. She shot a look over her shoulder, objection rising hot and wrathful in her chest.

Then she saw the same look of exhausted resentment in Grace's eyes. "…Fair enough," the sorceress relented.

They reached the far side, rattled from the height and the precarious balance. The sounds of groaning winds and crumbling rock faded into the distance as they slowly approached the flat face of unremarkable stone towards which Elias Leblanc was drawn.

Aimee reached out her hand, pressed it against the rock. This illusion was strong. Over a year and a half ago, she'd watched as Harkon Bright wove a well to hide a downed *Elysium* from the pursuit of Lord Azrael. Even then, she'd known that a person daring to walk through it would run into the real thing, dispelling the magic. Illusions failed when physical reality clashed with their projections.

Except here. Aimee's fingers brushed against rock and dust that she knew wasn't real—or at least not real in the way she believed. The core of illusion magic was showing the viewer something they plausibly expected, or wanted, to see. Roping their very expectations into the effect and weaponizing them against the viewer's eyes.

"I don't understand," Aimee whispered. "I'm…touching the damn thing. Why isn't it breaking?"

Her fist clenched. Another spell of detection. The threads just wove themselves tighter together. The sight grew more elusive. She looked back at Elias. "I don't get this," she growled. "Am I wrong? Is this not—"

The look on his face. The mournful mix of pain and realization in his green eyes, cut her to the core. "No," he said. "That's just it." The green-eyed man gulped. "It's really, really strong, and old…and it's latched on to the fact that you don't want to find what's on the other side."

Aimee froze. "T-that's ridiculous."

"No, it's not," Elias said. The look on his face made her chest clench. "We're both pretty sure whatever that is has to do with Oath of Aurum and whatever—" he clearly hated the word he said next "—destiny is associated with it."

"We don't know that," she snapped.

That washed over him, and she immediately felt a swell of guilt as he closed his eyes and let out a breath. "...My point exactly." He paused, then opened them again. "I can't see through it either."

He paused. Aimee's eyes were drawn to the sword on his hip. The blade over which so much had been made. "...Maybe we've been overlooking the key."

Elias glanced down. Both Helena and Grace took steps back. The former's eyebrows raised as she seemed to come to the same internal conclusion as Aimee.

"That would explain why Collum couldn't find anything here," the old woman shifted her hand on her hip. "The blade wasn't awakened."

Slowly, Elias drew Oath of Aurum from her sheath. The long, straight steel glimmered with its inner light. He held it up before his face, and as Aimee watched, the unease that so often covered his sharp features softened. His dirty fingers shifted on the hilt, then he took several steps forward, looking up at the rock face. "And if this place has to do with the blade, then it would make sense that it's necessary to gain access.

Still he hesitated.

Aimee shifted close to him. Again, his proximity was a heated sensation she was keenly aware of, but she had to focus now. Later. She'd worry about complication and pain and ambiguity later. "Are you alright?"

"Just..." he trailed off before taking a deep breath. "I've wondered, for over a year now...What all this meant. Now that we're here, I'm not sure I have the courage to find out."

This time he looked at her. Eyes mingling uncertainty, fear, and the slightest touch of an innocence that really shouldn't have existed. "I'm scared," he finally said.

Reaching down, Aimee laid her hand over his on the steel. Her hands felt a warmth on the parts of the hilt his fingers didn't touch. A warmth from him, or from Oath of Aurum. Possibly both. Her fingers wrapped around the pommel, and she helped him lift his arm.

"Together, then," she said.

The apprehension on his face didn't fade, but joining it she saw the ghost of a smile. A nod.

"Together."

The glowing blade's acute point slowly raised in their entwined hands, and pushed forward. The moment it met the illusion, a crack split the air, and a white glow blazed straight upwards. Bisected the cliff-face. Cracks split the illusion, spiderwebbing glass-like.

Then it came apart with the ring of a bell and twinkling embers of lingering magic drifted harmlessly about them in a rain of soft light.

In the place of the smooth stone face, an inward divot in the stone A notch surrounded by a diamond shaped series of carvings that culminated in an arched doorway in the stone. Aimee felt a chill run through her as she took careful steps forward. She knew the inscription just above the entryway. Identical to the one she'd seen in Port Providence, well over a year ago, but far better preserved, and here written in full:

CHILDREN OF HEAVEN NO MORE. BY THE WISDOM OF THE WHITE CHALICE WE STAND. NOT FOR THE FIGHT THAT BRINGS CERTAIN VICTORY, BUT FOR THE FIGHT THAT MUST BE FOUGHT.

9

THE BEACON

Elias Leblanc slowly approached the door. Aimee's hand slipped from Oath of Aurum and he lowered the sword. The words burned across his mind, setting his heart pounding and his recollection of the book Belit had given him racing through his mind. He didn't understand the references immediately, but it was familiar.

All of it.

As he approached the iconography, Elias remembered the somber, sad face of a statue in Port Providence that had stared down on him as the personality of Azrael cracked and shattered under the weight of his crimes mingled with the wrongs done him. Reaching out, the palm of his fingerless gloves brushed over the stone. Traced the lines of the words *Children of Heaven.*

"I know that phrase," he breathed. He squinted. Pulled his hand back and pressed it to his forehead. "I think...I think it was in those books I... Only a passing reference."

"I..." Helena's voice suddenly cut across his thoughts. "I remember... myths. Something about a God that was a Tree or something. It's all very old."

"Elias," Aimee said, and turning, he followed her gesturing hand to where a notch lay in the door, an outline shaped perfectly like the sword in his hand.

Slowly, he stepped forward, and exchanged looks with each of them in

77

turn before turning to face what was in front of him. *You wanted answers,* he thought. Then he turned the blade point down and inserted it into the notch. There was a rumble, a sound of grinding stone, and the blade released before the stone doors split on a central seam and slowly grumbled outwards. There was a flicker, and a light bloomed in the darkness into the illumination of a vast stone chamber.

Elias sheathed Oath of Aurum. The familiar weight of the sword settled at his hip, and he stepped through the door and into the shimmer.

A chamber greeted him, its interior a pyramid, stretching upwards toward a small hole in the distant ceiling that functioned as a sort of skylight from which issued a single beam of daylight onto a simple rectangular stone sarcophagus.

Elias drew in a breath. "This," he breathed, "is a tomb."

Aimee stepped in beside him. Out of the corner of his eye he saw her blue eyes sweeping the chamber's interior before she took three steps past him to run her fingers carefully over the upraised stone. Her fingers traced what looked like writing, and as Elias approached, the sorceress read the words out loud.

"Ophilia the Defiant, Last of Heaven's Children. First of the Free."

A beat followed, then Grace said, "Who in the abyss is that?"

Elias glanced over his shoulder and shrugged. "I have no idea."

"There's art on the lid," Aimee said. "Come look at this."

Elias's footsteps were hesitant, each one filling him with a sort of dread—as if the moment he saw what he was headed towards, there would be no going back to not knowing. He walked until his boots nearly touched the base of the stone, and looking down, beheld the effigy of the women entombed within. She looked ageless, her head was wrapped in a mail coif that fell to her shoulders, joining the rest of the plate that swathed her form. Her eyes were grey, her expression stern, but neither of those things arrested him as much as the other two details that jumped out:

Her armor was in the same style as the Eternal Order, save that it was a gleaming white…and in her hands was Oath of Aurum.

"Here lies Ophilia, Last of Heaven's Children, First Knight of the White Chalice," Aimee read. "Her defiance echoes down the ages."

Panels abruptly sprung to light around the sides of the chamber, projecting further light into the dim space. Elias turned in a circle as a shimmering mystic projection appeared in the air over the sarcophagus. They looked like schematics.

"What…is this?" Elias asked, walking around it.

"I don't—" Aimee paused, considering, "—hold on, let me look at this for a second. The writing is really archaic, but I think I recognize some of the mechanisms."

The White Chalice.

He looked up again at the projection slowly revolving in the air, then let his eyes carry his sight up and up towards the ceiling, where the lines of steel holding up the roof of the cavern met in a single five-pointed star entwined around a large crystalline structure. Stretching across the walls were faded paintings and pictographs depicting…something. A broken tree. A host of swords. A beam of light lancing down onto a blade. Wait.

It was Oath of Aurum, he was sure of it, etched into the wall in the air above what appeared to be Ophilia's outstretched hands. Writing was carved beneath. Reaching out with his hand, Elias traced words that he somehow understood.

"…And in the beginning there was the Twelfth Night, and the Children of Heaven were His servants…" his mouth dried and his breath quickened. "…but when He commanded them purge the Plains of Aurum of all life, Ophilia, first among them, stood defiant against her siblings and her god alike. He commanded her yield, and into His face she hurled a vow to defend the innocents he'd bid her slay. And the vow cracked the earth and became an oath."

Elias's eyes rose to the depiction of the blade at his hip, hovering just above Ophilia's heroic grasp. "…and the Oath became a sword."

Turning, he saw everyone staring at him.

"Elias," Aimee said after a moment. "These schematics…this tomb is some sort of control center for an engine that sends some sort of signal out into the Eternal Sky. A big one. I've never seen one this powerful, or this simplistic. I just don't know what it's for."

"…I think I do," Helena said, and she turned her eyes to look at Elias. "And I believe you do too."

Elias stared, eyes wide and heart hammering in his ears. Memories from the *Iseult*, of Belit and her old book.

"There's another order," The green-eyed swordsman finally said. "Or there was, once. Knights dedicated to fighting the Eternal Order. The White Chalice." Hope sparked in his chest for the first time in a long, long time. Then he looked between Helena and Aimee.

"And this thing—this beacon—is how we call to them."

The words left his mouth, and the ground beneath their feet rumbled and shook. Elias turned on his heel and bolted for the door, the chasing sounds of the others in pursuit with their noises of confusion rattling in his ears. Another set of stairs cut its way up the canyon wall just beyond the hidden door. Ghostly embers of lost memory chased his footsteps all the way to the flat expanse of earth beyond the stone steps. Elias staggered as he cleared the final hurdle, nearly fell. Careened onward. *No. Not now.*

In the distance smoke from a rapid landing slowly dissipated into the vastness of the sky. Moving forward, Elias crouched behind a boulder before peering around its edge. A landing ship, tear-shaped and dark-paneled, rested at the center of a dust-cloud of its own making. The impact had damaged some of the landing-gear, but as the hatch opened, Elias's chest froze and his throat dried up.

A cluster of figures exited the entryway, one by one, clad in the armor of the Eternal Order's mortal troops, plated and bearing flame-lances. Stylized. United by the death's-head shape of their helms. Behind them in the far distance, another drop ship was starting its approach.

And leading those soldiers, a knight that was all too familiar. *Gods,* he thought. How had she survived the collapse of the Iron Hulk in Port Providence?

Whatever means had saved her life, it didn't matter now. This was an Order kill-team. Rapid drop. Likely to be retrieved once the mission was over. The mission that couldn't be anything other than killing him.

The mission commanded by Sir Kaelith.

It was more than enough to massacre the survivors of Port Providence. The others didn't know. Elias felt his limbs freezing in place as the troops fanned out. He had to get back to his companions, and quickly. Rapid footsteps deadened by what few stealth spells he knew carried him across the open ground before he nearly slid-skidded into the canyon to find the others halfway up the steps.

"They're here," he said in low tones. "The Eternal Order."

Helena's eyes widened with a flash of what could only have been fear. "How many?"

"A large kill-team," Elias answered. "Led by Sir Kaelith."

"Who?" Aimee's hands twitched at her sides. Ready to fight.

"My former third in command at Port Providence," Elias said. "She's powerful, capable, and nowhere near as unhinged as Malfenshir."

"So worse," Aimee grimaced. "Fuck."

"Well," Elias gulped. "She doesn't have an Iron Hulk. Just troops."

"How long until they're on the settlement?" Grace asked.

"An hour, once they find it," Elias said. "And that's if she decides to move with her troops, she could be there in far less time going alone."

"We need to get back," Grace said. "Now."

The choice flickered wisp-like before his mind's eyes, and Elias made it. There was no pause at all. "I'll go with you," he said. "You won't stand a chance without at least one of us there, and they're looking for me."

"No!" Aimee's demand was immediate and loud, blasting his thoughts away. She took three long steps. Crossed the distance between them and grabbed the collar of his shirt. In an instance, her blazing blue eyes were all he could see. He tried to think around it. Refocus himself, but their touch burned through him like a torch to tinder.

"You know I can't let them do this."

Her grip tightened. "And I won't let you offer yourself up as a sacrifice. I know that look."

Her other hand folded in his. Gripped so tightly it made his heart spike.

"I can hold them off." He insisted. Gratified that his voice only wavered a little. "I know Kaelith's moves. How she'll fight. What she'll do. This is a necessary stand."

"It's also an opportunity for you die." Her words knifed through him. Allowing no equivocation. No room for denial. "I'm not letting you do this." Her voice softened. Just a little. "Not without me."

"He won't be alone," Helena said. "I'll be with him."

Aimee closed her eyes, let out a deep breath, then murmured "Fine. But before we go, there's one thing we have to do—I don't know that it will help us short term, but if circumstance led us to this place, we can't pass it up. We have to figure out how to activate that beacon."

Elias hesitated. Looked from face to face. Helena nodded. "It's a long shot, and it might not help now...but it's all we've got."

Aimee slowly let go of Elias's shirt, dropped down to one knee, planted her hands on the sides of the plinth, and bit her lower lip. "Okay," she said. "Okay I might have some spells that could unpack this. It shouldn't take too long—Helena, help me get this open."

There were sounds. A panel sprung open. Aimee's fingers wove in the patterns Elias recognized as the telltale precision of her spellwork. Grace moved towards the doorway.

And flew backwards as a bashing fist struck her in her center of mass.

The shadow stepped through the entry, sheathed in familiar black armor.

"It's been awhile, Lord Azrael," Kealith said. Her grip on the immense black axe she carried was casual, and her gait stepping through the door was slow and deliberate. Patience caging incredible violence.

Elias exploded forward. Oath of Aurum sang through the air. No reply. No defiant words. Her weapon flipped upwards and caught the edge of his blade with a shriek that sent sparks cascading across the walls.

The blow drove her back, out the door and skidding on her armored heels across the dusty ground. Elias chased, the world at the edge of his vision a blur pinpricking around the cold face readying itself as he drove at her. Kaelith bent her knees and exploded upwards with a burst of magic-powered strength. Elias dashed sideways. Kicked off the canyon wall. Oath of Aurum sheared upwards.

They met in the air.

1 0

THE FIGHT THAT MUST BE
FOUGHT

A storm of blades broke the air outside Ophilia's tomb. Inside, Aimee pushed down her fear and desperately wove spells through the air. She'd have killed to have Vant here now, his brilliance tearing through the puzzle of the beacon with masterful strokes, but in the moment there was only her and an ancient machine whose answers felt just beyond her reach. Meanwhile the man she loved was fighting for his life just outside the door.

She looked back over her shoulder. A ripple of light flashed beyond the tomb's doorway, tearing sound, and the shriek of blade on blade that tore at her heart. Elias was outside, facing Kaelith alone, and she wasn't helping.

Focus, Aimee, focus. How long would it take to get this beacon going?

Not enough time. Fuck.

No way out, no way around. And if she got it going, there was nothing saying that the monster fighting Elias wouldn't come rushing back in to smash everything within this temple-tomb to pieces.

Unless…

She slowly stood. Looked outside.

"Aimee!" Helena looked up from Grace's wounded side. "She's alive, but she can't stay in the middle of a battle. Get the beacon goi—"

"Stay here," Aimee cut her off. "And get to work on it. The instructions are there. Follow them."

Turning towards the door, she started running, casting one last look at Alahna's champion. "And whatever you do, don't leave this room."

Pulling a spell from her repertoire, she pointed behind her, and her eyes were filled with the image of the door collapsing. Rocks burying the entryway in a deafening rumble of debris. Ahead of her, Elias and Kaelith crashed into one another twelve feet over her head, filling her vision with a shower of sparks. The force of the crash drove them back, away from each other. Kaelith landed on the ground near the lip of the gaping hole in the center of the canyon, rolled, and came back up. Elias nearly fell as he staggered to a stop just ahead of Aimee. Sweat stood out on his brow. His eyes were intent with focus.

As Kaelith straightened, Aimee's hands flashed through a series of gestures, and she unleashed a massive bolt of lightning with a word like a primal scream.

Kaelith's eyes widened. Her axe flashed up into a defensive position, and the vast head of the weapon took the burst like a mirror. Aimee saw Kaelith's face set with strain as crackles and snaps of coursing power danced across her weapon before she held it high, and the bolt burst into the sky with a roaring roll of thunder.

Panting, steam rising from her shoulders, the immense woman stalked towards them.

"The traitor and the sorceress. Lucky me."

"Aimee," Elias breathed, his eyes refusing to move from their mutual enemy. "What the abyss are you doing?"

Aimee stepped even with him, her rage pushing down a mad, trembling terror. She swallowed. Her eyes flicked to where he stood just to her right. "What I promised: standing beside you."

The moment cost them. Kaelith was suddenly there. Aimee scrambled left, skirting along the edge of the gaping hole, Elias to the right and towards the canyon wall. The axe blasted earth from the place it landed between them. Size slowed their enemy not at all. Aimee barely got her shield spell up as Kaelith's hand spewed fire even as her axe forced Elias backwards. They were in it, now. Aimee's hands flickered from one motion to the next, flowing with desperation, barely quick enough to defend, a hairprick too late to attack. Kaelith was a relentless blur, flashing between the two of them. Dizzying. Her blows forced Aimee to stagger backwards even as her defenses barely stopped the hatcheting chops of the huge blade.

Elias came at her from the right and the canyon wall. The swordsman was a shearing whirl of jagged light. His enhanced speed keeping him just out of reach. There was no time to think, and only Aimee's periodic bursts of flame, lightning, and radiance, kept Kaelith from tearing him apart.

Sweat came now. Speed slowed. Aimee wasn't made for this. She'd faced the Order before, but never in a protracted duel in dangerous, slippery dust, and never so surprised. Kaelith's implacable pace made her fingers ache with the gestures required to maintain protection.

The shadow was a tornado.

And Aimee.

Just.

Wasn't.

Ready.

Kaelith's blade hammered her shield so hard it split down the center. Aimee staggered backwards towards the edge. Elias closed, tried to use the opening to bind and seize Kaelith from behind with a sudden infusion of strength so desperate and strong that the surge of magic made Aimee's teeth rattle. He let out a shout and unleashed a bolt of lightning directly into the monster's armor.

It wasn't enough. Kaelith screamed as bolts of crackling light crisscrossed the skin of her face, vomited from her mouth. And through the pain she wrenched one arm over her shoulder and seized Elias, sending the power of his own spell ripping back into him.

Elias screamed.

Kaelith heaved his limp body, still crackling with his own lightning, over her shoulder. Man and enchanted sword hurtled past Aimee and into the depths of the hole in the vast canyon.

Aimee didn't even think. She turned and leaped off the edge. No time. The wind whipped past her. A spell shot up into the air behind her, transforming into a vast lattice of magic she desperately hoped would work. Elias was falling beneath her. He thudded against the wall of the stripmine. Bounced. She kicked off the same wall and hurtled downward. Almost.

Her left hand seized Oath of Aurum by the hilt and jammed the blade into the stone. Her right closed around the cuff of Elias's leather breastplate. A second spell loosed.

They came to a stop twenty feet above the hole in the bottom of the earth. The force of the sudden stop ripped something in Aimee's back. She screamed in pain.

High above her head, Kaelith stood at the lip of the vast crevice. She lingered a moment, then she walked away.

Aimee let out a breath, then gulped. There was a ledge a few feet below her. Her grip was slipping. She angled then towards it, then let go of the sword. The drop was short. They landed with an audible thump. Aimee cried out as pain exploded through her shoulder. Nonetheless, she rolled. Fighting through it with gritted teeth and scrambling to Elias's motionless side.

He wasn't breathing.

No. No no no no no!

Aimee searched his neck for a pulse. Nothing. *No!*

She desperately scrambled for what she knew of emergency resuscitation. Hands closed together, and whimpering through the pain, she began to furiously pump his chest up and down. Kneeling to breathe forcefully into his mouth. The effort sent agonizing ripples of pain through her back and upper arm. She cried out again. Tears sprang spontaneously from her eyes. Nothing. His eyes were closed. Lips slowly darkening.

Aimee pulled back, summoned a spell not meant for healing into her mind, and cried out at him as she rubbed her hands together, crackling with light. It would save him or kill him.

At this point it hardly mattered. "Damn all the gods, you son of a bitch," she cried, dropping her hands to his chest. "Elias Leblanc, you are not leaving me!"

Elias's whole body jerked violently as the crackling bolts tore across him a second time. His eyes snapped open and his mouth glowed with light before he spit up a wad of phlegm and rolled onto his side, coughing and spitting and shaking.

Alive.

His eyes searched the sky. Found her. Gasping for breath, he finally found words. "What...Happened..."

"Kaelith electrocuted and threw you off a cliff," she answered. "You stupid, reckless, idiotic—"

He kissed her.

This wasn't like the tentative kiss in the spice shop. There was no restraint now. She didn't care about the stain of blood on his lips, or the pain still arcing across her back. Nothing mattered but the hunger with which he devoured her mouth, the taste of his tongue, the urgency with which his fingers threaded into her hair. For a blazing moment, she was utterly drunk. Her hands went to the nape of his neck, pulled him towards her as a tingle shot from her toes to the top of her head.

They broke, forehead to forehead. Breathing labored. Fingers gripping one another as if they might each vanish if given the chance.

"You—" she breathed finally "—really should've done that awhile ago."

"Technically you did it first."

"We did," she whispered, fingers ghosting along his cheek. "But fair point."

"Where are the others?" He asked as they slowly separated. Later. They'd revisit this later. *In detail.* Aimee promised herself. *Exhaustive detail.*

Gods, everything hurt.

"They're still in the tomb."

"Why did you collapse the entrance?"

Slowly, Aimee's wry smile crossed her face. "I didn't."

"And why did Kaelith just...leave? She shouldn't have, unless she believed us dead."

Aimee's smile—still pained—widened. "She did."

Elias's brow furrowed, then his eyes widened. "Oh, you sneaky sorceress. You used illusions, didn't you?"

"I banked on one possibility," Aimee said. "That she wanted us dead enough that she'd be more than willing to believe she'd succeeded. She thought she saw us fall to our deaths through a hole in the earth."

Elias let his head drop back to the dirt. "Gods," he swore. "You're fucking brilliant. How hurt are you?"

"Shoulder hurts like hell," she answered. "Tore something in my back. I can heal myself, but it will take some time, and I can't do it down here."

He rolled onto his hands and knees. "Then you'll have to be on my back. Give me a minute, and I may be able to climb us out." Looking some distance up, he spotted where Oath of Aurum jutted from the stone.

"...Come on," she said. "Let's get moving."

They crested the lip of the vast pit what seemed like an eternity later. Elias collapsed. Pitched forward, sweat soaking his face. They lay on the ground for a long moment, before Helena suddenly emerged through the illusion, making it fade slowly but surely into flickering motes of light that dusted the ground.

"Oh, thank the gods," she breathed. "You're alive."

"G-Grace," Elias coughed. "Is she?"

"Alive," Helena said. "In the care of her men just inside. She was hit hard, but she's still breathing. Aimee, do you have any healing spells?"

"A few, only the basics," Aimee answered, pulling herself up. "I need you to hold my right arm while I do something quick for myself."

Helena took her forearm, and Aimee let her weight fall into it, turning her body away until she felt her shoulder give a slight click. She gestured with aching fingers, then reached behind her shoulder to the source of the pain, releasing the spell with a word. It hurt. Burned for a moment... then the balm began to spread through skin and torn muscle. A breath out, and with a nod Helena released her arm. Better. She could move without agony. Still tender, but functional.

"Take me to her."

A few moments later, Grace lay on the top of Ophilia's sarcophagus, the blow she'd endured mended as best Aimee could manage, but still asleep.

What in the abyss were they going to do now?

Elias leaned heavily against the wall, still not fully recovered. Oath of Aurum hung from his hip.

"We can't leave all those people at their mercy," Helena said. Grace's men, gathered behind her, nodded. "Those are my people, and Eternal Order or no, we can't let them suffer what's coming again."

"It's possible they'll leave?" One of the men said. "You said they were after you—" he looked at Elias.

"No," the swordsman said. "Just on the off chance that we survived, she's going to go into that settlement, and she's going to hurt people. Moreover, if she was sent by the Eternal Order, she's going to slaughter anyone she thinks helped us." His eyes were haunted. "A lot of people are going to die."

"Then we go," Aimee said. Her fingers balled into fists by her sides. "How long do you think we have?"

"Before she starts killing people or before she leaves?" Elias asked.

"Either."

He looked sick. "Hours for the former. The latter...I don't know. Probably when she gets bored."

"Then it's simple," Aimee said. "We take a breather—we have to. Elias and I need a few moments rest, and we do the best thing we can do for everyone: we activate that beacon."

11

A DARKLY PLANTED SEED

Silas stood in an antechamber off Coulton's shipboard solar. The King rested, exhausted by his ordeal and sleeping off the immediate effects of the magic that had bound him to the Tireless. The sage stared at the man across from him. The origin point of all his loss and misery, and said "Why shouldn't I immolate you on the spot?"

Roland leaned against the wall, his large arms casually enfolded across his chest and his expression annoyingly amused.

"Well, for one, because I haven't actually done anything to harm you."

Silas' lips curled. "The invasion of my home was at your command. You are literally responsible for every misery that has befallen my people over the past year. Personally."

Roland shrugged. "And yet you haven't tried to kill me. Because you know I can help you."

"How?"

"Your King doesn't know how to wield those soldiers. They are of ancient Varengard, and if he puts too much into a given command, the effort will kill him."

Silas's eyebrows raised. That hadn't been his intention. In a flash, Silas was across the space between them, cold fire in his outstretched hand, the crackling flame inches from Roland's face. "You fucking monster. You're lying."

Roland didn't so much as move. One eyebrow arched over his cold gaze, and he shrugged. "You know I'm not, and if we're being candid…tell me Silas, after everything you've done for what you want. After every sacrifice and profane declaration, would it have truly made a difference if you knew the truth?" the dark knight laughed.

Silas snarled. In fury. In frustration. In indignance that his enemy, after everything the sage had gained, still seemed to fear him no more than an aurochs feared a gnat. "I would've saved my King," he lied.

Roland's face creased with a self-satisfied smirk. "Oh, I don't think so."

At length, Silas stepped slowly back. Extinguished the flames.

"And there's one more thing," Roland said. "Your magic. It's powerful beyond reckoning, outpacing my own, I admit. But—"

"But?"

"You have no idea how to wield it."

Silas bristled. The arrogance of this worm who had wrought so much destruction…was unfortunately correct. "I've only possessed it for a few weeks," he admitted.

"It is Intuitive Arcanism," Roland said. "Only far stronger than the variety your average member of the Eternal Order possesses. So, you need not fear my thinking that I can simply strike you down. I assure you, I cannot."

Silas stood back, regarding the taller man with a contemptuous sneer. "You think I don't know that? Do you imagine that I haven't made a study of your order and its methods and resources?" The sage placed a hand on the nearby wall. Willed frost to creep across it in interlacing lines that rippled towards Roland, a giant, razor icicle piercing outwards abruptly directly across from his head and stopping just short of his temple.

He neither moved nor flinched, but neither did he smile. At last.

"What do you want?" Silas asked. "What possible benefit could the alliance of an exiled people be to one of the senior knights of the Eternal Order?"

"That's simple," Roland said. "You want revenge. I can help you get it."

"And if I want revenge against your order?"

The dark knight threw his head back and laughed. Caustic and deep. "Then you're taking aim at the wrong target and forgetting who wounded you the worst."

It wasn't hard for Silas to follow the path being set out for him. He knew it was manipulation, knew that Roland was simply trying to draw his attention away from the Order.

It was also—at least from a certain perspective—true. "The list of those who have wronged my people is long and distinguished," Silas said. "You're going to have to be more specific."

"Who actually took the diamond?" Roland arched his eyebrow. "Who fled Port Providence with the object of your revenge in tow? Who promised aid, only to run when the time came to make good on their vows?"

Silas's fists clenched. Some part of him recognized the manipulation at play. The attempt to divert his hate to a target more suitable to the other man's ends. A distant voice begged him to walk away.

Let it go. You have everything you need. Go home, and finally grieve.

But there was another voice in his head.

It was no less soft, yet its sharp edges somehow drowned everything else out. Washed away his conscience with the dismissing hand of its simple words: *If you let this go, they will live their lives unaware of your pain. Going about their existences, blameless, unfettered. Unpunished.* Abruptly the voice became louder. Burned with the flame of his terrible resolve. Scoured away the agony he didn't want to feel.

That. Must. Not. Stand.

Silas looked Roland in the face, and said "The crew of the *Elysium* must pay."

Roland smiled.

"I couldn't agree more."

Silas breathed out. "Finding them is the problem. I've—" he paused. Something struck him, as Roland watched.

"She sent a letter," he remembered.

"Who?"

Silas felt his smile twisting into a smirk as the voice in his head egged him on. Urged him towards the conclusion that he was finding ever more palatable by the second.

"The Queen Mother."

Silas walked through the gilded hallway of the ship, his boots thumping on the wooden deck beneath its crimson rug. The doorway was guarded by two of the king's men, and both shifted uncomfortably when Silas arrived.

He waved his hand. The door opened, and he stepped into the dimly lit room.

She sat with her face away from him, in a chair before the window that looked out across the sky with its ripples of distant thunder. Her hair was ragged, frame withered and worn from age and time. Some part of Silas's dwindling conscience felt a twinge of shame for what he had done to this woman…but it was rapidly washed away by the ocean that was the voice deep within his soul. She didn't understand. She'd tried to undermine everything he was trying to do. In the face of that, there was nothing he could do but keep her confined here, away from where her treacherous mouth could do his cause more damage.

But now, Gods, why had it never occurred to him before? Now even her treachery could serve his ends.

"I don't have anything to say to you," she finally said.

"You sent a letter," Silas continued, stepping fully into the space. "To the crew of the *Elysium*. I sent assassins after the messenger, but they never came back, which means they were stopped."

She slowly turned her eyes towards him. They were red-rimmed. Exhausted. And yet there was a defiance in them that made the sage stop walking forward.

Silas gritted his teeth behind his lips. She still refused to fear his power. "What was in that letter?"

Alahna took a long, measured moment, then lifted her head and said, "Hasn't anyone ever told you that it's rude to read some else's mail?"

Silas snarled, and his hand flicked up reflexively, black flames dancing about his fingers.

Roland caught his wrist. "Now, now," came the quiet voice. "Let's not get carried away. It's unbecoming to raise a hand to an old woman, and a one-time queen, no less."

When her eyes fell upon him, they widened, and Silas realized in that moment that something had changed.

Alahna recognized him.

"…You," she whispered. "After all this time."

"Hello, Alahna," Roland said with a casual familiarity. "It's been a long time, hasn't it?"

"You…know each-other?" Silas lowered his hand as Roland released it.

"Oh yes," Roland said. "It was in another life, of sorts. I was a different man, and she was still a queen."

"And you," Alahna seemed to draw herself painfully to the maximum height her chair would permit. "You were nothing."

The faintest twitch passed across Roland's controlled features.

"And yet," he said. The smallest ghost of menace echoed in his words. "You remember me."

"I remember you," she snapped back. "I remember every one of your crimes, Ma—"

Roland twitched his fingers. Alahna's words died on her throat with a choke.

"No," he said quietly. "We shan't be using that name. I don't think so."

Her eyes were wide with fear, now. Roland knelt opposite her. His eyes fixed upon the features and lines of her face, and he tilted his head like a cat watching a particularly curious mouse. She tried to speak, but only a choking noise came out.

"It's not pleasant, is it?" he whispered. "Being denied your voice. The only thing you have left in all the world. The only thing you can use freely." There was a glint in his pale eyes. "Fortunately, you don't need to talk for what comes next. And it doesn't matter. You're brave, and I believe that even under the worst sort of torture, you'd just lie to me anyway."

Silas felt his throat go dry.

"So we're going to skip all that," Roland said, "and just go straight for your mind."

He reached out and took a lock of her hair between two callused fingers. Her breath trembled as her eyes focused on his. Silas felt the knight's presence fill the entire room. The daylight darkened. Thunder without grew louder, and flashes of lightning painted the room with bizarre, twisting shadows that echoed to Silas the darkness he'd seen within the bowels of the decapitated tree.

Then Roland pressed two fingers to her temple, and she screamed.

Silas clenched his fists. His own words to her, snarled in a sky ship bay a mere few weeks ago, echoed in his head. *And you will watch.*

Light flashed in the room. The shadows on the walls laughed.

Silas looked away.

OF UNFINISHED THINGS

Elias leaned against the wall of the cavern, the overwhelming weight of it all crushing down upon him.

Died. He had nearly died. His eyes closed for a moment. The others were talking, and their voices were a continuous din from which he could only parse the edges of individual words.

They needed to activate the Beacon. That much he was sure of. As certain as any part of him had ever been about anything, but he didn't know how. Couldn't begin to guess at the strange mechanisms displayed above Ophilia's tomb.

Kaelith was loose among the people of Port Providence, and he had failed to stop her. That ache was almost as torturous as the physical pain still lingering from her redirection of his own lightning. Fuck. Grace lay unconscious nearby, and the sight of her brought back the painfully sharp memory of his own sword taking her sister's head from her shoulders when he'd served under the constructed persona of Azrael. *Not again,* he thought. *Not again.*

History was rhyming. He should've been more thorough in his efforts on the *Iron Hulk* over a year ago. Would it have been so difficult, to find Kaelith before Malfenshir, to have finished her off before he'd traveled to the bowels of the lethal mountain fortress? The answer, he knew too well, was yes. He'd had only moments to spare, and it had been almost by chance that he'd arrived in time to enable Aimee and Vant to destroy the vast metadrive that had powered the weapon called the Silent Scream. There was no way he could've stopped both of his former lieutenants. But all that meant was that the job was even clearer, and its results all the more overdue than when he'd barely survived the aftermath of Port Providence.

They had to activate the Beacon. He had to recover some of his strength in what little time they had left.

And then Sir Kaelith had to die.

Aimee looked at him from across the sarcophagus, her hands moving amidst the projected magic glyphs, shifting and touching bits and pieces. Her eyes burned for a moment, and the kiss flashed through his mind. An unfinished conversation on the verge of boiling over between them if they weren't given a chance to sit and talk.

Helena emerged at his side after a few moments, laying a hand on his shoulder. "How are you?" the older warrior asked at length.

"I failed," he finally said, not meeting her eyes. "I had one job: to kill her."

Helena gave him an odd look. "You're still thinking like one of them, on some level."

"What do you mean?"

"I mean that only an evil bastard thinks in terms of how many he kills. Frames his wins in terms of enemies slain and threats destroyed." She tilted her head to the side. "The good man cares only for who he saves. Defends. Shields against harm. The only calling of the good warrior is to save lives. As many as he possibly can."

She smiled. "Your enemy escaped, but we're alive. You did not fail."

Elias stared at the opposite cave wall. The words rolled over him. How many times had Belit said something similar as they trained in the dark hall of the *Iseult's* Captain's Guard. *One light in the dark, keeping the demons at bay.*

She'd been right then. Helena was right now.

It was quite a thing, how slow the mind could be to come around even when presented with hard evidence that its previous assumptions were wrong.

Elias hurt everywhere. He straightened from the wall as Aimee hit a last glyph and stepped back. "I..." she took a deep breath. "I think the only thing left is for it to charge."

"How long will that take?" Helena asked.

"I wish I knew," Aimee said. "It needs to gather ambient energy from the land itself, and I have no idea how much this isle has left to give."

"And in the meantime," Elias started.

"—We have to stop Kaelith," Aimee nodded.

"You're both damaged," Helena interjected. "Beat to hell. You're in no condition to fight."

Elias straightened. The aches in his body tried to drag him to the floor of the cave, but there was no time. "We have to. People will die."

Helena seemed to accept that. She drew in a deep breath and let out a slow sigh. "Look," she said. "You've faced Kaelith once already, and failed to defeat her, and that was before you were injured. If you mean to bring her down, you need a plan."

They exchanged looks. A silence hung in the air between them, and Elias watched Aimee's face fall slightly. "I…I don't know how to overcome it," she said. "The power she has, that you have. I know my magic is theoretically stronger, but that hardly matters when she can cast faster than I can think."

"Is that how it works?" Helena considered.

"Intuitive Arcanism is the gift of the Eternal Order," Elias nodded. "It's not as outrightly powerful as traditional sorcery, but it can be performed as fast as we can think it. Speed of thought. It's difficult to outmaneuver," he looked at Aimee. "But not impossible."

She looked at him. "How?"

Elias took a deep breath. Leveled his eyes at her. "Don't give her a chance to think."

"What do you mean?"

"Plan your attack. Know the repertoire of spells you will cast well ahead of time. Attack the environment. Trip her up. Get inside her head." He folded his arms across his chest. "When we can't think, we can't use our magic."

She appeared to take that in. A slow nod followed. "Okay," she murmured. "Okay, I can do that."

"And you won't be alone." Helena said. "What can we do to help?"

All eyes were momentarily on him, and Elias opened his mouth again, before closing it. He looked around the room.

"A rifle," Aimee suddenly said. All eyes shifted to her. "We get her tied up fighting us," Aimee continued after a shift of her foot. "Someone takes a shot at her while she's occupied."

"Can you get her away from her troops?" Helena asked.

"She will pursue me," Elias said with a nod. "As soon as she recognizes that I'm alive. Trust me. Kaelith will chase me to the island's edge."

"Who does the shooting?" Aimee asked.

"I will."

The voice was small. Weak and tired. And it took Elias a moment to realize that it came from Grace. The young leader was propped up on her side, a dizzy look on a face that was no less determined.

"My lady, no," Helena started.

"I am the best shot of all the people gathered on this island," Grace calmly insisted. One of her men helped her into a sitting position.

"You're still injured," Aimee cautioned.

"So are you," Grace answered.

"I'm a sorceress," Aimee said. "A portalmage. Gods, you're sixteen."

Grace leveled her eyes at Aimee de Laurent. "I can pick a hellchicken's eye out at the three hundred yards." She took a steadying breath. Her eyes burned. "Keep her busy, and I'll kill the bitch."

Elias hesitated. In that moment, all he could think of was the painful memory of the moment when he'd slain captain Gara in Port Providence. The sick memory of a crime committed when Azrael had been his name kept playing in his head on loop. He couldn't give the girl in front of him satisfaction for that wrong.

But he could give her the next nearest thing. So he pushed the conversation along to the next logical statement. "We'll need a way to occupy her troops."

"Buy me time among the people," Helena said, "and I'll have them rallied. Our people are done with being occupied and kicked around."

Silence fell. Elias swallowed a lump of fear in his throat.

Aimee gave a slow nod, looked from face to face, then settled her gaze on Grace.

"How long until you can hold a gun?"

Elias stared at the moral along the wall of the tomb, as if he could draw some sort of succor for his battered body from the images of the defiance etched above him. A defiance he barely understood, but that he must now emulate.

He'd never intended to spend the rest of his life fighting the Eternal Order, and despite the understanding that facing Kaelith was now unavoidable, he felt the hand resting on Oath of Aurum tremble with fear. *I lost*, he thought. *I threw everything I had at her, and I still lost.*

And now he had to do it again.

The beacon thrummed behind him as Aimee worked its archaic mechanisms. Elias felt a ripple pass through the floor beneath him. Magic like a tease at his senses. He breathed out, shaky. Uncertain.

"Almost," Aimee breathed. "C'mon, c'mon." Focus was writ across her face. All the energy the sorceress possessed was tied up in trying to keep her fear under control by focusing on what she had to do. Helena bent over the other side of the sarcophagus, following Aimee's directions. Grace leaned against a wall, recovering her strength and drinking from a battered canteen.

He closed his eyes. Tried to center himself. Tried to remember everything that Belit had taught him back aboard the *Iseult*. *Focus, Elias. Focus.*

Lord Roland's face swam before his vision, eyes like cold stars and twisted smirk the echo of the one Elias had once worn as Azrael. *Fear is weakness, weakness is death.*

He gritted his teeth.

No.

And then he was jolted out of it. Arrested by the sudden clunk of something shifting beneath his feet. Far below and deep—oh, oh there were lights flashing now. Running up the sides of the room through previously unseen channels, five lines of gossamer shimmering towards the apex of the tombs ceiling. Aimee slowly stood back from the sarcophagus and Elias watched as a thousand translucent pieces of projected magic slotted together like the self-assembly of an incredibly complex three-dimensional puzzle.

The lines of light converged in the ceiling, and the ground shook. Dust shook loose from stone and chips of paint cracked and slid from the mural along the wall. Abruptly, Elias turned and dashed for the doorway, past the illusion and out onto the open ground where he'd fought Kaelith less than an hour before.

High above the top of the cliffs into which the tomb was built, far off, emanating from the giant pillar of stone around which the survivors of Port Providence huddled, a beam of brilliant white light shot into the heavens.

Elias gulped. Thinking of their enemies, and what they had to have seen. They hadn't thought this through. Hadn't thought any of it through. He looked back through the door.

"We did it!" Aimee exclaimed. Only for the look on her face to die as she put together what he'd just done.

"…Okay," she said. "Time to get fuck out of here."

They fled. Closed the doors behind them, this time. Then they began the hurried trek across the base of the canyon floor, back the way they'd come. Fast and deep. Hoping against hope to avoid Kaelith realizing they were still alive before they needed her to. Elias's booted footfalls crunched with terrible echoes on the stone and the dirt. The oppressive chorus of remembered pain assailed his senses, and he could swear that this time he moved through the echo of past battles and screams as something unimaginably vast moved over his head, its presence blotting out the sun.

The sensation made his head hurt. Time passed. They saw no sign of the enemy, eventually reaching the base of the cut stone steps and making their way slowly upwards. Grace leaned on Helena's shoulder. In the distance behind Elias, the sun was starting to set, and the line of light grew more visible against a darkening evening sky.

Would this work in the dark? Grace could barely be expected to shoot without daylight. They'd have to wait out the night…somewhere.

Where?

"There's a cluster of tall rocks a half mile from here," Grace said. "We should be able to hunker down and make a proper plan. Helena, is there any way you can get us a signal once you've infiltrated the camp to let us know that it's time to go?"

"No, I can't imagine that I will," she answered as they moved. "But I can give you a time window past which I'll almost certainly be either successful or dead."

"How long?" Aimee asked.

"One hour."

Aimee, Grace, and Elias exchanged a look in the fading light.

"Do it," the sorceress said.

"Here's where we part ways, then," Helena said. She shifted her cloak to loosen her retractable spear at her side. "May the gods bless you all, and may we kill these bastards quickly and with minimal casualties."

Then she was off into the darkness. They had one hour.

Elias did his best to relax. Forced his breathing into even measures as he stared at the lights of the immense encampment from around one of the tall rocks. The men were resting, and high overhead, the stars were beginning to come out. He wondered how the rest of the crew was doing.

Whether they'd managed to escape the *Atrocity*. Whether they were safe. He hoped they were.

"I don't know if I can pull this off," Aimee's voice abruptly said beside him. He hadn't noticed her approach. Too lost in his own, consuming thoughts.

"What?"

"I threw everything I had at her," she said quietly, and her voice sounded small. Uncertain, in a way it rarely ever was. "It wasn't enough."

Elias was silent. He needed to say something. Needed to help her find her feet. And yet his own were so shaky beneath him that he could barely stay steady on rock-solid ground.

"I know you can," he said, finally.

"How?" She asked.

Elias took a deep breath and turned his head to look at her face. The starlight cast it half in shadow, half in a silvery edge that framed her features and glinted off her blue eyes. Her gold hair drifted faintly in a soft breeze.

"You defeated me."

"Are you sure you weren't just distracted?" she asked and tilted her head to the side.

Elias laughed. More than a little nervous. "I assure you. I had other things on my mind. But you did it all the same."

She frowned. Absorbed that, and he could almost hear the complex wheels of a mind that had only a short time ago discerned the mechanisms of an ancient beacon turning as she reflected on the statement.

"Don't forget," Elias said. "We'll both be back from the dead as far as she's concerned. That will shake her. The more rattled she is, the less well her magic works." He grimaced. "I would know."

Her hand found his in the darkness. Fingers laced between his own. She didn't say anything. Just looked at him for a long moment as they stood together on the edge of life and death.

Oath of Aurum hanging by his side, Elias walked towards the camp. His breath echoed in his ears. Step. Heartbeat. Another. The lights drew near, and he could hear shouting. In the darkness, the beam of light they'd activated, the beacon, shot into the heavens.

He would not run. He needed to arrive in a certain way. He needed to pull as much attention as he could. The name of the game was to draw her away, not to fight her in the midst of a mass of people who could easily become collateral damage. Get her away. Get her near the rocks. Keep her from seeing Aimee until she was ready to turn one on one to two on one. Dogpile. Attack. Attack. Attack.

Only fools wanted a fair fight.

It was not hard to find her. Her voice carried, and he recognized the cold, dead promises of twisted necks and pulverized spines. He didn't catch exactly whom she was menacing, nor how they responded. The whimpers and the noises of fear were all too familiar, and at once he was back at Port Providence, among these people, watching their suffering. Knowing his responsibility for it.

Elias's pace quickened. Nobody noticed him, because they weren't expecting him. He made his way past the edges of the tents and through the crowd. People turned as he approached. Uncomprehending faces shifting to looks of shock as he suddenly emerged at the edge of a sea of bodies. Kaelith stood in the center of the mass, her axe-head planted in the ground. Before her, a man knelt, blood pouring from his broken face that mirrored the splatter on the knuckles of her gauntlet.

Elias stepped out of the crowd. "Kaelith," he said.

The look of surprise was still registering on her face as the first of her soldiers stepped towards him, a flame-lance rising in threat. Oath of Aurum swept free. A white line of light cut through his center of mass. Two halves of a man fell as a swell of blood splashed across the sandy ground.

Elias leveled the blade at his enemy and spoke, loud and concise.

"We're not finished yet."

This is **Harkon Bright.** They call him the Mage that Meddles. Harkon Bright. Professor, Warrior, Adventurer, and dissident. The last, perhaps, most of all. Ever since his early years—a period of time as tightly wrapped in secrets as only a powerful man can make them—he has used power to oppose power. His path has left a swathe of victories that have made him a legend far grander than he prefers, for every success erases the truth of the ten tragedies from which he learned before. And Harkon Bright learns. It is perhaps his greatest strength; the knowledge that every action carries a recitation to be absorbed. A truth to be teased out.

It is a lesson more powerful even than magic itself.

But by itself, learning is not enough. It is more than just the rote absorption of knowledge or the taking in of facts, that matters. It is the understanding. It is the grasping of the weight of matters and of why they fall as they do, that makes the difference between a wise man, and a man who simply knows things.

Harkon Bright has made wisdom a life study, and it has cost him over the years. In failures. In missteps. In every loss and through every trial. He is a fighter by nature, made resilient by every one of his mistakes. The lesson he has taken is not that error is equivalent to failure, but that every error carries an opportunity to grow. Now Harkon faces dangers beyond what he's faced in the past, for his position, and the position of those he loves and would see protected, balances upon the edge of a knife. The world sits at an inflection point, and can be pushed towards goodness and decency, or into the nightmare that yawns beyond terrible decisions.

To stop the nightmare, Harkon must do the impossible again.

And it starts with surviving the next day.

13

THE SPARK THAT LIT THE SKY

Harkon Bright's footfalls echoed through the central corridor of the *Elysium* as he headed towards the engine room. He prayed Vant was wrong. He probably hoped in vain.

The hatch opened, and Harkon found Vant taking readings from the metadrive. It wasn't smoking, at least. That told him that this wasn't the worst position his beloved ship had ever been in. "How bad is it?"

"She'll recover," Vant said. "I've set her to vent the buildup of chaos through the dampeners, but that means that we've got no power beyond the minimum until that's finished."

"How long?"

"A day if I had to estimate."

Harkon sighed. "What do we still have in the meantime? Is there any way to speed up the process?"

"I mean," Vant said, "I suppose we could vent everything through the guns, but I don't think you want to blast raw chaos across a port. Kinda a bad idea."

Harkon scratched his chin. "I'll keep that one in mind."

"Sir?"

"Hmm?"

"That's disturbing."

"I keep everything in mind, Vant. You know that. How safe is the vent?"

"Safe enough," Vant said. "Since the Harbormaster agreed to take our money, I'd guess on a gentle one we'll be here about two days."

Harkon drummed his fingers on the bulkhead. If the *Atrocity* caught up with them before then…well, they were in the Violet Imperium, now. The Eternal Order might hesitate to attack outright.

Then again, if The Order believed they could strike quickly enough to destroy the dock-front and leave before the Imperium navy arrived…

Ogier was always a bit of a question mark, as unpredictable as he was sadistic. Harkon sighed. Naturally The Order had bequeathed its finest ship to a capricious, mad dog of a man. It made a twisted sense: if you wished to test a weapon, give it to someone you could trust to use it. Someone who could be abandoned to his fate, if he became inconvenient.

"Keep working," Harkon said. "I'll see to Vlana's progress."

Vant gave a nod and went back to taking his readings. "Just tell everyone to stay away from the engine exhaust, okay? It's not dangerous to anyone dockside, but anybody climbs up on the wing and stands too close and they might, I dunno, grow a third eyeball."

Harkon arched an eyebrow. "Indulge me, why is someone climbing close enough to huff the engine exhaust something you're earnestly worried about?"

"Just covering my bases, boss."

He found the Quartermaster on the bridge. She was crouched over some papers that looked as if they'd been neatly pressed a moment ago.

"We have enough money for two days docked," Vlana didn't look up. "And I don't know how long that will last when they learn that we're being actively hunted by the Eternal Order."

"They'll be here before then," Harkon sighed. "The question is simply whether Vant will have been able to vent everything safely and have readied us to get out of here before they arrive."

Vlana finally met his eyes. "And if he can't?"

Harkon's mouth drew into a taut line. "We buy him time."

Vlana gulped. Slowly nodded. "Oh."

They came sooner than Harkon anticipated. It took the better part of a day—time spent meditating and preparing himself—but they arrived. The horizon line of heaven was painted a red-gold, and the distant crack of an opening portal preceded the appearance of the vulture-like shadow of the

Atrocity, smoothly flying towards the port. Harkon stood at the end of the skydock, the heat of the evening surrounding him like a suffocating blanket that mingled with the scorch given off by the softly venting engine exhaust ports.

The ship glided closer, and the Mage Who Meddled crossed his arms, contemplating the realities behind a reputation for power. Ogier was not Roland. He was a legendary monster of no small infamy. The maker of Malfenshir, who had tried to turn Port Providence into a pile of floating, shattered stone before Elias killed him. Ogier, like Malfenshir had been, was bleak monstrousness incarnate...but he was also just that. A blunt object that knew no language but the most straightforward sort of force that he could summon.

Bjorn slowly approached. He wore his immense two-handed sword, his eyes locked on the specter of the approaching dreadnought where it hung in the sky.

"You're really set on fighting this time, aren't you," the bearded warrior said. A statement, not a question.

Harkon folded his arms. The ship grew in his vision. "They've put us in quite the corner."

"Could fall on the city for protection," Bjorn shrugged.

"Perhaps," Harkon answered. "But that would hardly stop a monster who believes his due is vengeance. He'd retreat to the edge of the port's claimed territory and wait until we eventually had to leave." A sigh escaped him. "And in any case, I'm tired of running."

"You're not a young man anymore, Hark."

"No. But my strength hasn't faded. Not yet."

A simple laugh escaped Bjorn. "Like old times, then. Jump in the pit and get it over with."

"The son of a bitch has been barreling towards a rightful death for a long time," Harkon shrugged. "If the hard wall he dashes his brains against is me, so be it."

This time Bjorn threw his head back and laughed. "Then let's send him to hell."

Harkon walked to the edge of the skydock and stood where his boots brushed against the lip of wood that was all that stood between himself and the formless eternal drop into the abyss. Then he reached for the spell in his mind and shaped it with quick gestures to form the magic before releasing the spell upwards into the sky with the word that loosed it. *Gestures summon, words release.*

A bolt of gleaming, radiant light shot upwards from his upraised palm. It climbed higher and higher, rising above the top tiers of the port and high above the spires of the city beyond. Then it burst and filled the heavens with a brilliant, blinding light that dimmed to a single whirling glyph that hung in the sky, slowly fading.

"Gods," Bjorn said after a moment. "You sure know how to keep it subtle. Didn't think you'd use your mark."

"A formal challenge is best," Harkon said. "Draw him out in person."

"He's a fool if he accepts."

"Yes."

"I'm going to guess that you don't want the rest of us involved directly in this."

"Oh, I do," the Mage who Meddled answered. "I've made plans with Vant. I'm going to need you to man the rear guns and wait for the order to fire."

Bjorn looked back at the engine vents, and for just a moment his eyebrows raised. "...Oh."

"Quite."

The old warrior turned and jogged back to the ship. The vulture-like specter of the *Atrocity* grew in Harkon's vision as the sun set. He was a speck before a beast slowly devouring the clouds with its maw of a silhouette. He raised his chin, clasping his hands behind his back as he waited.

It wouldn't be easy, but he'd killed worse.

It filled his vision. Up close, the immense ship was a ruinous vision of black and red, swooping lines and avian appearance. The red horizon painted the edges of her wings a bloody gold that contrasted with the *Elysium's* silver. He watched at a distance as a hatch opened and a gangway descended, figures exiting the vessel and moving onto a dock some distance from where the *Elysium* hung moored in the sky. Dockworkers got out of their way. A cluster of harbormaster's enforcers jogged towards them. Harkon saw the bloody exchange happen at a distance. Silhouettes of men gored and splattered against the sunrise. His fists clenched. He couldn't stop it all. Could only meet Ogier in a place of his choosing. He strode down the length of the dock, past the *Elysium's* exhaust ports and away from its lowered ramp. He caught

Clutch's eye as the pilot stood just inside the bay doors, and she nodded, understanding.

As far as plans went, it was risky, but there weren't any other options, just now. He moved as if in a dream. Screams were filling the air as the Eternal Order's troops moved along the dock front. Flame-lances and swords shone in the sunlight that dusted armored soldiers and fired the edges of visors with death's head symbols. Harkon ascended a flight of stairs to bring himself level with their approach as a press of civilians fled inland, toward the safety of hard rock and tall buildings. Harkon's boots crunched upon the wood of the platform, and his hands twitched through the opening motions of a spell.

Knights of The Order were the dangerous ones. Lethally fast intuitive arcanists who could cast at the speed of thought. The troops were chaff. There to soften him up. Distract him. There were times for fighting subtly and deftly, and then there were moments like now. Harkon felt the power building as he moved his fingers, slower than once they were, but still quicker than even the best of these could dream. Their lances lowered.

Harkon walked forward, and released his spell with a single word: **"Part."**

A hurricane ripped apart the advance of the Order soldiers, and scattered bodies into the open air like strips of falling paper. Harkon walked through the eye of his own tempest. Right. Left. Up. Down. His fingers flashed too fast for even his own trained eyes to follow. Nets of light caught bodies and saved his enemies from tumbling into the abyss. There they hung, suspended, separated by hundreds of feet and deprived of their weapons.

"Good. Now stay."

The first of Ogier's apprentice knights came rushing forward. A sword was moving free, and Harkon could almost see the thoughts forming spells in his mind. A jet of fire. Harkon swatted it aside, took control of it with a word, and sent it spiraling back around at the knight with three times its strength.

The knight parted it with his sword. Staggered back. Harkon snapped his hand out, snake-like, and graced a knuckle along the blade's edge before shifting sideways. **"Melt."**

The man screamed as molten steel burned away his hands, and fell shrieking to the dock. Harkon stepped over his frame and stopped.

"Ogier," he addressed the chaos of the dock, and gestured at the screaming knight on the wood at his feet, "I believe this one belongs to you."

And Ogier came.

It had been years since Harkon had beheld the monster, and then at a distance. His head was shaved, these days. He had a harsh face, pitted and scarred by many fights. His nose was hooked, and his eyes were dark. Almost black in the recesses of their sockets. His armor was all horror and projected violence. Plate covered in spikes, stained red with what Harkon knew to be paint in the style of splattered blood. Even among the Eternal Order, Ogier was ostentatious in his bearing. In his left hand he held the haft of an immense, barbed glaive whose blade glowed green. They stood facing one another under the apocalypse glow of the setting sun.

"Where is Azrael?" the lord knight demanded.

"Far from here," Harkon answered. "Beyond your reach."

"Oh, I doubt that," Ogier said. "No matter. I'll show him your corpse when I see him at last. A final gift before his end." His hand graced across a seal affixed to his breastplate, and then Harkon saw it. His heart seized up. That was the glyph of Guild benediction.

Ogier was hunting them in the capacity of a representative of the Guilds.

Well. That would make the consequences of this difficult. Nevertheless, it didn't matter.

"No," Harkon said. "You won't."

A wind picked up between them. Harkon's robes stirred in the air.

"My Gods," Ogier laughed, low. "You truly mean to fight me, old man?"

"No," Harkon sighed. "I mean to kill you."

Ogier's smile was the only warning, and then the beast erupted forward.

Harkon's shield was already prepared. It blasted outwards and upwards in every direction. Tall as a city spire, wide as a thoroughfare. The spear struck its center, splintering the magic in glass-breaking spiderwebs.

But the purpose of the shield had never been to stand for more than a moment. Harkon sidestepped as he let it shatter. Ogier's momentum carried him forward, the spear missing the sorcerer's middle by inches. Harkon summoned a cutting wind. Ogier vaulted backwards. Swept the spearbutt at Harkon's head. The sorcerer swept one heel back. The spear missed him by inches. The razor-edged air cleaved a spike from the shoulder of the knight's armor. Ogier roared and swept his spear in a blur at Harkon's body, the glaive's head abruptly everywhere at once. Harkon's hands had started moving a half second before. And abruptly, he was no longer there.

He was nowhere. Done. Finished with petty spells and the little magics with which he'd matched this creature of darkness up until this moment.

Harkon reached into the space between breaths. The interminable vastness that comprised time and potential. A swirling mandala of potential outcomes appeared in the air surrounding him in the place between places. The breath between breaths. And his eyes swept the outcomes. The myriad ways and methods by which this conflict could be ended. Three mirrors hovered before his gaze. Three ways forward.

Harkon reached into one of them and clenched his fist.

He reappeared on the dock, thirty feet away from Ogier.

The monster turned. His weapon swept up.

The wind dusted across a grassy field. A chattrang board sat between two children. The children were concepts, and they were also real. The first reached out his hand to touch his knight. A carved horse head forged of black moonlight.

On the slatted wood of the skydock, Harkon Bright's boots shifted against the grain as Ogier charged.

The first child smiled. The second frowned. And they sat opposite each other.

Ogier's glaive severed the supports holding the two levels above him. The collapsing scaffolds spilled machinery and cargo into the empty air.

The white Empress aggressed in the second child's hand. It was a direct move. Forceful and daring. And Ogier's pounding feet and enhanced speed carried him into a leap that blotted out the sun above Harkon's head. A spear descended, trailing arcs of red light.

The first child simply smiled. And Harkon was not there. A spear punched through wood and blasted the ochre-dust of agisstone upwards into the air. The first child shifted with his feet beneath him. He closed his eyes, and the knight moved in his hand. Forward. Left. The second child's eyebrows raised.

Harkon appeared again. Ten of him. Twelve. Forty. Manifold palms traced the symbols of Unending Force. Ogier's eyes filled with the reflection of eighty-four descending fists.

The Empress toppled sideways. The wind was gone. The children were gone.

Harkon bright looked down.

Ogier's bloodstained, shattered hand twitched one last time.

Harkon reached down to pluck the seal from Ogier's broken breastplate and the bloody ruin of the flesh beneath. The Guild seal was cold in his hand. He raised his eyes to where the *Atrocity* was detaching from the docks. Her guns slowly turned.

Harkon felt the first weight of exhaustion begin to push down on him. The cost of immense magic. He ran. Barreling towards the *Elysium* despite the complaints of his knees. The ramp was still down, and the first blasts from the aether canons ripped up the docks behind him, sending splinters racing past his face as he summoned a shield at his back. Bjorn ran down the ramp. Harkon leaped as the *Elysium* began to pull clear. For a terrifying moment he hung over the edge of the abyss. Mid-air. Plummeting.

Bjorn's hand slammed into his forearm, the grip like iron. Screaming with exertion, he hauled Harkon aboard.

"Raise the ramp!" Harkon screamed. *Elysium* was still unvented. They couldn't fly free with their engines overloaded.

But there was one way to vent everything at once. "Get to the ready guns," Harkon said, then, breathing with increasing difficulty, made his way forward. "Don't fire until I give the order!" He shouted behind him.

Moments later, he burst onto the bridge. Vlana looked terrified. "Sir, we're right in their sights!"

"Vant," Harkon said into the tubes. "I need you to redirect all the chaos venting through the rear batteries."

"Are you fucking insane?" the engineer shouted back.

"It's our only shot."

Clutch looked at him sideways as she gripped the wheel. She was sweating, her eyes filled with real fear. "We're sitting pigducks."

"We're sitting pigducks with a hand-cannon."

"If this doesn't work, we've got nothing but a fried set of rear guns and an engine that will still take a second to cycle up before we can get out of here."

"And if we hit them, it'll be months before that ship can do more than limp home. Now bring us rear facing."

They turned. The open sky glimmered before them, an expanse of beautiful cloud and the last twinkle of a sun before it vanished.

"Ready!" Vant yelled.

"We're flashing our ass!" Clutch shouted.

Harkon heard Vlana praying. "Bjorn," Harkon said into the tubes. "Target their guns. Wait for them to glow. Don't miss."

A breath followed. Another. Harkon could see nothing but the sky. The *Elysium* drifted through the heavens. If this was to be the end, there were worse ways.

Then a roar ripped out of them. The entire ship shuddered from nose to tail. Harkon grabbed the railing. Clutch screamed. For a half second the sorcerer didn't know if they'd dealt harm or taken a mortal blow. Then Bjorn screamed back across the connection.

"She's burning! The son of a bitch is on fire!"

"The vents are clear!" Vant yelled. "Hard burn! Go go go!"

Clutch spun the wheel and the *Elysium* veered left. Through the side of the main viewport, Harkon saw the frame of the *Atrocity* shuddering. Her main gun was a smoldering ruin twisting up the nose into burning shrapnel just below the bridge. Then they were moving forward. Slower than Harkon would prefer. Still fast enough. He dashed up onto the portal deck as the lenses descended. Swept through the motions of summoning magic with exhausted fingers. An eye tore itself open across the sky and the *Elysium* limped through. It slammed shut on the other side.

Harkon sagged against the rail, looking down at the bridge crew as Bjorn emerged from the hall and embraced Vlana, who was now openly crying.

"For real, though," Clutch said. "When we get back to Lia's Rest we need to let the girl breathe. Put her down and do some maintenance."

"We'll only have so long," Harkon sighed.

"Why?"

Harkon pulled the seal out of his pocket and tossed it down. The pilot caught it in a dark hand and held it up to the light. Her eyes widened. "Oh. Oh, fuck."

"Yes," Harkon sighed. "It seems that whatever the Eternal Order is doing, they have official Guild sanction this time. Which means as of now, having killed one of their official representatives, we have made an enemy of the entire Guild."

14

BY THE GODS' GRACE

Aimee broke into a run. She ran through the list of spells in her head. *Don't let her think. Don't give her time or a chance to form her thoughts.*

Ahead of her, Kaelith straightened. The crowd had parted before Elias, who now leveled his sword at the enemy. A dead soldier lay at his feet, and others were moving to take him. He exploded forward. A flat struck one man's head. A pommel another. He swept a leg. Kaelith moved forward. Elias pivoted back. She was open. Aimee loosed a spell. Crackling lightning tore outwards between the parted crowds. This time it struck Kaelith in the shoulder, and she veered sideways, shouting in pain.

Her axe whirled overhead and Aimee heard her scream. "Drop your fucking sword or I will kill every person in this crowd."

Elias blurred forward, just past her defense. Caught her off guard. He wasn't in a position to stab or cut with Oath of Aurum, but he was able to deliver a heel-kick to the center of her breastplate that sent her flying backwards and into a crowd of her own soldiers. Aimee was nearly upon the group now. They had to draw Kaelith away. Into the open. Away from the crowds. Where Grace's gun could reach her.

She just hoped the girl had gotten herself into position.

Kaelith burst upwards. "Fine," she said. "Crowd-killing it is."

Aimee's hands twitched in concentric circles. Swept up. Out. To the side. She got the shield up a moment before Kaelith loosed a wall of fire in all directions, and it slammed down around her in a containing barrier that trapped her with her own flames.

An inferno erupted into the night sky. Aimee heard Kaelith scream.

Then a blow slammed into her shield. A second. A third. Aimee winced. Her feet slid backwards on the dusty ground. The shield snapped in half, and Kaelith emerged from the firestorm, flames dissipating from her pauldrons. Half her hair had burned away, but her skin was somehow untouched.

"So, you both survived," Kaelith said. "Well, at least this won't be boring." She gestured at her men. "Kill these people."

The first of the Eternal Order's soldiers, recovered, hefted a flame-lance, only to lurch suddenly at the crack of a gunshot. He dropped. Aimee's eyes flicked to the source of the sound. An old man of Port Providence held a long-gun, smoke issuing from the barrel.

"No," the tired, ragged voice said with a ferocious defiance. "Never again."

Kaelith exploded towards him. Almost faster than the eye could follow. Elias was suddenly there. The ringing of his sword against the immense axe was a bell in the dim light.

Aimee charged. A gust of wind slammed into Kaelith from her outstretched hands. The knight flew backwards. *Don't give her time to think. Keep on the pressure.*

Kaelith came to a stop outside the edges of the crowd. Dirt billowed upwards in twin clouds to her left and right. She opened her mouth to issue another threat, and then the crowd surged. Helena's spear took one of Kaelith's soldiers through the chest, and then the woman was there with a cluster of armed, furious people.

Elias pushed upright, hefted his sword, and said, "Time to go."

Kaelith roared, this time. She barreled past people, coming straight for the two of them.

They ran. Kaelith gave chase. Aimee didn't have the advantage of being able to match Elias's enhanced speed. She gained on sorceress and the swordsman quickly, and Aimee abruptly turned on her heel, loosing another blast of wind to drive their enemy back. This time the Order Knight was ready. Kaelith was barely driven back enough to keep her counter-swipe from cleaving Aimee in half.

Elias barreled into her. The sword struck from high. Kaelith caught it on the haft. Her free hand set a bolt of lightning ripping through the air towards Aimee. The sorceress stagger-stumbled out of the way, a scorch mark burning the corner of her blue coat. She swept a leg back, set her teeth, and sent a bolt of her own crackling back.

Elias saw it. Jumped clear. And this time, finally, it struck home. Kaelith roared in pain as the jolts of electricity surged over her body, sending her lurching backwards.

Then she turned the stagger into a spin and brought her axe down into the earth, blasting a huge, loose boulder up into the air. Kaelith leaped. Her axe blurred in two directions as she hewed it into four chunks and kicked each one of them at the pair in succession with a series of blows that sent shockwaves rippling through the air. Aimee dropped, sent a whirl of wind upwards, and muscles straining, spun it around her frame and back towards her enemy.

Elias's sword burst through his own boulder, sending two halves falling on either side of him. Kaelith nearly dropped her axe on top of him, only to be forced to kick off Aimee's boulder as it sailed towards her. The knight landed in a crouch ten feet away.

"What is this?" the knight grunted as she straightened. Aimee's mind raced, trying to pull more useful spells to keep on the tip of her tongue. To stay even and be useful against an enemy that seemed almost two breaths ahead.

"The Azrael I knew was unmatched," Kaelith continued. "Even fallen as he was, he still bested Malfenshir. And now even with this bitch's help it's still all you can do just to survive against me. What are you now?"

Elias was breathing hard, the strain painted across his features. White knuckles gripped Oath of Aurum's hilt as he slid into a guard. "I..." he breathed. Then straightened. Jaw clenching. "I am Elias Leblanc."

Kaelith rolled her eyes. "You're a pathetic, crawling, soft thing. And I will put you out of your misery. You and—"

BANG.

The crack of the gunshot was simultaneous with the ping as the bullet glanced off Kaelith's pauldron, making her stagger. Elias exploded forward. The Knight blurred back and swept her axe across the space between the three of them. It trailed a wall of fire that bloomed out in all directions. Aimee summoned a shield. Elias stumbled, and Kaelith was racing off in the direction of the gunshot.

"Oh, you sneaky little bastards."

Grace. She was going to kill Grace.

～

The young woman had crouched one hundred feet away, propping her long gun up on a rock. As they caught up, Aimee watched as two of the last remaining Port Providence soldiers rushed to get in the way. Kaelith killed one with the axe, the other's head she crushed with a bone-shattering blow to the temple. Aimee couldn't loose lightning or wind at her, that close to Grace.

Stupid brave, the girl swept her gun high to fire point-blank. Kaelith sidestepped before it could fire, grasped it around the barrel, and hammered the stock so hard into Grace's shoulder that she fell back, screaming and clutching at the broken bone with her other hand. Kaelith stood over her. Derisively tossed the rifle away where it clattered somewhere in the dark.

"How many bullets were in that thing, you little snake? Never mind. It's gone now."

Something. Do something. Anything!

The spell Harkon had taught Aimee for dealing with the dead back in *Iseult's* depths sprang to her mind. Kaelith wasn't dead, but she bet it would hurt anyway. Aimee leaped free from Elias's back as he came up short, vaulted sideways to put distance between them and bring herself profile with the knight, then made the symbol and loosed the spell. Too slow. Kaelith pivoted. The spell glanced off the face of her axe, forming a beam into the night that petered out.

"You make each other so weak," the knight said as she hammered Oath of Aurum aside a half-moment later. "I'm not even battling two enemies. I'm fighting two people dividing their attention between defending themselves and defending each other, and that's before finding the energy to fight me."

Aimee saw the bolt of fire coming, but this time her shield was too slow. It shattered mid-summon. The broken shards of magic hurtled back at her. She dropped to the ground, landing painfully on one elbow as razor edges lashed her leg. Kaelith caught Elias's next sword strike with her axe head, grabbed his arm, and physically hurled him into the ground. He let go of Oath of Aurum and grabbed onto her arm as he fell, body flipping her.

Suddenly, Kaelith was down. Aimee forced herself up as two combatants rolled away from each other. She couldn't see Grace. Hopefully the girl had gotten away. She fired a cutting wind at Kaelith's frame, and the other woman rolled away, grasped a rock and hurtled it at Aimee's head with all her strength. Aimee barely dodged. Kaelith was nearly up when

Elias slammed his shoulder into her armpit with a cry. They went down again. Kaelith ended up on top, her hands clamped around Elias's throat. He choked. Gasped as Aimee rushed to reach them, lifting a rock of her own and hurling it at her enemy's head.

Kaelith let one massive arm free, the other still crushing Elias's trachea, and the boulder stopped mid-air between herself and Aimee. Aimee stopped it from hurtling back at her with a spell, and it hung in the air between the two women as both exerted their wills upon it. Sweat stood out on Kaelith's features as she strained between holding the boulder and choking the life out of Elias. Aimee couldn't move. It was all she could do to stop the rock from coming back at her. Her feet trembled in her shoes and her fingers ached from making the sign of warding.

"This," Kaelith snarled through her teeth "is where it ends. Choking, gasping in the dirt."

Elias's face was darkening beneath the stars. His hands flailed and his body heaved under his enemy's iron grip.

"And they died happily ever after," Kaelith snarled. The en—"

BANG.

The gunshot cut across the night. Kaelith lurched back from Elias, letting go. He rolled to the side, gasping for breath, The knight's large hand reached up to her neck. Red covered her palm. "...What?"

Ten paces away. Grace crouched. The long gun was braced against her unbroken shoulder, the barrel perched on a rock. "Six," Grace said. "Six bullets, bitch."

BANG.

BANG.

BANG.

BANG.

Kaelith's corpse hit the ground with half a head.

Aimee let her arm drop and fell to her knees. She felt the blood of the dead Port Providence men stain her pants. Elias's breathing was returning, and high overhead the stars were achingly beautiful. It felt horrible to be aware of that, just now. Grace's gun clattered to the dirt, and she rolled onto her back. There was a moment of dragging silence, and then Aimee heard her sobbing.

At length, they made their way back to the massive encampment, cautious. Unsure of what they would find. They were greeted by Helena on the outskirts. Tired, with a cut on her brow, but otherwise unhurt.

Kaelith's soldiers were either dead or captured. They worked through the night to see to the dead and the wounded, then retrieved Grace's fallen guards.

Kaelith they left for the rats.

The beacon illuminated the night, a shimmering line of white lancing up into heaven from the center of the encampment, its source an orb of white light seemingly summoned beneath the spire when they'd activated the mechanism in Ophelia's tomb, whatever that meant.

Aimee no longer had the energy to care. She slept terribly, when the time came. She slept most of the next day, and woke from nightmares of Kaelith's melting face, and the terrible pillar she'd once seen on the day she'd failed the test of the Axiom Diamond in Port Providence over a year ago. It was dark out, and the brutal heat of the day had faded into a cool, quiet night.

And then both she and Elias rose to the sound of shouting that it took them a few moments to decipher. A ship had been seen in the sky, arcing in a slow turn around the island before beginning its slow descent to the ground at the edge of the vast encampment. Aimee emerged from the doorway to where they'd slept in time to see it land. Silver, forward swept wings, and more beautiful in that moment than any vessel she'd ever seen.

The *Elysium* had returned.

15

A BARGAIN OF BEGGARS

Silas dreamed of the tree. It glittered in the heavens, made of a thousand strands of upraised light branching out in every direction. Coursing bolts creased up its length, flickering starlike in an interconnected vastness that defied description when viewed all at once. Silas was a gnat on the surface of a rose-window. Aware only that he touched something greater than the sum of all human parts.

And then fire. A blazing, crisping pain ripped through its form. Darkened its parts. The trunk crumpled and crunched and broke halfway up. A scream beyond words wracked through the sage's form, and he awoke sweating in his cabin. His chest itched as it hadn't since the first day after he'd made his bargain. He pulled himself from his bed and aching, crept across the floor until he reached the mirror with its wash basin. There he opened the neck of his shirt. The dark patch in his chest had grown. In all directions from its center, ropey, veining threads branched beneath the skin. Silas tilted his head sideways, and wondered what fate awaited him when this affliction spread further.

It was irrelevant. Soon he would have vengeance, and none of it would matter anymore.

Alahna's screams still echoed in his mind. He splashed water on his face and took a shuddering breath. These were the sacrifices one made to attain one's goals. The fact that none of them understood simply meant he was forced to work around them.

And in any case, the information they'd learned had been invaluable. Now he had only to meet with Roland and plot the next phase. The thought of working with the Eternal Order Lord made him shudder, but the benefits would be paid in treasure and accelerated gains. His chest hurt and the voice in his head surfaced from the place it lurked beneath his thoughts.

Stavrophore, you're so close.

He just had to grit his teeth and bear through the horrors. That he would endure. That he would commit. That would accomplish what was necessary.

The knock came abruptly at his door, and Silas straightened, pulling on his robe. "Enter."

The soldier's uniform was stained and worn. His long gun was strapped over his shoulder and he looked exhausted. "His Grace wishes to see you."

Damn. Had word gotten back to Coulton yet of what had happened with his grandmother? "But of course," Silas said, and following, closed the door to his quarters.

Coulton's audience chamber was a long hall that had once been beautiful and ostentatious but was now crowded with soldiers and exiled nobles. This was the room in which the crew of the *Elysium* had stood and accepted the quest to recover the famed Axiom Diamond for his grace. A task they'd accomplished, but whose dictates they'd betrayed, once they'd acquired the prize. How much more easily might the past year have gone, had Coulton and his people had the jewel? Had the Violet Imperium not abandoned them as unwanted refugees without a home?

Coulton sat in his chair, flanked by two of the Tireless, and for the first time since binding his King to the automaton soldiers, Silas felt the slightest twinge of fear. The immense beings stared into space with their inscrutable faces, not moving. Between them, Silas's King sat in a chair once owned by some noble who'd lost his seat, which now served his master in place of his life. Pausing amidst the assembled rags of a royal court, Silas bowed.

"You sent for me, my King?"

"You asked my helmsman to change course," Coulton's voice was worn and tired, but there was still strength in his words. That was good. His Majesty could not afford to fold under the pressure yet. "Why?"

Silas's eyes flicked across the assembled nobles. He knew they didn't trust him. Knew that they resented his influence over the king. Which of them, then, was whispering in the young King's ear when Silas was else-where? He needed to keep a tighter rein on this.

There were five of them. Had Coulton's court dwindled that much?

"My king," Silas said. "It is important to constantly remain in motion, lest our enemies find us. I am seeing to a meeting soon between ourselves and a number of Guild Representatives who have agreed to assist us in our efforts. It was necessary to take us to the rendezvous point."

"Sage," the foremost of the nobles said. He was a Duke of the House of Vierce, not that his house mattered anymore. His lands had been scorched and were now overrun by those things that had escaped from the *Iron Hulk* when it collapsed onto Port Providence. "We have an army now. One unlike anything the skies have seen in a generation. We must go home and retake our isle. Yet you persist in all this…irrelevance."

"My king," Silas began. "I bid you be patient. I have only done what I must do to secure ourselves the best position. Our allies in the Violet Imperium rejected us. Our home is badly ravaged, and our place in the heavens is far more tenuous than perhaps your advisors believe—"

"Do not ignore me!" the Vierce demanded. "Majesty, this man has been indulged long enough. He has secured these warriors for you, for a certain, but now he dawdles about with new advisors and talks of events that have little to do with us. We have power, and we must use it, or we are no better off than we were the day we fled our kingdom."

New advisors. So Vierce and his cohort had not yet guessed the identity of Lord Roland. Not that it would've mattered. The high-ranking member of the Eternal Order would have killed them all easily without breaking a sweat. Just as Silas was now able. The hand by his side absently twitched, practically aching to set the Vierce's head on fire. Ignite the deck beneath the feet of these arrogant nobles before they could interfere with his plans. *Patience,* the voice in the back of his mind whispered. *Soon they will suffer.*

Once, he'd sworn to obey and listen to these men of status, but if they were going to put foolishness ahead of his own plans for restitution and justice, to the abyss with them. "Duke," Silas kept his voice carefully even, "with all my respect, you are thinking too small."

"With respect," another noble—the count of Eastedge, Silas thought—said, "Home is what matters. Yes, the isle is infested with those things, but as the Vierce has said, we have an army, now."

"And would you rather attempt this alone with our limited resources, foodless, friendless, on limping ships creaking with war-damage?"

Silence fell for a moment, and Silas took a few steps forward. He didn't fear physical violence. Only the loss of his King's favor. That he had to keep at all costs. "Majesty," he said, kneeling before the throne. His dark robes pooled on the floor. "I have ever been your advisor and confidante. Trust me now as you long have. I wish to secure us allies and supplies. I wish to make our position in the heavens unassailable. Surely this is something with which no reasonable advocate for our survival could find issue."

"Have you not been listening?" Eastedge demanded. "We have an army, now—"

"His majesty has an army," Silas saw the opportunity and took it. "An army to which none of you contributed and with which you can only think small thoughts. You would have us use it without allies. I would have us use it with powerful allies. You would have us limp back to our corner of the sky to lick our wounds and accept our decline." He clenched his fist. "Majesty, I would have us take this age by the reins and give ourselves the sky."

"You're insane," the Vierce replied. "My King you cannot put your trust in this…this…" he stuttered. "This cynical apostate. He is using you to further his own power and to harness his own strength. You cannot—"

"If you please," Coulton's voice was tired, but surprisingly resolute, "I will be my own judge of whose council I take. You wanted a question asked, and he has answered it. And answered it to my satisfaction."

Silas kept his face carefully neutral as the Vierce turned his furious eyes upon him. "If your grace has doubts, I will happily see them assuaged when we meet with the representatives of the Guilds."

"Who is your new friend?" Eastedge demanded. "And why has he been granted free reign to go wherever in the abyss he wants on our King's flagship?"

Silas slowly turned his head and looked the nobleman in the face. "A harbinger of the great things I bring you." At the obvious look of sudden fear on the man's face, Silas let his eyes roll, exaggerated and amused. "Just a Guildsman," he said. "Come now, what do you take me for?"

"If I am honest?" Vierce eyed him, level and concerned. "I take you for a man so consumed with whatever it is you have done to yourself to secure what our people have that you have forgotten why doing so was virtuous." He folded his arms. "I have known many wise men, Silas. I have seen sages and priests come and go. I am not a learned man, but I have heard every prayer and every philosophical platitude that someone with my years might possibly encounter. None of the ones worth listening to have the lilt of your voice now. And nobody who speaks of owning the whole sky should be trusted by people who just want to go home."

For just an instant, the sage was taken aback. A painful ache formed in the back of his throat, the faintest touch of shame ghosting along his spine in time with the memories of teachers who would have turned their faces away, had they seen what he'd become.

In that moment, Silas made a quiet decision. It might not be now. Might not be tomorrow. He might have to count the days until it was possible, but one way or another, he would have restitution for those few seconds of guilt and anguish. Vierce had made him feel it, and for that, the duke would die screaming.

∽

"Tell me, majesty, how do you fare?" It was a short time later, and Silas stood beside his king, watching as the Tireless shifted only in response to the ebb and flow of Coulton's mood. Even those movements were taxing. The strain the King was under was intense.

And Vierce thought we could use this army to simply conquer. They're a means, you fool. A means to a very specific end.

"I've been having strange dreams," Coulton said. "I dream of a tree falling and a field of fire. I can hear my brother amidst the parted flames, begging me to stop..." he trailed off for a moment, and it took Silas a few seconds to realize that the seventeen-year-old monarch's voice was breaking. "...and then I can see him, and I try to tell him that I don't. I don't know what I'm doing, and he looks at me with such sadness in his eyes." He gulped. "And then my brother turns away from me."

Silas felt his teeth grit as the memory of the prince filled his vision. A weight hanging over his head. Would Collum have agreed with what he was doing? Would the storied hero-Prince of Port Providence have given his blessing to the vengeance they were soon to secure on his behalf? Likely not.

But that was precisely the point: he was not here to object. His life had been taken from him, along with countless others, and in the end, only Silas seemed to care.

"My king," Silas said with a heavy voice after a long moment. "Whether...whether or not the dead would approve of what we do is less important than that we pick a course through our grief and keep moving forward. Nobody can take away our pain, but we alone decide what to do with it."

Coulton closed his eyes, and Silas saw a tear trembling above his cheek. *This is wrong,* some little part of him begged. *He is a child.*

Yes, but the world was broken, and the blood price for what was done had to be paid in full. Sacrifices were needed, and even children could not be spared from twilight.

"Have no fear, my king," Silas said, and laid a hand upon Coulton's shoulder. "All will be well."

It was a lie, he knew. Nothing would be well. Nothing ever again.

But with effort, and just a little more time, all would be avenged.

Two days later, they saw the Dreadnought. Silas stood on the bridge as the helmsman gulped in naked unease. None of them had been prepared for the size of Guild ships.

Beside it, Coulton's flagship was little more than a small cruiser. By contrast, the Guild dreadnought was a gray lance tapering to an impossibly narrow point. More sculpture than ship. Silas let his gaze linger for only a moment before turning to look at the rest of the crew manning the bridge. How many of them had so much as seen a Guild Dreadnought before? The wonder would captivate them for a while. It might even keep some of them from noticing the nature of the people they were about to meet. Silas did his best to hide the deep breath he was taking. This would be the delicate balance.

The ship grew in their vision, Silas rehearsing the words of his communication as he walked down the halls towards the docking port. They slowly drew alongside the dreadnought, and the stravrophore met with his King near the doorway. Coulton looked nervous and tired, all his emotions tangled up around his feet, making it difficult for him to put one foot in front of the other.

"What you are about to see and hear," Silas said, "may frighten you. There will be things that seem paradoxical and at odds with our goals before now, but I assure you, we will leave this meeting in a place of tremendous strength."

The mechanical thunk of vessels connecting and the locks sliding into place echoed in their ears. Coulton looked at him, apprehensive...but then he took a deep breath and said "I have trusted you as long as I've known you, my friend. I will trust you now."

The doors slid open. Silas felt the faintest pang of guilt, but that voice was little more than a whisper, now.

A dozen people stood waiting. Foremost among them was a robed man with a sallow face that looked as if it didn't get much sunlight. The glyph of the Functionaries—those people who attended to the everyday relationship between the Guilds and their immense Behemoth trade-ships—rested just above his left eye.

"King Coulton," the man said in a smooth, quiet voice. "Welcome. My name is Dietrich." He stretched his hands out wide. "To put you at ease, let us say that we understand well ahead that you and your people have a specific grievance with the crew of the skyship *Elysium*."

"More than that," Coulton's red-rimmed eyes burned. "My people have been cast adrift and abandoned to their fates by our allies. Our property has been taken. Our lives destroyed." He squared his shoulders. "We need our home returned to us. We need to recover what was lost."

Silas watched the Functionary with his dark eyes. Dietrich smiled. "I fear I must tell you that Port Providence is an overrun ruin, and her recovery is unlikely, even with the army you have acquired... but there is something we can give you in its place. That and much more."

Coulton absorbed the bad news with a hard expression that bespoke pain. Then, after a moment, he took a breath and regarded the functionary with a kingly grace. "I am listening."

"First hear our proposal," Dietrich said as the wind whipped behind him. "Your people will deliver the Axiom Diamond unto us when it is taken from the dead hands of the *Elysium's* crew. You and your advisor Silas will bring the Tireless to bear as the spearhead of a war against an enemy that we will lure to a place and time of our choosing. In return we will give you a new home. A place of strength that will place your people at the center of commerce in all the heavens, and all with the Guild's blessing."

Coulton's breath let out as he stared at the functionary in front of him. "Which enemy?" He asked. "And which place?"

Dietrich inclined his head. "The enemy is an infamous independent Skyfarer who would make herself a ruler in defiance of Guild law. Her name is Belit the Red, and when the *Elysium* calls for help, her Behemoth, the *Iseult*, will answer and pull them from a trap that will snap shut around her and her precious ship-that-would-be-a-country."

Here he smiled, and it was a mirthless expression of pure hunger. "The place is a nation that has harbored your enemy. A state that has marked itself through its patronage of Harkon Bright. Majesty, we speak of nothing more and nothing less than giving your people the jewel of the unclaimed." His eyes glittered. "We will give you Havensreach."

16

TOGETHER AGAIN

Elias stared up at the ceiling of *Elysium's* infirmary. He really needed to get better about not getting the shit pounded out of him every time they confronted a serious enemy. His ribs still ached, but the healing spells had done their work, and what had been multiple broken bones and a nearly crushed throat were now simply pains and the strain of a magically sped recovery. He closed his eyes for a moment, breathing out the confirmation he'd made in his head for the thousandth time.

Kaelith was dead. The bitch was dead. Her body was left in the dusty wilds for the scavengers.

The last of his Port Providence invasion crew was slain. It wasn't the vengeance that these people deserved, but it was something. Malfenshir. Fenris. Kaelith. The others whose names he'd honestly forgotten, which the bastards fucking deserved. He closed his eyes. Dead, dead, dead, dead, dead, dead.

Slowly he straightened. He was alone, with only the occasional creak of the wind against the hull reminding him of where they were. At length he shifted the blankets off his legs and grabbed his pants before stretching and heading in the direction of his cabin. The central hallway was empty, but he could hear the sounds of conversation from the common area. Elias hesitated for a moment, torn briefly between curiosity over what had happened while he slept and not being fully awake enough to understand what anyone was saying yet.

Eventually he opted for risking confusion and made his way towards the common room and galley with its bay window view of the terrain surrounding their landing spot. In the distance, the beacon still blazed into the skies. Elias wished he knew what it was calling for, or what help might arrive in response.

A group of faces looked up at him, and all the talking stopped. Vlana blinked several times. Bjorn sat across from her, and Aimee made up the third in the trio. All three had steaming mugs of coffee in their hands, and looked to have been in the middle of what wasn't a deep conversation.

He should've paid them all equal mind, but Aimee was the only one he saw, for just a moment. Her blonde hair was down, freed from the braid she usually wore. She was dressed in a loose-fitting white shirt she must've thrown on quickly, and he did his best to avert his eyes from the neckline to focus on her face. Her breeches came to midway down her calves, and she'd doffed her boots to go barefoot. More than any of those physical details, though, was what they told him. She was tired—probably more worn down than he was—and had thrown on whatever was clean before coming out to get the cup of coffee. She seemed a little groggy, and for just a moment when she saw him he couldn't tell what spirits she was in.

Then her blue eyes widened just slightly, and the brightest smile he'd ever seen spread across her face. Like he was the only thing that existed in the heavens, for just a moment.

For Elias, it was like looking at the sun. He lifted a hand and in a sleep-graveled voice, muttered "Hi."

"How you feeling, kid?" Bjorn asked. The older warrior had a simultaneously concerned and amused look on his face. "You took a hell of a beating."

"Throat still kinda hurts," Elias murmured. "I imagine I won't be singing for a little while."

Aimee opened her mouth. Then she appeared to belatedly realize something. Her face turned beet red, and she bit her lower lip and cleared her throat. "You...um. You forgot your shirt."

Vlana snorted. Elias looked down. Apparently he had. He looked back up at the trio and shrugged. "It's hot."

Aimee's face burned a little redder. She looked away for a second and he nearly tripped over words that almost came out. He didn't say them, instead trying to clear an awkward patch of space between them by not touching on something they needed to talk about in private.

"What did I miss?"

"We interrogated one of Kaelith's men," Bjorn said, "and the people of Port Providence captured her frigate. We've got an extra ship and a bit of perspective on what's going on, now."

"Please," Elias said, sitting. "We've been in the dark too long."

Vlana took a breath. "It...turns out Silas has made common cause with the Eternal Order."

Elias's mouth hung open. That made no sense. "What?"

"If Kaelith had survived, we might have learned more," Bjorn said. "Not that we had the means to restrain her, or that she didn't deserve to die. But yes, it seems Silas has somehow enmeshed his goals with..." here he paused, and Elias could see the hesitation on his face. He didn't need to let the man finish. It jumped to the forefront of his mind, summoned from the depths of his worst fears.

"With Roland," Elias finished.

Bjorn's mouth closed. He and Vlana exchanged a glance.

"It's alright," Elias lied. He felt his heart hammering as his every panic impulse rose, bringing bile almost to the back of his throat. He pushed it down. "It was inevitable, right? Gullrats have to come home to roost."

"... Elias," Aimee started.

"It's fine," he cut her off, barely keeping his voice from cracking. "What's the plan?"

"We still don't know why Kaelith turned to killing the people her boss is trying to manipulate when she thought she'd killed you," Aimee sighed. "But we did glean the coordinates of a place where Coulton's flagship returns every week to meet with resupply ships. With that plus the frigate we stole from Kaelith... we might be able to sneak aboard and get both the King and his mother away from that monster."

Elias watched her for a long moment. At length, Dame Helena entered the room, mid-conversation with Harkon before the two of them paused. Elias looked at them, and there must've been something in his face that spoke volumes, because Harkon's own expression twinged briefly with a painful resonance the moment their eyes met.

"I see they told you," he said simply.

"And it makes no difference," Elias said as quickly as he could. "I made a promise to help them." He gulped. Could barely say the name. "Roland or no Roland." He ran a hand through his dark hair, swearing quietly. "And that's before we have to even think about Ogier—"

"Ogier is dead," Harkon said with blunt finality. Elias looked the older man in the face. For a moment, he almost couldn't think of what to say, then he breathed out a sigh he didn't know he'd been holding in as the mental book of Malfenshir's evil closed itself with finality in his mind's eye.

"Good."

"We'll take the frigate, with the Elysium following in its shadow," Helena said. "We should be able to dock with them, and Grace knows the interior of the ship. Where His Majesty and the Queen Mother will be located. We take two separate groups. One for the Queen Mother, one for Coulton. It's our best shot. Especially given new complications."

Elias looked from face to face. Now he felt even more in the dark. "Spill."

"The Eternal Order appears to have changed its relationship with the Guilds," Harkon sighed. "Whereas before they were merely occasional employees with the ability to apply a certain pressure to the Council... well, now they seem to be operating as its officially sanctioned agents. To cross them is to cross the Guilds, and to cross the Guilds, is, well—"

"—'To court the wrath of heaven,'" Elias repeated the well-known phrase.

"And Silas has made common cause with both." Helena said.

And they'd killed a Guild representative. There was nowhere to run, now. Except maybe back to the *Iseult*, to shelter with Belit. But they weren't going to do that. They were going to fly into the teeth of their enemies and try to abduct them. Well, one of them. Alahna wasn't their enemy.

He should've managed this better. Should've handled it stoically, but in that moment, it was all more than he could handle. He took a breath. Took another. The eyes on him were dizzying. He felt nauseous and in a flash of an instant, nothing was more important than being literally anywhere else.

"Great," he said, running his fingers over his forehead. "Let me know when we're due to take off. I'm going to sleep and get ready."

"... Elias," Aimee started. He could hear the concern in her voice, and while he appreciated it—Gods was some part of him ever thankful—he just couldn't do it. Not right now.

He stopped in the door to the hallway. Paused. Wanted to say something meaningful. Intended to say something like *'I need to lie down and process this'* but instead, he just sighed and said, "Need pillow now."

~

Elias stood alone in his cabin. His heart was beating so fast that it was physically uncomfortable, and had his ribs not been mended they would've creaked at their breaking points with the repetitive blows. He took several steps further into the space, putting a hand out to catch himself before he fell. Cold metal greeted his fingers as he steadied his frame before catching his other hand on the wood panels of the wall. *Deep breaths. Get it under control, Elias. Handle your shit.*

But it wasn't just the fear of pre-battle jitters or the dangers of bullets or lightning bolts. In his mind's eye, Roland was almost more storm than man. A bleak shape looming terrible and large, recalled as the danger between doorways and the punishment for every missed step. The man who'd killed his mother, raised him as a reflection of his own desire for dominance and control. The man that had broken Elias Leblanc and stitched the personality of Azrael together from the warped reflection of the broken pieces.

Roland was involved, now. Elias had faced monsters and people who were worse than the monsters. He'd faced sorcery and sword and skyship gun…but in the face of the man who made him, his trembling hands were no stronger than those of a shaking, frightened boy.

He looked down at the cold metal under his hand and found it resting on the black pauldron of Azrael's plate armor. His expression shone back at him from the polished steel, and all at once, he couldn't take it anymore.

Elias fell to his knees at the feet of the armor he'd worn as a broken, enslaved monster, and sobbed. It didn't last long. There wasn't as much left in him as he'd expected — too burned out on fear, on repressed terror and things undealt with and unconfronted. On—

—A knock at his door. He almost didn't answer. Could barely summon the energy to stand…but he did it. At length, Elias found his feet and walked towards the door, cracking it open.

Aimee stood there, and the look on her face forestalled objection. She looked worried in a way that cut through his heart, her eyes wide and the concern writ on her features growing as she took in the state of his own face.

"I—" she started, faltered "—can I come in?"

He didn't answer. Just stepped to the side, and closed the door behind her as she stepped through. She took several steps forward as the door closed behind them with a click, and slowly turned, fidgeting with her hands absently. "I wanted," she almost gulped. "I wanted to make sure you were…"

"Okay?" Elias asked quietly. "I'm really not, but…thank you anyway."

She nodded slowly. "I don't presume to know what you're going through," she paused, words separated by an awkward breath, "But I…I'm here if you want to, you know, um." She paused. "Talk."

He looked down for a moment. It was hard to think, with her right there. A confusing surge of emotions rushed through him. "Talk," he echoed at length. "I…yeah, we need to do that."

"I didn't mean to impose upon you," she blurted out. "And I realize now that kissing you might have been presumptuous, given what you've been through and oh Gods now I'm talking about that when we should be talking about what's going on with y—"

Elias crossed the distance between them, took her chin between his thumb and forefinger and craned his neck down to kiss her. Her lips were soft. Warm. There was a half-second of stiffened surprise, then she made a sound that sent a thrill from his neck to the base of his spine. Her fingers slid up his chest to bury themselves in his hair, and the thrill turned into an aching want. Their kiss broke and he opened his eyes, their faces inches apart. His hands were on her hips and he felt her trembling.

"Do I," she breathed, "do I need to go?" A difficult pause followed. She swallowed. "Do we need to stop?"

Elias felt his breath shake. His knees were weak, and his thoughts were a warm flood of fever-haze. Part of him was afraid. Felt the menace of his own experiences circling like a prowling predator in the recesses of his mind…but the jingling of a frightening belt and the presence of those who had hurt him was growing distant.

Her every touch was burning those memories away.

"The only thing you need to stop doing," he murmured, "is apologizing."

Her answer was an aching moan, then her hands were on him. He felt her nails lightly graze his back as her fingers dragged down the length of his frame. They pressed together, lips joined, fierce and desperate. His hands moved on instinct, curling into the hem of her shirt and forcing them to separate long enough to pull it over her head. She threw it on the floor and stepped into him, groaning as they pressed skin to skin for the first time. The sound of her voice made him shiver, and before he knew what he was doing his hands shifted beneath her thighs to lift her up.

She wrapped her legs around his waist and they stumbled in the direction of his bed. Her fingers threaded into his hair, gripping the strands as she stared down into his face, eyes wide, shoulders heaving. Her lips trembled and she kissed him furiously again, her tongue stroking desperately against his. The kiss broke, and Elias moaned before his face dropped to her chest, where her breasts strained against gray satin. He slid one hand up over the smooth skin of her belly, her ribs, peeled aside the fabric and closed his mouth over her left breast, feeling her shudder, loudly groan, and curse as his tongue curled eagerly around a diamond hard nipple. "Fuck," she gasped. "Elias. Gods above. Abyss. Please don't stop."

The backs of his legs hit the baseboard of his bunk and he sat down with her in his lap. He was so hard it almost hurt. Elias's heart hammered in his chest. All he could smell, see, and taste was Aimee. Her skin slid against his as his fingers made quick work of the bra, pulling it off her chest and closing his mouth over her right breast in turn. He groaned low in his throat and sucked until she whimpered. Her hips rocked against his cock through their pants and his mind almost whited out.

Making space between them with a gentle push against her hips, he started undoing her pants with shaking hands as she made a moan of frustration before dropping her fingers to help with his own. He peeled her pants down. Her underwear was black, cut to emphasize the arch of her hips, flaring wide from her narrow waist. Looking up into her eyes he flashed a grin before a shudder raced down his spine as her hand pushed his pants and underwear down and her fingers wrapped around the base of his cock. Her eyes widened for just a moment. "Oh. Oh well alright then."

"Just a moment," Elias half-breathed, half-groaned. "You first."

His fingers curled into the straps of her underwear and slid it off her pale legs. He pressed a kiss to the fluttering skin of her middle before his lips made their way down to the juncture of her hips. She gasped and he went to work with lips, teeth, and tongue. She arched and words tumbled out in incoherent murmurs. One hand was buried in his hair, the other gliding up and down his cock. Then she was letting go of his hair, pushing him back onto the bed. Her fingers wove the intricate motions of a simple contraceptive spell, then they awkwardly, urgently shuffled out of the rest of their clothes, throwing them across the room. She straddled his hips. Elias stared up at her. The light from outside the cabin porthole fired the edges of her hair, her skin. Her blue eyes burned into his, and her hand reached down between them, taking his cock between her slender fingers again, and slowly, sweetly, guiding him between her legs. "Are you alright?" she asked between hard breaths. His mind almost went blank at the rush of sweet sensation. "Is this…okay?"

Elias put his hands on the smooth skin of her ass and slowly sat up, curling his hips upwards and into hers as he did, until they were flush with each other and he was buried deep. His breath left him in a gasp and he murmured, "Does that answer your question?"

Her lips parted and her eyes squeezed closed. Her fingers clenched against his shoulders. "You bastard," she gasped loudly. "Oh Gods. Elias I've waited for this for so long. Don't you dare stop."

Her eyes opened. She pressed their foreheads together and grinned as he coiled his arms around her and drove his hips upwards again. It was adrenaline. It was desperation and hedonistic indulgence and bright, aching wish-fulfillment. They twisted together, entwining and—eagerly, finally—fucking in a knot of hastening movement and quickened breath. Elias held her to him as they trembled and clung to one another in exhaustion and hunger. Her lips made him drunk and the feeling of her skin against his, her knees on either side of his hips, her breasts against his chest, filled him with dizzying fever. They moved together, urgency burning hotter. She rode him furiously, words tumbling incoherently from her mouth between kisses. He rolled her onto her back and arched over her and they made the headboard rattle against the wall until a tingle raced from the base of his spine to the back of his neck and her back arched like a bow and her heels dug sharply into his ass and he stifled their screams with a kiss and felt himself let go. His mind was perfectly blank and blissful for just a few moments.

They came back to reality slowly, pressed together in a sweaty tangle. Her fingers grazed the side of his face and her blue eyes stared into his with wonder and unabashed joy.

"Well," she nervously laughed. "That escalated quickly."

"We were inspired," he breathed. "To say the least."

She was about to say something else, her fingers still caressing his face, when a deafening knock sounded on the door to Elias's cabin, nearly sending them tumbling from the bed in a pile of limbs and surprise.

"Elias," Helena's voice came. "We need to talk."

17

THE FARMER

When he was chopping up vegetables, Bjorn could almost pretend that he was young again. Before the war. Before prophecy destroyed the first home he'd ever known. The knife moved up and down. The board beneath was the same as it had been back in a small farmhouse where light and laughter had chased the children running around his feet. The blade was the same too, one of a handful of things from the farm that still existed. Re-handled five times, now. Carrots came apart under his skilled repetition. He studiously kept up the work and tried not to look directly at his hands, the only things in his field of vision that prevented him from forgetting the vast gulf of years between that life and this one.

His home was gone because of a war almost nobody remembered. There were times when that seemed like an appalling injustice, but the rest of the time the old farmer was just glad that the world had moved on, even if some part of him never would. That was what the world was supposed to do, after all; continue. New generations stepping up to history and leaving the grief of their fathers and mothers behind. It was his preference to live in a world that was moving on.

And that was precisely why Bjorn's heart was now filled with fear. The others hadn't realized it yet, though Harkon likely knew, but the Eternal Order was playing for so much more than hunting them down, now. Ogier had secured the badge of a Guild representative. For a Lord of the

Eternal Order to be granted that status, they had to have wrested a level of control and influence over the Council of the Twelve that put them in a position of incredible power.

Guild representatives could command the obedience of kings. Could make emperors pause and republics shake. The Eternal Order—once a mercenary organization that frequently served at the behest of high-ranking Guild members—was now at least partially calling the shots. It wasn't just a disaster for the nations the Guilds moved between and the ones over which they held sway, it was a potentially lethal blow to every independent skyfarer plying the heavens. Seated at the reins of such a massive corporate apparatus, there was nowhere in the known heavens that the Eternal Order could not reach.

And Harkon had just killed an instrument of that power. A symbol of its might.

The others had born witness to war's edges. They had known politics and tasted the edge of power lashing out. None of them but Harkon knew what it was to have the full force of that might turned against them and aimed squarely at their backs.

Bjorn knew. Hell itself was coming for them.

"You okay?" Vlana's voice interrupted his brooding. He grunted in response at the person who was as near to a daughter as one could be without being the daughter he'd lost. She leaned in the doorway, tilting her head and looking at him. "You're not even chopping anymore. That slice of galley wall that interesting?"

"Thing about being my age," the farmer sighed, "is you never really stop thinking. There's so much garbage of a past for you to noodle on and your body makes you sit for ever longer periods of time between your little bursts of doing things. If you ever wonder why old folks are cranky, it's because all they do is think. Think, think, think."

She laughed, the sound bell-like and pleasant. The twins were Bjorn's private joy. "I'm serious, though," she said. "Are you alright?"

"Definitely not," Bjorn sighed. Then he looked at her and squinted. "But it's rather beside the point. We've bitten off a hell of a chomp, girl. I'm not sure we can actually chew it."

She folded her arms and considered. "I just..." she paused. "I can't think about it. If I let my mind go to what's coming I just..." a breath followed and she gripped the insides of her folded arms with fingers tight against her fatigues "We're going to get Coulton and his grandmother," she said, mostly for herself. "And then we're going to put an end to this."

Then she shook her head. "Gods. No, that's wrong. There's no putting an end to any of this, is there? We've started something that I don't know we can finish."

Bjorn watched the fear flit across her features. He had a meal to make, and it was as if the act was almost pointless on some level. They were up against something so much bigger than just a mercenary operation in a small kingdom, or a cult aboard a city-ship. "Help me cook," he said at length. "Whatever we're going to do next, we shouldn't do it on an empty stomach."

"Have you seen Aimee or Elias?" Vlana asked as she slid gratefully into the galley and started donning an apron. She reached for a cup and filled it with water from the sink.

"They're off fucking their tension out, I expect," Bjorn said.

Vlana spit the water into the air. "Bjorn!"

"What?" the old farmer laughed as he fetched the sealed packets of meat from the ice unit. "It's not like the way they look at each other has been exactly a secret."

He tossed her a packet. Vlana snipped the corner with the shears, shaking her head. "Yes, but not all of us want that image in our hea— Francesco, dammit!"

There was a blur of color and fur and tentacles as Vant's adopted squitten shot through the door to the galley and bent at the middle, furiously attempting to wrest the meat-packet from Vlana's hands with tentacles and thumbed paws. "Oh hell," Bjorn grunted. "Damned squat. Where's the fucking net?"

"Bjorn you can't just throw him in a net!"

"I'm not going to throw him in a net," the farmer grunted as he grasped around the galley. "I'm going to put him in the net. I'm going to throw him into Vant's cabin."

The squitten, denied his desired prize, had backed off Vlana now, and floated impatiently about her head in an orbiting circle of irritable mews. The navigator smiled and stroked his cheek as he passed. "There, see? Who's a cute little would-be-thief?"

"Big bastard is what you mean," Bjorn grunted. "He's a big bastard. Because people won't stop feeding him enough to double his size in the past year."

Vlana had put the packet down and gotten her hands around the squitten's midsection. She laughed delightedly and made a kissy face at the animal's feline head. "Nooooo, how could anyone hate Mr. adorable fuzzybelly fart-stink!"

"Maybe because he inked them in the face." Bjorn said. "How come he never inks you in the face?"

The navigator and quartermaster grinned as Francesco started purring. "Because he knows I love him!"

"Take him out of the galley already!" Bjorn answered. "Put him in Vant's bunk. Let him ink his bed."

"Come on, littlest skyfarer," Vlana cooed, wrapping the ship's pet in her arms and carrying him out of the kitchen, taking her offer of assistance with her.

It took Bjorn a bit longer to get the stew simmering, but once the job was done there was nothing else for him to do for a little while. Slowly, he made his way down the spinal hall of the ship towards the cargo bay, only to slow as he heard voices coming from the main hold. One was Helena's, and that brought the old farmer up short. The Grayspear wasn't a woman he knew well, thus far, and they could not have been more different despite similarities in age and occupation. Helena was a born warrior and showed it in every inch of her poise and ability.

Bjorn was a farmer who had taken up a sword by necessity. Taken it up and failed. That Harkon saw him as more, that anyone did, was their prerogative. He considered wandering back up the hallway and spending some time on the bridge, watching the sunset before necessity brought him back to weapons maintenance in preparation for the upcoming rescue operation.

He didn't. What they were saying was another thing entirely.

"I've never put much stock in prophecy," Elias answered to something muffled. "I just picked up a sword, and touched a diamond, and I—"

"—and you still don't understand that the very fact that you restored Oath of Aurum to its former strength means that it's about you," Helena's tone was insistent and reserved. Bjorn immediately felt himself intruding on something private. Nonetheless, he felt a pang of annoyance at the warrior woman's words. *The boy's suffered enough, dammit. Carries enough on his shoulders. He doesn't need this, even if it's true. Prophecies tend to take care of themselves, when they turn out true. And even then, many don't.*

Elias was quiet for a moment, then Bjorn heard his voice, quiet. "Prove it."

"Who were your parents?"

Elias's voice faltered. Bjorn could hear the pain. "I don't know who my father was," he finally said. "My mother was Theliana of New Corinth."

"Which makes you the last living descendent of the kingdom's royal line."

"I am not a prince—"

"Absent a legitimate heir, you are."

"I am not going to chase a throne, Dame Grayspear."

"Did I say that you must? Your criteria makes you the object of the prophecy. It's not about reclaiming crowns or destroying great evils. It's so much more than that."

Bjorn had heard enough. He walked through the doorway to the cargo hold and cleared his throat. Elias's shirt was disheveled, hastily donned. Helena's arms were folded across her chest. Her hood was down, her steel gray, short hair catching the light.

"I think the boy's heard enough," Bjorn said. He couldn't quite keep the irritation out of his voice. "Or do you imagine that dumping an irrelevant bit of word salad on his shoulders will help?"

Helena's eyes flashed as she turned to face him fully. "I'm sorry, I was not aware of the fact that you were this man's father."

That stung him. Bjorn would never have expected them to. He wasn't the lad's father, after all. A year ago—when he wore the persona of the dark knight Azrael—Elias had nearly killed him. But it had been Bjorn who took the knife from his hand when he'd contemplated taking his own life in Ishtier. It had been Bjorn who symbolically cut his hair, and who, had trained with him in the year since. Watched his pain. Seen him grow through painful fits and starts.

Father? Maybe not...but Elias Leblanc was Bjorn's responsibility, and whether for good or ill, their fight in the valley back in Port Providence had connected the two men by a thread of understanding. Bjorn had been the first to see, and know, his pain.

"Just someone who knows a man's right to have his own life, free of the blatherings of seers," Bjorn said. Then he looked Elias squarely in the face. "Listen to me, you just got your life back a year ago. I know you feel all sorts of obligations to spend it in recompense and restitution, and I know that some part of you would give anything to lose it in a redemptive blaze if you believed it would make a difference, but I am begging you—"

his voice cracked "—don't do this. Don't let the words of a prophet take your life away from you. Not again."

Helena's expression turned from incredulous to annoyed, to shocked. It took Bjorn a few moments to realize why: in her heart of hearts, Helena Grayspear was a woman who believed in destiny and in the importance of seers. He'd just slapped her in the face.

"And what would you know about seers, soldier?" She didn't use the word with contempt, but with the clear bite of someone who held herself above that rank. A person accustomed to command and to position.

Bjorn folded his large arms across his broad chest. "I'm from Skellig."

Her mouth, opened to snap out a retort, stayed that way. Then after a moment, it closed.

"…Oh."

A tension hung in the air between them for a long moment. Then Elias broke it.

"Right now, I'm just focused on a rescue mission," he said quietly. "Not on prophecy, and not on Prince Collum." For just a moment the younger man's voice caught on the word. "I just want to save Coulton and his grandmother. I owe them that."

Helena fell silent. She appeared for a moment to awkwardly struggle, then she said "I'm…forgive me. I lost sight of the here and now. I just. Please understand that even if the prophecy has nothing to do with my people, that doesn't mean it's not important, and it doesn't mean that we won't have to contend with it sooner or later."

Bjorn sighed. There was the familiar lingering frustration that always emerged when someone he'd readied himself to argue with backed down, leaving those emotions swirling, churning and furious, without a destination. He swallowed it along with his pride. He was entirely too old to add further chiding to someone who didn't need it. If he'd known when he was younger that older people were no more innately reasonable or wise than when they were twenty-two, he might not have taken so much pride in every passing year.

"Get through one thing before the next. If it's true, it'll come to us regardless," he said. "If it's not true, it hardly matters what the seers said."

Helena folded her arms across her chest, looked between the two of them, then finally said "Just…please don't forget."

"I won't," Elias said, and Bjorn's heart ached at the tone in the much younger man's voice. He was what, twenty-two? And Aimee was twenty, now.

Nobody so young should've been shouldered with all this. Yet it was what it was, and the old warrior and cook knew he could no more take the burden from their shoulders than he could make dead earth new again, or return the crowns of kings whose time had passed. The world deposited its weight where it would, and such things were not easily moved.

The Grayspear nodded solemnly, then said "I need to make ready. I'll see you soon."

Then she was gone, walking down the ramp and into the sunlight. Bjorn was about to say something more when there was a small creak of the door behind Elias, and Aimee emerged, looking more disheveled than Bjorn had ever seen her. Her shirt had been hastily pulled on, and her hair was wild. She didn't see him at first, instead touching Elias tentatively on the shoulder and embracing him fiercely when he turned.

For a moment, the farmer awkwardly averted his eyes with a small smile. A long time coming, and well-deserved.

After a second, Bjorn awkwardly cleared his throat, and Aimee looked up from where her face was buried in the taller man's shoulder and she turned briefly red. "Oh," she said. "I...um. Hi."

"Good," Bjorn said. "Take the time you have."

They both reddened this time.

The farmer shook his head, then said, "Food soon. Listen, the coming days are going to be harder than they've ever been for us, and I need you to both know..." he struggled for a moment, then reached out and put a hand on each of their shoulders "...that you are both so deeply, truly loved. And that whatever happens, you were, are, and always will be, enough."

They were silent for a moment, clearly not expecting the words that had just come out of the old farmer's mouth. Then abruptly, both of them were wrapping him in a fierce hug. It took Bjorn off guard. He almost staggered. Then he hugged them back, squeezing his eye shut. He couldn't take this burden off them, but there and then he made a silent vow.

If he could keep the hammer from falling, he would.

18

INTO THE TEETH

Aimee felt stupid brave. Like her feet could carry her through a thousand hurricanes without fear of falling, and like the lightning would only make her stronger. She tried to keep a level head as she buckled on her boots in the relative silence of her cabin. Focus.

They had a shot at cutting off Silas's ability to control the people of Port Providence through access to their king. She wasn't sure what would happen next. With them being enemies of the Guild, everything got harder. She vacillated moment by moment between real fear and the elation of her stolen moment with Elias in the bed of his cabin. She took a breath as she donned her blue coat, knowing that soon they'd be facing off against what were likely to be innocent protectors of a king who had lost his way.

Or so the idea went. Aimee remembered Coulton from their brief encounter in Port Providence a year ago, and her recollection of the then-sixteen-year-old Prince was the unflattering image of a spoiled boy who despite being rattled had lost none of his entitled nature. That he was being led astray she didn't doubt. That he held the keys to saving his people...in that she had less faith. She'd seen the leadership of which Grace was capable, of which Helena was capable. She'd read the Queen Mother's words with their elegance and strength.

Coulton held power because tradition—and tradition alone—dictated that he should. Tradition was what made him, and Silas through him, able to do all the harm they were doing. To hell with tradition.

She finished buckling on her boots and walked down the hallway towards the gangway. The plan was simple: take the Eternal Order's frigate to the rally point where Coulton's flagship would be waiting. Link up and divert their attention while the *Elysium* slipped in from below and docked with the secondary gunboat bay that Grace reported was currently unused due to battle damage taken back in Port Providence. Quick in and out. Rebalance the scales. How exactly they'd extricate Coulton from his small army of automaton soldiers she wasn't sure, but they'd attempted more dangerous things.

She buried her fear and the unease roiling in her stomach. In and out. Quick and clean. They were going to be fine.

Then she saw Elias standing in the main cargo bay and her heart lurched.

He was wearing the black and gold armor that he'd worn as Azrael. The steel melded to his frame, and he was self-consciously adjusting the straps holding the arms about his forearms, flexing his fingers inside a gauntleted hand. The sight of the man she'd finally made love to only a few hours ago dressed in the garments he'd worn as her enemy stopped her dead in her tracks and open her mouth to say words that never got out.

Sensing her there, he raised his eyes to meet hers and reading the expression on her face, closed his eyes in obvious pain before saying, "It's the best armor I have. I'd be a fool not to wear it, today."

She paused. Then slowly descended the stairs into the bay proper. Stopping just in front of him, she reached up and touched the side of his face with her hand. He leaned into it, and for just a moment it was as if she was holding the weight of an entire world in her hand. "You're you," she whispered. "Always you."

"Alright, break it up, break it up," Vant's voice came from the far end of the hold as he approached. A shock-stick hung from each hip, and Grace was approaching up the gangway at the same time. She was looking better, after rest, and Helena walked strongly by her side, the older woman's hand resting on her shoulder as she continued explaining something they must have been talking about on their way to the ship.

Aimee couldn't help but think of how much better of a leader either of those two would've been for the people of Port Providence than its easily dominated, spoiled king. And now Elias was going to try and save the boy, and she wasn't sure she even wanted him to.

In a flash, an undertone of barely suppressed fear gripped her. Bubbled to the surface with a sharp, fresh ache that momentarily robbed her of breath. She refused to give voice to it. Refused to validate it by speaking the words that tormented her heart in a whirl of what-ifs. It wasn't going to happen.

Wouldn't. Couldn't.

At length she pulled her hand back and turned to face the newcomers. "Ready to go?"

Helena nodded. "As near as we can be."

Aimee looked at Grace. For just a moment she was about to object again, but then she remembered the bullets dropping Sir Kaelith when all their magic and steel failed. She'd earned her place on this mission, and Aimee would not argue.

Helena looked Elias up and down, then her mouth drew into a thin line. "You sure you wish to try and rescue Coulton looking more like his hated enemy than you have since I met you?"

"I don't." Elias answered. "But if we encounter Silas and Roland, I have to be protected...and this is the best armor I have."

Helena looked at him and sighed. Seemed to roll that around in her head, then at last gave a nod. "Can't fault you for that. We'll want to grab him quickly. I somehow doubt he'll be amenable to a kidnapping even if he were to trust you implicitly. The armor makes no difference."

"There you are," Bjorn's voice cut across Aimee's thoughts as he emerged at the top of the stairs. "It's time to hatch-up and head out."

"Aimee," Elias asked as the others went up the stairs. "I...can I hold the Axiom Diamond, just for a moment?"

She almost hesitated. Not for fear, but for concern. Knowing what he'd seen the last time he held it. Knowing the trauma that memory they both shared carried. "Are you sure?"

He nodded, and there was a sincerity in his green eyes, albeit nervous, that she couldn't deny. Reaching into her coat, she gently produced the glimmering jewel, and pressed it into his hand.

Elias's eyes closed as his fingers curled around it, and for the briefest of moments his eyes went blank, as if he were seeing something else. Then he let out a breath, and handed it back to her. She caught a glimpse of tears at the corners of his eyes. "Thank you," he murmured quietly. "I... thank you."

She nodded quietly, and they climbed the stairs together.

~

The Portal slammed shut behind the Elysium and Aimee lowered her hands. The sky was sunset-tinged, with beams of gold and red slicing up the massive cloud formations, larger than Havensreach or the isle upon which her home crouched.

There was a loud buzzing noise, and the larger frigate moved past them, taking the lead while Clutch pulled slightly back on the wheel. "Slow throttle, Vant," she said. "Time to run nice and soft."

Aimee descended the stairs. Harkon stood near Vlana's navigation console. "Scan again."

The navigator's fingers flew over the buttons and dials. Aimee turned her attention out the viewport. The sky was beautiful in its manifold expanses. She could almost forget their dire circumstances, but that wasn't an option. *Keep your head on straight, Aimee. It's not the time for getting distracted by pretty clouds.*

The frigate turned in a slow graceful arc around a cloud bank, the sheen of the sun running its dark length, and then Vlana spoke up. "They're here."

Aimee didn't need to ask. They rounded that same bank of white tinged with gold, and there was Coulton's flagship. Gods, but she'd seen better days. If Coulton's throne was the last vestige of a rotted aristocracy held together with pride and grief, this ship was the perfect reflection of that. From nose to tip, pockmarked with battle scars and battered from impacts. A tall superstructure sprouted from the outdated chassis, the pennant of Port Providence flapping in the same breeze that rustled the walls of *Elysium's* hull.

Aimee knew that flag, and the same thought passed through her head now that she'd had the moment she'd first seen it on the hull of a Port Providence gunboat just over a year ago while they fled for their lives: *kings who lost their crowns seldom got them back.*

Why were they doing this?

"Take us low," Harkon said. "We're going to dive below the cloud layer and rise slowly from beneath."

The nose of the *Elysium* dipped down as they slid silently into the frigate's shadow and towards the darkness of the abyss. Up above them Aimee watched the wedge-shaped, knife-like silhouette of the Eternal

Order vessel pass overhead as two gunboats departed Coulton's flagship and slowly limped through the air towards it. Maybe the King did have an army of tireless automaton soldiers, sure, but how exactly he was planning on successfully landing them anywhere that wouldn't make swift work of his paltry fleet before they could so much as disembark, she didn't know. Something about this felt wrong. They were missing something. She just wished she knew what.

Remember, you're enemies of the Guilds, now.

And the Eternal Order had moved to a position of ascendency—mastery even—over the Guilds. Aimee's eyes swept the sky. No signs of any other ships. The clouds moved away from around them as they dropped down low, and Aimee heard Clutch counting under her breath. Her fingers fidgeted at her sides as she waited in the low light.

Then the pilot said, "Alright boss. We good?"

"Take us up," Harkon said. "Slow and smooth. Minimal burn."

"You heard the man, Vant," Clutch said into the tubes. "Minimal burn. We're going up slow."

The rumble of the engines followed, and the *Elysium* began its slow ascent through the clouds. Soon the underside of Coulton's flagship appeared as they moved up beneath it. The frigate was in the process of docking with the ship on the other side of the bay. Closer. Soon the bay was looming before them, and Aimee looked at her mentor.

"Get to the bay," he said with a nod. "It's nearly time. Remember the plan?"

She ran over her memorization of the route they needed to take. Descended the stairs in a haze of focus and concentration and grabbed her shock spear as she stepped into the bay. Elias stood staring at the un-lowered ramp, still and stone-like.

"We're going to pull this off," Aimee said, stepping up beside him.

A seam of light split the back of the ship, and the bay ramp descended. They slipped into Coulton's flagship with Bjorn and Helena behind them.

The corridors were close and confined, made mostly of battered metal that had seen better days. They made their way up, moving quickly and quietly. The docking of the frigate would have drawn most of the soldiers' attention by now. She didn't hear the sounds of fighting yet, but she could only assume it would happen soon. They had to be quick, before this errand cost more lives.

Stairs led them up to a floor with carpeted hallways and doors of fine hardwoods that retained the ghost of their splendor even in their shabby state. Aimee looked from left to right, then finding the door she was looking for, made hastily down the hallway with the others hot on her heels. This was the Queen Mother's suite. It was the one they'd come to first, and it was their best shot at getting her. Aimee paused before touching the door. Too easy. They'd barely run into a single person since entering the ship. Certainly no guards, no skyfarers. No soldiers of Port Providence. Not even a single Tireless.

"This isn't right," she murmured. "I don't like this."

"It has a wrong feeling about it," Bjorn said. "Trap?"

"There are no guards on this door," Aimee said. "Nobody to keep us away. They can't be so shorthanded as to have nobody watching over someone so important."

"Open the door anyway," Elias said. "If she's in there, we can't afford not to try and pull her out."

Aimee looked back at the door with trepidation, then she summoned and released a simple spell of detection, seeking whether any traps were set upon either door or lock. Nothing. That satisfied she crouched, summoning another spell to undo the mechanism and releasing it with a whisper. It slid open, revealing a sizable stateroom furnished with a four-poster bed and a writing desk. Yet what Aimee's attention focused on immediately was the silent form of what she could only assume was the Queen Mother. She was an old woman who looked as if she'd recently lost a great deal of weight. Annoyance with their mission immediately fled Aimee's system, replaced with a touch of shame.

They had to get Alahna out of here. "Bjorn," she said. "Can you?"

The big man moved through the doorway and past her, as Helena drew in a sharp gasp. "My lady," Aimee heard the older woman whisper. "What have they done to you?"

"She's breathing," Bjorn said. "But it's shallow. We'd best get her back to the ship before we go looking for anyone else."

They stepped back out into the corridor, backtracking until they emerged back in the bay, and Aimee breathed a tangible sigh of relief.

Elias made a sharp noise, and abruptly Aimee was shoved hard against the wall in time to watch as a blast of black energy ripped down the hallway, slamming into the black-armored swordsman with a force so great that her ears popped and her skin prickled. Elias slammed into the steel wall at the far end of the bay, so hard that the metal crumpled inward. She staggered back. Twenty soldiers armored in familiar livery emerged from behind the black-robed figure that strode into the chamber. They moved quickly, putting themselves between the group and Elias.

"It's been a long, long time," Silas said as he emerged at the hallway's far end. "Let's catch up, shall we?"

19

FOREVER VALIANT

Hours ago

Elias stood in the darkness of an empty cargo bay, holding the Axiom Diamond in his hand. The room had gone dark, absent everyone else as the gem took him deep into the recesses of his mind. He took a deep, shuddering breath in an effort to drive down the fear.

"Hello, Elias. It's been awhile."

The light in his hands pulsed with the warmth of life. Elias still couldn't begin to fathom what this thing was. Where it came from or how it had the sentience and power to touch hearts and minds as it did. He only knew that right now he desperately needed that power. Was it for knowledge? Comfort? He wasn't sure. He just knew that if anyone had the answers, it was the Axiom Diamond.

"I need to know something," he said quietly. "I...I've recently learned some things about my predecessors. About the first knights who broke with what became the Eternal Order. I have a feeling you know something about them."

A long pause followed, then with a certain quiet reticence, the voice answered *"I think I know what you need to know, but I will let you give me the words, yourself. Truth is always best found, rather than given."*

"I need to know," Elias said, his voice catching. "Because I'm about to face something…if not worse than they did, at least something that terrifies me. I need…courage. I need to know, what were they like?"

The diamond pulsed in his hand. *"Do you want the truth?"*

Elias gulped. "Yes."

A sigh followed, and the voice was earnest.

"They were afraid."

Now.

Elias barely managed to summon his durability before his back met the steel wall. The deafening sound filled his ears with the ringing shriek of crumpling metal as it caved beneath his impact. He almost dropped his sword. Breath left him, and dissipating arcs of black lightning sizzled and cracked across the surface of the enchanted steel that had barely saved his life.

Walking purposefully across the bay, Silas's frame filled his vision. The man was gaunter than Elias had last seen him, draped in sable robes that couldn't hide the black veins creeping up his thin neck. His eyes vacillated between pale and ordinary and rimmed with darkness.

"I didn't expect to find you so easily, nor for you to take the bait so readily. I suppose I shouldn't discount the desperation of a man so thoroughly broken."

Elias pried himself loose. The blow had left him tingling and disoriented. He prepared a burst of speed only for the sorcerer to summon a blazing wall of flame that surged towards him in a line of scorching heat twice his height. Elias desperately and reflexively summoned a wedge-shaped shield centered on the point of Oath of Aurum. His defenses shook violently as the flames parted on either side and left him rattled. No sooner had he taken one step forward than Silas was loosing bolts of lightning that he barely managed to parry. One struck him in the shoulder and only the enchantments in Azrael's armor kept the electricity from frying his flesh. Silas kept coming. One spell followed another in rapid succession, each one greater than the last. This was a degree beyond Intuitive Arcanism. This was speed-of-thought casting mingled with a terrifying breadth of power greater than anything a knight of the Eternal Order could command.

Silas's magic broke all the rules.

Fire blazed out of the corners of his eyes as Aimee's magic ignited. He couldn't see what she and the others were doing. Could only concentrate on the inferno of magic in front of him. Silas stepped through guttering embers. The one-time-sage's expression was a twisted mask of hate. "Did you honestly think we'd just let you take her?" the robed figure asked. "Did you imagine we'd let you take our fucking king?"

Elias held his sword point before him. He'd fallen prey to his own tactic. He'd let Silas get inside his head. Now his own thoughts were murk and mud and his reactions barely fast enough.

"If he fully understood what you were," Elias said, "he wouldn't follow the twisted lead you've set before him. What in the abyss have you done, sage?"

Silas face abruptly changed into an expression of grief and rage. "Don't. Don't you dare. The destruction of my country, my people, is your fault. You bear the blame. You and you alone."

The words cut through Elias's mental armor, incisive and harsh. He barely managed to summon a shield when the next spell struck home. The shield came apart, and Elias hurtled backwards. He turned the fall into a roll, the sound of armor scraping across the metallic floor of the bay, coming up in a crouch as shards of broken spell sparked against the ground around him before dissipating into nothing. Elias took his sword in both hands, held before him as a ward against a man he couldn't protect himself from.

"Silas," he breathed. "I don't know what you've parlayed with for this sort of power. I don't know what darkness has twisted your mind, but I'm begging you. Don't do this. Don't make common cause with him."

The one-time-sage stood before him, hands lowered yet still guarded, dark eyes locked upon his. "Go on," he whispered. "You did let me speak, back when you took Grey Falcon. Do you remember that? Before you showed me that sword, and broke my King's gracious heart."

Silas's eyes narrowed. "So go on. Do as I did. Plead, Azrael. Beg."

"Silas?"

The new voice cut through the inferno of the fighting. Somehow audible above the chaos. Elias's eyes flicked past the black robed man in front of him. Tired, bedraggled, and looking like hadn't slept in days, Coulton stood in the bay.

Elias had dreaded this moment for over a year. Had sought to avoid it before the promise that had brought him here was made. A spike of fear cut through him, but with it came enough awareness to recognize the fact that Silas had briefly looked away from him.

The black-armored swordsman exploded forward. Two thoughts burned in his brain. First: if he killed Silas now, the prince would never be brought around to see reason. Second: he had to get to Coulton. The black robed figure's hands rose to loose another spell. This time, Elias was faster. He turned a dashing step into a turn and drove his heel into the center of Silas's mass, folding him in half with an explosive exclamation of pain before the man crumpled to the deck. Elias sped forward. Determined to reach the—

WHAM.

The impact hit him so hard from the side that he lost all sense of orientation. The world twisted on its axis, turning end over end as his body flew through the air. Oath of Aurum slipped from his fingers and he heard it skitter across the floor before the metal panels rose to meet him. He managed to tuck his chin, but the impact still sent pain blasting through his body. Elias rolled over two, three, four times before sliding across the metal with a shriek of his complaining armor, and finally came to a stop. He spit blood onto the floor, trying to push himself up on his arms. Desperately looking about for what had hit him.

Lord Roland stood twenty feet away, slowly straightening from the extended position of the armored punch that had sent his one-time apprentice flying. Elias's eyes widened. Azrael's former master was armored in a black that mirrored his one-time student. His voice sent fever chills of terror through Elias's blood.

"So inattentive. Tsk. My Azrael, you should know better."

"Elias!" Aimee screamed from across the room. He glimpsed her twist away from a duel with three Port Providence men, her face a vision of rage and fear. A bolt of lightning tore outwards towards Roland.

The dark knight shifted his hips, and it passed him, petering out in the empty sky of the bay. His fingers flicked, and a ripple of magic burst in the air between himself and the sorceress. Elias physically felt the pressure change, then a concussive blast of air exploded a half-breath after he saw Aimee summon a shield. A ball of fire bloomed in the open space. Obliterated three of Coulton's men. The shield shattered and Aimee fell backwards, rolling and landing awkwardly. Elias couldn't get to her, and he was now hemmed in. Roland to his right, and Coulton, somehow, straight ahead.

The King looked frightened as they made eye contact.

He regained his crouch. He had no weapon. Breathing was difficult, and by the blooming wet sensation in his chest he had several broken ribs.

Maybe worse. Roland casually strolled towards him. "That's enough of that, now."

There was only one thing to do. Elias held out one bloodied hand towards Coulton. His words came out a choking rasp. "Coulton. Coulton listen to me. Don't do this. Whatever they're telling you, it's a lie. Whatever they're asking of you, it's wrong. Don't. Go with my friends. With your grandmother."

He struggled to his feet. Roland stopped ten feet away. "Azrael," the soothing voice tormented Elias's mind. "It's time for you to come home."

"I..." Coulton swallowed. His eyes were wide with horror and fear. "You don't understand. You don't..."

"I do," Elias said. "Please, it doesn't matter what happens to me now. Don't do this. Don't become me."

The King's mouth hung open for a moment. The world seemed to hang upon a pin.

Then Silas got to his feet. The black-robed figure bled from the corner of his mouth. His hands snapped up, and Elias heard Aimee scream his name.

He didn't hear the spell. Snaking lines of darkness filled his vision. The force of it hit him full in the chest. Ripped across his body, rattling loose his armor. Pain sent his senses sparking, and his feet left the ground. He sailed through the air, falling backwards as Silas screamed, maintaining the spell that sent Elias backwards. The bay mouth passed over his head and he hurtled backwards, body still crackling with lines of darkness, into the cold and empty air.

Then Coulton's flagship was rapidly shrinking in the distance. And the sky. The *Elysium*. Even the clouds were fading tufts of white, as the shadows rose to claim him.

Elias Leblanc fell down, down. Into the endless dark.

20

GONE

o.
Aimee scrambled to her feet, her heart hammering in a mad panic in her chest.

No.

A Port Providence man barred her way.

She didn't even think. Her hand snapped out as he drew back his sword for a strike. She grabbed his wrist and her other hand swept out in a half-second gesture. "Boil."

The man fell screaming to the deck as his blood killed him from the inside. She knew it was too late. But maybe he'd grabbed onto the lip of the ship.

This isn't real. This can't be real.

She couldn't see a hand. She was running towards the edge, disregarding any semblance of safety or reason.

*It's not real. I won't **let** it be real. **Please**, by all the Gods, **Please.***

"Aimee we've got to go!" Vant was shouting behind her. Somewhere. Did it matter? She was almost at the edge. When Harkon had fallen off the catwalk between the spires on the Iseult, she'd caught him. Saved him from plunging into the abyss. She'd done it before. She'd done it.

But not this time.

Bolts of magic whipped past her. Screams echoed as she reached the ledge. Even knowing what she would find with a terrifying certainty, the nothing that greeted her cut deeper than any blade. The empty clouds were a carving knife, hollowing her heart and punching deep into her gut.

Gone.

"Aimee! There's nothing you can do now!" Bjorn screamed.

She whipped her head around to look behind her. Beyond the charred corpses the King stood in what looked like a state of shock.

Oath of Aurum had landed at his feet. Roland stood facing her, still a short distance away. Silas leaned against a nearby bulkhead. She felt the kernel of energy she still possessed bloom into a blazing pillar of rage that filled her limbs, and recalling the enhanced gestures Harkon had used in the *Iseult* against the hordes of the dead, her hands swept together. Then both palms turned flat and she cut across her body in a sweeping X, screaming the word of the spell.

"Radiance"

A blazing wave of white light roared outwards from her, a crescent of burning daylight bigger and stronger than any she'd ever cast before. She saw Silas summon a shield that physically cracked and shook at the impact. Roland vaulted upwards, over the top of the wave, and landed in a crouch before he started walking towards her, sword held in one hand. "Are you the one, then?" he asked simply. "The one who twisted my Azrael's mind, who took my greatest masterpiece away from me?"

Aimee's face was wet, though she didn't know when the tears had started. There was only the terrible, despairing fury coursing through her veins. "It doesn't matter now, does it?"

Her lightning bolt took him slightly off guard, and only a snap of his sword into position allowed him to deflect it. Gods, but he was fast. Silas recovered and fired off a bolt of searing flame. She summoned a shield and deflected it, sweeping one foot back. Roland burst forwards towards her. She couldn't pivot in time.

A wall of flame erupted between the two of them, easily three times her height. It shot from one end of the room to the other. Through the flames she saw Roland move backwards as Harkon Bright now stood at the base of the ramp. The Dread Lord of Ashes swept his sword up in an arc and down. The flames parted on either side of him, and his pale eyes narrowed lethally. "The old man shows himself."

Aimee had never seen her teacher thus. Harkon's normally serene face was set in an expression of harsh contempt, his eyes fixed on his enemy with complete and total focus. "And the boy still has not learned," he answered.

Roland's slight crouch was the only warning he gave, then he exploded upwards, hurtling towards the old mage like a hammer from above. The floor shook where he launched himself, and Aimee struggled to keep her footing.

Harkon summoned a shield above his head, and Roland's sword dropped onto it with a force that sent a shockwave outwards, knocking her off her feet. She rolled over twice. There was no more time to watch. Silas had recovered. She barely dodged the giant flaming skull that erupted from his hands, scorching the floor where she'd stood a moment before.

Aimee threw a bolt of fire in his direction. Then another. Another. She could hear the words of the releasing spells flying at her enemy, hatred filling her voice in tune with a terrible grief she'd break herself to keep at bay, if only until this pointless defiance killed her. Fight. Kill. Rage against the impossible. Anything to keep the wall of horror from overwhelming her mind.

Then arms were wrapping tightly around her frame, pinning her elbows to her side. She screamed. In rage. In pain. Bjorn lifted her and started running towards the bay door to the Elysium. "Grieve later," she heard him say through the haze. "Live now."

Harkon's shield forced Roland back. The dark knight landed in a crouch, and Aimee recognized the air-blast he was summoning.

So did Harkon. Her mentor summoned a half- sphere of hardened light around the pinprick of igniting air the moment before it burst, directing the blast back at Roland and Silas. Both men were propelled backwards, the latter summoning a shield to protect Coulton.

"Time to go," Harkon said. They were dashing up the ramp. The bay greeted them, and the ramp was closing, taking with it every promise of getting back what she'd just lost. The *Elysium* was lifting off. Moving away. Leaving two dark lords, and their victory, behind.

Aimee limped up the hallway. The others were talking, but she couldn't process any of the words. She knew she was crying. The tears stained her face and made her shake even as she struggled to keep her footing within the sharply turning ship. She made it to the galley with its observation ports giving her a view out of the side of the ship. The sight took her breath away.

The frigate was burning. Limping away from the battle. Gleaming like blades in the heavens, three Guild dreadnoughts hung in the sky, hovering above Coulton's flagship like protective silver ravens.

The grief spiked through the numbness. They'd suspected that it could be a trap. They'd taken precautions…and they'd still walked right into it.

Elias.

Aimee felt sick. The first blasts from the forward guns of the enemy erupted outwards, falling just short of *Elysium's* frame and painting the sky with pockmarks of bursting flame and wreathes of smoke. "Hang on everyone!" Clutch yelled over the tubes. "And if either of you sparklefingers could get up there and make with the portaling, that would be great!"

She followed the command without thinking. Something to do. She needed something to do. She moved onto the bridge, stepping into the familiar open space that somehow reeked of emptiness. Vlana glancèd over her shoulder and must have caught the look on Aimee's face, because her own expression paled. "Oh no."

"No time," Aimee managed. She pushed herself towards the dais, her feet seeming to move through watery muck. "I need…we have to get out of here."

She got to the top of the Portal Deck. Caught herself on the rail and nearly crumpled before clenching her fist and snarling to herself as she forced her feet onto the dais. *Grief is for the living,* she thought. *You have to be alive to grieve.*

The lenses lowered, and she felt the familiar surge of magic from beneath her feet. For a terrible moment as her hands assumed the position and she started making the gestures, she felt a horrible wave of nausea overwhelm her. He was gone. He was gone. But if she left now, she was abandoning him to a fate from which he couldn't be saved. She almost couldn't say the words.

Her eyes opened. Flicked down to the bridge below where Clutch stood behind the wheel, and Vlana stared up at her with her bright, worried eyes. Think of the others. Save who you can.

It was what he would've done.

Aimee said the words, and the blazing eye of the portal ripped open. The *Elysium* shot through it, and with a wave of her hands, it snapped closed behind them. The silence of the other side was crushing. She stepped off the dais as if in a dream, walking back towards the stairs. Each footfall felt surreal. At the bottom she just stopped, her feet abruptly made of lead. One hand reached out and pressed against the grain of the wooden panels of the wall. It was real in a way that made it all somehow worse.

"Aimee…" Vlana appeared before her. Her eyes were wide and questioning, but she stopped when she saw the look on Aimee's face. It must have been a sight to see, to render her so suddenly silent. Then one hand slowly raised to cover her mouth. She took two steps forward and wrapped Aimee in a fierce hug.

The sorceress was dimly aware of Harkon and Bjorn returning to the bridge. She heard things being said, recognized broken tones and disbelieving voices. Words were exchanged, and she couldn't make sense of any of it. Eventually she broke away from Vlana's hug and let her forehead rest against the wall as she struggled to master the well of grief that wouldn't stop flooding her.

"…Those fucking bastards," Clutch swore, and Aimee had never heard so much venom in her voice.

"I'm going to kill them," Aimee said, straightening from the wall. Her voice cut across further conversation. She turned and the others were looking at her. The words had given her something concrete to hold onto. A promise that set fire to the kerosine-soaked paper of her pain. She put one hand on the brass rail at the bottom of the portal-deck. "Coulton lives," she said. "Elias died trying to save him, and I won't disrespect his last efforts that way." She felt her teeth clench. "I will grab that little snot by the collar of his shirt and drag him back to the light no matter how hard he screams. Fine. Whatever. He lives."

She was shaking, now. "But Silas? Roland? Their soldiers? The people they've allied with? I'm going to kill them all. Every last fucking one of them."

And that was when Helena arrived on the bridge, just in time to take in Aimee's words with a look of mingled concern and anger. It vanished swiftly as she pushed aside whatever had put her off and said simply "Her majesty is awake."

21

THE PLAINS OF AURUM

Coulton swam through an ocean of confusing nightmares. He sat in his throne in the audience chamber of his flagship. *Oath of Aurum*—at last—lay across his lap in a borrowed sheath. Azrael —or Elias, whatever he'd called himself—was dead. The hated enemy he'd spent so much of the past year dreaming of in murky nightmares, was gone.

Coulton shouldn't have felt this deep disquiet in his soul. He shouldn't have. A cloud of fog overlaid his vision, voices unceasingly whispering in his mind. He should've been celebrating in the depths of his heart.

But if that were so, why couldn't the King stop shaking?

Silas and Roland stood before him, the Guildsmen that had welcomed them—his name was Dietrich, Coulton remembered—and he was only now able to absorb their conversation, heated as it was.

"We've done what you wanted," Dietrich said. "*Elysium* was ambushed."

"And yet she still got away," Silas snarled. "With Alahna, do you under-stand that? With Alahna, who knows our plans."

"Do you know that for certain?" Dietrich soothed, his expression even and measured. "Was she not kept confined to her quarters for the entire time of her stay on this ship?"

"She's not stupid," Silas countered. "And she doesn't need to have confirmed what we're doing. She merely needs to suspect." He flexed his fingers.

"In any case," Silas continued, "I'm surprised to find you so blasé about the *Elysium's* escape. Did they not only just murder one of your representatives? Have they not been marked as an enemy of the Guilds?"

Dietrich's expression twitched. Coulton sensed the barely suppressed tension beneath the surface of the functionary's words. "The *Elysium* is a problem, but you know quite well that it is far from our most immediate concern. They're a useful enemy, one that can be used to bait our real adversary."

"Yes, yes," Silas waved his hand dismissively. "We're all aware now of Belit the Red. The Guilds are mighty beyond imagining. Why in the abyss are you worried about a renegade flotilla?"

Dietrich's eyes flashed. "If you cannot grasp that, then you're unfit to play with children's blocks and magnetic letters, to say nothing of advise a king. How in all the Heavens can you be so stupid? Belit is the entire reason for our allegiance with the Eternal Order, and with you. I'm shocked that you don't yet understand why the *Elysium's* escape and your bumbling incompetence is the best possible outcome."

"If the *Elysium* is able to warn Havensreach," Silas started, "the city will be ready for us. They'll have time to prepare—"

"And if you think that matters, you are a fool," Silas was cut off. "We have more than enough resources to crush the city just using the Eternal Order alone. The principal concern has never been crushing Havensreach and it never will be. The concern is using the *Elysium* to draw Belit and the *Iseult* out. If they call for help, which they will once they know what we're plotting, the *Iseult* will come to rescue them. We will be waiting, and we will decapitate that bitch's rebellion against Guild Authority before it begins. Without Belit, and without the *Iseult,* Flotilla Visramen will return to our control."

"And *Elysium?* What about them?"

"Do you honestly believe they will survive having their rescuers destroyed by the combined firepower of a Guild fleet? The *Iseult* will be destroyed. You got your revenge, Silas. Be pleased with it. Harkon Bright's little yacht escaping can only benefit us all."

Coulton's head hurt as he tried to process everything that was happening around him. Ever since being bonded to the Tireless, his brain was a constant mess of complicated sensory inputs. Silas had said that it was the consequence of being able to sense what any of them were seeing and hearing at any one given time. A legacy of the ancient times, when Varengard commanders had used those inputs to detect everything their forces were seeing and hearing at once, and to allow their armies to act as a seamless force with the reactive speed of thought that one man possessed.

Coulton however was not trained in such things, and the constant dull noise gave him a massive headache that had yet to abate.

Roland remained a short distance away from the other two men, his back to the arguers and his hands clasped behind his back. Coulton watched him through half-lidded eyes, aware on some level of the fact that he should hate this man. Yet hate, like everything else about his emotions, didn't seem to be functioning. He felt dampened, overwhelmed and unable to process anything.

"You should've captured him," the Dread Lord of Ashes finally said. Silas and the Guildsman fell silent at the same time. "Not killed him."

Coulton raised a hand to brush against his hurting head. Azrael's—or was it Elias's—words echoed in his head.

"Please, it doesn't matter what happens to me now. Don't do this. Don't become me."

"I took our people's rightful vengeance when I had the chance," Silas said. "I put my King's sword back in his hands."

Coulton reached down with one hand to touch Oath of Aurum's hilt, only to feel the dangerous heat that burned the crewman who had tried to pick it up for him. He could only touch the scabbard, not the sword. "Not exactly useful to me, Silas," he finally said.

The sage flashed him a look of distinct irritation before his expression shifted. The fists balling at his side unclenched. "My king," he started, "do you imagine that we have cells that could hold a warrior such as him?"

"Don't do this. Don't become me."

"In time," Silas soothed, "we will find a way to return that sword to your hands. I promise you. All things bend to sufficient power."

"Enough," Coulton dismissed him, his own annoyance rising. He hoped the Tireless were worth it. He tried to force down the uncomfortable memory of the green-eyed man in black armor. His enemy, pleading with him. Asking not for mercy on his own behalf, but for Coulton to show it to himself.

"Where," he managed, "are we going now? Is it time to march on Havensreach?"

That was the plan as he understood it. Move on Havensreach. Use the Tireless to take her level by level, while supported by the Guild Fleet. All this business about someone named Belit was strange to him, and trying to plumb its depths only made his head hurt more.

"No," the sage in his black robes said. "First we must see to the last and most important phase of the plan. And for that, we must return to the Plains of Aurum."

~

"I don't understand," the helmsman said, slowly stepping out from behind the wheel. "Where are all the people?"

Coulton straightened, walking to the viewport. The Plains of Aurum were a vast expanse of flat earth bisected by an immense canyon, and a tall thrust of rock jutting into the empty air. It was at the base of this that the refugees of Port Providence had erected their camp. This was where Coulton had left them. To keep them safe. At once he was moving forward, crossing the bridge with its ornate fixtures and leonine imagery to stand before the viewport, staring out across what was undeniably the encampment that had held his people. The camp was still there.

The people were gone.

"Get me down there," he said.

"My King," one of his soldiers said, "we don't know what has happened. Someone else should—"

"I command an army of powerful automated soldiers that act at my whim," Coulton snapped. "Get me down there. Now."

"My King," this time it was Silas, his face notably drained of color and his expression disturbed. "If what we are seeing is true, then there is no telling the risk you might be placing yourself in. I remind you, that you are still young and—"

"Tell me," Coulton found his voice, staring down his advisor. "Which is us is King, Silas, and which is not?"

The sage's eyes actually flashed for a moment, and Coulton felt—in a way he couldn't describe—the rising of a power far more terrible than what Silas had let him see prior to now. The King almost took a step back. Almost walked back to his throne upon the bridge.

Almost.

Out of the corner of Coulton's eye, the monster named Roland raised an eyebrow.

Silas's hands flexed by his sides, then the dark look upon his face faded away, and he clasped his palms together, nodding his head. "Will your majesty allow me to accompany you at least?"

~

The lander hummed towards the ground. Coulton gripped a handle on the upper bulkhead, keeping himself steady despite the nausea in his stomach. The nearer they drew to the dusty earth, the more his unease burned. He could feel the presence of Silas and Roland behind him, and the Guildsman at their backs. More than anything, with each passing moment the presence of all three made his skin crawl. What had he agreed to? What had he allowed to happen to his people?

Don't become me.

Coulton's free hand went to his forehead. His memory of Azrael's sneering face in the throne room of Falcon's Rest over a year ago clashed with the still-fresh recollection of Elias's desperate green eyes. *My enemy begged me not to do what I am doing. He **begged** me.*

He didn't turn his head to look back at the three men behind him, but all at once, the King felt incredibly alone.

What have I done?

The landing gear hissed as the small ship put down on the ground outside the encampment. The door slid open, and the small ramp lowered, and the King bounding out before the other three could keep pace.

"My King—" Silas started.

Coulton's fingers snapped and his two Tireless bodyguards walked with him, nearly shouldering the sage out of the way. At least they responded quickly to commands, even if every one he mentally gave drained him further. He coughed, held his head high. He would not be seen tripping. Would not fall when he was struggling to find a way out of the circumstances in which he'd found himself.

The camp was empty. Coulton walked past lean-tos bereft of occupants. Tents and small shacks and ramshackle ruins in which people had sheltered themselves. There was no sign of violence, nor of struggle. There weren't possessions or clothes left behind. It was as if the entire encampment of people had simply left.

The King wheeled on his advisors, flanked by the Tireless as the three men approached. "Where the fuck are my people?" he demanded.

Silas wasn't looking at him. His eyes were fixed upon some point in the distance at his back. His expression was set with a look of consternation, and turning to follow his gaze, Coulton beheld the beam of light lancing upwards from the center of the tower of rock and high into the heavens.

Silas didn't answer him. Instead he simply walked past Coulton, headed for the immense thrust of rock. "Perfect," Coulton heard him murmur. "They couldn't have handed me a more concrete victory."

"What the abyss are you talking about?" Coulton demanded. His irritation rose to surpass his fear, the fog on his mind less intense in the face of his anger. "Silas, our people are gone. What in the name of all the Gods gives you the impression that this can be called a victory?"

"Follow me, majesty," Silas said, absently gesturing behind him. "All will be revealed."

Coulton snapped his fingers and the Tireless flanked him. He felt the specters of Roland and the Guildsman behind him as they drew closer to Silas's destination. At length they came to doors carved from the stone and steps dusted with sand. Coulton's breathing was heavy as they climbed. He felt dizzy, as if every motion was a drain on his body. Somewhere deep down he knew that allowing the sage to bond the Tireless to him had been a mistake. As the uncertainty once more flooded his veins, he wondered how many other great errors he'd made.

The interior of the chamber spread out around them, and a brilliant light, the source of the beam lancing into the heavens, greeted him. Its origin point was an orb like a lamp hovering in the geometric center of the room.

It was one of the most beautiful things Coulton had seen in a long time. Silas approached it, walking in a slow circle around it.

At Coulton's back, Roland paused, and the surprise in his voice was evident. "They did it."

"They did," Silas breathed. "Did I not promise you results, Dread Lord?"

"I never thought I would see the beacon lit in my lifetime," Roland murmured, walking slowly towards it. He stopped a foot away and rested one hand on the pommel of his sword with a murderer's casual ease. *Who have I fallen in with?* Coulton thought. *I didn't want this.*

Silas took a step forward and thrust his hand into the heart of the light. "And now," he breathed, "we take the first step in our vengeance for the wrongs both ancient and recent, that have been done to us."

The wave of magic that burst outwards from the sage made Coulton stagger where he stood. He caught himself on the arm of the Tireless. The cold automaton didn't move. As a creeping horror frosted his limbs, Silas's hand turned dark within the light, and bled a shadow that slowly turned it blacker than a starless night.

A ray of darkness shot into the heavens, burning away the light and making the ground shake. Coulton gripped Oath of Aurum's scabbard. The light was gone, now, and he could only see in the chamber by the daylight lashing across the floor from the entryway. A great and terrible roaring filled his ears, like land shuddering and ripping away from land. For a terrified moment Coulton believed that the ground under his feet was about to sunder and break away. He wanted to run for the door, was abruptly nothing more than the boy who had watched his kingdom burn at the hands of the Eternal Order.

He was witnessing something horrible, though he couldn't articulate what. The very air acquired a terrible weight. He tried to force himself into a standing position. Fought through the lack of clarity clouding his mind, and demanded, "Silas, where are my people?"

He did not say 'our people' for he no longer had any faith that the sage cared. Did not believe that the fate of the remnants of Port Providence, for whom Coulton had given and sacrificed everything, mattered at all to whatever his one-time advisor had become. Only one thing mattered, all at once. If even a shred of truthfulness remained within Silas, Coulton needed it now.

Silas didn't answer at first. His hand remained caressing the darkness, the expression on his face set with a predatory ecstasy. Coulton took a breath, clinging to the Tireless with one arm, and shouted, "Silas. Your King demands an answer."

Silas slowly turned his face to look at him, and with a lackadaisical shrug, simply said, "I don't know."

Coulton straightened himself, white anger burning through him. "And how in the abyss are we supposed to find a new home for them when none of them remain?"

"My King," Silas started, "have faith, soon we will—"

"No!" Coulton snapped, and for just a moment, he thought his voice sounded like his older brother's. "I have listened to you since I was a child, have always followed your advice, have never once wavered in the faith I placed in your wisdom. But this... Silas I don't know what in the abyss you're doing, but if your plans—which are supposedly in the name of protecting my people—require me to ignore the fact that they have all gone missing, then those plans must cease until such a time as we know what happened here."

Silas's face was blank for a moment, then it twisted into a look of contemptuous arrogance. "Boy," he finally said. "You would do well to remember that your role in this carries a cost. Expend yourself too hard, and I might not be able to protect you from the consequences."

And there it was. The threat. Coulton's mouth hung open as the last protector he had in the world proved himself so irredeemably false that there was no sweet lie which could make him look away. Everything he'd done since leaving Port Providence came crashing down on him at once. All the choices made in the name of justice, of protecting what little he had left, of trying to chase the foolishness—he now saw—of recovering what had been lost when he should have spent every moment gathering up the precious grains of what remained and holding them in his hands before the terrible wind that Silas had become blew them all away, all of it, fell upon his shoulders, and almost crushed him.

Almost.

Elias's green eyes stared back into his own. *Don't become me.*

Coulton's hand twitched at his side as he sent the mental command to the Tireless. Silas saw it coming, and pulled away from the center of the room, both hands extended. The two automatons stopped in their tracks as the sage held them at bay with his terrible magic. "Now, now, boy, don't be a fool—"

But the Tireless had never been Coulton's plan. He summoned what little physical reserves he had, and rushed forward. *I'm sorry*, he thought. He had no other weapons. No other means to do harm. He was not a warrior and he was not a skilled athlete. He had only the desperate fear and anger of his seventeen-year-old self, and a sword that wouldn't let him touch it. *I made this mess. I let this monster loose. I don't know if I can even stop him, now.*

Coulton's hand went to the hilt of Oath of Aurum. Pain seared through his palm and tore up his arm. He pulled as hard as he could. *I just need to do this once. Let me do this. Just once.*

Collum's sword came free. Screaming in pain, Coulton took the burning blade in both hands and with the awkward arms of one unused to its weight, he swung it as hard as he could at Silas's face. As hard and fast as the young King had ever struck.

There was a ringing clang, and Roland was between them. The steel of the glimmering blade snagged upon his own. The cold eyes of the Dread Lord of Ashes filled Coulton's vision. "Very brave, child. But too late."

The blow of the armored fist hit Coulton so hard that the breath burst out of him all at once. Oath of Aurum flew free from his aching hands, and he slammed into the floor, rolling over twice before he came to a stop, lying on his side. Everything was blurry. Sound was cloudy and indistinct in his ears. A ringing overlaid his senses, and he had trouble breathing.

Roland slowly walked towards him and said in a low voice "Ironic. He told you not to become him, and it seems that you did anyway. A pity."

Silas had recovered. Coulton saw the monster standing just behind the dark knight, slowly lowering his hands. Coulton reached for the Tireless, but they were still immobilized. He could barely breathe. The sage wore a look of hurt, of rage, of agony, as he stalked towards him. One hand flicked and Coulton found himself rising into the air.

"I did everything for you," Silas snarl-sobbed. "Sacrificed everything. Gave my life. My power. My years. And now, when I am on the verge of gaining vengeance for our people, you repay that favor with that."

"You," Coulton choked, suspended in the air, "said…you would…save us…all."

"Fortunately," Silas said through his furious tears, "I don't actually need you to finish this plan. I only need you breathing. And if breathing is the minimum necessary to play your part in the plan, then, my King, breathing is all you will do."

A hand snapped out and grasped Coulton's forehead. Pain. The breaking of every doorway and the shredding of every barrier. Coulton saw a dark tree beneath a sky of alien stars, and a bleak shadow beneath the waters of a mirror river. Terrible black roots rose up to pull him down deep into the recesses of his mind.

Coulton screamed, then silence fell.

22

THE EVER-BEATING HEART

Vlana felt cold. The loss permeated the air around her, a tangible musk that suffused her ability to perceive anything at all. She'd been here before. She'd faced this...but it didn't matter how many times it happened. She'd never get used to the fact that grief had a physical taste.

She pressed her forehead to the wall. It was eerie, how quiet it was now. How little sound permeated the *Elysium* other than the low and steady thrum of her metadrive. She was in the hallway and nobody was around, and it was hilarious that she didn't want anyone to see her weep when everyone else was already doing the same. Slowly she steadied her breathing. Why did he have to die when she was just getting used to him?

She straightened at length. The others would be seeing to the Queen Mother, now. She needed to at least try to be on the same page about what was happening as everyone else. Slowly she started walking down the hallway. The only person who wouldn't be at this little meeting was Clutch, who was still swearing at the wheel on the bridge, getting out her frustration and grief with curse words directed at innocent clouds. There were certainly more harmful ways to get it out of your system, Vlana reflected.

I never accepted him. Did he die thinking we would never be friends?

She could hear words at the far end of the stairs, and only belatedly realized that they'd put Alahna in Elias's empty cabin. That somehow made this worse. Her boots thumped on the deck of the cargo bay, and she slowly stepped through the door and into the room she'd not set foot in since Elias Leblanc joined her crew.

Vlana wasn't sure what she'd expected of the Queen Mother of Port Providence, but what she saw did not match up. Alahna was an unnervingly thin woman with long snowy hair framing a matronly face worn to exhaustion. Helena sat beside the outline of her legs on the bed, slowly helping her drink a glass of water. After a moment and a small cough, the Queen Mother of Port Providence opened eyes that were difficult to look at: piercing and bright.

"...I'm sorry," she finally said. "Nothing I can say will make up for what you have lost."

Vlana saw Aimee shift where she stood just at Harkon's back. The portalmage's apprentice had her arms folded across her chest, her long blond hair braided behind her head. Everything about her posture was furious, but Vlana could see that the anger was holding the grief back. The sorceress sensed that she was being looked at, and shot her tear-stained blue eyes in the quartermaster's direction. Vlana did her best to give a pained smile, then stood to the back and out of the way as Harkon started speaking.

"And I am sorry that we could not secure the escape of your grandson."

"I don't..." Alahna coughed. "I don't know that it matters now. Not after what I've seen." Looking at them, her eyes acquired a terrible fear. "Listen to me. Your home is in greater peril than even Port Providence was."

"What do you mean?" Aimee asked.

"Silas," Alahna started, "has set in motion a plan to bring the might of the Guild and Coulton's army of the Tireless down on the city. He sold it to my grandson on the promise that Havensreach would become our people's home...but his goal has never been to occupy the city. He intends to destroy it."

Aimee was suddenly alert. "What do you mean?"

"I mean exactly what I said," Alahna breathed, sinking back to the pillow of Elias's bed. "He has some sort of ritual planned. I don't know all the specifics, but I know those automaton soldiers he's bound Coulton to are part of it. As is the Plains of Aurum, and that black jewel embedded in his chest."

Harkon's attention was suddenly focused directly on the old woman. "What jewel?"

"I only saw it at a distance," Alahna closed her eyes. It's like a cyst of black stone, and every time he uses those new powers he's somehow acquired it grows. When I last saw him, its veins were nearly grown to the top of his neck."

Harkon's face remained carefully neutral, but Vlana knew that look perhaps better than anyone on the crew other than Clutch. The Mage who Meddled was worried.

"When did it first appear?"

Alahna scrunched up her face. Clearly in pain. "A month or so ago. It wasn't long after that that he started throwing around new and frightening magic that allowed him to quickly consolidate his place of power at Coulton's side. Nobody else could stand up to him, or reach Coulton. Not his other mages, not the court." Her eyes cast downwards. "Not me."

"I need you to try as hard as you can to remember," Harkon said, kneeling at her bedside. "What preceded this. Do you have any information that might suggest how he acquired it, and his magic?"

"I don't know," Alahna said. "I only know what I saw when Roland touched my mind. I—"

"What?" Harkon's eyes sharpened.

"He reached into my mind," Alahna wrapped her hand around Helena's, and she closed her eyes tightly. "I tried to fight him but... he took everything I knew. Including the warnings I sent you. Including my request. It's how they were able to anticipate you coming, I think." She paused. Took a shaking breath. Then she pressed on. "I saw the depths of his mind I...Harkon," she paused. "You know him. You know who he was. You know he won't stop." A head shake followed. "I saw a dead tree, Harkon. Bigger than any I could've imagined. A mirror river and alien stars. I saw..."

"You saw the Twelfth Night," Aimee said. Harkon turned and looked at her. Vlana did as well. "What's that?"

"It's," Aimee looked like she was having a hard time finding words. "It's a god. Or it was a god, or something like that. It...created the people who preceded the Eternal Order. And then it commanded them to destroy innocent people. Instead of obeying, some of them, led by a woman named Ophilia, rebelled. I thought from the myth that it was destroyed, but the iconography we discovered was of a tree. That can't be a coincidence."

Silence fell, then Vlana finally broke it. "We're up against a fucking undead God?"

"That would explain Silas's power," Harkon said. Then he shook his head. "This is beyond vengeance," he finished. "This is an extermination. Genocide."

"Don't forget the Guilds," Bjorn said quietly. "This is genocide backed by the Eternal Order and the Guilds."

Vlana's mouth went dry. Fear rippled across her skin, and she folded her arms, as if gripping her triceps would make her less cold. "Then a force unlike anything we've seen in the modern era is about to descend on our home."

She gulped. "What in the Abyss are we supposed to do about this?"

"We put out a call for help," Harkon said, decisively. "As far and as loud as we can. It will take a day of burning the metadrive to power our communication spells. Then…we go home, and we get ready to fight."

Vlana walked towards her control station, trying to calm her pounding heart. *Elysium* had only sent out a distress signal a handful of times in the years that she and her brother had been a part of its crew, and never had they had to broadcast something this big. The travel speed of spells was swift, almost instantaneous, if the vessel in question had a powerful enough metadrive. *Elysium* had a unique one, unlike any other Vlana had ever encountered in all her years of skyfaring.

But was it powerful enough for what they needed to do now?

She adjusted the tube next to her own station and spoke into it. "Vant, we've gotta send out a distress signal. We're going high for this one."

"How high?"

"As high as we possibly can."

A pause followed, then came, "Gods. That bad?"

"Hark's doing the spell," she said. "Clutch is taking us up—how long do you need to give us the requisite power?"

"Um. That depends on how much you need."

"All of it."

"I was afraid you'd say that. You do know we still need some to, y'know, not tumble out of the sky?"

"Yes," she snapped. "We know. How long do you need?"

A pause followed, then a slightly more empathetic tone reached her ears. "Give me an hour to make sure we're not damaging key systems. Take us high and you'll have everything that you need."

"Thanks, little brother," she whispered.

Another pause followed, then she heard her brother answer "We're gonna get those sons of bitches, yeah? We're gonna get them for what they did to him."

Vlana took a shuddering breath, then smiled through wetted eyes. "Yeah," she said. "We might lose, but we're gonna make them pay."

The tube went dead, and Vlana heard footsteps behind her. She knew it wasn't Clutch, who was still stoically standing behind the wheel, maintaining a steady heading.

Aimee stood a few feet away, her hands white-knuckled on the railing at the edge of the bridge before the viewports, just staring outside the window. Vlana paused. It was hard for her to look at her friend, just then. She'd only known Aimee de Laurent for a year, but that was long enough in close proximity to bond deeply and become incredibly aware of someone's habits. Mannerisms. The ways about which they went and the things they held dear.

Aimee had always been a fiercely independent soul but seeing her without Elias by her side physically hurt Vlana. Not because one was incomplete without the other—no person was not a whole on their own —but because the absence of their crewmate left a hole in their midst. An empty space that should've been occupied by a living, breathing soul. It was the absence of presence that hurt the most, and Vlana almost couldn't process it.

"I..." she started. Trailed off. Then she found words again. "...Do you need anything, Aimee?"

Aimee stirred after a moment, then slowly turned around to look at her. Her blue eyes were bloodshot and her heart-shaped face was stained with dried tears. "I couldn't stop him," she said at last, looking down at her slender hands. "All my magic and I wasn't fast enough to stop Silas from..." she couldn't seem to spit it out. Vlana watched as the sorceress's eyes closed and her hands balled into fists. "And Coulton," she nearly spat the name. "We came there to save him. All of this was for that. Elias gave everything he had, for that. And in the end the little snot-nosed fucker did nothing. He stuttered and stammered and let Silas send the man I love into the abyss."

Her mouth drew into a tight line, and she opened her eyes. "Maybe it's not charitable of me, V, but right now...I want to kill them all." Her teeth clenched. "Roland. Silas. Coulton. Their soldiers and their court. The Guilds. Every last fucking one."

Vlana took an impulsive step forward, and then Clutch broke her long silence at the wheel. "Yeah," she said. "Me too. All of those sons of bitches. Fuck 'em. Fuck these bastards and their genocidal dreams." Vlana watched her friend's dark hands tighten on the wheel. "It's long past time someone put every last one of them in their goddamn graves."

"There's a lot more of them than there are of us," Vlana murmured.

"That just means it's a target-rich environment," Clutch deadpanned through tightly clenched teeth. "Plenty for each of us."

Aimee was looking forward through the big viewport at the clouds moving by. At length she took a deep breath and said "They took him from me. They're not taking my home, too."

"No," Vlana finally said. "They're not."

She felt the presence of Harkon Bright before she saw him step onto the bridge. Vlana had seen Harkon resolute. Had seen him tired and worn and determined. She'd even seen him angry, once or twice.

But not like this. The Mage who Meddled was furious. Clutch was taking them up, now. Higher and higher into the heavens. Wisps of cloud passed the main viewport as the heavens swallowed them up. Harkon walked towards the dais.

"Vant, are you ready?"

"You got it boss," the engineer's voice returned to them via the tubes.

Vlana felt the surge moving beneath her feet. Harkon climbed the stairs up to the portal dais, but rather than summon the lenses, he wove his fingers through the air in complex patterns. Summoning a globe of light in front of his face. It shimmered, fluctuating, and Vlana shifted to the communications panel, ready to use the ship's power to amplify Harkon's message.

The Mage who Meddled opened his mouth and started to speak.

"People of the Drifting Lands, this is Harkon Bright, aboard the skyship *Elysium*. The Guilds have allowed the Eternal Order to take the helm of their power, and now they threaten the city of Haven-sreach with bloodshed and hellfire. Countless innocents are about to die. This is a desperate call for any who will render aid. Who will stand up to corporate tyranny and the violence of coin against an unsuspecting nation. You will find us in the sky before the walls of the white city. I know you are afraid. We are all afraid. But if we do not stand now, a power that has long dominated our lives will begin to massacre innocents on a scale not yet seen with absolute impunity.

Our only recourse is to fight. Come to Havensreach. The lives of every free Skyfarer, and every landborn person depend on it."

As the message flowed forth from the ship, echoing across the heavens, Vlana felt a chill run through her. And looking over her shoulder she saw the same fear reflected on the face of each member of their crew. Perhaps their fate had been sealed when Harkon killed Ogier. Or when they'd stood against the Guilds aboard the *Iseult* a year ago. Perhaps earlier than that, when they first involved themselves in the war of Port Providence. Or maybe it had been the day they left Havensreach with Aimee aboard, on a crash-course towards the conflict that could no longer be avoided.

The Guild had just picked a fight with Havensreach. With their home.

They were at war.

lias Leblanc falls. Clouds whip past him, wisps of immaterial mist pass by his face and the light recedes into an impossible distance as he descends into a vast, swallowing darkness. His body has stopped rotating, now. Or perhaps it's simply too dark to tell. His fingers are all but invisible, discernible only as outlines against the deeper black. The roar of the wind is constant, an unending din screaming against his ears, and he can't even hear his own shouts of grief and anguish. He stopped what seems like a long time ago.

When Elias was a very small child, before the Eternal Order took and broke him, he heard the same stories that every child in the Drifting Lands does, of the endless abyss that swallows ships and devours people who fall forever. Some of the myths speak of it as a sentient thing, an endless maw that devours the world from the root. He used to tremble in terror of it, but now it is not the fear of an unknowably vast leviathan that surges through him, but the knowledge that he is falling, and that there is now, truly, no way out.

And for the first time in his life, Elias realizes that he does not want to die.

He doesn't know what lies in the depths. Cannot know. And as he falls every moment of his life flashes before his eyes. Perhaps that means that he is dying, or that his body thinks his death is inevitable and imminent. Bits of horror and violence twinkle about his mind's eye along with pockets of joy, spread out like a constellation of mirror-shards. He almost feels as if he can reach out and touch them, pull recollections beautiful and agonizing from an ocean of stars. He sees Port Providence burn. Takes Oath of Aurum—now lost—from Collum's hand. The sword that he murdered to take pulls him towards a fate that shouldn't have been, and the Axiom Diamond strips away the persona of Azrael. Bits of his black armor, shredded to uselessness by Silas's magic, dislodge and rip away from his body as he tumbles downwards.

It's fitting, he supposes. As the shell breaks off and hurtles away from him, he sheds the remnants of Azrael for the last time. At least if he dies, whether by sudden impact or the starvation of falling forever through nothing, he will meet the end as himself. As Elias.

He closes his eyes, and the memory he touches last is of Aimee, her lips on his, the two of them standing before a sunset. Dancing beneath a field of endless stars.

When he opens them, his world fills with blinding light. Running lights. As dazzling as the sun, fill his vision. A ship! A sliver of white opens in the shadow between lamps. A figure reaches out. A voice screams, "Take my hand!"

Elias Leblanc desperately throws his hand forward, and for the first time he can remember, grasps for life.

2 3

A HAND IN THE DARK

The powerful hand heaved Elias forward, pulling him through a hatch and onto a hard surface. Onto the deck of a ship. Lying on his back. Staring up at bright lights that blinded him after the darkness of the abyss. He blinked several times, acutely aware of just how badly every part of his body hurt.

"Get him out of his armor," a voice he didn't recognize said.

Hands started undoing the buckles that remained on his body, stripping away bits and pieces of Azrael's shattered armor. Elias closed his eyes. His mouth was parched. Someone lifted his head and put water to his lips. He gulped it down, then choked. Sputtered. Rolled onto his side.

Then he was being picked up and hurried down a hallway or something like that. He felt a cot beneath him as he was laid down. Indecipherable voices buzzed in his ears. The world began to fade. He knew he was injured, knew that he was at the mercy of whomever had pulled him from death, but he couldn't stay awake. Couldn't keep his eyes open.

"It's alright," a familiar voice he couldn't place said from close by. "You're going to be okay, boy."

The world faded to strange dreams and dark, thundering skies.

When he awoke, the world came into focus only slowly. He was lying on a cot under a blanket in a dimly lit room of cold steel and exposed piping. Slowly he sat up, glancing down at himself. He wore his undershirt and pants, scorch holes still evident where Silas's lightning had coursed through his body. And yet through them no wounds could be seen. Only pink stains and bruises where healing magic had apparently mended him while he slept. He raised a hand to a sweat-stained forehead. He had dreamed of a dark, broken tree upon a plain of black glass and an ocean of mirror water under strange stars.

He was alive. He couldn't reckon on exactly how it had happened, or how this ship—he assumed it was a ship—had found him, but he was alive. The only question now was what to do next. What could he do next? He was weaponless, isolated, in an unfamiliar place where he wasn't even sure if he should open the door to the small room that presently formed his world.

But that was no reason to be a coward. He swung his legs over the edge of the cot and slowly stood, feeling the echo of ache flood through his body. How long had he been out? He strode toward the door and turned the latch.

It opened before he could push it outwards, and he found himself staring into the face of a shorter man wearing a homespun tunic, with big, knotted arms and a grey beard. A longsword hung at his left side, and his right forearm bore the simple tattoo of a cup. He eyed Elias up and down, then said "Good. You're not dead. Come on, the others want a word."

Elias opened his mouth, then closed it. The man was already walking down the hallway, with no gesture for him to follow. About ten feet away he stopped, not looking back. "If you want the answers to your questions, Elias, you're going to need to trust the path."

"Wait," Elias said, hurrying to catch up. "What's your name? Where am I?"

"My name is Bendis," the man said. "And you are aboard a ship called the *Nine Stars Shining*."

The interior of the ship was anything but shining. Exposed piping and cables carrying mystic energy were everywhere. A low thrum filled his ears, and the path they were taking briefly became a catwalk suspended over what looked like an armory below. Elias saw swords in racks side by side, and behind panes of glass, armor with a shape and style that was familiar.

White armor, affixed with the sigil of a cup.

"Who are you?" Elias asked. "I don't mean your name. I mean you. All of you. In this place. Why did you save me?"

Bendis kept walking. "We are the Order of the White Chalice, some-times called Ophilia's Children. Once upon a time, we and the Eternal

Order were one." He looked over his shoulder with a half smile. "But that was a long, long time ago. Now we are their foes. Steadfast and implacable." He paused. "As for why we saved you, well. That is simple, Elias Leblanc: you are on the path, and you called out to us. We will always come for our own."

Elias's mouth hung open for a moment, his mind racing and his heart rate increasing by the moment. The memory of Belit's old story from near a year ago rebounded in his head. *And White Knights came from the Deep Sky...*

But one thing held him back from following. A burning question that arose as soon as the initial wave of wonder receded. "Where have you been all this time?"

Here the first flash of guilt appeared on the other man's face, and he sighed, turning to regard Elias fully. "Seeing to a duty so important that it required us to let the Eternal Order run amok. Please understand, we opposed them in every way we could while not abandoning our sacred charge."

"And what was that?" Elias answered, trying to keep the skepticism from his voice. In that moment, memories of his mother's murder boiled to the surface. "What could you possibly have been protecting that would justify a thousand years of letting the Eternal Order do whatever it wanted?"

Bendis's answer chilled him.

"Life itself."

He didn't wait for Elias's answer. He just turned around and kept walking.

At length they came to a door wrought from distressed wood and iron, and Bendis pushed it open. The room beyond was unmistakably the bridge, full of lights blinking on uneven surfaces, and just as in the corridors that preceded it, everything was exposed. Unfinished. As if this place had been cobbled together from the bones and viscera of other forgotten ships, long ago.

Elias sucked in a breath at the vision beyond the viewport: the darkness was almost total, and only the thrum beneath his feet told him that the vessel was moving, and at an appreciable speed.

Bendis kept walking while Elias stopped, approaching a helmsman who stood at the iron wheel in the center of the room. "Progress?"

"An hour above the deadman's line," the helmsman answered, his hands moving deftly along the spokes. "Absolutely below any possible detection."

"And the Guild dreadnoughts?" Bendis followed up.

"Long departed. They didn't even try to chase the skyship that fled the Port Providence flagship."

Elias let out a breath. "The *Elysium*," he said. "Thank the gods, they're alive." Then the realization that they must all believe him dead struck him, painful as a knife through the back of his shoulder blades. "I have to get back to them," he said. A hand ran through his hair. "I have to get back to them. Please. And Gods, Coulton has Oath of Aurum, now. I lost Ophilia's sword. I—"

"Relax kid," the new voice was familiar. So familiar that Elias knew it before he even turned to confirm its owner. The one-eyed, dark-skinned man named Rachim, the *Elysium* crew's host aboard the Behemoth *Iseult*, stood just off to the side, grinning at him. "I'm glad you're not dead, Elias LeBlanc."

"I..." Elias trailed off, disbelieving. "How? How are you here? What's going on?"

"Let me explain," the older man said. "Sometime after your ship left the *Iseult*, these people came to us. Apparently Belit's dismissal of the Guild representatives and the potential freeing of an entire flotilla from Guild control got their attention. They've been working with her in confidence for the past year. Then, on their last visit, they were alerted to the activation of some sort of beacon for which they've long kept watch. Belit told them it had to be you, and we set out to find you. We arrived at the battle where you fell too late to affect the outcome." He looked at Elias. "But not too late to save you."

"How did you even find me?" Elias asked. "That's like snatching a coin out of a tank of dark water."

"Not like that," Bendis said. "Was that. Specifically. But the beacon, it turns out, leaves something of a mark on the people who activate it, and our sensors were able to pick you up as you fell. Getting you was no easy task, and you'd been so beat to shit that it took a lot of healing spells to bring you back from death's edge. "I get the sense that you like to push your limits, Elias. Be careful of that. Someday it may cost you something permanent."

Elias turned and looked at him, inexplicably and suddenly annoyed. "There are things more important in this world than my life."

"I didn't say it would be your life," Bendis answered.

"Let's not get lost in the weeds," Rachim said. "There's more important things at play here, like, oh, I don't know—the fate of the entire Drifting Lands."

"You said you were gone because you were protecting Life Itself," Elias said to Bendis. "What do you mean?"

"If you've activated the Beacon," Bendis answered, "then I'm going to guess you've been to Ophilia's tomb. You've seen the story writ across that wall."

"The Twelfth Night," Elias breathed. "The… God… thing, that Ophilia and her fellows killed?"

"And destroyed the Empire of Varengard that it ruled, with it." Bendis affirmed. "Creating the Maelstrom and scattering much of the survivors into what became the successor states that now rule most of the known territories. Yes. Killed is the best way of putting it," he continued. "Certainly the closest thing to a state of being that we would understand. But when it comes to things this vast, dead is a misnomer. The Twelfth Night was immense. A consciousness of countless components and vast power that wasn't limited to one physical space or even time. Killing it was no mean feat, and even inert, it still…dreams. Thus contained—powerful but unmoving—it has remained for over a thousand years. But it's not gone. It still possesses a certain cognizance. It still remembers, and it still hates."

He let that linger in the air. "While we would have gladly spent our countless years fighting the evil the Eternal Order metes out upon those it is paid to hurt," Bendis said, "the truth is we have been guarding the physical and metaphysical places in the Drifting Lands where the doorways to its tomb can be accessed. We have, at great cost and for many centuries, been ensuring that it remains as 'dead' as it can be."

Elias felt his throat go dry. Suddenly the creeping darkness consuming Silas's form made a disturbing sense. His dreams of a strange tree and a terrible darkness. "Silas," he said after a long moment. "He's made contact with it. Struck some sort of bargain with it, for power. And for…something else." A terrible creeping sensation spidered down his back. "I don't know what, but it can't mean anything good."

"No," Rachim said. "It can't. This Silas has managed to lash together the Guild, the royalty of Port Providence, and the might of the Eternal Order into a force that apparently has one goal: the destruction of Havensreach."

"How the fuck does the death of a city serve a dead god that's mouldering hidden away somewhere in the darkness?" Elias asked.

"Souls," Bendis said.

"What?"

The White Knight's expression drew into a hard line. "The Twelfth Night is, as I said, a being of component consciousness. Or at least it was, once. Feeding it countless living souls in one terrible flash of blazing destruction would not be enough to return it to the power it once possessed in life, but it might be enough to let it do something it hasn't been able to do in a thousand years: act on its own. That, alone, is too terrible to contemplate. If Silas has somehow managed to slip our watch and make contact with this thing, he has the power—I believe—to enact a ritual that will use the conduit between himself and the Twelfth Night to kill every person in Havensreach, feeding their souls directly to his master. Thus empowered, it may be able to shake the walls of its tomb, and that might be more than enough to let it tear loose."

"…Oh," Elias said. "Yeah that. That's bad."

Rachim's smile was grim. "Fortunately, it seems that Harkon has done the exact opposite of running. Shortly after the battle ended, he sent a message to every independent Skyfarer in the Drifting Lands, calling them to Havensreach to fight. As for how many will show up, who fucking knows?"

"…not for the fight that brings certain victory," Elias said.

"But for the fight that must be fought," Bendis finished. Then he gestured for Elias to follow. "We're traveling deep right now, but we will be at Havensreach soon. You have only a brief time to meet your fellows, and if you are not made ready for this, you will be chaff before the reaping."

"Can I follow?" Rachim asked amusedly. "I've always wanted to see something like this."

"Something like what?" Elias asked.

"The ritual," Bendis said. "The one from which we take our name. Here is the hard truth, Elias: the Twelfth Night created us. The touch of its power marks every single person possessed of the Intuitive Arcanism that the Eternal Order and the White Chalice share. If it awakes, it will be able to touch your mind. We can offer you a ritual that will prevent that from happening. Believe me, as one who has stood near enough to the seals upon our progenitor's tomb to perceive the whispers, you do not want them in your head."

Bendis led him downward. There was no way to tell if this was into the bowels of the *Nine Stars Shining*, or even how big the ship itself was. Elias moved through a world new to him with every step, on a path that accelerated as air currents were pulled violently into the swirl of a storm. At length they reached the bottom of two flights of metal stairs, and into an open chamber lined with weapons and armor. Armor of a familiar style— similar to what he had seen on Ophilia's tomb, and set with the symbols of chalices and pale roses.

Elias stood in the stark room with its exposed wires and piping, in which the only things that appeared pristine were the tools these people used to keep watch over their order's original charge. It was only looking now that he realized some of the armor was damaged. In one breastplate, perforations had worn its structural integrity to the point that they now surrounded a gaping hole in the side. Another was missing its arms, and there were stains of blood upon the mesh between plates. Elias took another step forward.

"These are memorials, aren't they?"

Bendis did not look up. "To the ones who added their blood to the sacred stains of memory." He walked to where a breastplate was split open down the center. "Every drop of blood upon these armaments is a debt that we must honor."

He turned and looked at Elias, finally. "Death builds upon death. Every loss in the service of a cause is a weight. A door closed that makes it harder and harder to turn back. This can be a virtuous thing, driving people forward...or it can be a chain that shackles them to a terrible course for which they have paid too much to consider turning back. That is why we must all be sure that the causes we fight for are worthy."

A sigh followed. "This is what your prince Coulton has done, and this is why you need to let go of your grief and your guilt."

"I killed his brother," Elias answered. The guilt bubbled to the surface as he spoke. Fresh and sharp. "I destroyed his homeland. The least I can do is try to save him."

"Which you cannot do so long as what you're doing is about you and your need to erase the weight upon your conscience," Bendis said, and his expression was unyielding and unforgiving, thoughtful eyes turned hard as flint waiting to spark a flame. "Give that up. Your guilt is pure, distilled selfishness. You will never atone. True service is not in trying to wipe slates clean. It is in building something new, for the sake of those who cannot do it alone. Atonement is a trap, Elias, and we are at war with the oldest and greatest evil in the world. Let go of your need for it and focus on what you can do next."

Elias stood in stunned silence, staring at this stranger in the room full of memorialized weapons and armor, connected to a legacy he barely understood but that hummed with the echoes of purpose. "How do you know all this about me?" he finally asked.

"I told him," Rachim said behind him. "And Belit told him. She suspected they'd take an interest in you, and that they might have what you were looking for. This is the fight, kid. The one that matters."

One by one, other knights of the white chalice were entering the chamber. Elias saw people of a dozen different ethnicities, sizes and shapes. All of them scarred. All of them with a war-weary look of resilient determination.

"This is the path," Bendis said. "But only you can walk it, and if you're going to make that choice, you need to make it soon." He gestured to a table nearby which—Elias noticed for the first time—held a small, plain-looking chalice.

"What happens to me if I drink from that?" Elias asked.

"Pain," Bendis said. "You will be cut off from an ancient connection rooted in the power you have inherited to the one who created it. That process is…unpleasant. When it is done, you will find your mind clearer and your senses sharpened. Other than that, your power will remain mostly the same. It will not alter your thinking or exert influence over your mind. This is not a trick, and it is not a trap." He paused. "But it is necessary, if you are going to be free and survive what is coming."

Elias's throat was dry as he regarded the cup and all its promises and dangers. This decision, this sudden choice, had come so much sooner than he had ever expected. It felt risky, making such a leap, but then again…

"You're going to have to trust the path."

And this was where the path had led him.

Elias swallowed his fear, took a leap of faith, and said, "I'll do it."

Bendis slowly took the cup with both hands. A woman handed him a pitcher of what looked like water and he filled it. "There is nothing special about this cup, save that it's banged up and we've grown sentimental about it," the knight said. "It's the symbolism that matters, and it will be the symbolic act you make in drinking from it that will make the ritual work."

He passed it to Elias's hands. It was surprisingly heavy.

"Repeat after me," Bendis said.

"Children of Heaven no more.

By the wisdom of the White Chalice we stand.

Not for the fight that brings certain victory,

But for the Fight that Must Be Fought."

Elias looked down into the liquid. It seemed to spark with a faint life. He looked from face to face, taking in the people around him, and along with the stoic determination and the reserved calm, he saw hints of something else. A humanity embodied by the phrase the Axiom Diamond had said in his mind when he asked the question alone in *Elysium's* bay.

They were afraid.

None of these people knew if they would survive, or even expected to. But they knew they had to fight, as their predecessors had fought. Elias looked back down at the cup. *As I have fought.*

"Children of Heaven no more," he said. And the cup was heavy in his hands. "By the wisdom of the White Chalice we stand."

He lifted the cup to his lips. "Not for the fight that brings certain victory," and the Queen Mother was suddenly at the forefront of his mind. Her, and every other person caught up in the struggle to which he now joined himself. "But for the fight that must be fought."

Elias drank. There was a moment where he cleared a breath after he gulped it down. Then he immediately started screaming. It wasn't like swallowing fire. This was worse. Worse than Kaelith's lightning. Worse than Malfenshir's blade punching through his guts. Worse than hands around his throat. For a terrible few seconds, every ounce of Elias Leblanc's being was simultaneously on fire. He didn't remember what happened next. The world went white, and he was aware of hands catching him as he pitched sideways, shouting so loudly that his throat went raw.

Eventually the world came back in fuzzy patches and lattice-like cracks through the glass of his vision. It coalesced until he found himself sitting on the hard metal floor, his back to a cold wall. Several blinks followed as the world came back into a focus it had never had before.

"Can you breathe, Elias?" Bendis asked.

"I..." he managed. "...Yes. I can breathe."

"Welcome," Bendis said, clasping his hand. "To the Order of the White Chalice."

24

THE DREAD LORD OF ASHES

It did not matter how many times he replayed the past seventeen years through his mind, Lord Roland would always come away from the recollection frustrated. Power acquired over and over again. Control established. His desires bound up in cords and chains that were impossible to break, only for outside interference to throw the entire affair...out of balance.

Silas was not supposed to kill Azrael. Had the Dread Lord of Ashes not still needed the idiot stravrophore, Roland would have killed him on the spot for that act of singular foolishness. *Careful,* his good sense reminded him. *He is powerful enough to incinerate you with a gesture.*

True enough, but even the tool of a God was not invulnerable, and in contests of power who was stronger mattered far less than who was faster. He stood in the empty bay, the mess of battle having been long cleaned by frightened crewmen trying to reclaim some sense of normalcy on a battered ship they were only now beginning to see was on the 'wrong' side.

It didn't matter. In the end, Roland did not need the people of Port Providence at all. He needed Coulton's blood, expertly bound by Silas to the Tireless. And in truth he didn't even need the Tireless for more than the formality of protecting a ritual that was soon to make at least half of Roland's problems go away. He would do what he had to do. Crouching by the lip of the bay door, he squinted out into the darkness below. When he closed his eyes he could still see Theliana in all her court finery staring out from the palace window of the alabaster spire of New Corinth beneath the gleaming light of the sunset. The boy had looked so like his mother. Was the only thing left of her.

Roland had burned an entire kingdom down for the chance to possess her. That what remained of her also held the spark of the memory of the man she had mistakenly chosen over him was an offense that he could barely stand. Roland had broken Elias of that spark, and in its place built his beautiful Azrael. The memorial to everything that he had lost.

The son that Roland should have had with the woman who should've been his own. When the time came, he would kill Silas himself, claim the jewel growing in his chest, and be done with all this farcical disaster. He would have his revenge, and he would have everything that he sought.

But first he had to kill another group of people.

The slow walk back into the interior of the ship was punctuated by people getting out of his way with all the scurrying haste of drowning rats. They knew who he was, now. Recognized the name that rippled through the Drifting Lands as a symbol of fear. Roland, Dread Lord of Ashes. Breaker of spires and flayer of kings. They knew only terror at his presence, which was as it should be. At length he came to a finely decorated corridor that led to the audience chamber where the remaining nobility of Port Providence was gathered. When the door opened, they raised their eyes from the table around which they'd gathered, allegedly in secret to plot Silas's murder and regain their King's freedom.

It was such a pathetic effort, made so completely late, that Roland laughed out loud. He closed the door behind him.

"What are you doing here?" the most senior among them asked. "This is a private meeting."

Roland put his hand on the lock to the door and summoned a spell of heat. The metal melted under his gloved hand, sealing the only exit. His smile turned knife-like. "I suppose from a certain perspective, yes."

"This is outrageous," a woman said, getting to her feet. Her hand lingered near her sword. "You can't—"

Roland crossed the room in a blur. His right hand pressed down on her own, holding the sword in its sheath. One of the younger men drew a blade of his own and leaped over the table. Roland gestured with his other hand and blew a hole through the man's torso. Red guts splattered across the fine tapestries hanging on the far wall.

"I do as I please," he said simply. The hand at her sword snapped up to her throat, and he unceremoniously broke her neck.

Two more were brave enough to try and hurt him. One pulled a well-designed, ornately carved flintlock out of his coat. Roland side-stepped the bullet and strode towards the shooter. The second brave man tried to stab him in the back and Roland stopped, grabbed him by the back of the head and smashed his face into the table. Once. Twice. Three times. He stopped twitching. Everyone else was running by the time Roland reached the man with the gun. First, he broke the gun. Then he broke the shooter's legs with two strength-enhanced kicks to his knees.

The man crumpled, and for the first time Roland saw the realization in his eyes. That he was going to die horribly and that there was absolutely nothing he could do to prevent it. Roland idly wondered for a moment if he would try to meet it with courage— few people did—or die blubbering and screaming like most. Mid-thought he decided he didn't care, and proceeded to beat the man to death with the butt of his own pistol.

Turning, the Dread Lord of Ashes watched as the remaining nobles clustered around the door like ants clinging to one another amidst rising water. Blood dripped from his face and he walked slowly across the room. No need to hurry, after all. Ordinarily one of these gnats presuming to threaten him would've been reason to flay them all and fly their skins from his banner like flags. This was not a personal matter, however. It was the business of the Eternal Order, and despite his position, he had an obligation to be prompt.

He reached the first of them, grabbed a fist-full of finery, and hurled him all the way across the room. Heart his spine snap as he hit Coulton's throne. "Everyone always runs," he said. "They always imagine they will be brave, but they never are."

A sudden jolt of pain burned up his side. Minor. Like the swift bite of a stinging insect. Roland looked down. One of the nobles, a man who couldn't have been any older than eighteen, had somehow gotten his hands on a shock-spear, striking Roland's armor with it. He blinked as he looked down. Something in him snapped. The Dread Lord of Ashes gripped the haft of the weapon and ripped it out of the boy's hand. Took the blunt butt and rammed it into his middle so hard it punched through both his gut and the wall behind him. "Stay there."

He killed the remaining people by the door without ceremony, then slowly returned to the youth impaled to the wall. His breath was coming more quickly, now. His eyes wide. Blood leaked out of the boy's mouth. A hero, apparently.

"Y-you," the boy choked. "You…will not…win."

Roland heard Theliana's voice knife through his mind. Decades past.

"I could have a thousand choices for a thousand years, and still I would never choose you."

Roland put one hand on the spear and sent a charge of lightning through it. It blazed across the boy's body, sending him rigid and making him bleed from the ears. "I have won every war I have ever fought!" Roland screamed. He sent another jolt of electricity through the dying man. "Do you hear me? Every! One!"

He sent another jolt through the boy. The youth's body convulsed. His teeth crackled with arcs of light and his eyeballs melted down his face as he screamed. Roland did it again and again and again, loosing the spell over and over, even after the boy was dead. Until there was only a charred mass staining the wall, vaguely human in shape.

He took a moment to compose himself, alone in the empty room. The clouds passing outside the window were striking in their ephemeral beauty. He walked to the nearest viewport and lifted a carafe of dark golden liquid and smelled it. Some sort of brandy. Likely made some place that no longer existed. He raised the dark drink to his lips and tasted it. Smoke and honey and the kick of something potent. He wondered how many of these people had died with that taste on their lips. The idle reflections on the nature of those he killed could drive him to occasional distraction.

He wondered what Harkon Bright's last thought would be, before he killed the old man and tore his ship apart bolt by bolt. Before he had his crew tortured and maimed and turned into preserved-flesh sculptures for his private gardens.

Roland wondered many things.

Turning his eyes downwards through the viewport he beheld the fruit of their labors: the Isle known as Lia's Rest was under way. The whole island was moving under the power of Silas's magic, escorted by the two Guild dreadnoughts and several Eternal Order frigates. Soon they would meet up with the rest of the Guild Fleet, and make the jump to Havensreach. At this point, Coulton's flagship was practically an afterthought that had existed only to house the nobles Roland had now killed. Originally it was needed as a rallying point for the rest of Port Providence's people once they were brought to Havensreach—to inspire them as they took the city with the help of the Tireless. Given that the citizens were missing, now, it hardly mattered at all. At best, Port Providence was a shell of a hollowed-out idea to be used as a pretext for the fulfillment of the Twelfth Night's thousand-year plan. A plan Roland had long been aware of, but whose culmination had still managed to surprise him.

Now the only thing that remained was to communicate directly with his superiors within the Eternal Order, and report that it was time to bring everything to bear.

He took a single, longer drink from the carafe, then poured the rest of the liquid out onto the floor before cutting the lock and leaving the room.

Roland took a small gunboat down from the flagship to Lia's Rest. The Isle was dusty and empty as before, the single spire the only noteworthy landmark on the large plane of rock. At its foot, the Tireless stood in rank and file, now controlled directly by Silas through Coulton. This was not going to be the most comfortable place to do his communicating, but it was the place where Roland had the best shot of success. He stretched out his senses towards the beacon. Felt for whence its power originated, and finding that place, he followed. Alone, Roland made his way through the canyon filled with the psychic echo of those that had died here before the Tireless were entombed. Before Ophilia and her misguided rebellion put them all upon the path at whose end they had now arrived. He passed the echoes of Knights of the White Chalice battling against impossible odds to vanquish the thing that had made them. The thing that had successfully reached out to Silas and begun to initiate its return, if you could call it that. Roland still wasn't sure that one could.

He found the doorway hidden by a paltry illusion that was likely the work of Harkon's whelp of an apprentice. He dispelled it with a gesture and paused a moment to stare up at the doorway's etching of the White Chalice's oath. It was ironic, Roland thought. A year ago, he had sent Azrael to find the Axiom Diamond with the precise hope that the jewel would lead him to the hiding place of the Eternal Order's oldest enemies, and now it was entirely possible that they would come to him as an act of providence. Walking slowly and deliberately, he entered Ophilia's sacred tomb.

It was humbler than he imagined. Its only ornamentation was her sarcophagus and the story of her triumph over the Twelfth Night spread across the walls. Roland turned in a circle, taking it all in. There was a private joy, to being in this space. Knowing that his mere presence desecrated it in the eyes of those that had made it.

"It's ironic," he said to the empty space. "So much has existed between us for so long that I once despaired of ever finding your order." His hand graced along the edge of the lid of the sarcophagus. "But now the board has been cleared, the very protections you built are turning against you, and one by one the peoples and forces that stood between us are being swept away. Everything, and everyone, that kept my sword from you is dying. Wilting away before the heat and the storm."

He looked up at the wall with its murals. A smile spread across his features. "You will all be with me, soon. And the original crime that split you away from us will be washed away in the rivers of your blood."

He walked to the back of the room, and pausing beneath the depiction of the Twelfth Night, he knelt. There was no dais here, but Roland had no need for one. Closing his eyes he drew upon his inner strength and reached across distance and time towards the minds of the Eternal Order's elders.

Silence fell, and then with it came a sudden and powerfully oppressive weight, pushing down on him. Roland was immediately aware of the pressure difference in the air. "You are late," they said as one.

"I have found Ophilia's tomb," Roland said, leading with an offering of success. "Silas is doing as I bid. Harkon Bright and his crew are enemies of the Guilds, and Oath of Aurum is within our possession." He smiled. "I have succeeded beyond our wildest expectations."

There was a long pause, and then the question he'd dreaded was asked. "And Azrael?"

Cold settled into Roland's gut. He knew what the council had wanted since the failure at Port Providence. He knew they craved his former student's death. Well. At least he could answer it with what was not a lie to the best of his knowledge.

"Dead," he said. "By Silas's own hand."

He felt them probing his mind. Skirting around places he'd learned to protect by careful trial and error. If they came to know the fullness of his plan, they would crush his soul out of his body and leave him a husk here on the dusty ground. To make contact with the elders was to be open to them. It was only through careful and thorough effort that Roland had learned to lie.

"Still you lack the Axiom."

His brows twitched and he bit back the urge to retort in anger. *Careful.* "Temporarily," he said. "I offer much in compensation. See what I have given you over all these years: Oath of Aurum, the end of Port Providence, the nearest we have come to total Guild control. New Corinth was my gift to you—"

The weight of the combined minds of the Eternal Order's elders bore down suddenly and abruptly upon him with such a force that he gasped for breath.

"No," the voices declared. "New Corinth was our gift. To you."

A pause followed. The weight receded slightly. Roland breathed again.

"It is time to do as you promised," the voices said. "It is time to deliver."

Roland's eyes stayed closed. *Breathe. Control yourself.*

A chorus of whispers echoed around him, filling his mind and his conscious ears. Though his eyes were closed he could feel the paint of the murals around him curling and crisping off the walls from the sheer corruptive force of the elders' violent thoughts.

"This errand has cost us dearly already. We remind you, Lord Roland, that every knight you have thrown at this task from the very start of the Port Providence affair is now dead. Even Ogier lies slain by the hand of Harkon Bright."

Roland tried to suppress his amusement at that. Of course Ogier had imagined himself able to kill Harkon Bright. Of course he had paid for his stupidity in blood. Still, it had been enough to begin Roland's war. That was enough.

"But what results you have," Roland answered. "And such as none of us have dreamed of are coming. There is much more I can squeeze from the stone of this task. I need only your patience."

"You test that sorely, Roland."

"I have won more victories for you in seventeen years than the Eternal Order had seen in a thousand before me. Elders, I can give you the White Chalice, at long last."

There was a pause, and then came the reply. "What do you need?"

Roland paused. Here was the gambit for which he had so long prepared. The leap across the chasm that there was no avoiding taking. If he played his cards right, his war would be won, here and now.

Roland, Dread Lord of Ashes, took a deep breath, and answered.

"Everything."

I t is the biggest Guild Fleet the Drifting Lands has ever seen. Silver-spike dreadnoughts fill up the pocket of sky above the House of Nails. The tortured landscape of tall, deathly spires set amidst the ruins of a lost wonder burns blood red under the apocalyptic vision of a crimson sunset.

The skydocks swarm with activity. Vessels are loaded before their engine exhaust ports flare and they rise like vultures into the sky. A thousand black crows with gleaming contrails flooding the sky. Not since they first conquered this place has the Eternal Order moved in such force. But it is not the ships that are the true source of the horror. That distinguished honor belongs to the two immense shapes rising from the far side of the isle once called New Corinth. Splitting away from the very earth, setting wedges of land crumbling and breaking away, two mountains break free and rise into the air to join the fleet.

Iron Hulks. Two of them. Two is more than enough to break Havensreach over the Eternal Order's knee, though perhaps the fight would be difficult. But this is two Iron Hulks mingled with the might of the Eternal Order and the power of the Guilds. Directed against a small city state in the middle of the Unclaimed, it is overkill to an absurd degree. Ascendent and overwhelming in its violence. As the vessels move towards the edge of the airspace controlled by the House of Nails, portalmages on countless bridges watch as lenses lower, and the burst of lights fill the sky as numerous portals flash into existence all at once.

Seventeen years ago, the storm of ships appeared over New Corinth's skies. Today they appear at the edge of Havensreach's airspace. Flashing through portals, immense, deadly knives venting glowing exhaust stabbing towards the city's white walls.

And then a massive, final portal tears open behind the main fleet. What comes through is neither a ship, nor an Iron Hulk.

It is an island. Crowned with an immense spire of rock and blotting out the sun, the whole of Lia's Rest emerges from the iris of the blazing eye in the heavens. As it moves, chunks of stone split from its edges, moving in different directions. As Havensreach's defense forces scramble, as her skyships take to the air in a much smaller flock of birds, these errant, smaller isles slowly begin to encircle Havensreach. Atop each one is a carved circle of black, scarred magic, and a single Tireless standing in place at its center.

While the first flashes of gunfire break out between the Havensreach Defense Forces and the terrifying power arrayed against them, the dancing lights flicker off the face of the figure atop the spire at Lia's Rest. Silas's hands are extended over a massive ritual circle, a terrible glimmer glowing up from within its lines. At his back, his King is chained to his throne with shackles mingling with the pool of terrible magic before him, Oath of Aurum strapped mockingly to his hip.

Silas smiles.

"And now," he whispers. "The End Begins."

25

A RACE TO THE FINISH

Aimee stood near the stairs to the portal deck as the ship hurtled through the heavens on the way to the next jump. The clouds moved slowly by, but she knew for a fact that they were going so fast that the engines were in danger of overclocking. She felt nauseous, vacillating between wanting to come apart from grief and feeling a spike of rage so intense she might burn everything down if she allowed the point to touch anything at all.

Her hands fidgeted at her waist, fingers clammy and twitching occasionally as she pulled the spells she knew out in her mind and leafed through them one after the other. Silas had far more powerful magic than she did. He was connected to something truly terrible and appallingly strong. Her magic took time to execute, she knew less than he had access to, and she was not backed by an army of automaton soldiers or the might of the Guilds. Nonetheless, she had to find a way to kill that son of a bitch if she got the chance. She just didn't see any way she could conceivably get anywhere near him before she was obliterated by aerial gunfire or overwhelmed by unfathomable numbers.

She didn't even see how they lasted more than a few moments against a fleet of that size. She knew the Havensreach Defense Forces. She knew —at least in general terms—what the city could bring to bear for its protection on short notice.

It didn't stand a chance.

Aimee took a deep breath as the image of Elias hurtling over the lip of the bay door flashed through her mind. Were she someone else, she might have run from it. Pushed it from her mind and tried to wall it off behind a barrier to keep the grief at bay, but that was not Aimee de Laurent.

Instead of running, she embraced the memory. Used it. Let it roll over and through her like a wave. And in the memory's wake? Rage. A fury more potent than any she'd ever felt before. She was not going to run from this. Not going to allow it to paralyze her or render her weak and helpless.

She was going to get her hands on the people who had done it, and if she was going to die—and somewhere deep down some part of he knew she was—she would do so with her enemy in front of her and the loved ones she still had at her back, protected until the bitter end.

My classmates. My uncle's grave. My friends. My parents.

She clenched her fists silently. *You took Elias from me. You won't take them too.*

Bjorn walked up beside her, surprisingly quietly given his size. "I won't say are you ready," he said. "Because nobody is. I'm just going to ask; are you good and pissed?"

Aimee looked at him. "Fucking irate."

His smile was wry. "Good, because you're gonna need that."

Vlana was at her control station, and Clutch was at the wheel. It was eerily calm as they stood, hurtling through the sky and waiting, waiting. "Can I ask you something?" Aimee said.

"Anything," the old warrior answered.

"Your home," she said. "The farm on Skellig. What...what happened to it?"

He gave her a sideways look, then sighed. She saw his jaw tighten for a moment and was about to apologize for even presuming to ask when he shrugged and said, "What happens to every beautiful place when powerful people decide it's worth killing over." Then he turned to fully look at her. "My home was destroyed. My wife. My children. Gone. That is why I fight." He looked back at the window. "Today and always. I can't get back what I lost, but maybe, even old as I am, I can keep it from happening to one more person."

He fights for me, she realized. *For my family. For everyone we love.*

"Do you understand?" Bjorn finished.

"I thought I did, once," Aimee admitted. "But that was before they came for my home. Once I imagined that I would feel righteous indignation. A powerful nobleness of spirit." She shook her head. "Now? I'm just fucking pissed."

Bjorn nodded, then folded huge arms over his broad chest, adjusting the baldric that kept the immense sword across his back. "Then let's do this thing."

Harkon walked past them, striding up to the portal deck. Aimee's teacher wore an expression that mirrored the fury in her heart. She watched as the lenses descended. Felt the thrum of Vant adjusting the metadrive under her feet as the powerful magic was directed to the dais of the Portalmage. She couldn't help but think of her first portal-casting over a year ago, when the sabotage of their ship—still unsolved—had sent them hurtling into the conflict at Port Providence. *Someone in the home I'm defending wants me dead.*

But it didn't matter. The spell complete, the beam of light lanced out from the Elysium. The portal ripped open with a deafening crack. Clutch yelled "Vant! Hard burn!"

There was the nauseating sensation as the portal washed over them. The world tilting on its axis and the engines roared as they burst out the other side and into the crimson light of a dimming sky filled with flickering, blinking lights. Aimee took several steps forward and the breath left her. Two Iron Hulks. A host of Guild warships...and the might of the Eternal Order. And arrayed against it, the Havensreach Defense Forces, fighting and bloodying the nose of an enemy far bigger than themselves. And losing. She could see it even from this far away. Ships burst and burned and fell.

It was every story she'd heard of New Corinth.

It was Port Providence, all over again and writ larger.

The same story. The same violence. She clenched her fists and her teeth set. Then she heard Clutch gasp. "Holy fuck."

And turning her gaze to follow the pilot's, she saw it: the immense, sun-blotting form of Lia's Rest, the entire isle hovering higher in the heavens than the city she menaced, propelled by some terrible force that Aimee could only imagine. Isles should not move as this one did. And yet.

She stepped further onto the bridge. A ring of smaller isles encircled the city, far ahead of the gun battle, unseen by the Defense Forces. Bursts of magic crackled around the spire that crowned Lia's Rest, and the Isle was in the absolute thick of the warships, surrounded and guarded on all sides.

Clutch gulped, and Aimee heard her say "Orders, boss?"

"Straight for that Island," Harkon answered. "That's where Silas is. That's where we go."

"Vant," Clutch took a deep breath. "Full burn and get me power to the forward guns. Bjorn, get in the rear turret. Boss, Aimee, we're gonna need some shields."

They shot forward so fast that Aimee had to grip the rail to keep her balance.

"Alright you sons of bitches," Clutch said. "If it's a fight you want, it's a fight you've got."

They were halfway across the sky when the first gunboat spotted them. Aimee watched it turn. She summoned the shield spell and projected it far out in front of the *Elysium*. The beam from its turrets lanced across the heaven and crashed into her protective magic. Clutch turned and hit the trigger. Aimee felt the deck beneath her roar, and the metadrive-powered bursts of crackling light crossed the crimson sky. They cut across the gunboat's flank, tearing the vessel's skin open and bursting men and debris screaming into the sky.

Clutch gunned them up and over the falling wreck and let out a whooping cry. "Come on, you corporate bloodsuckers. Show me something new!"

Harkon shifted his feet on the other side of the bridge, and his shield turned aside a powerful beam of light.

A massive Order ship was turning slowly towards them. Aimee gritted her teeth. Its spinal turret swiveled in their direction, and she audibly gulped. "I don't think we can block that one!" she shouted.

"I know!" Clutch yelled back. "I'm waiting!"

"For what?" Vlana shouted back.

"For the glow in its center! Ignites one second before it fires. I twitch down or to the side and the whole thing misses. Their gunners can't adjust that bad girl on the fly!"

"Fuck, fuck fuck," Vlana's hands flew over her console. "Bjorn!" She yelled into the tubes. "We've got two gunboats swinging round our rear!"

"I see them!" Bjorn's voice came back. A half second later the dull thump of the rear guns made Aimee's teeth rattle. Then Clutch yelled "Hold onto something!" and *Elysium* dove as a huge beam of light sizzled over their heads, big enough to envelop their ship. Aimee grabbed the rail but lost her focus on the shield spell. They were hurtling down, now. Towards another capitol ship below. A forest of light beams punched upwards towards them, and Clutch moved the wheel. *Elysium* started spinning. Aimee fought the urge to vomit as they pulled up what felt like inches from impact with the hull. Roared along the length of the huge vessel and shot upwards again, the floor steepening as they climbed. Lia's Rest was above them, now, and they were in the thick of the battle. Blasts of fire erupted from the sides of ships. Bodies fell past them and into the depths. They were no closer.

"We have to veer off!" Clutch yelled. "We can't get at them this way!"

"Regroup with the Havensreach forces!" Harkon shouted. "We'll go high and drop down!"

Elysium shuddered as something struck the hull. It veered off course, then Clutch wrenched the wheel and brought them back around towards the falling-back defenders. "Hey hey hey!" She yelled. "Stop shooting at my girl!"

"Could you hold a steady course for two seconds!?" Bjorn shouted through the tubes. "It's hell trying to get a mark on those boats when we're spinning like a top!"

A loud boom echoed somewhere behind them. "Got him in the cockpit!" Bjorn yelled. "Second one crashed into the first. Our asses are clear for the moment!"

Harkon moved to Vlana's side as Elysium once more turned in a fast arc that leaned the deck. "I'm going to send a communication spell, clear the chatter!"

Aimee pulled herself back up, shaken but still stable. Through the viewport she could see Havensreach, now, surrounded by a vast ring of miniature isles that crackled with some sort of terrible energy. Then a massive pulse of magic rippled outwards from Lia's rest and Aimee's teeth chattered. Another followed a few seconds later. Then another.

Every one of the stone pylons surrounding her home pulsed with darkness.

"Havensreach Defense Forces!" Harkon's voice echoed through the sky. "This is Harkon bright of the skyship *Elysium*! We're pinned down by a constant barrage. Can you clear a column for us to reach that huge island floating in the thick of the enemy?"

A half breath later came an answer. "Harkon Bright? What in the abyss is on that island that's worth more than the two godsdamned Hulks and the fleet of warships bearing down on us?"

"The greater threat," Harkon said. "And if we don't get there immediately, Havensreach may not survive to know the face of its would-be conquerors."

"With respect," came the reply that made Aimee's heart sink. "We're barely holding our own line. You want to help? Get amongst us and start shooting."

The communication spell cut off, and for a terrible moment the bridge of the *Elysium* was silent.

"Clutch," Harkon said. His voice was heavy but fierce. "Take us towards the island. Full burn. Straight shot."

"We'll never make it," she said, but the ship started to turn at her command.

"Nevertheless," Harkon said. "We have to try."

"I want you to know," Vlana breathed. "That I love you all very much, and it has been an honor serving with you."

"Stuff that talk," Clutch said as they turned towards the teeth of a vast fleet. "If I'm going to die it's going to be cussing out the ones who finally pulled it off."

Aimee dashed forward and summoned a shield. A storm of blasts greeted them. She moved to the front of the bridge, and a heartbeat later lances of light were dancing off her summoned defenses. Her fingers started aching from the pressure needed to maintain it. *I'm going to fail,* she realized. *This shield is going to fall and we're going to take a hit directly to the bridge.*

In a flash she pictured Elias falling over the lip of the bay door and into the empty sky. *I'm going to die.*

She set her jaw, feeling the realization hit her even as she fought to hold the spell against an angry burst of aerial fire. She'd always thought that the knowledge of her imminent demise would bring peace or determination. A stoic fury that would carry her through the worst until the end. Instead she felt only grief. Grief and frustration and an impotent anger at the unfairness of it all. The knowledge that everyone—not just her, but everyone—was going to die was so crushing that she almost dropped her defenses.

We—they— all had so much more to do.

"... Abyss..." she heard Clutch say, and looking past her own defenses, Aimee stared down a Guild Dreadnought that had moved into their path. So close that it nearly blotted out the viewport. Its gun apertures were glowing. Aimee could almost feel the imminent heat. This was it.

A beam of light that dwarfed the *Elysium* shot overhead from somewhere behind her. It struck the Guild warship directly in its center of mass. Punched through armor-plating and internal structure, coring the vessel at the halfway point. The vessel shuddered, twisted, and a burst of fire bigger than some of the smaller ships erupted in all directions, splitting it in half.

A half second later the sound reached her ears. A terrific bang that rattled her teeth and shook the whole bridge.

"Cloud-Cracker," Vlana shouted. "That was a Cloud-Cracker!"

"What ship in Havensreach's service has one of those?" Clutch said, veering them closer to the burning hull to use it as cover against oncoming weapons fire. Yet even as she did so Aimee saw the other ships turning, moving in their formation at the arrival of some unseen, new enemy not visible from the front of their ship.

"Who in the abyss did that?" Vant's voice came up from the tubes. "What the fuck is going on out there?"

"Gods," Bjorn's voice answered from the rear of the ship through the tubes. "Gods, it's the *Iseult*. It's the *Iseult!* It's the entire fucking flotilla!"

Aimee's mouth hung open for a moment as it settled in. Hope.

Belit had come.

The corona of a blazing sunlight cuts through the window of the *Iseult's* wheelhouse as Belit rises from her chair. The Guild dreadnoughts fill the sea of the open sky. No less than two Iron Hulks move inexorably towards Havensreach's high walls, its meager defense forces dancing against the tide of loosed gunboats in flashes of intermittent light.

She strides towards the wheel where her helmsman steers the vessel, one hand resting upon the pommel of a sword that itches for war. These are the powers that have kept her people under the boot of their authority for generations. This is a trap, intended to bait her and her newly freed polity into the teeth of a waiting Guild. They expected her to take it. Knew she would come. But as the *Iseult* moves forward under full power, a flash erupts in the sky to the ship's starboard side. Another to port. Another behind them. Another. Another. Another.

The might of Flotilla Visramen erupts through a wall of portals bursting forth across a sunset sky. Belit has taken the bait, but she does not bring a fleet. She brings a nation.

And every one of these city-ships is armed with cloud-crackers. With heavy guns and grapple-lines bristling from every scaffold. A year has been a narrow time in which to prepare for today. She wishes she'd had longer…but this is enough, and the time was here.

Flipping a switch on the central console, the Red Queen signals her fleet as she surges forward into the greatest aerial battle the Drifting Lands have seen in five hundred years.

"Flotilla Visramen, first wave," her voice carries across the channels.

"Fire."

26

THE WHITE CHALICE

Elias picked up the breastplate. Tried to calm his pounding heart. He'd dressed in the mesh to which the metal adhered before being fastened with buckles and straps. Slowly he lifted the white enameled steel to his body and let it adhere into place with a soft thumping noise. Next came the buckles. It fit well enough. Not perfect, but enough.

He finished putting on every piece, until he stood resplendent in white armor from head to foot. The last thing he added was the sword-belt with its longsword. There was a moment of sadness as he was acutely aware of Oath of Aurum's absence. The blade had carried him for a year with its constant reassurance and presence. Now, he would simply have to do without. He just hoped this sword's edge was up to the task.

He turned. The other knights were similarly arrayed, hilts gleaming in scabbards at hips. A woman with an undercut and dark eyes walked up to him and checked the straps on his armor. Satisfied after a moment, she regarded him, then reached out, touched the chalice symbol on his chest and said "This armor was previously worn by a warrior named Karim. He died at the fringes of civilization facing horrors of which most folk will never know. Nobody remembers him but us." She gave him a solemn look. "And now you. Wear it well, do you understand?"

The armor at once felt a little heavier, and Elias gulped. "I can't live up to that," he said. "But I will do my best."

She held his gaze for a moment, then nodded, and struck the symbol on his chest with her closed fist, hard enough that he felt it through the steel. "For the fight," she said.

Elias nodded. "For the fight."

The ship shook, and Elias was dimly aware of the brief and strange sensation of portal transition as the *Nine Stars Shining* made its jump.

"We're going to join Belit," Rachim had said. *"We're going to give the Eternal Order something they can't ignore, cut our way to the heart of that ritual, and in so doing, give Havensreach a fighting chance."*

"There are far more of them then there are of us," Elias had answered. *"I know the Eternal Order's strength. We're looking at horrifying odds, if this gets up-close and personal."*

He would remember Bendis's answer for the rest of his life with a cold chill.

"Remember our Creed. If Silas succeeds, all is lost. Not just for us, but for everyone. If this is our end, there is no worthier place to stand."

The other knights began to move, and Elias followed, keeping an eye out for Bendis. He did not have a place within their rank and file. Knew nothing of his role in this. Only that he had to follow as they were going. Once more Elias found himself swept up in a tide and unsure of his place within it. He looked down at the sigil set upon his chest, and at once something Belit had said to him in one of their training sessions sprang to his mind.

Each generation picks up the fight where the prior one put it down. It never ends, Elias LeBlanc. Just your part in it. Do well, to honor the ones who came before, and to ease the way for those who come after.

Elias put his hand on the pommel of his borrowed sword. There was no warmth as he would've received from Oath of Aurum, but that didn't matter.

I am the fire, now, he thought. *The heat is within me.*

Trust the Path.

He saw Bendis at the front of the group, and the senior knight raised a hand. "The stavrophore sits atop the tower of Lia's Rest, the Plains of Aurum before him. An army of Tireless is arrayed against us, and likely the might of the Eternal Order. We must face this if we are to have a chance to stopping the ritual of the Twelfth Night's return."

A voice arose from the assembled knights. Clarion clear and bright in the hold of the large vessel. "This is what we have trained for," Bendis said, and his voice was filled with a sobriety that put chills through Elias's soul.

"This is the time and the place to spend everything we have. Each and every one of you has given more than I could ever ask. You have sacrificed everything to face the darkest horrors in anonymity, and many of your friends and beloved fellows have died forgotten at the edge of the storm. Now I must ask for beyond the most."

There was a loud sound of a clanking as the locks hissed into place. Bendis drew his sword.

"We are the White Chalice, and this is the Fight. In Ophilia's Name, for the ones who have fallen and the ones who have yet to come, today we will stand."

"When we land," the woman Elias had spoken to before said to him. "We will surge out this door and make for the base of the spire." She looked at him. "My name is Ilara. If I fall, remember it."

Elias met her eyes, and every memory of the battles he'd been in before flashed through his mind. Of warriors jockeying for position and glory and the chance to create fear. This was everything that Azrael's battles were not.

"I will not forget," he said. Then offered "But you're going to live." He left the last part unspoken.

And so am I.

There was a rushing sound accompanied by a series of dull thumps, and the *Nine Stars Shining* shook beneath Elias's feet. He recognized the distant whumps of explosions and the sizzle of beams blasting past the vessel's hull. The sense of the bottom dropping out of his stomach told them they were in a descent.

"When the door opens," Bendis said, "stay close to one another. Fight in conjunction. Do not let one of our number face an enemy alone."

It was everything the Eternal Order—invested in individual power, prowess, and personal glory—was not.

A seam of light split the far wall, and a ramp lowered, spilling daylight and the sounds of violence into the chamber. Elias drew his borrowed sword and flexed his fingers inside borrowed gauntlets. *For the fight that must be fought.*

The Order of the White Chalice erupted out through the opening bay and onto the dusty ground of Lia's Rest, and Elias charged with them.

He poured on speed, tried to stay near Ilara. At first all he could see was the dust kicked up by the large vessel's landing. There wasn't even time to turn and get a sense of what the *Nine Stars Shining* looked like. He did cast a glance up, and the heavens above him were a kaleidoscope of aerial violence. The sky was on fire. Immense vessels blotted out the sun, exchanging apocalyptic blasts of light with one another. A smaller gunboat, Elias could not tell on whose side they fought, absorbed a burst of crackling energy from a much larger vessel and blew apart in a shredding rain of debris that crashed to ground some distance away. Then an explosion went off barely twenty feet away, and he was showered with dirt and grime. Turning his face ahead, he saw a line of figures through the heat-haze of the flat plain. At their back, the central spire of the isle, its apex nearly blotting out the setting sun. Ilara was moving. Bendis jogged at the head of what was rapidly turning into a V-shaped wedge moving forward under power of magic. They picked up the pace, running. Thundering forward. Elias felt his boots pound the ground and kick up dust behind him. It took a few seconds to realize that for all their smaller numbers, the impending wall of the Eternal Order did not actually realize what was happening. The nearer they drew, the more he heard shouts of surprise echo in his ears.

They were almost upon the enemy when behind them, the *Nine Stars Shining* ignited her guns and fired over their heads and into the thick of the Eternal Order's soldiers. A haze of vaporizing red blasted upwards into the air as bodies became gas. The earth roared into a thick, churning cloud of dust through which they charged into the thick of a press of bodies.

The Eternal Order soldiers never knew what hit them. Elias's sword snagged on a shock-spear and he compensated for his lack of Oath of Aurum by leveraging it out of the way with a shot before delivering an enhanced-strength thrust into the armpit of the man's armor. A scream tore through his ears, but Elias was already ripping the weapon free and moving to the next. The wedge carved forward through the foot soldiers, Elias barely had time to mark each man as more than a blur through or around which he moved. Weapons scraped off his armor. He turned aside blows and dodged blazes of light. Through his mind as the chaos reigned, the single thought coursed: where were the Order's knights? They should have been here.

Then a spell nearly took him in the back, and turning, Elias saw them. They were walking. A casual stride drawing closer and closer to the members of the White Chalice. Elias heard their death-chants grating across his ears, bleak with the ashen kiss of dreaded familiarity. The fear seized him and for just a moment he was paralyzed. Then he looked to his left and to his right. Bendis. Ilara. Others, with faces as diverse as any collection of Skyfarers.

Elias wondered if the *Elysium* was up there above him, in the constellation of dying lights. Then he forced his attention back down to the battle before him, right as the Knights of the Eternal Order charged.

He shot into the thick of them, and everything was instantaneously chaos. A sword swept over his head, fast enough to cut wind. Elias sidestepped and loosed a bolt of lightning that sent the attacker veering away. He was abruptly fighting someone else. Steel rang against steel, and he gripped his sword halfway up the blade before moving in for a thrust at the throat. His enemy tried to drive a strength-empowered fist into his breastplate to set him off balance, and Elias hardened himself, taking the force of the blow and wrapping the armored man's elbow before rotating it with a burst of superhuman speed. A scream followed as the knight's shoulder ripped in the wrong direction.

A bolt of fire blasted the dirt at his feet, and he pivoted. Found himself on the edge of the battle, rolling several times before he came up in a crouch. He could see the spire. And between himself and its base, nothing. He'd somehow cleared the edge of the conflict and…

…And he could see people there. Flashes of light. A struggle unfolding that he'd been unable to see before. A flash of a blue coat. Golden hair. Aimee. Elias hesitated. He watched as she hurled a bolt of lightning at a figure that swatted it aside with the ease of a titan batting aside a gnat. Elias's eyes were on the figure, now, and frost chilled his gut.

Roland. She was fighting Roland. And Roland was winning.

There was no choice. He didn't have Oath of Aurum. Wasn't equal to this fight. The last time they'd briefly faced one another, Elias had wound up thrown into the open sky after being bloodied and beaten half to death.

His mind raced. If Aimee was trying to make it to the top of the spire, there was a chance she could stop, or at least delay Silas. And Roland would do anything to stop her. Only one thing could possibly draw him away. The only thing in the Drifting Lands that the Dread Lord of Ashes wouldn't be able to ignore. Elias felt his throat dry and his hands sweat. Nothing for it.

He set his feet and blasted forward with the hardest burst of speed he could muster. His feet pounded the ground. Dust blasted in his wake. He closed distance. Nearer. The figure grew in his vision. Roland's sword was out. Aimee was retreating. Faster. Come on. Faster. Elias's mother's eyes watched him in his mind's eye. Aimee was blown backwards. Hit the ground.

Noble and Brave, Gentle and Kind.

Elias Leblanc slammed his feet down as hard as he could and leaped the last hundred feet. The ground cracked and split in his wake. He took his sword in both hands as he hurtled downwards. There was a blast of thunder as he burst through some unknowable barrier of sound.

"Roland!" he screamed as he descended. "This is for my mother!"

27

ONE DESPERATE SHOT

Earlier

The second Cloud-Cracker tore a massive chunk off the body of the nearest Guild Dreadnought, and the *Elysium* surged downwards, narrowly avoiding a beam many times the smaller skyship's width. Balls of fire taller and bigger than Havensreach's tallest peaks bloomed into the bloodied heavens. "We have to get to the spire," she said to Clutch. "Harkon and I have to get down there somehow."

"Why can't we just turn our guns on that fucking rock tower till it turns to mist?" Vlana yelled above the chaos.

"Because he's engaged in a ritual," Harkon answered, his shield turning aside a blast. "If we blow him up without knowing its contingencies it could accelerate the process to conclusion or unleash magic that could wipe out half the city or any number of worse outcomes." Aimee heard him growl, "I hate ritual magic."

"That spire is right in the middle of a conflagration," Clutch shouted. "We're going to need shielding if we're going to land." The pause was terrible. "Unless we're putting down and staying down, only one of you can go."

"Put us down," Harkon said. "As near to the Spire's base as you can get us."

209

"There's Tireless down there," Clutch said over her shoulder. "We're gonna be wingless gullrats."

Aimee's eyes flashed to Harkon, where he stood at the fore of the bridge. "Aimee," he said. "Get to the bay."

She felt a rush, a combination of the rabid thirst for revenge and the certainty that she wasn't ready. Couldn't possibly face down the monster alone. "...Teacher," she started.

"I'm going to be right behind you," he said. "I just have to ensure that we're covered while we touch down. Clutch, can you stick close to the spire after we've put down?"

"I can do my damnedest. Might not work for shit," Clutch said "but there're less noble ways to die."

"By far," Harkon answered.

"Just don't stage your own grand finale," Vlana said. "We need you. Both of you."

"Hang on," Clutch said, and the Elysium's nose dipped towards the plains of Aurum. "We're coming in like fire."

The last thing Harkon did was press the Axiom Diamond into her hands. "You're going to need this. Now go."

Aimee's stomach jumped into her throat, and she gripped the rails. It didn't matter how many times Clutch flew low and fast, her gut would never be used to it. Her hands went white-knuckled as visions of a charnel battlefield roared beneath them. A large ship had landed on Lia's Rest, disgorging figures racing across open ground and into the mass of what appeared to be Order Knights. Aimee could barely make sense of it before they were past the melee.

The spire grew in their vision, crowned with coruscating light high above.

"Aimee," Harkon said. "The bay. Now."

She ran the length of the ship, bouncing into walls as the vessel pitched and turned and sped. Loud explosions ripped overhead, and staccato shrieks narrowly missed their silver hull.

She erupted into the cargo bay and for just a moment she was there again, as she had been back at the beginning, moments before descending into the Iron Hulks to face Esric and Malfenshir. The battle where she'd see Elias—truly—for the first time. Her eyes caught sight of his cabin, and the shock of grief mingled with imminent danger sent her adrenaline surging. She was going to fight her way to the top of that spire and kill the bastard before he could touch her home.

The sound of the landing gear lowering ground in her ears and Aimee grabbed the shock-spear she'd taken from the *Iseult* a year ago. A seam of light split the back of the bay as the ramp started to lower and then, just as she had on the Iron Hulk a year and a half ago, Aimee ran down its length and leaped the last few feet down to the dusty ground.

Then a blast of fire tore up the ground a short distance away and the *Elysium* lurched. Aimee summoned a shield to ward off the shower of debris. Her feet tore up furrows in the ground as she was pushed backwards. The ship was warded by Harkon's shield, but it couldn't afford to drop the protection. In an instant, a terrible realization struck the portal-mage's Apprentice: she was going to have to do this on her own.

Looking upwards at the rear gun turret where Bjorn was seated, she started waving the ship off. "Go!" she screamed. "Tell them to go!"

The ship shifted. And then the rear ramp started closing, rising upwards. Aimee watched it go, feeling her hand tense around her weapon. The *Elysium* roared upwards and away, and she turned towards the spire. The first time she had touched the Axiom Diamond a year ago, it had tested her by showing her a spire of dark rock rising from the ground. The spire on Lia's Rest had been warped, twisted and maimed until it now resembled the tower she'd seen under the diamond's influence

"Alright," she breathed. "Make for the stairs."

And then he was there. A figure taller than her, swathed in black armor. A black sword in his fist that glimmered with a pale light. Even if she hadn't seen him before, Aimee would've known him by the cold eyes set in a cruel face. Lord Roland strode casually towards her.

"Miss Laurent," he said. "Welcome."

Aimee's hands flew through the motions of a lightning spell. Roland was nearly upon her before the spell was cast. Ironically this bought her a breath. To avoid being struck, the knight had to twist away at the last second, leaping backwards and veering off the base of the spire before loosing lightning at her so fast that she barely got a shield up in response. The explosive force of his spell sent her propelling backwards. Aimee rolled, feeling her shoulder hit the dirt and trying to maintain her grip on the spear. She came up, weaving a spell of fire with one hand and using the other to channel its release through the point of her weapon, then she swung it like a club as she came up in a crouch. A wave of flames screamed outwards in a semicircle with Aimee as its origin-point. The blaze parted around a sword, and there Roland stood.

"So violent," he said quietly. "I just want to talk."

"I have nothing to say to you," Aimee said, and this time she loosed a stronger Radiance, driven by all her fury and her hate, directly at his center of mass. She saw his eyes widen, and he didn't quite get out of the way. His sidestep caught the edge of the blast on the pauldron of his armor, and She thought she saw the slightest twitch of pain cross his features.

"For a whelp," he continued, "you have spirit at least."

She summoned her shield reflexively, and the impulse saved her life. It flashed into existence just as he summoned that sphere of churning air and ignited it. The resulting explosion struck her defenses so hard that her fingers ached and her shoulders almost collapsed from the effort of trying to hold it together.

Roland blurred through the smoke and shattered her shield with his fist. "The old man has run out of tactics to teach his apprentices, I see."

Aimee felt her balance going, toppling backwards. A sword-blow would come next. She remembered from Elias and Bjorn's lessons. She let herself fall onto her back, weaving the rapid motions of a lightning spell as she went down, then released it with her feet right as she landed. She saw Roland blur backwards and sweep his sword in an arc. He dealt with the spell, but it gave her time to regain her footing with an over the shoulder roll. She grasped for the shock-spear just in time to turn aside an air-splitting cut from Roland's sword. The weapon rattled her down to her feet.

"He taught me plenty," she said through clenched teeth.

His weapon came off and she jumped back just before it lashed through the air in front of her, barely clearing the space. She evaded the cut, but not the crackling burst of exploding air pressure that erupted in its wake. Aimee was blown backwards, the air leaving her lungs in an explosive whuff.

She hit the ground and skidded to a stop, body rolling end over end over end. *Get up. Aimee, get up.*

Aimee forced herself up to one knee. Roland started walking towards her, then started running. She raised her spear. Braced it against the ground and shouted a defiant cry that she was certain would be her last.

There was a deafening boom, and Aimee heard a familiar voice burst her heart with sudden shock and hope.

"Roland! This is for my mother!"

And Elias Leblanc shot downwards like a white-clad meteor from heaven. Roland blurred out of the way and the knight slammed into the ground, his strike obliterating earth and stone and blasting a shockwave outwards. Roland was thrown back, and Elias rose from the crater. He stood tall, clad in white steel from shoulder to boot. His face was resolute, fixed on their mutual enemy with a look both frightened and determined.

God, but he had never looked so beautiful. "You," she almost choked. "You're alive."

"You have to go," he said. "Aimee, get up the spire, Stop Silas. Go."

"I'm not going to lose you again," she said. "Not—"

"No," he said. "You're not. I will find you again, no matter what. Now Go!"

"Azrael," Roland said, and his eyes glinted with a predatory focus. At once, Aimee understood what Elias was doing. She saw his jaw tighten. Saw the fear and the courage on his features.

"You have returned to me," Roland finished

This wasn't going to end well.

But she had to do what she could, because now she was the only one who could even try.

Moving around behind him, aching to take him in her arms, to kiss him one last time, she instead shouted "I'll hold you to that!"

Then she took off, towards the steps of the spire, and began her climb.

The steps ascended slowly, and she could only run so fast. Aimee drove herself forward, as dark waves of crackling magic burst overhead and warships killed and died all over the skies in every direction. Deafening sound was everywhere. She was alone.

And it didn't matter. Maybe she could scuff his ritual circle. Or free Coulton. Or do something. She had to try. She couldn't see the *Elysium* anymore in the clouds or amidst the aerial knife-fight between both fleets. Aimee didn't dare look backwards to see how the battle between Elias and Roland was going. There was only the climb, now. There had to be.

The nearer she drew to the summit, the stranger the sounds. There was the howling of the wind and the cacophony of battle, but also a lower sound. Something she could feel more than hear. She couldn't tell if it was an animal roar or the growl of some distant voice echoing as if from a vast cavern. At once her mind was filled with the image of blackened, twisting roots moving rapidly through the soil. Writhing and dead as they pierced the surface of the earth. Searching. Hungry.

Aimee turned on a reflex to look back at her home, and the vision that greeted her filled her gut with scrambling terror. The smaller isles that had broken off from Lia's Rest now encircled the city, rotating in slow arcs. And from within each of them, an immense, building-dwarfing root of faintly translucent smoke had emerged, curling towards the city walls. Havensreach was like a flower surrounded by flames, and the terrible, sheer presence of the thing that was being turned against her home made her teeth chatter and her legs shake. Aimee had stood before a storm kraken at the edge of the Maelstrom less than a year ago... this was nothing like that. Aimee stopped, leaning on the wall of the Spire, at once frozen with a deep terror that almost pulled her ability to stand from within her.

This is so beyond me. I am not equal to it.

But if she didn't do something, everyone was going to die. She thrust her hand into her pocket to warm it.

And found the Axiom Diamond. *"You need to keep going,"* the voice echoed suddenly in her mind. *"I will be with you, but you have to hurry."*

Aimee pushed herself upright. Kept walking. It felt like an eternity, but suddenly the lip of the apex was above her, and she could hear a voice now, clear above the cacophony of the aerial battle.

"If you had only listened, my king," Silas's voice said. "If you had only tried to understand me, to understand what I am trying to do for our people."

She crept closer, one sweating hand gripping the shock-spear. She couldn't quite pinpoint where he was. Needed to get closer. Down on her hands and knees, now, she inched closer to the ledge as quietly as she could. Silas was rambling again, but this time it didn't sound as if he was speaking to his king.

"No, no, I said that I just need more time. This will finish. You will have everything."

Silence fell, and Aimee pushed her head up the last few inches to bring her eyes over the lip of the spire's flat apex.

At the far end was a throne, and Coulton was chained to it, Oath of Aurum strapped to his side. Silas was on the other end, and Aimee had to suppress a gasp at the sight of him. The blackened veins had transformed into something almost calcified, like black stone stretched across the left side of his face. His robes were ragged and stained with blood, and Aimee's gut lurched when she saw the bodies encircling the ritual circle, arranged in a pattern line a mutilated series of broken roots.

Nothing for it. She had to get on the offensive, right away. Aimee was not one for prayer, especially now that a god threatened her home, dead or otherwise. So instead she put one hand on the Axiom Diamond for fortitude before weaving her fingers in the shape of the best spell she had. Pouring it into the shock-spear, she summoned every ounce of courage that she possessed, and leaped over the edge of the spire's top.

"That's my home, you son of a bitch," she said. Then she loosed the spell with a single word.

"Lightning!"

oulton dreams. The King is chained to a throne in a mockery of his position, perched upon the rock high above Lia's Rest. Every ounce of defiance has been bled from him. Leached by the one he trusted most. Coulton can barely tell one moment from the next. Chained by magic to the Tireless, used by Silas to fuel their commands, he is barely more than a vessel. The King experiences the titanic struggle happening about him, everything from the sorcery to the war in heaven, as a blur of light and sound of which he can barely make sense.

Yet through the haze, he begins to feel a prick of heat. A small spark of flame. And the King's mind lights, bit by bit. Something is happening. Something so immense that even the most wounded of minds cannot sit out the struggle and maintain conscience. Even the beckoning siren call of oblivion cannot hold in the face of transpires before him. Elias Leblanc battles on the Plains of Aurum and Coulton feels it as a tangible thing, as if it were unfolding directly in front of him.

And strapped to his hip, Oath of Aurum begins to shake in its sheath.

The King is exhausted beyond measure. He hears the sounds of battle, of catastrophic conflict shaking floating earth and expansive sky. It is all too much to process. The chains upon his mind pull him downwards, bidding him sleep off pain and confusion. Offering him the comforting darkness of oblivion.

"Brother."

The kings eyes open, and for the first time it is neither Silas, nor struggle, nor the endless expanse that he sees.

It is Collum. The brother he lost. The King who never was. And Coulton's parched lips part, a hundred apologies wanting to tumble forth from his mouth. He has come so far, destroyed so much in his ignorance and in his youth and in his fear.

"Brother," he cries. "I am so sorry. All of this is my fault." He croaks and sobs and the tears won't stop coming. "I was a coward," he chokes. "What have I done? I have never been brave when it mattered."

An eruption of color and terrible light blasts through the sky above him, and Coulton's eyes are wide with horror.

And Collum's hands slowly reaches out, resting on the young King's shoulder. Coulton doesn't know if it is a dream. The words, however, are real enough. The dead prince's eyes are full of pain and sadness.

And hope.

"Be brave now," he says.

Coulton can feel Oath of Aurum rattling at his side, now. Insistent. Tugging away from him. "How?"

"There is a saying our father was fond of," Collum says. "Do you remember it? A true King is not a master. A true King is a servant. A true King," he pauses, "is a sacrifice."

Coulton's eyes close. And he feels his brother's hands upon his shoulders. "Let go, brother."

The King draws in a breath. Oath of Aurum rattles violently in its scabbard, and Coulton feels its tiny connection to him. His own grief, holding what does not belong to him in place. And he feels something else: the Tireless, moving at Silas's command. Through him. Another order echoes in his head, and he knows at once what his brother means.

A true King is a Sacrifice.

He just has to time this moment right. He needs Silas distracted. Needs a breath to summon what will he has remaining to him.

And then Aimee de Laurent clears the lip of the apex of the tower, screaming her battle cry. Coulton feels Silas's focus suddenly shift. He closes his eyes, lets go of Oath of Aurum. And the sword rips free from its scabbard and hurtles through the air.

The King takes a deep breath as a battle of terrible sorcery breaks out mere feet away from him and screams a single command to all the Tireless to which he is connected. He cannot end the violence, but he can end his part in it.

"Stop!"

28

ONE LIGHT IN THE DARK

His hands shook, sweating inside his gauntlets as he gripped the sword, fear and determination a mingled tonic that felt as if it would rattle him to pieces. Elias stared down Roland, hoping that Aimee had managed to get clear.

"What," Roland said, staring at him with a casual smile. "So silent? Have you no words for your father?"

Ice crept down Elias's neck. Every blow. Every word of rebuke. Every ounce of a dark and horrific upbringing was racing through the front of his mind. His legs felt frozen to the spot.

"You," he managed. "Are not my father."

Roland rolled his eyes with absolute confidence. "Azrael," he soothed. His feet took him in a slow arc that forced Elias to shift his position to stay facing him. "I am as near to one as you have ever had. Who watched over you, day and night, lovingly molded you into the paragon of greatness you became? Come home, child. You've been errant for long enough."

Elias felt the fear freezing him. Felt his will crumbling like so much gauze in the face of a flame. Cold and hot at once. Unable to escape and desperate to hold his ground. "You mistake freedom for errantry," he finally said, and his voice sounded stronger than he felt. "And with respect," his enunciation was perfect. "Stop using that name. I am Elias Leblanc, and I am no son of yours."

Roland's lip curled. Elias felt the weight of the other man's presence abruptly upon him. The power of his will a tangible force. **"Yield,"** Roland commanded.

He almost did it. The power of the word swept across his mind, finding the cracks in his resolve. He felt his arm slackening. Felt the strength of his legs beginning to buckle. In his mind's eye, he sank to the ground, kneeling before the master he could not defy.

Noble and Brave, Gentle and Kind.

"No!" Elias exploded forward and cut at Roland's head as hard and fast as he could. "Never again!"

Roland's eyes widened just slightly. Then he was moving. Their swords met as each leaped from the ground, and the resulting clash sent them rebounding away from one another, half bellow and half shriek. Elias had barely a breath before his former teacher was upon him. Their swords rang together. Twisted at one another. Edges snagged and snaked and feet shifted and churned up dirt. For a moment they strove as each tried to leverage the bind. The ground cracked, then cratered beneath their feet.

Then they split apart, and Roland stood, sword held loosely in one hand. "You sly boy," he said. "You found a teacher."

"Who taught you to hate this much?" Belit's words from a year ago echoed in his mind. Roland knew his every move, except what he'd practiced for those few weeks with her. Except for what he'd learned from Bjorn. Except, perhaps, for what he'd read in the manual of the Varengard sword-style.

"I found purpose," Elias answered. "Something you never gave me."

This time Roland's expression twitched, a hint at what lay beneath the false calm that Elias recognized all too well. There was a momentary tic as his only warning, then Roland exploded forward. Elias jumped back. He had to get the monster away from the spire. Had to—

Roland smashed into the ground in the middle of the space he'd just occupied, and the shockwave of his impact drove Elias back so hard that he flew through the air. His body rotated end over end, and he saw the ground shrink away before he could process what was happening.

He was mid-air when Roland burst upwards from the crater and leaped skyward. "I will teach you," he snarled, driving a fist into Elias's breastplate, "to mind your tongue."

Elias summoned his durability. It was all that kept him alive. The force of the impact echoed with a horrible bang from high in the air, and he was being propelled downwards again. He was out of control. Airborne.

But so was his enemy. Elias brought his hand on-line as the wind whipped past his ears, and screamed in defiance as he shot a bolt of lightning ripping upwards at the foe who couldn't dodge him.

It struck Roland full in the chest a breath before Elias hit the ground. Even with his durability keeping him from splattering on the earth, he still lost nearly all his breath. He rolled onto his side, gasping. Couldn't see Roland through the dust cloud.

He saw a rising silhouette through the cloud and charged towards it. Roland readied his sword as Elias bore down on him, and they crashed together with a deafening clang. Elias swept back, hammering aside Roland's counterstroke and trying to make space for a spell. It did not appear, and they struggled about each other, churning up dust and ripping through the air with sword strokes that made thunder with sparking specks of dirt.

Elias could feel the rhythm of the battle as a tangible thing through the overloaded rush of his senses. Roland was nowhere and everywhere at once, overwhelming and inexorable. Elias leaped back, making space to redirect the fight. He blasted the ground between them before Roland could close the distance and angled their battle further away from the spire. Into the open ground, where he could move. Roland bore down upon him and the resulting storm of cuts burned away all conscious thought.

Through the haze of exertion and dancing swords, A single impression crystalized in the back of Elias's furiously focused mind: he was not ready for this. Outmatched and outmaneuvered. His skill was a patchwork built on the frame of a shaking spirit. His enemy was relentless. Confident and powerful, and not yet past his prime. A shadow and a storm with a sword in its hand.

Bit by bit, the shadow and the storm were overwhelming him.

The darkness abruptly blotted out all daylight, and both men risked a glance up just in time to watch as the burning frame of a collapsing Guild Dreadnought fell out of the sky on top of them.

The body of the gigantic warship split apart as it fell, spilling wreckage and belching fire. Elias put on a burst of speed, only to feel Roland catching up. He twisted as he ran, barely parrying the cut that dropped down upon him and kicking off a piece of wreckage that slammed into the surface, blasting earth in all directions. His momentum carried him end over end, and if it weren't for his armor and his own mystically enhanced durability, the next impact would've shattered his legs. This time Roland landed too close for him to evade, and as the vessel hammered into the ground, Elias took a kick to the chest that sent him smashing backwards into the hull of the broken vessel.

He burst through the wall, trailing fire and debris, through the ruined, corpse-like interior of the obliterated vessel. He hit the far wall, caving in steel and cracking a rib in his back. He coughed for breath, his entire chest burning with a wet, cracking pain. He dropped to one knee on the broken floor. There were screams everywhere, mingled with the sounds of breaking machinery and a ruined hull on the verge of collapsing into itself. Elias's borrowed sword was notched in a dozen places and he had no notion of how much longer it would hold together. Out. He had to get out.

Roland slow-walked through the flames towards him, the fire parting at his will. "Amazing," his one-time master sneered. "To think you threw away everything I gave you, to become this. You can barely stand against me. How broken are you now, boy? Are you ready to return to the fold, yet? Or do I have to keep beating it into you until you pass out and drag your body to an Iron Hulk for reconditioning?"

Elias coughed painfully, still down on one knee. The shadow and the storm loomed over him now. Roland's will once more pushed down like a lead weight. The notched sword felt heavy in his hands and his breathing was labored.

"I," he managed finally, "could have a thousand choices for a thousand years...and still, I would never choose you."

Elias's sword hand began to tingle. It was minuscule at first. A subtle warmth in the center of his palm, but as he spoke the words it grew. And at once his mind was filled with a mental picture so clear that the under-standing was immediate. A chance. A *chance.*

Roland stared down at him as the words landed. His face was utterly blank. Almost unseeing, and Elias felt himself being stared through. As if the man before him looked at a vision behind his back.

The burning in his hand was so intense he could no longer hold onto his borrowed weapon. It started to slip from his fingers. Twenty or so feet above them was a rent in the hull of the vessel, edged in fire. Above it, Elias could see sky.

"You," Roland's voice had suddenly dropped lower, its edge turned nearly feral, "arrogant, petulant little cunt."

He felt the blow coming. What he was about to do would cost him, but it was his best shot at making this fight last. Roland's sword swept down, and Elias pushed off with his foot, leap-rolling sideways, dropping his sword with his right hand as it passed beneath him and reverse-gripping it with his left. Roland's steel sparked off the floor, leaving him open and Elias landed on his right foot, calling on his speed and surging up.

The borrowed sword swept upwards reversed, the pommel catching Roland under his chin and knocking his whole body backwards. That crack would've pulverized anyone's spine, but Elias knew his one-time teacher would survive it. Still. Bent backwards was all he needed. As he moved upwards he planted his other boot on Roland's chest and hammered down with every ounce of power he had as he let go of his weapon.

Noble and Brave, Gentle and Kind.

There was a cratering boom, and Elias shot skyward. He passed through the nimbus of fire. Soared higher. He had seconds before his teacher would follow. Desperately hoped this would work.

One light in the dark, keeping the demons at bay.

From atop the spire, a golden bolt of light streaked towards him through the air. There was a crashing sound from below, and Roland hurtled upwards after him, his sword ripping the air apart as it sheared upwards.

Not for the fight that brings certain victory
But for the fight that must be fought,

The bolt flashed into Elias's hand, and with the familiar warmth flowing through him, the white knight twisted mid-air and met the sweeping upward cut with the glittering blade of Oath of Aurum.

The resulting shockwave blew them in different directions. Elias hit the ground and bounced, barely keeping his breath as he rolled, came up in a crouch, and skidded to a halt, casting around for his enemy.

Roland emerged from the dust and the chaos, walking now. He stopped perhaps twenty feet back, and his eyes were different. The false veneer had been stripped away. Before Elias was a feral man with wide eyes and a blazing nimbus of power so potent that it almost pushed Elias back.

"You ungrateful child," he snarled. "Bastard waste of flesh. After everything I gave you, you throw it away for a prophecy and a bitch in a blue coat. So be it. I will teach you consequence. I will break every bone in your body, and make you watch as I visit special torments on every member of your crew." He gestured at Elias up and down with his blade. "I think I'll start with your neck."

Elias raised Oath of Aurum. He didn't give a shit about prophecies, and for the first time in forever, he didn't give a shit about threats. The warmth of the blade calmed his fear as chaos reigned in the heavens. "You'll try."

They met in the air. Steel crashed and screamed, and Elias gave ground. Away from the Spire. As far as he could get them. It didn't matter if he lost. If in the end his enemy hammered him into the dirt and broke his spine or carved his heart from his chest. What mattered was that he do what he set out to do: face Lord Roland on the open field and keep him from interfering in the confrontation that really mattered.

Save Havensreach.

Save the *Elysium*.

Save Coulton.

Live.

I made her a promise.

Elias checked a cut and twisted in for the thrust. Roland turned it aside before it could reach his face and tried to lever the blade out of Elias's hand. The white knight swept his foot back and grabbed Roland's arm in turn. They grappled and strained. Then Roland overextended himself. He was too close to use the sword, so Elias grabbed his arm and levered him into an over the shoulder throw that sent him rolling. Elias couldn't cut quick enough, and the force of his blow tore a three-foot deep trough into the rock. Roland was on him again, and this time Elias's parry fell short. The shadow's sword slammed into his breastplate. The armor stopped it, but cutting through the metal was never his enemy's intent.

Roland loosed a spell—something similar to his sphere of exploding air—and an explosion struck Elias's body full-on. He felt a cascade of pops burst through his body and he hurtled backwards, barely summoning his durability in time to keep from being completely dashed on an outcropping of rock that stopped his flight. The stone cracked and burst apart behind him. Elias dropped down to the ground from midway up the crumbling stone and spit blood into the dirt. His breath came in painful gasps, now. Multiple ribs broken. Probably bleeding badly beneath the armor. He could barely keep his aching hands on the sword. Roland suddenly stood over him.

"What a putrid waste," the dread lord of ashes said. "I suppose I'll need two demons to control you, next time."

Elias raised his eyes. His enemy was backlit by the sun, only his terrible eyes visible amidst the shadow. He'd done all he could, and it still wasn't enough.

Then a blazing burst of light erupted from the top of the spire, ripping outwards in all directions. Roland's eyes abruptly widened.

"You," Elias cough-laughed. "Are so predictable, teacher. All that strength. All that power, and you still don't get it. This was never about you."

Roland's face turned fully towards the spire, and he let out a roaring scream. "No!"

Elias saw his chance and took it. His hand grasped around Oath of Aurum's hilt and his mind seized on the words he desperately needed. *One light in the dark, keeping the demons at bay.*

He swung his sword upwards at Roland's face, as hard and as fast as he could.

Roland saw it coming. Pivoted backwards with a blur that was frighteningly fast…but not quite fast enough. He evaded the worst of the blow, sparing his life, but the point of the gleaming sword traced a line across his face, cutting him from his left cheek, across the bridge of his nose, to just above his right eye.

Elias fell sideways from the effort. Couldn't force himself up. Roland staggered, screaming, then pointed at Elias with his right hand, still shrieking obscenities. Light gathered around his outstretched fingertips. This was it.

A massive beam of light slammed into Roland from their right. It hit the Dread Lord of Ashes with a terrible flash and a deafening bang, and Elias watched as his one-time teacher was hurtled backwards through the cloud of dust and towards the wreckage of the dreadnought.

The *Elysium* descended from the sky like a silver, avenging angel. In the rear gun bubble, Elias glimpsed Bjorn's face.

"Bet it takes you a bit to get up from that one, you son of a bitch."

A seam of light split the rear of the ship, and the ramp slammed down. Vlana came running down the gangway, a rope tied around her waist and secured in the hold far behind her. She slipped an arm under Elias's right side and with a grunt, hauled him to his feet. "Come on," she said. "Please tell me you can walk."

"That won't kill him," Elias choke-coughed as he let her haul him to his feet, limping and leaning on her shoulder. "We have to get away from here. Now."

"That's why we gotta hurry," the quartermaster said. "Come on, hero. It's time to get going." She grabbed the speaking tube. "I've got him! Go!" The bay door slammed closed, and the roar of the engines filled Elias's ears as the ground fell away behind them.

2 9

ATOP THE BLACKENED SPIRE

Silas summoned a shield surrounding him from all angles. Aimee saw what was coming and summoned one of her own before the lightning bolt glanced off it. *Keep your focus. Stay on him.*

They faced one another across the expanse, Coulton on his throne between them. Aimee took in the state of the king, and for the first time since they'd accepted the mission from Alahna, Aimee felt a spike of pity for the younger man.

Nobody deserved whatever had been done to him.

"The gall of you to show me your face, de Laurent," Silas spat. "The sheer cheek to imagine that you have any right to stand in my presence after everything you did to my people."

Aimee turned as he moved, trying to keep her eyes on him while also assessing the ritual circle. *Remember,* she thought. *Killing him is nothing if we can't stop whatever he's trying to do.*

"I didn't do anything to your people," she said. "You're fucking insane."

Silas's face twitched and he took two steps forward before unleashing a massive column of fire directly at her shield. "Didn't do anything? Didn't do **anything?**"

The fire wreathed around her, blazing past her and making her sweat. Aimee's shield held.

"You stole the Diamond!" Silas bellowed. "You took our people's sacred property, after promising to help us! You spared the life of the monster that destroyed our kingdom, then you **gave him a place on your crew!**"

The flames intensified, and Aimee had trouble keeping her feet. She dug her boots into the stone, sweating. Silas's flames died, as if he'd run out of breath. Before she could properly shift her posture, he sent out a lance of crackling darkness. She dropped her shield, redirecting it sideways into the oncoming spell as she dashed right, out of the way. Silas was already raising his hands by the time she landed, too fast for her to weave a spell of her own.

But not too fast to use the weapon in her hand. She gripped the shock-spear and sent a crackling bolt of static straight at her enemy. Silas batted it out of the way with a swat, but he couldn't summon another spell before she sent another bolt his way. She had four more charges before this thing ran out. Silas stepped back and swatted it away again, and this bought Aimee enough time to dash behind one of the pillars on the surface of the dais. A bolt of lightning bisected around it from the other side, and she heard her enemy screaming obscenities. She leaned on her shock-spear, breathing hard as a bolt of fire struck the rock behind her. And then another. The stone at her back slowly heated up.

She tossed a glance over her shoulder, daring to peek. Two more pillars of this same obsidian colored rock rose behind Silas at the far end of the ritual circle. As reflective as those were, she wondered...*fuck!*

Aimee noticed the spell almost too late. A flat disk of shadow lanced towards her, whirling through the air. She barely pulled back, so narrowly escaping that she felt the frigid razor ghost against the side of her neck. Her head got suddenly lighter and there was a splash of blood. She pulled back behind the pillar and reflexively touched her neck. The cut wasn't deep, but her hand came away red...and her braid lay on the stone a foot away, perfectly sliced from the rest of her hair. Too close. She was shaking now. With fear. With shock. With the terror that she wasn't equal to this.

"*Aimee,*" the voice was suddenly in her head. "*Aimee, listen to me.*"

She sucked in a breath, recognizing the voice of the Axiom Diamond.

"If you're going to help me," she breathed, "please no riddles. I'm going to die here if I fuck up. Not just me, but me and everyone else."

"*You are dealing with a man riddled with grief that has turned his soul bleak and cold, If you want to defeat him, you must destroy his ability to focus.*"

"I'm going to take everything away from you, Aimee," Silas snarled beyond the pillar. "Your love. Your ship. Your home. I lost everything in

Port Providence, and you will know my pain." She felt another spell hit the back of the pillar. "Do you understand now?" Silas roared. "Do you?"

Aimee closed her eyes.

"Answer him." The Diamond said. *"I know it is difficult, but nothing disrupts the flow of the mind like words."*

A breath out followed. Aimee opened her eyes, clenched her fist so tightly that it hurt, and answered.

"No," she said. "I don't."

Silence greeted her. She took another deep breath and kept going. "I'm a privileged brat," she said. "I was a rich child who got whatever she wanted growing up. I've never known want and I've never known true peril before this past year." She started weaving a spell in her hands. "You've suffered beyond what any person should have to suffer, and you've been faced with trials I can't even begin to fathom."

She needed him off balance. There wasn't going to be any margin for error when she did this. She was going to have to prep the spell, turn, look, and loose in the same moment.

"But that doesn't mean," she said, "that you're free from responsibility for your actions. Pain doesn't make you a saint, Silas. And it doesn't excuse what you've done." She forced her voice even. "And it doesn't mean that you have a right to kill millions of people."

Aimee held the summoned spell in her aching fingers. This was a one in a million shot. She couldn't do anything to him from far away. Not without careful work to throw him. She pivoted her foot and swung out from the opposite side of the pillar. Silas's body was angled slightly away from her. She sighted her target and loosed the spell in the same breath. "Radiance!"

The beam shot over Silas's shoulder. He laughed.

It struck the mirror-like obsidian surface of the pillar behind him, ricochetted off, and struck him full in the back. Silas stopped laughing. He lurched forward with a cry of pain. Whatever magic connection he had with the Twelfth Night clearly made him vulnerable to the spell, but he was still mortal enough that she couldn't tell how badly it hurt him. It didn't matter. She didn't need the spell to kill the old man, and an old man was precisely what Silas was.

She needed him to hold still long enough for her to close the distance and beat the shit out of him with her bare hands.

Silas lurched forward and started to straighten right as Aimee's fist smashed into his face. At the same moment, Oath of Aurum ripped free from Coulton's side and hurtled through the air and into the distance.

Silas's head cracked to the side as Aimee laid into him. He staggered back, raising a hand to blast a spell at her. She sidestepped as Bjorn had taught her and smashed the shock-spear into his hand, sending the blast veering into the distance. His other hand swept upwards at her face. She dropped her weight underneath as a burst of darkness crackled above her head, then she drove upwards with an uppercut underneath his jaw. She wasn't the best hand to hand combatant. Wasn't anywhere near the boxer of her teachers, but Silas was old, and she was young, and if you needed to stop someone thinking, nothing worked better than a fist to the face.

Silas twisted away, but this time he managed to loose another cutting spell. Aimee got the shock-spear up between them. It stopped the spell with its innate enchantments, but the head burst apart in a shower of sparks, leaving her holding a rod of inert metal. Better than nothing. In the end a cudgel was still a cudgel. She closed with him again, and this time she pulled the stave between the two of them and rammed the broken end into the center of his chest. It struck something neither flesh nor garment, clinking off a hard and jagged surface.

This time Silas screamed in pain, and as his robes fell aside Aimee saw the jagged protrusion of a black stone jutting from the center of his chest.

"That is the source of his power," the diamond said in her mind. *"The manifestation of his connection to the Twelfth Night. Separate it from him and he's finished."*

"Will doing that kill him?"

"Very possibly."

"Fine by me."

She sidestepped as Silas summoned flames beneath her feet. No time for another spell. She didn't have the space or the time. She leaped off the fire, feeling it singe her boots, and swung the broken shock-spear at his head like a bat. The impact into the stone-encrusted side of his face rattled up her arm, and he staggered.

"Come-on!" she shouted. "How many times do I have to fucking hit you before you go down?"

Silas spit blood and reached up with his hand, grabbing the stave in a stone-crusted hand. "You don't get it!" he growled. "I am utterly beyond you, child. Now die!"

She realized what he was going to do a half breath before he did it. Just enough time. As Silas poured the lightning directly into the rod in her hand, her other hand swept through a single gesture of channeling, releasing the spell with a whispered word. The shock jolted through her. Made her hair stand on end, and she felt her heartbeat hammer unevenly through her shaking chest. She couldn't let go with her right hand, and the searing pain of the electric shock blazed across her body and burned her fingers. Aimee screamed as the charge traveled along the angles of her body, moving up one arm, across her back, and through the other before she swung her hand forward and slammed it into the stravrophore's chest. Her fingers grasped at the gem, and she let the magic go, turning it back onto its source with a shrieking crack.

Silas opened his mouth in a wordless shriek, his whole body going rigid and his back arching. Aimee let go of the staff with a cry of pain and slammed her other hand into his chest, grasping at the jagged jewel and pulling with all her might. It moved. Silas's body jerked violently. Aimee lifted her leg and jammed her boot into his middle, giving one last straining effort.

It ripped free in a splatter of blood and a burst of darkness that sent her hurtling backwards, landing painfully on the dais and rolling over twice, nearly pitching off the edge of the spire's apex. As she scrambled into a crouch, she watched as Silas staggered. The sage stood, a gaping, horrific wound in his chest. The jewel lay between them. He lifted a hand as if to cast a spell, and nothing happened.

"You," he choked. "You can't. You can't stop it. Nothing can."

He dropped to one knee. "Can't stop."

"Can't stop."

"Can't."

"Ca—"

The sage fell sideways and lay still. His lips kept moving for a moment. Then he was gone. Aimee looked down. Her coat and clothes were covered in blood and scorched holes. Her right palm was burned red and raw and bloody, and moving her fingers hurt.

She was bleeding from the side of her neck, but it wasn't severe. Staggering forward, she fell to her knees at the edge of the ritual circle as the aerial battle played out. By the blessings of whatever gods watched over them, the Guild was in retreat, moving away from the forward roll of Belit's flotilla.

The circle pulsed with light. Half of it was in a language she couldn't read, but the essence of it was apparent after a few moments of study. Aimee's chest froze and her eyes raised to distant Havensreach, surrounded by a rising mass of titanic, ink-dark roots.

Silas was right.

She couldn't stop this. The circle was powered by dozens of other circles, each on one of the small stone outcroppings floating about the city. Each one of those independently strong and watched over by one of the Tireless.

Aimee turned to look at the barely sensate form of the King on his throne. She could feel the connection between the King and his automatons. Her stomach turned. Should she kill him? Was that the only option? "How do I stop this?" she helplessly murmured out loud.

"You can't," the voice of the Axiom Diamond was sad.

"What?" she gasped. "No, no no no I have to, I have to—"

"Aimee," the voice continued. *"You cannot stop it because it is not your job."*

And as she looked at the King on his throne, her mouth opened, and she took several halting steps forward. "Coulton," she said, reaching for the king. "Coulton, please, wake up."

He didn't respond, and abruptly her world was filled with light. Running lights, sweeping across the apex of the spire as a silver ship descended from the sky.

The *Elysium* was here.

30

THE LAST KING

Elias limped toward the lowering ramp. The brief healing Harkon had given him had taken the edge off his wounds, but he still moved painfully. One hand clutched Oath of Aurum, welcoming the balm that he'd missed. Booted steps took him down the ramp and then he was faced with the aftermath of whatever had just happened.

Aimee was alive, though a hairline cut dripped blood down her neck and her hair had been chopped off below the chin. Silas's corpse lay a short distance away, and Elias paused for just a moment to stare at the man who had done so much to him, and to whom he had done so much. He didn't feel grief, exactly, or rage or pain. Just weight.

Just resignation.

So. That's done.

Aimee turned towards them as Elias descended the ramp. Her face was a mask of horror. "I can't stop it," she said. "Harkon, I don't know how,"

Harkon walked past Elias towards the circle. It crackled, unstable. High over Havensreach a warship attempted to fire on the sky-rending roots reaching up to envelop the city. The appendage swatted it in half with an explosion that rained wreckage into the abyss.

Elias turned and looked at the King and his heart sank into his feet. Coulton was emaciated, bound by chains to the chair into which Elias had put him by killing Collum a year ago. And even though Silas was the one who had done this to the boy, who had twisted the boy and abused him into this position…without Elias, none of this would have happened at all. Without him, none of this would've been possible.

Helena was saying something, her tone alarmed. Harkon was talking behind them, and the ritual circle was pulsing with light. Elias walked across the apex of the spire towards the throne, and got down on his knee, bringing him eye level with the boy-king.

He'd promised Alahna. He'd promised.

"Coulton," Elias said, tentatively touching the King's hand. His voice broke. "I'm so, so sorry."

"It's tied to the other isles," Aimee was saying behind him. "And each of those has a Tireless watching over it. There isn't time to shoot any of them down. Certainly not enough."

"I can't break what's been set in motion," Harkon breathed, and Elias had never heard his voice sound so heavy. Still he stared at where Coulton sat, and the wind blew across the spire with the cruel weight of a world's ending.

"Majesty?" Helena's voice was tentative. One aged hand reaching out to touch the King's …and then his eyes opened.

"I… can…" he croaked.

Helena froze, and Elias felt his gut constrict painfully.

"…What?" Helena asked.

"I can…stop it." Coulton's cracked lips moved. "Just need…help getting out of this chair."

Harkon and Aimee had turned. The group of them were a blasted, soot-stained rabble mired in blood and battle-damage. Before Coulton could get another word out, Elias drew Oath of Aurum and severed his chains with the magic sword. Coulton sagged forward and Helena caught him. The King grunted in pain and breathed hard before slowly straightening, leaning on his grandmother's champion.

"What are you talking about?" Harkon said.

Aimee looked at Elias, then at the king, and he felt the sudden devastation in her voice as she spoke.

"…The Tireless," she said. "He can command them."

"The circles are empowered, now," Harkon said, his brows drawing together. "Even if the automatons were able to start destroying them, the ritual is too far along to disrupt by—"

Coulton coughed. "Silas was very clear in his ranting. I couldn't stop this without giving a command I wasn't prepared to give." He took a deep, obviously pained breath. "I'm prepared now."

Elias understood what he meant before anyone else. If his body was connected to the Tireless, if his life-force flowed through them... the feedback of that much destruction all at once would be unsustainable. Even at full health and in peak physical condition, there was no way Coulton would survive it.

"Coulton," Elias said. "...This will kill you."

Another sound echoed behind them and turning, Elias watched as a second ship lowered itself towards the spire. This one was older, battered. One of the gunboats attached to the Iseult, its sides pockmarked with blast scars and battle damage. It landed at the spire's edge and a new ramp lowered, Rachim emerging with a cluster of Belit's soldiers. The one-eyed politician took in the scene before him, then fell silent, holding up a hand for his men to lower their weapons.

The King looked up at Elias, and in his blue eyes the white knight saw a world of possibility expressed in a glance. So many things yet to see, yet to do. And all of it about to be willfully snuffed out.

"One person for several million seems like a fair trade to me, doesn't it?"

Elias couldn't disagree. There was no way to argue with that level of calculus.

"I can command the Tireless to destroy themselves," Coulton continued, addressing Harkon now. "All of them will self-destruct next to their circles. Will that...will that be enough to stop this?"

Harkon looked as if he had aged a hundred years in the span of a moment. He was quiet for a long time as Elias watched, then he said "Yes, that should do it."

"What will the backlash do to the city?" Aimee asked, looking at her teacher.

"Nothing," Harkon said quietly. "If the ritual circle's power breaks, the Twelfth Night will lose its point of contact with the city. It's not physically here. It's still trapped in its own tomb dimension, deep within the Maelstrom."

"How long do you need, boy?" Rachim broke his silence. "And do you need any help that we can give?"

"I just..." Coulton leaned heavily on Helena's arm. "I just wish I had the chance to see my people again. To know what happened to them."

"I can answer that well enough," Rachim said. "Flotilla Visramen picked them up, shortly after the White Chalice made contact with us. Your people are safe, Majesty. They are taken care of."

Coulton sagged against Helena. Then he squared his shoulders with resolve and said, "Help me to the circle."

Every step appeared another effort. Elias stepped under Coulton's other arm and the King leaned on him, spreading his weight between both his carriers until they reached the edge of the crackling circle. There the young King stood, and Elias heard him murmur under his breath "A King is a sacrifice."

"My King," Helena said quietly. "I will not tell you not to do this, but you grandmother will grieve beyond words."

"Convey my best wishes to her," Coulton breathed. "Along with how very, very sorry I am. She warned me, and I did not listen."

Elias couldn't keep the words in, any longer. They tumbled out, one after the other in a jumble. "If it weren't for me, you never would have been in this position," he said. "I did not do what Silas did, but had I not done the wrongs to you and your people that I have done, you never would've been set upon this path."

Coulton slowly turned to look at him, and the younger man's blue eyes were pained. Filled with resignation and fear. He could've rebuked Elias or forgiven him in equal measure, but neither of those things came out of his mouth. Instead, the seventeen-year-old boy who was about to die simply asked, "Will you stay with me?"

Elias felt his heart constrict, and he closed his eyes, tears stinging at their corners. Then he took a heavy breath and answered, "Till the end."

Coulton closed his eyes, and Elias felt the King's hand tighten against the pauldron on his shoulder. Coulton looked down, body sagging beneath the weight of the magic to which his one-time-teacher had irrevocably shackled him. Then, just when it seemed as if he would collapse, he straightened, and stared into the distance. His eyes locked upon the sunset painting the embattled heavens the color of blood and treasure. Then, as he stared, his breathing hastened, a rasping sound heavy in his chest. A golden light blazed from his eyes, and his teeth set with the signs of obvious strain.

One by one, every one of the severed isles encircling Havensreach began to glow. Columns of golden light lanced into the skies. Coulton's breathing was labored now, his body shaking. "Brother," Elias heard him say. "Brother, I'm coming."

Coulton's body became an outline of incandescent light, and the root of every glimmering column burst in crackling waves of cascading fire.

The ritual circle snapped and cracked. Faded, glowed, then faded again. The heat at Elias's side was almost too much to bear.

There was a flash, and then the King was gone.

Elias heard a roar echo from somewhere far away, distant, terrible, and frustrated beyond words.

The roots surrounding Havensreach vanished. The light of the ritual circle died.

Between Elias and Helena, Coulton's crown dropped and fell to the ground with a clang that might as well have been a gong. It rolled a short distance away, then it lay still.

3 1

BLOOD FOR A STONE

Aimee knelt at the edge of the deadened circle, and for the first time since fighting Roland, cast her eyes over the plains of Aurum, where a battle had unfolded and the field was littered with dead and ships crouching like vultures.

Near as she could tell, the Eternal Order was evacuating, and the silver hawk of the White Chalice ship still stood, an island in the sea of chaos.

Then she heard the whispers. Almost at the edge of hearing. Aimee staggered for a moment, catching herself on her teacher's shoulder with her good hand. She pressed a hand to her forehead as words murmuring in a scratchy, distant voice grated across her thoughts.

Then she heard the much clearer, calmer voice of the Diamond. *"It is exactly as you fear."*

Turning slowly, and realizing that Harkon was moving the same way, Aimee lowered her eyes until they fell upon the jewel she'd pulled from Silas's chest.

She took a step towards it, not realizing until she'd taken another that her hand was reaching out.

"Don't touch it," the voice suddenly cut across her thoughts. *"Aimee, I am a font of thousands of years of collected knowledge, and I don't know what that is."*

Aimee's perception snapped back into focus and she realized she was already down on one knee reaching out. Her hand recoiled as if struck.

Just behind her Harkon had brought it up short. Looking at the others he immediately asked, "Can anyone else hear that thing speaking?"

A chorus of worried expressions greeted them. Elias then looked up from his silent contemplation of Coulton's absence. "I...distantly. Until you pointed it out, I didn't realize."

"The diamond doesn't know what it is," Aimee said. "I don't know what it is, just that I almost picked it up without meaning to. That thing cannot go on the *Elysium*. It's a hazard to all three of us."

"It's a hazard to anyone who uses magic and hasn't had the training to resist it," Harkon said.

"I'll take it," Rachim said. "Can I touch the thing without it burning me or hollowing my soul out or some such business?"

"It might be safest aboard the *Iseult*," Harkon nodded. Then he came to an internal decision. "Take it. Get it away from here as fast as possible. Let's clear out, before this spot becomes a target for somebody's aerial guns."

As he spoke, Aimee watched Helena slowly crouch to the ground. All that remained of the King was a burn mark upon the stone and his golden crown, shifting in the wind. Slowly, gingerly, she lifted it in both hands, staring at it with a look of intense, painful grief.

"What should we do with Silas's body?" Aimee tentatively asked. She knew what she'd have done herself, but for better or for worse he had been one of Helena's people. The decision wasn't Aimee's to make.

Helena raised red-shot eyes, the first sign of her own tears, and slowly stared at where the old man's corpse lay across the apex, its hair blowing threadbare across an unseeing face.

"Leave it for whatever beasts roam this place," she said. Then turning, she made her way up the ramp and into the *Elysium*. Bjorn came down the steps inside the cargo hold and started ushering the rest of them up. Harkon walked past him and into the ship, making his way to the bridge. Behind her, Rachim slowly removed a cloth from inside his coat and lifted the dark jewel from the stone beneath him. Aimee looked at Elias. He stood a short distance away, still staring at the burn mark on the edge of the now-defunct ritual circle. A tremor passed beneath their feet, and she had the feeling they needed to move quickly. Crossing the distance, she reached for his right hand with her left, taking the gauntleted fingers in her own.

"There was nothing you could've done," she said. When he didn't respond she pulled on his hand until he turned to look at her, his eyes red-rimmed and tear-stained.

"We did so much," he whispered. "And the one thing I was asked to do. The one thing that put us on this path, I failed."

"Come on," she said, and started to pull him towards the ramp. "We'll talk inside. It's time to go."

He resisted at first, but eventually, at long last, followed. Their boots clanked up the ramp as they entered the cargo hold, and Bjorn signaled the bridge as Vlana appeared at the top of the stairs to the spinal corridor. The *Elysium* rose slowly into the air, and looking behind them, Aimee watched as Rachim and his men started to fall away into the distance. The one-eyed man carried the jewel back towards his ship at a brisk pace.

Then Lord Roland burst over the lip of the spire and rammed his sword through the seneschal's back. Aimee screamed. Roland was like a human scythe. He tore his way through Rachim's men, leaving his first kill to bleed out on the rock. Blood stained his face from a wound stretching from one cheek to above his opposite eye, and it soon mingled with the splattering and the screaming as he carved through every last man on the spire's apex. As Aimee watched in horror, the Dread Lord of Ashes knelt and lifted the jewel from Rachim's dying grasp. Then he raised his eyes to look at the *Elysium* rising into the sky.

And then he leaped. Aimee had proper use of only one of her hands. Hadn't had time to heal herself. He closed the distance in a terrifying burst of speed, landing on the back of the ramp. Elias turned and reflexively fired off a bolt of lightning that whipped past her. Roland parried it and stalked up the ramp as the *Elysium* rose ever higher.

"What was that I promised you again?" Roland addressed his former student. "Ah yes: break every bone in your body and visit special torments on every one of your crew." His eyes were wild, and his footsteps heavy, bloody sword in one hand and jewel in the other. Harkon was on the bridge at the other end of the ship. There was no time. Someone screamed and she didn't know who. Maybe it was even her.

Then there was a blur to her left, as Bjorn came rushing through the cargo hold. She knew what he was doing before it happened, but she couldn't stop it. The old warrior set his shoulder as he ran and slammed into the Dread Lord of Ashes with all his might. The two of them went tumbling backwards, over the lip of the ramp and into the sky, over a thousand feet above the ground far below.

Vlana screamed, and it was unlike any noise Aimee had ever heard.

The horrible, wounded sound of a child losing a parent and a woman losing her best friend all at once. The two of them veered towards the end of the ramp. Aimee glimpsed Roland catch himself on the edge of the spire with one hand, lose his grip, then slam his sword into the stone itself, carving his way down until he came to a stop in a crouch on the spiral stairs winding up its base. They were too high for another leap, now, but Aimee saw his hateful, wide eyes staring up at them.

Bjorn was not so fortunate. The last time Aimee saw her friend's body it was sliding slowly off the apex of the spire, broken like a distant doll, and into the empty air at its far side.

Vlana was near the edge on her hands and knees in the open wind, screaming. "No no no no no no Bjorn, **Bjorn!**"

Aimee wrapped both arms around her crewmate, hauling her backwards kicking and screaming. Vlana was sobbing violently now, her whole body shaking as Aimee turned to Elias. "Close the ramp!"

Elias hammered the switch into place and the ramp began a torturously slow ascent until it slid into place and the terrible sound of the clamps locking in with a hiss filled Aimee's ears.

"Aimee? V?" Clutch's worried voice came through the tubes. "The whole ship just shuddered. What in the abyss happened down there?"

Aimee reached out for the tube, her good hand shaking. Vlana was on her hands and knees, still violently sobbing. Elias leaned against the wall, his eyes wide and staring into nothing. Aimee's voice shuddered and shook.

"I...Roland...jumped onto the ramp. I couldn't. Clutch I couldn't stop him and Bjorn, he..." she couldn't say it. Couldn't make herself say it. That would make it forever real in a way that would leave scars across her heart for the rest of her life.

She didn't need to. The sudden agony in Clutch's voice told her that the message had been understood.

"Oh...oh no..."

"We'll. We'll be up soon," Aimee said. "I..."

She just hung up the receiver. Couldn't say anymore and couldn't bring words to speak. They were moving up and at length she slid down to her knees beside Vlana on the floor. The cargo bay felt cavernous and empty. She wrapped her arms tightly about her friend and after a few moments the sobbing became contagious.

They held together in the empty room and cried together as the ship steadily rose into the heavens.

32

THE END OF THE BEGINNING

After his healing, Elias slept for what felt like three days. He didn't track the rising or setting of the sun, didn't register when one day bled into the next. His room on the *Elysium* was occupied by Alahna still, so he moved himself to Aimee's quarters. Sharing the bed with her calmed some of the terrible guilt wracking him, and they held each other desperately through the night. Pain at their loss and relief at having one another back mingled in a potent tonic, and even sex didn't alleviate everything, though it took the edge off and let them both forget for a little while. Neither of them made it into Havensreach even when awake, and they saw the other crew seldomly.

On the morning of the third day, neither of them could ignore responsibility any longer, and as Aimee rose from the sheets to push aside the blackout curtains that obscured the viewport, Elias slowly sat up, staring at the mirror opposite the bed at his exhausted face and the dark circles under his green eyes.

"We have to go," she finally said, looking over her shoulder at him. She'd since cut her hair short under the top, shaving the sides close but leaving the rest thick. It fell across her eyes in a tangle as she looked at him, and he nodded after a moment.

"Where first?" he asked.

She looked down, clearly thinking, and he thought for a moment about how even through the pain it was beautiful to watch the wheels of her mind work.

"The others first," she said. "We've been hiding long enough. You need to talk to Alahna, and I need..." she sighed. "I need to talk to Harkon and then I need to report to the Academy of Mystic Sciences." She pulled on a robe, but shivered anyway. "And I need to go home. I haven't seen my parents since I left."

He silently nodded, then swung his legs over the edge of the bed. Looking down, Elias stared at the calluses of the hands that had failed to do so much. In his memory he felt the weight of Coulton against his shoulder. It would never, ever leave him. Some part of him would always stand upon the apex of that spire beneath the apocalyptic heavens as the boy he'd vowed to save died in front of him. Every day. Every hour. Every minute.

"Let's go, then." He stood, crossing the distance between them and kissed her. She melted into him for a moment, then they separated and started getting dressed, mostly in silence. At length they stepped out of her quarters and into the ship that was uncomfortably quiet.

Bjorn's absence was everywhere. As tangible as the pots and pans in the unoccupied galley. Elias stopped in the doorway at the sound of a small mew, and found Francesco the squitten slowly circling the air, looking for the man he'd made a habit of annoying since he first arrived on the ship.

And Vlana. The quartermaster was very carefully cleaning one of the old warrior's pots, left with the remnants of the last dinner he'd cooked. Her hands moved a brush back and forth over the metal in a thoughtless pattern. "He," she started. "He was always so fastidious. I just needed to see it clean. I needed." She put the brush down and took a shuddering breath, not looking at either of them.

Elias wasn't sure what to say. Some part of him believed that it should've been him leaping out the back of the ship and into the open sky, but the old warrior had beaten him to the punch, never hesitating to protect his family.

Never once.

"I'm sorry," Elias finally said. It felt so empty.

Vlana was silent for a long moment, still not turning. Just when Elias was about to excuse himself, she said in a very small voice "I hated you for a long time. This ship is my family—my only family—and you were an outsider. You tried to kill us."

Elias closed his eyes. Took a breath. "I know."

She was quiet for another painful moment, then she slowly turned and looked at him with red-rimmed eyes. "I was wrong, Elias." A pause followed. Then she said "And I'm done hating you. My family has…gotten smaller," her voice was pained. "But the truth is… you're a part of it. I'm not going to live the rest of my life hating people my friends love. And I'm not going to waste the time I have left with the people I still have."

She hesitated for a moment, then looked at him, and slowly extended her hand. Elias took it, letting out a quiet breath. She gripped his fingers. Then he said, "Family."

The memorial for the Battle of Havensreach, as it was being called, was held a day later, at sunset. Elias was moving better, by then. And as he exited the *Elysium* in the company of her remaining crew, he was greeted by the sight of the skydocks stretching as far as the eye could see, lit by so many floating lanterns that the base of the walls was an ocean of glimmering stars. Out in every direction, the mass of Flotilla visramen spread, a second ocean of Behemoths at rest, and each of them glimmering with countless lamps. There was no formal service. No bright words spoken by some priest of distant and unfeeling gods. Every cluster of people was speaking their own benedictions, giving voice to their own grief and memories. The sound could be heard like the soft murmuring of a vast crowd. A chorus of voices united by loss.

Loss, and hope for a better tomorrow. The Guild had fled. Havensreach stood. A God had been defied.

And the number of people lost was too high for Elias to count. There was more to do, still. He had to reconnect with the Order of the White Chalice. Had to see to the wellbeing of the people of Port Providence. He had to talk to Belit.

But here and now, first and foremost he had to grieve.

Harkon stood by the edge of the skydock, looking as if he'd aged a hundred years in a day. At his side was Vlana, holding the lantern for the whole crew. Vant was next to her, one hand on her shoulder and stoically staring into the distance. Clutch leaned against a set of crates and watched the sky with its fading sunset. Aimee stood next to Elias, slightly back from the others. Vant spoke first.

"You were always there," the engineer said. "Even when I didn't want you to be. Even when I didn't know that I needed you. I'm never going to forget that."

"You were crazier than all of us, deep down," Clutch said. And Elias realized as he watched that she was holding the old warrior's flask in her hands. She reached out over the lip of the skydock and poured the dark liquid into the abyss. "This is for you, big guy. Skyfarers remember."

Silence fell, and Elias realized it was his turn. He didn't know why he hadn't understood, but with a twist of the knife he realized that he'd been waiting for Bjorn to speak. Elias's throat dried up, then he forced himself to say something as the old man's words from their first fight echoed in his head. *"You poor boy, what have they done to you?"*

"You were the first to see me," Elias said. Thinking of a day in Ishtear when he'd held a knife in his hands. A knife that Bjorn had taken away. "And you took the knife when I needed you to." A lump formed in his throat. "I will always be grateful."

Aimee spoke next. Elias could hear her voice quavering, and she gripped his hand tightly. "You saved us all," she said. "And I can't repay you for that. And it hurts, and it's unfair." She steadied herself. "But for you, my friend, I will try."

Vlana's fingers curled around the base of the floating lantern. "I'm not ready to say goodbye," she finally said. "You're my like my father and you're my friend, and there's no making this right. I want you back." Her shoulders shook for a moment, then she squared them. "I'm not the cook you were, but I'll remember what you taught me."

Harkon was the last to speak, and for a long time it seemed as though he wouldn't. Then, finally, he simply said "You were the best of us, my oldest friend. The best, and no less than that."

Vlana held up the lantern, and gently let it go. As countless other people let their lamps go, a second sea of stars rose from Havensreach's walls, from the ocean of the flotilla. From the ships of independent Skyfarers. They rose and floated amidst the ships and spires, and the candles of heaven drifted among men as the sun set, and the world grieved together.

Alahna had been moved from the *Elysium* to a better lodging within the city shortly after the ship returned, and that somehow made Elias's guilt worse. The first time he walked Havensreach's white streets, he went alone despite Aimee's offer to come with him, and the stone streets with their overhanging signs and the sheer normality of this comfortable, prosperous city was jarring. A war had just touched its borders, stained the innocence of the place, and yet life continued as normal in a way he had never experienced in his life.

Nobody knew who he was, here, and he wore his long coat that partially obscured Oath of Aurum at his side. He was just another swordsman in a cosmopolitan city where any number of such people could vanish into the press, and occluded thus, he made his way slowly up the main thoroughfare to towards the building called the House of Respite, a whitewashed building where Helena had arranged to see Alahna watched over by the finest physicians in the city. Elias's understanding was that even this was unlikely to be enough. The Queen Mother was approaching her last days.

When he gave his name and his appointment to the healers, they didn't fight him. He was led through a set of hallways until he reached the doorways to a suite with a beautiful view of the Skydocks and the heavens beyond with their ocean of behemoths. Helena was the person who greeted him, and when she saw his face, her eyes passed through a series of emotions, each more difficult for Elias to meet than the one before it. At length, the woman called Grayspear simply said "I can't promise that she wants to see you. If she bids me do so, I will have to see you ejected. I hope you understand." Then she stood aside, and with soft footfalls that nonetheless felt heavy, Elias made his way into the room.

Alahna was siting up in bed, her eyes cast towards the window, her back propped up with pillows. She looked as if she'd aged a hundred years since last he saw her, as if pride and resilience were the only things keeping her alive, now. And grief. He saw the red rim around her eyes and knew at once that this would be the most painful conversation of his life.

So Elias did something he had never done before. He stopped several feet from the bed, and he knelt.

"Majesty," he said quietly. Then he lowered his head.

The voice that finally answered him was neither kind, now cruel. More than anything else, it was tired beyond words. "Kneeling does not make it better, son of Thcliana."

The use of his mother's name knifed through him, and Elias closed his eyes, squeezing them tight against the tears. Slowly raising his gaze, he found the Queen Mother still not looking at him. "Nothing," she said, "can make any of this right. I do not say that to be cruel, but some hurts cannot be mended."

"I am so sorry," Elias said. Nothing else felt right. Felt proper. Yet it also felt hollow. The cheapest of phrases. Rote and too often repeated.

"Helena tells me that he was himself, at the end," Alahna answered, still not looking at him. "I suppose I cannot ask for more than that, though it does not console me. To live to see the end of my House, the displacement of my people, to be left making these last decisions myself." She took a breath before continuing. "The nobility of Port Providence is all dead. Grace will see to the people's leadership in absentia, when I am gone. She will do this with Helena's assistance, and may she do a better job than we have."

At long last, she looked at Elias. "Come closer, boy. I can barely see you over there."

Slowly he rose, crossing the rest of the short distance until he stood beside the bed. Unexpectedly, the Queen Mother reached out and took his hand. "I'm sorry, Elias," she said. "But I can't make this go away, for either of us. It's going to stay with you, and in that way it will be harder for you. You've a lot of life left to live, and there is no making this right."

Elias held her hand. The pain weighed heavier on his shoulders, never to leave.

"I cannot be angry with you," she said. "For nothing I might say is worse than what you are already saying to yourself. I'm sorry, Elias Leblanc, but this is a weight you and I must carry, for the rest of our days."

They sat together for two hours, after that. In silence and in grief.

Alahna died the next morning.

33

THE COUNCIL

It had been a full year since Aimee had been in the council chamber of the *Iseult*, and this time the room was emptier, hollower than it had been when last she saw it.

Belit sat in her chair at the far end of the table, dressed in red from head to foot, but for the black stripe of a sash of mourning for Rachim resting across her chest. Her gold eyes burned, and one hand rested on the table. The past year of leadership had changed her, making her both more confident and stronger.

And angrier, Aimee noticed. Though she did not comment on it. Opposite Belit was Harkon. Aimee's teacher had been fortified in the last few days by time taken to privately grieve. Elias was there too, and a man he'd pointed out as being Bendis, the head of the Order of the White Chalice. There was Grace, representing the people of Port Providence, and Helena was by her side. The rest of the seats were empty. There would be few, if any witnesses to what happened here.

"Roland has the stone," Harkon finally said. "This is far from over."

"We didn't even know about the Twelfth Night until shortly before the Battle of Havensreach," Belit answered with a sigh. "We set out to fight the Guild, and we bloodied their nose, but now the Eternal Order controls the levers of their power, and now you tell me they have control over an enchanted stone that gives them access to a God."

"Not just a god," Bendis spoke up. "Their god. The being that created their progenitor's power, and whose thoughts even now guide the council of their elders. I don't know what they're going to do with that thing in their possession, but I can guarantee you that it has only made them stronger." He shook his head. "There is no putting it back in the bottle that Silas has uncorked."

"It's getting worse," the man beside Belit—Vallus, her consort—said. "This morning, the Violet Imperium declared itself for the Guild, and the Kiscadian Republic declared against. It's only a matter of time before the great powers of our age are at open war."

"Which serves the Eternal Order," Harkon said. "Which is why I called this council. All of this will have been for naught if the Order is able to repeat what Silas did, but on a grander scale. If the heavens descend into open warfare, how many more opportunities will there be for mass sacrifice? How many more chances will they have to bring their dead god back?"

"We're going to need time," Belit said. "Flotilla Visramen endured that battle, but we lost two ships to the abyss, and the ones who remain have sustained damage. We have yet to calculate the full loss of lives, and my people need time to recover."

"We may yet have some," Harkon answered. "The Eternal Order will need to lick its wounds. Roland will need to figure out how to use what he has acquired. And there is concern over where Havensreach will fall in the unfolding politics. The Guild was once the prime trading partner of this place. I do not know what the leaders of the inner ring will decide, though I doubt they will turn against the flotilla floating outside their gates."

"If they ask us to leave we have to," Belit said. "But this is the safest place for us, right now. The Guild won't try again until it has the Imperium at its back." She ran a hand down her face. "Gods, this has all gotten so complicated."

"Then what's next is research," Aimee spoke up. All eyes turned to her. "All of us. We need to have a better understanding of what we're up against. We need information, and we need to build up our strength."

"My order will tell you everything you know," Bendis said. "Our history is not complete, but it is long… and we have been watching over this enemy since time immemorial. Where we can help, we will."

"My people need a home," Grace spoke up. "All this talk of Gods and ancient foes and new wars is all well and good, but my people are not natural born Skyfarers. We come from earth beneath our feet, and mountains and streams. Lakes and rivers. We can't just stay on Behemoths."

"I can't speak for Havensreach," Harkon followed, "but I do not believe they will turn you away. Not in the short term. You'll have some time, to figure out what your next moves will be."

Grace fell silent, after a nod.

"Research it is, then." Belit said. Her eyes drifted to Elias. "Research and training."

Aimee saw the first hint of a faint smile in days flicker across his face. It fortified her heart, a little. A small sliver of hope that light could be found still, even in the midst of all this darkness. Her mind turned to Bjorn again. What he might have said to them now. She didn't know what it might have been…but she knew that he wouldn't want her to go without the joys in life that could be gotten even in the midst of grief.

She vowed, silently and seriously, to remember that. And when the meeting ended, she resolved to do one last thing. Something she'd been putting off since she returned.

Aimee walked up the streets of the upper ring. It was midday and the tall houses of the wealthy ward of the city rose around her, rooftops crested with gullrats and catching the sunlight high above her head. Step by step she made her way towards the familiar gate, pausing only at the top of the hill to look down over the city. The charm school where she'd learned high society, and beyond it the dome of the Academy of Mystic Sciences, where all this had begun, what seemed like a lifetime ago. And maybe it was. Aimee didn't know why she was here, and on some level she still did. The *Elysium* had become her home and her family in less than a year… but this was where she was from. Would always be from. And after so much loss, she needed to return.

The gate slowly swung open, revealing the walkway she'd played on as a child so many times. Dreaming. Making. This was the first place she'd conjured magic from thin air in a shower of sparks to the delight and shock of her parents. And as her booted footfalls passed the garden, she noticed that the roselotus was in full bloom. Her favorite flower.

She climbed the steps and rapped twice upon the door, not having to wait long before it swung slowly inward. Aimee took a breath.

"Hi, mom. Hi, dad," she said with her best, sad smile.

"I'm back."

EPILOGUE

THE GOD IN THE BOWL

Roland ascends the steps to his manse. The cold lashes across the former palace grounds, its red trees wafting in the frigid wind. The Dread Lord of Ashes has succeeded beyond his wildest expectations, and yet his fury knows no bounds. He forces the doors open, not bothering with locks. The braziers have gone cold in his absence, servants sent to other duties leaving the central building that he once built on the bones of his enemy's palace cold and empty. There are priceless works of art upon the walls, and relics he took from the bones of the place that he destroyed. Trophies. Mementos. Last sentimental remnants of a life he discarded when he assumed his name and his place within the Eternal Order.

And there is one above all others that Roland cannot escape. It is a painting he secured, not from New Corinth, but from a gallery of art to which he tracked a hated enemy, only to find the man gone and the painting left behind. Its significance is known only to him. It depicts a woman with dark hair and green eyes, dressed in a simple peasant gown, in a rustic, simple house somewhere far away from here, long destroyed without pity or mercy.

On her lap is a child with a laughing face that may as well be a clone of his mother. Of Theliana, the last princess of New Corinth. Roland stares up at the painting, and at length his hand reaches up to brush across the scar from the healing that covers his once immaculate face. At the base of its frame is a simple name. A title placed lovingly by a man that Roland hates above all others.

"The Last Roses"

He takes a deep, drawn breath, and then he lets out a primal scream of hate before he shatters a mahogany chair with all the force he can muster. The chair breaks apart, hurtling shards across the room and knocking over a brazier, cold and empty, onto the stone floor.

Roland turns and reaches into his satchel, and with his right hand, removes the jewel that Aimee so graciously saw fit to harvest from Silas, killing the madman in the process. The Dread Lord of Ashes never hedged his bets on the old man's success, and his long-term plans had always ended in the old man's death...but he had not expected his brief ally to fall so swiftly. Harkon's apprentice is growing in power, which will need to be contended with, sooner or later.

But first, it is time to do what he set out to do. He holds the jewel before him and walks deeper into his sanctum, until at last he arrives in the cold room with its raised dais. Not long after New Corinth fell, he had this place constructed to the specifications of the dream he received before he joined the Eternal Order. Before he was Roland. The dream that gifted him purpose. Power. A means to acquire what he wanted above all else.

Roland places the jewel in the center of the dais, and after a few moments of silence, lights stir around it, blinking in familiar patterns that slowly spread outwards from the base of the plinth, twisting across the walls in ghostly lines like a tangle of vast, interconnected roots.

Roland smiles in the depths of the darkness, and as the Dread Lord of Ashes reaches out to touch the jewel he hears, for the second time in his life, a dark and cold voice, rising up from the dust of the ages.

THE END

The tale of the Drifting Lands will continue

ACKNOWLEDGMENTS

It is very rare for a series to get a second chance like this, and there were numerous times over the last seven years when I thought I'd have to lay it aside and do something else. Many people played a role in keeping me from giving up, and I'll try to thank them all here.

First, to John Hartness, for picking up the series and ensuring it has a new home. For the assistance and the encouragement all the way. To Neal and Greg and everyone else on the Mongoliad crew for telling me not to give up. To Meaghan, for believing that this, and I, had a future. To Alice, Nick, Dean, Lyn, and Matt, for being constant sounding boards, and to Nik for making art of characters I never thought anyone would want to draw. Thank you, all, from the bottom of my heart.

To the music of Yasuharu Takanashi, Two Steps from Hell, BTS, and every other artist whose music pulled me through to the end of this book. To James and Evelyn for being amazing kids who believed in their dad, and to my parents and sister who never doubted.

And to you, every Drifting Lands fan knew and old, the ones who waited for seven years and the ones who are just discovering the story. Thank you.

ABOUT THE AUTHOR

Joseph Brassey lives in the Pacific Northwest with his wife, two children, and two cats. In his spare time he trains in and teaches Historical European Martial Arts in his native Tacoma. He has worked everywhere from a local newspaper to the frame-shop of a crafts store to the smoke-belching interior of a house-siding factory with very questionable safety policies.

josephbrassey.wordpress.com

FRIENDS OF FALSTAFF

Thank You to All our Falstaff Books Patrons, who get extra digital content each month! To be featured here and see what other great rewards we offer, go to www.patreon.com/falstaffbooks.

PATRONS

Dino Hicks
John Hooks
John Kilgallon
Larissa Lichty
Travis & Casey Schilling
Staci-Leigh Santore
Sheryl R. Hayes
Scott Norris
Samuel Montgomery-Blinn
Junkle